NEW YORKISH

and Other American Yiddish Stories

NEW YORKISH
and Other American Yiddish Stories

by

SHIMSHON APTER

FISHL BIMKO

MEIR BLINKIN

DER LEBEDICKER

BORUCH GLAZMAN

PERETZ HIRSHBEIN

DAVID IGNATOV

LEON KOBRIN

KADYA MOLODOWSKY

ISAAC RABOY

MIRIAM RASKIN

AVROM REISIN

L. SHAPIRO

I.J. SINGER

SHEA TENENBAUM

Selected and translated by
MAX ROSENFELD

Published by
SHOLOM ALEICHEM CLUB PRESS, PHILADELPHIA
CONGRESS OF SECULAR JEWISH ORGANIZATIONS

ISBN 0-9610870-1-3

for ROSE
life-long companion

Contents

FOREWORD

New Yorkish and Other American Yiddish Stories, a collection of stories chosen and translated from the Yiddish by Max Rosenfeld, has been published by the Congress of Secular Jewish Organizations and the Sholom Aleichem Club of Philadelphia.

The Yiddish literature presented here is not to be considered as an heirloom of a bygone age but as a guidepost to a thriving, self-conscious Jewish community life in North America.

The Congress of Secular Jewish Organizations (CSJO) is a federation of like-minded community organizations and supplementary Jewish schools dedicated to developing a vibrant secular and humanistic Jewish life on this continent and, in conjunction with groups elsewhere, wherever there is a Jewish community.

The schools and adult and youth groups of the CSJO carry out programs of education directed towards understanding our people's past and enriching our present Jewish lives. These programs include study of our tradition, history, literature, music, art, languages (Yiddish as a vital instrument of expression of a significant period of our history; Hebrew as it relates to modern Israel; and other languages created out of the Jewish experience). Creative approaches to holiday celebrations provide an opportunity to reflect upon our cultural historic heritage and to relate their significance to present-day life.

The CSJO has published *Mame-loshn — A History of Yiddish Culture,* by Rakhmiel Peltz of Columbia University, and a holiday book geared toward a secular celebration of Rosh Hashona, Yom Kippur, and Sukkot.

The Sholom Aleichem Club is one of twenty constituent members of the CSJO, which in turn is a constituent member of the North American section of the International Federation of Secular Humanistic Jews. Similar organizations exist in Israel, Argentina, Uruguay, Australia, Belgium, France, and the countries of the former Soviet Union.

For over 40 years the Club has served its members through its social, cultural, and educational programs. It has sponsored the *Haggadah for a Secular Celebration of Pesach,* now in its fifth edition, and an earlier translation by Max Rosenfeld of Yiddish stories from America, *Pushcarts and Dreamers* (now in its fourth printing).

For information on these and other publications, write to the Executive Director, CSJO, 19657 Villa Drive N., Southfield, Michigan, 48067, or to the Sholom Aleichem Club, PO Box 27648, Philadelphia PA 19150.

Editorial Committee
Lawrence Schofer
Jane Schofer
Jack Rosenfeld

Cover design by Ruthie Rosenfeld

Lawrence Schofer has served as co-chair of the Congress of Secular Jewish Organizations and as editor of its *Newsletter*. He is active in the Sholom Aleichem Club of Philadelphia and was president of the parents' group of the Philadelphia Jewish Children's Folkshul. Larry has a Ph.D. in history and has published numerous articles and book reviews in the fields of Jewish history and German history.

Jane Schofer serves as conductor of the holiday chorus of the Sholom Aleichem Club of Philadelphia and for several years directed the music program at the Philadelphia Jewish Children's Folkshul. She is the librarian of the Akiba Hebrew Academy in Merion PA.

Jack Rosenfeld has served as co-chair of the Congress of Secular Jewish Organizations. For many years he has designed dramatic presentations and holiday programs for the Sholom Aleichem Club. He is chairman of the Club's Book Fund Committee.

Ruthie Rosenfeld, a graduate of Carnegie Mellon University, is a graphic artist and director of special effects for television in New York. She was the illustrator and calligrapher of the Sholom Aleichem Club's award-winning *Haggadah for a Secular Celebration of Pesach.*

From the Translator

The 20 stories in this book have two basic elements in common: they were all written in Yiddish and they take place in "America" — more accurately, the United States. The time period is roughly 1920-1950. Most of them first appeared either in the periodical called *Zukunft* (*The Future*) — about which see below — or in one of the literary magazines put out by groups of the younger Yiddish writers themselves.

The stories have something else in common: the action is driven by the complex relationships that have always existed between men and women — sexual, emotional, economic. In that respect, they could have been written in any other language, but they happened to immigrant Jews in this country, and since the participants expressed their deepest feelings in Yiddish, they are in that respect unique. Also for that reason, we considered it essential that certain Yiddish and other foreign expressions remain in their original language, and we have provided a glossary for them.

Zukunft, a Yiddish monthly founded in New York in 1892 (and still published), was one of the first serious Yiddish periodicals to appear anywhere in the world. Through the years *Zukunft* was edited by some of the most distinguished Yiddish literary figures in America. Its pages have been open to all sections of opinion in American Jewish life, while remaining secularist itself. Under the editorship of Abraham Liessin, from 1903 to 1938 *Zukunft* published the work of practically every Yiddish writer and thinker of note. At present it is a bimonthly edited by a volunteer committee of six.

Note on transliteration

The transliteration of Yiddish words presents a problem. Should they be presented "scientifically" (as in the YIVO system), or should they be presented in a common-sense (though often inconsistent) manner? We have chosen here to spell the words phonetically, though in a few cases a Germanized spelling has been used because that is how the original publishers spelled the

iii

Yiddish. For example, the editors of the magazine *Zukunft* chose to use the German *Z* rather than the phonetic *ts* for the first sound.

Yiddish has no capital letters, but in this book the first word of a title of a book or story is capitalized. Every word is capitalized in the names of literary movements and of people.

Max Rosenfeld

INTRODUCTION

Sanford Pinsker

Shadek Professor of Humanities, Franklin and Marshall College

Yiddish writers did not have an easy time in America. Caught between memories — sometimes warmly nostalgic, sometimes bitterly critical — of a world they had left behind and an uneasy accommodation to the America they found, it is hardly surprising that discontinuity became both their defining posture and congenial subject. What Tevkin, the marginalized Hebrew poet of Abraham Cahan's *The Rise of David Levinsky* (1917), says of the possibilities for an authentically Jewish art in America — namely, that "I am in a strange land. My harp is silent." — applies equally to those who wrote in Yiddish. But while Yiddishists may have protested their condition, their collective "harps" were hardly silent, and this is true whether they were poets, playwrights, novelists, or short story writers. For if American-Yiddish writers were guilty of anything, it was of protesting *too* much, of insisting that they had no place in an America of getting, spending, and philistine values. Unlike Hebrew, Yiddish emerged as the more supple medium, one better equipped to speak directly to the widest ranges of the immigrant Jewish heart.

Interestingly enough, scholar-critics have made considerable efforts to preserve the best work done by American-Yiddish poets and playwrights, but precious little to keep alive the names and short fiction of those who published their sketches in newspapers or literary magazines such as *Zukunft*. Thus, one looks in vain for some mention of Miriam Raskin or Shea Tenenbaum in standard literary histories like Sol Liptzin's *A History of Yiddish Literature* or Charles Madison's *Yiddish Literature*. To be sure, Kadya Molodowsky and Avrom Reisen receive well-deserved attention as poets; Leon Kobrin and Fishl Bimko as playwrights; Isaac Raboy as novelist — but their short stories apparently do not merit so much as a passing mention. Worse, even the most widely popular anthologies of Yiddish fiction (one thinks, for example, of those compiled by Irving Howe) pay scant attention to American-Yiddish fiction, preferring instead to concentrate on figures more closely associated with eastern Europe. I.B. Singer is, of course, the notable exception, but one that only serves to highlight the general rule.

The twenty previously untranslated stories collected in *New Yorkish and Other American Yiddish Stories* serve a variety of purposes. They are, first of all, an effort at cultural reclamation, a way of restoring a legacy not fully appreciated when the stories first appeared, and largely forgotten — or never known — during subsequent decades of escalating assimilation. In much the same way that Yiddish newspapers once provided a vibrant portrait of the immigrant Jewish world, so too do these stories serve as a large encompassing mirror. Largely couched in the aesthetics of social realism, they suggest how members of a discrete community worked, dreamed, fell in (and out) of love, and, perhaps most of all, dealt with the dizzying complications of being transplanted, hyphenated Americans. Such fiction wears a thoroughly human face.

That said, however, the stories must also stand firmly on their own artistic feet, and the good news of this collection is that they most assuredly do. For what a given story might sacrifice in layered complexity or radical experimentation, it more than makes up for in an unstinting regard for characterization. A brush stroke here, a turn of phrase there, is often enough to establish a character for an audience that smiled — or clucked — knowingly. A garment industry worker need only be described as one who believes in the essential unity of man and machine ("A good operator, when he works in rhythm with his machine, feels his limbs singing along too.") to establish the essential framework from which the complications of a story such as Miriam Raskin's *Generation of the Wilderness* will unfold. Bennie, Raskin's politically innocent protagonist, is forced to pit his definition of "unity" against others in the shop who define the term in sharply ideological ways. In other cases, it is enough to know that a character has light-blue eyes that "looked at you dimly, as through a glass, or even a sieve" for the necessary conditions of an ill-fated relationship to be set into motion.

Not surprisingly, the bulk of stories in this collection are set in sweatshops, or cramped tenement apartments. No matter, because as I.B. Singer liked to quip, if the Eskimos have many words for the intricate shadings of snow, Jews have an equally rich vocabulary to express aspects of disappointment. But that said, let me hasten to point out that it is the well-heeled who turn poverty into romance and squalor into the exotic. American Yiddish stories about the gritty world of garment workers could not avail themselves of such easy luxury, for protracted strikes, shortened seasons, exploitation, and backbreaking work came with the territory. In a word, this is a fiction that did not blink, much less sugar-coat.

At the same time, however, Max Rosenfeld, the volume's translator and principal arranger, avoids stacking the cards on behalf of special pleading or propaganda. Consider Shimshon Apter's *Mabel's Secret,* a story set in the unbearable August heat of the Eastern Frocks building: "Motors drove the sewing-machine cylinders with a weary, monotonous drone, spreading a foul odor of oil and grease. The workers — Italians, Greeks, Jews, Puerto Ricans, African-Americans, men and women — sat with their heads buried in the machines, sweat dripping from their flushed faces." In less skillful hands, the story might have gone on to count every bead of sweat, every aching bone, but Apter has larger, more intriguing notions in mind. For when the fiercely overweight Mabel suffers a heart attack, the "wine-colored dress" that lay before her at the sewing machine becomes transmogrified into a "panorama of green fields, lush hillsides of pine and maple trees" — a scene from her childhood in the Catskill mountainsides, where she fell in love, and her father subsequently disowned her. The reason, *Mabel's secret,* is that she has become attracted to Abner Hayes, a classmate whose mother worked at one of the area's hotels, and who is black. Ultimately, she marries Abner and lives in Harlem, forever separated from the family that insists she will "be lonely and miserable the rest of your life. You won't be welcome in our family — or in his — ."

The story's concluding lines are wonderfully ambivalent, cobbling a vision of reconciliation with her brother, Joel, to the hard facts of her impending death:

> The frantic tooting of a horn awakened her. She felt a searing heat all over her body. With a great effort she opened her eyes. Several faces hovered over her. She shivered. A pale, round face. Blonde mustache. Her brother Joel. So many years she hadn't seen him. She shut her eyes for a moment. No, it wasn't Joel, it was Dr. Saunders, a stethoscope hanging out of his ears and a stiff smile frozen on his thin lips.
>
> "Abner!" she called. "Where's Joel?"
>
> Joel appeared again. Not as clear as before. His rough hands were caressing her cheeks, her forehead.
>
> "Joel! You've come to take me home? I want to go home and see Papa," she babbled.
>
> She smiled and closed her eyes.

Like other Jewish-American protagonists who come to feel the loss of authentic roots, the pain of severing of family ties (one thinks of the long trail of such tears from David Levinsky's litany of regrets in the final lines of Abraham Cahan's 1917 novel, *The Rise of David Levinsky* to the painful family memories unpacked in Saul Bellow's masterful 1967 story, *The Old System*), *Mabel's Secret* investigates what might be called the sweatshop of the heart, that place where complicated sorrows last a lifetime, and perhaps even longer.

Granted, not all the stories in Rosenfeld's collection move in such surprising directions. Indeed, some are filled with the charms of easier recognition, of tensions that come to us with the force of insider information. Take, for example, Leon Kobrin's *Actors!*, a story that could only have been written by someone with wide experience in the vagaries of the Yiddish stage. Kobrin is, of course, best known as a playwright, a worthy successor to the likes of Abraham Goldfadn and Jacob Gordin. Early plays such as *Minna* (1899) and *Yankel Boila* (1908) made it clear that characterization was his strong suit, but also that he would have to reorient his material to the struggle for bread and love if he were to survive as a

Yiddish playwright in America. *Actors!* is partly an effort to settle certain scores — against backers, producers, audiences, and, most of all, actors — and partly an exercise in comic irony about the bitter ironies attendant on writing Yiddish comedy.

The story is narrated in retrospect, as the speaker (clearly modeled on Kobrin himself) remembers how it was to live among the high hopes and great expectations of rehearsal:

> This happened about ten years ago. One of the Yiddish theaters was preparing a production of a new comedy I had written. The leading actors in that company had good roles and spoke glowingly about the play during rehearsals.
>
> "It's going to be a hit!"
> "It'll run the whole season!"
> And so on.
>
> The cashier of the theater, who spoke only English when "business was booming!" and only Yiddish when "business was rotten" — he too, hearing what the actors were saying, stuck his black curly head out of the booth whenever he saw me and greeted me enthusiastically in English:
>
> "A double-G" he predicted, which meant, I assumed, Good with a capital G.
>
> Given this level of enthusiasm, why not have the company do the narrator's play in Hartford the Wednesday evening preceding the Friday premiere in New York City, rather than the old war-horse they'd originally scheduled? After all, nothing perks up actors so much as a live audience. Unfortunately, what sounds persuasive in theory often turns sour in practice. The Hartford audience had been expecting an operetta, but what they got was something very different indeed:
>
> The curtain goes up. The audience applauds the famous actors from New York. The play begins. Only the actors with minor roles are on stage. The audience is quiet. Then the blonde star enters. She is a favorite here and the audience applauds.

"Now!" says the manager, scratching his right cheek. "Now we'll grab them! If it was funny at rehearsals, the audience here will be rolling on the floor!"

But what is this? The blonde star is playing her heart out — and the audience is not even smiling.

"What's wrong?" the manager asks me, as if I know. "Why aren't they laughing?" I shake my head.

The comic enters. Same reaction. The audience applauds when he comes on stage, but his jokes fall flat. The entire cast has been on stage, playing their roles perfectly, but they might as well be giving this performance in a graveyard.

At that point, charges mount and the plot, as they say, thickens. The play is a "lemon" and the playwright little more than a swindler. What the production needs, some suggest, are more songs and dances; others remain convinced that the whole thing is too "litcrary" and that what bombed in Hartford will surely die a quick death in New York. In short, the very people who had praised the playwright to the heavens now gladly consign him to gehenna.

But as twist gives way to turn, the play turns out to be a hit, capital-G Good. Now, the "cashier spoke only in English," and "in the cafes, the people 'in the business' again came over to my table and inquired solicitously after my wife and children." Only other playwrights kept a cool distance — to which the narrator, weighing ups against downs, can only respond (in the story's final word): "ACTORS!"

By contrast, Miriam Raskin's *In the Shadows* comes at the self-absorbed world of artists and artistic pretension from the perspective of a narrator more comfortable on the sidelines — in the shadows, as it were — than on center stage. Annie is one of the solidly nondescript — "A moment after you saw her you forgot her, as if you had never even seen her." She labors uneventfully at her sewing machine during the week, but saves Saturday evenings for her visits with the Shermans, fashionable friends who fill their apartment with poets, writers, and, most of all, with bright, sophisticated talk.

Granted, Annie hardly fits in (indeed, she sits in her appointed corner, in silence, and "in the shadows"), but something about her attracts the attention of Isaac Lev, a poet who blathers on about how "art is like life," only more so because "it's even higher than life. If the artist doesn't like the world we live in he creates his own world."

He might well have been describing Annie, had he but the ability to see what was clearly at the end of his nose. That he doesn't is, of course, testimony to how far brittle artistic talk is from life. Annie is merely the quiet girl he took home one Saturday evening — the maker of his tea and the resident *balabosteh* of his apartment. For her part, Annie continues to admire Lev's brilliance, but becomes increasingly upset by a life spent under his long shadow. When friends knock at the door, they ask after Lev; when Lev speaks, they listen. Would her life "always be like that — always in *his* light?"

Only when Annie asserts both her independence and her self-worth — indeed, only when she announces that their relationship is over and that she has packed his suitcase — does the situation change. The woman in the shadows has come out from them, and even Lev is impressed: "I love you more than ever," he confesses, and Annie (who felt like "shouting for joy but didn't want to show her feelings so soon,") goes off to make a pot of tea. As the story's concluding line puts it, "She floated into the kitchen," into a realm where the claims of art have effectively given way to those of the heart.

Yiddish readers enjoyed a good story, one with lots of human drama and melodramatic punch. In some cases, the orchestration of a plot's twists and turns remind one of O. Henry, as is the case in Boruch Glazman's *The Hand of God* in which a ten-dollar bill is mysteriously found and then just as mysteriously lost; in others (say, I.J. Singer's *Bella Saradacci*), the protracted movement to ever-more exotic settings are what one remembers. But of the stories in Rosenfeld's collection, none is likely to seem more exotic, or more unlikely, than Shea Tenenbaum's *Among the Indians of Oklahoma.* Long before the affinity between Indians and Jews captured the attention of critics such as Leslie Fiedler (*Love and*

Death in the American Novel) or a Jewish-American novelist like Bernard Malamud (*The People*), Tenenbaum wrote about Norman, Oklahoma, in the mid-1930s, and the curious ways in which the lives of Jews and Indians were inextricably combined. Some years before, the narrator's brother had married an Indian woman. She returned to the small town of Seminole after his death, taking with her his tiny Psalter and a watch with a six-pointed Star of David engraved on the case. Nor was he the sole member of Norman's Jewish community. Tenenbaum's initial descriptions include a doctor who not only prefers Peretz to Sholom Aleichem, but is also eager to explain why, along with other solid Norman citizens. However, Tenebaum's plot takes its oddest turns when the narrator finds himself gravitating toward Seminole. There, he meets Soreh-Minke (a woman who "looked like a big duck that had been fattened for Pesach") and comes to learn of her *tsoris* [woes].

It seems that Charlie, her only son, who was such a desirable match for the bright and good-looking daughters of the local wealthy Jewish families, was actually in love with an Indian woman who was not even particularly pretty.

Perhaps not, but one could argue that she is more authentically "Jewish" than the official Jewesses in town, and more important, that her suffering and disenfranchisement speak to what binds, rather than separates, apparently disparate cultures:

> Her diminutive face was yellow and pockmarked, making her look like an old woman. When she laughed, it sounded to me as though she were crying. From her small brown eyes peered an ancient sorrow, the sorrow of her old, weary and aggrieved people, which had once owned an enormous territory — all of America — with its fields, forest and rivers, over which roamed the hunch-back buffaloes that let themselves be caught to serve as generous meals for the Indian tribes.

As if all this weren't enough, the narrator notices "certain Jewish features of ancient days, when King David ruled the Jewish country," and points out that "she sang sad songs filled with a kind of Jewish nostalgia." Those who imagine that is a recent invention would do well to consider Tenenbaum's story. Indeed, I can imagine it being briskly debated at synagogues and Jewish study groups.

No short introduction can do full justice to the sheer range and intrinsic interest of this collection, but let me say a few words about the title story — *New Yorkish,* by L. Shapiro. Best known as the Yiddish Kafka, Shapiro has written a story of an odd relationship — half obsessive love, half prostitution — between a world-weary (Shapiro's word is "grouchy") Jewish man and the non-Jewish, vaguely Hispanic waitress he picks up at an Automat. Played out against a backdrop of New York's movie theaters and bustling thoroughfares, the tenuous relationship between Manny "Lakritspletsl" and Dolores ends, as it must, in his apartment. Thus baldly put, the story might seem either too superficial or too sordid to merit serious attention, but Shapiro invests events with paragraphs that sing with lyricism even as they point toward significance:

> What is the moral of the story [Manny wonders]? Bought love is also — love. Show a person a shekel and he starts singing the praises of heaven. Bah! A bad joke. Am I so stupid? All my life I never understood that? That would be too simple. Too simple is not good. Too complicated is also no good. Where is the truth? Oh, hell! He spits, because he has just put the wrong end of the cigarette in his mouth. But also because his thoughts are in such a hopelessly tangled knot.

Finally, some thoughts about translation, a subject I have avoided purposefully until now. Granted, *any* translation, even a quite good one, can only provide an approximation of its original; but that said, I think the time has come to shift the argument from heated discussions pitting doggedly faithful translations against their more creative counterparts — and instead to concentrate on the obvious advantages that accrue when works now languishing in obscurity are able to acquire new readers. No doubt some Yiddishists would prefer that the stories appear in their original language, or at the very least in a bilingual edition of the sort that Benjamin Harshav provided for his magisterial volume, *American-Yiddish Poetry.* But given the realities of the publishing world, I doubt very much if a major press could be persuaded to join Rosenfeld in an effort to resurrect these lost stories. For one thing, short fiction simply does not carry the clout that poetry packs, even though one might reasonably argue that far less damage is done to a translation of a story than to one of a poem; for another, publishers rely — probably much more than they should — on name recognition. If an author has slipped through the historical cracks, perhaps the fate is deserved. For these reasons and many more, the task of turning dream into reality fell to Philadelphia's Sholom Aleichem Club and to the Congress of Secular Jewish Organizations, a national organization of which the Sholom Aleichem Club is an affiliate. Its members are to be commended for their vision, as Rosenfeld himself deserves to be honored for his tireless efforts. Yiddishists and English readers alike have much to enjoy, and learn from, in *New Yorkish and Other American Yiddish Stories*.

GLOSSARY

amkho sher un izen — the common people, the tailors (literally: Your people, shears and irons) (Yiddish)

baalebos — the boss (literally, owner of the house) (Hebrew)

bubba — grandmother (Yiddish)

Bund — Jewish Labor Federation (Yiddish). Jewish Socialist labor party influential in Poland prior to World War II

Bundist — member of the Bund (Yiddish)

chupah — wedding canopy (Yiddish and Hebrew)

chutzpa — brazenness (Yiddish and Hebrew)

Di grine kuzine — My Greenhorn Cousin (song title) (Yiddish)

Dubinushka — a 1905 Russian revolutionary song, satirizing the use of the *dubinka* (night-stick) by the tsarist police against workers' demonstrations

dybbuk — soul of a dead person residing in body of a living individual (Yiddish)

Eretz Yisroel — Land of Israel (Hebrew)

folkshul — here, secular Jewish school

freilakhs — Jewish circle dance; the music for such a dance (Yiddish)

genosse, pl. genossen — comrade; title once common in the American labor movement; here used ironically (German)

genossines — feminine form of genosse

goyim — non-Jews (Yiddish and Hebrew)

kheyder — Jewish elementary school (Yiddish)

kaddish — memorial prayer for the dead (Hebrew)

kalleh — bride (Yiddish and Hebrew)

katerinka — barrel-organ; slang for an old machine or car (Yiddish)

khosn — bridegroom (Yiddish and Hebrew)

khosn-kalleh — A couple recently married or about to be married (Yiddish) klezmer — musician (usually one who plays dance tunes); a klezmer band (Yiddish)

k'n'hora — "no evil eye;" uttered to ward off evil spirits while speaking favorably of people or events (Yiddish)

kretchma — tavern (Yiddish)

lantsman — someone who comes from same town as you (Yiddish)

lantsleit — plural of lantsman

latke, latkes — pancakes (Yiddish)

literatsia — "literary intellectuals" (derogatory — a made-up Yiddish word on the analogy of the word intelligentsia)

Litvak — a Jew born in or living in Lithuania

l'khayim — "to life!" A toast. (Hebrew)

masovka — mass meeting (Russian)

mazl-tov — good luck! (Yiddish and Hebrew)

mentsh — a person of good character (Yiddish)

miltsn — a fish delicacy (Yiddish)

minyan — quorum of ten Jews necessary for communal prayer (Hebrew)

od lo ovda tikvoseynu — "And we'll never lose hope" — from *Hatikvah*, the Zionist anthem

parnoseh — livelihood (Yiddish and Hebrew)

peyrek — "chapter" of the Mishnah (part of the Talmud); usually refers to a section of *Ethics of the Fathers* (Hebrew)

puzhalista — if you please (Russian)

Sefer Yosifun — Book of Josephus (Hebrew)

shlimazl — person who has bad luck (Yiddish)

shmaate — rag (Yiddish)

shokhet — ritual slaughterer (Yiddish and Hebrew)

shtetl — small town (Yiddish)

shvieger — mother-in-law (Yiddish)

shto za raznitsa — What a difference! (Russian)

tallis — prayer-shawl (Hebrew)

treyf — non-kosher according to Jewish dietary laws; hence, dubious, unethical, unscrupulous, rotten, corrupt (Yiddish)

u'mipney khato-eynu — "Because of our sins," a High Holiday prayer (Hebrew)

vey iz mir — woe is me (Yiddish)
yarmulka — skullcap worn by observant Jews (Yiddish)
yohrtseit — anniversary of someone's death (Yiddish)
zdravstvoyte — Greetings! (Russian)
zhlub — boorish person (Yiddish)

NEW YORKISH

L. Shapiro

L. (Levi-Yehoshua) SHAPIRO (1878-1948) — born near Kiev; died in Los Angeles.

Shapiro signed his works with his first initial and is always referred to as "La-med" (Yiddish letter for his initial) Shapiro. After his traditional Jewish education, Shapiro formally studied the Russian language. His early poems were written in Yiddish, Hebrew, and Russian. In 1896 he met I.L. Peretz, who recognized the merit of his first literary efforts and published some of his work in the Yiddishe bibliotek, *a Yiddish literary annual edited by Peretz.*

After the pogroms in Russia in 1905 he emigrated to America, with a one-year stopover in London, where he wrote for the Freie arbeter velt. *In 1909 his story* The Cross *aroused so much interest that he was welcomed onto the pages of the* Forverts *and* Zukunft. *He then returned to Europe, where he wrote for the Warsaw Yiddish press and translated various works by Dickens, Victor Hugo, and Walter Scott into Yiddish. Two years later he came back to New York and stayed until 1921; he then moved to Los Angeles, where he spent six years trying to develop a form of color film. In 1927 he moved back to New York but finally returned to Los Angeles in 1939.*

At the end of the title essay in his last book Der shreiber geyt in kheyder (The Writer Goes to School — *published in 1945), after discussing problems of the writing craft, Shapiro wrestles with his personal need to expose the rotten apples in his own community. "The participation of some Jewish criminals in the pogroms of 1919-20 in the Ukraine sticks in my flesh like a thorn..."*

Yiddish critics viewed him as a master of the novella and a leader in the post-classical tradition. Isaiah Spiegel calls him "the Yiddish Kafka."

New Yorkish *appears in* Nu-Yorkish un andere dertsaylungen (New Yorkish and Other Stories), *self-published in New York, 1931.*

L. Shapiro

New Yorkish

That evening the man with a grouchy look on his face ordered a portion of griddle-cakes at the hot table in the Automat.

A young woman with bare brown arms, in a white apron and with a linen cap on her hair, called out the order to the cook, turned around and suddenly threw the customer a broad let's-be-friends smile.

The grouchy face didn't change expression. The stooped shoulders tried to hunch together even more, to express even more grouchiness, but the little pouch at his waist-line did not allow it. The young woman's lips tightened again and the smile disappeared automatically, as befits that particular restaurant. She stirred one of the pots with a wooden spoon, then stirred another one. She raised her head with the long black hair and the longish, not-so-pretty face — and tried another smile. This time the smile was not as simple — it was more inviting, and at the same time had a childlike uncertainty. Childlike was also her languid, yearning look — as were her thin arms that ran pitifully up to her shoulders — as was the skeletal collarbone around her skinny neck. Her face — she could have been 16, but also 26, or even older. The grouchy guest stared at her for a moment with a confused look. Gradually the grouchiness receded from his eyes like the frost from a windowpane; his bulldog expression softened. On such a face it was virtually a smile — a "return smile." Thank goodness!

The young woman brightened, responded more swiftly and energetically to the requests of other customers. The man with the grouchy face got his griddle-cakes and syrup and butter and sat down at a little table not far from the counter. He proceeded methodically. First he placed the pats of butter between the hot-cakes, to give them time to melt, then he poured himself some coffee from the automatic faucet in the wall, then he took off his hat and coat and hung them up on a hanger. For a few moments he sat motionless at his table, his round shoulders slumped as if in weariness, and at the crown of his cranium appeared an ivory-yellow bald-spot which his slightly silvery hair tried in vain to conceal.

Then he ate his griddle-cakes. Slowly, thoughtfully. From time to time he glanced in the direction of the young woman.

Once he even shrugged his shoulders, as if to say, "Ah, forget it!"

He had already put on his coat, but the arm reaching out for his hat fell back to his side. He walked back to the hot-table and, without looking at her, pointed to the dessert trays. "When do you get off from work?" he asked nonchalantly. In the blink of an eye a wave of little looks and crinkles passed over her face like a soft breeze over a stream, and as her eyes darted toward the clock on the wall, she said:

"About an hour."

He nodded his head gloomily. Leaving his dessert untouched on the table, he walked out into the street.

2.

The street-lights were already on. The air was a bit tangier than it had been in the afternoon, but the evening was still mild. The streets were jammed with people and vehicles. The very apex of the rush hour.

He strolled along the streets around the Public Library, his eyes thoughtful, his brow unruffled. Relaxed. The noise and bustle all around him were separated from him as by a thin wall that he always carried with him. At one point his composure was shaken when he came face to face with a young woman with blond hair and gray eyes. Both he and the woman paled. He touched the brim of his hat. She said, "How are you?" and he said, "Thanks, how are you?" She asked him to accompany her, but he said, "Sorry, I'm meeting someone in a few minutes."

Behind the polite, restrained words their eyes glared hard and cutting, like rapiers in the hands of a pair of duelists. She walked along with her spine erect and her head high, and he — with his shoulders a bit more hunched and his face clouded. But a moment later his forehead was again unruffled, one corner of his mouth turned up in a little smile, and his expression stayed that way until he noticed by a clock in a window that he was already five minutes late. With unhurried steps he returned to the Automat.

She stood near the restaurant looking into a show-window. She was wearing a grey-brown coat and a little brown hat — and neither of them suited her. Her face was serious, with the expression that made her look 26. As she turned to meet him, a momentary smile changed the lines of her face and then disappeared. What volatility! Latin blood, or what?

They walked west on 42nd Street to Broadway. She walked in a well-mannered and "lady-like" way. At first glance you might have taken her for an impoverished middle-class Jewish matron. At second glance you would change your mind. At third glance you would see clearly she was from another world: Spanish, perhaps, and with a mixture of Indian blood.

"Do you have a regular job in that restaurant?"

"My tenth week. Half-days. Can't make a living this way."

What is she hinting at — "Can't make a living?" Must have an additional income. He grimaced.

"What's your name?" he asked.

Again her face changed with extraordinary rapidity, as from an internal explosion. These sharp transitions unnerved him a bit, as if she were nudging him or grabbing hold of him by a button. Actually she was quite modest in her movements; only the cut of her mouth kept moving like the strap of a whip, and in the corners of her eyes flickered a little smile.

"Jennie," she said. "My name is Jennie."

"Jennie indeed. Why Jennie?"

She pouted. "Why not? I'm American. Born right here in New York.."

"I'm not saying you weren't. But you — you look like you come from one of the Latin countries — Spain, for example, yes?"

Her swarthy brow grew darker.

"Well, my parents, yes — they come from California. But I'm a New Yorker. Born here. Right here in the city." Her left hand pointed southward.

That much is probably true, he thought. Her speech was incorrect, ungrammatical, but no different from that of any other working-girl — American, New Yorkish.

3.

He offered to buy her an ice-cream, and sitting at the table in the Ice Cream Parlor she again loosened up. She really doesn't know any Spanish, she admitted. Her "old folks," of course, they speak Spanish to each other, but she herself barely knows a few words. And of course, the prayers; but those are in Latin.

Now he too loosened up a bit. "But listen. What kind of name is Jennie for you? Really. Every Jane, Jean and Joan becomes Jennie. At least if you'd call yourself Juanita, or Isabella. And what's wrong with Dolores?"

She looked at him a little uncertainly.

"But I'm an American."

"Of course you're an American. Certainly. But say it yourself — Do-lo-res. It has a rhythm to it. So that's settled. That's what I'm going to call you — Dolores."

She laughed. With a big grin on her face, she reached across the table and put her hand on his.

"All right! Let it be Dolores, if that's what you want. And what shall I call *you*?"

Whatever formality had existed in their conversation now vanished.

"Me?" he said. For a moment his previous reserve returned, then he smiled again.

"You won't even be able to pronounce it. Let me hear you say LAKRITSPLETSL..."

"Lak — Go on, you're kidding me!"

"My name isn't important, Dolores. Call me Manny. Easy to pronounce and better than Morris or Sydney. What do you say to a movie?"

"Of course! Sure. I'd love it. Let's go!"

They went out into the street and headed toward Broadway. As they walked he caught her looking wistfully into the window of a flower shop. He went inside and brought out a rose — a single rose — not completely open, but a full, plump one, with much promise.

"Thank you, sweetie!" she exclaimed.

Inside the theater, after she removed her hat, she took the flower out of a buttonhole and pinned it to her hair at the right side of her head. Somewhere he had seen a painting — a Goya, perhaps — a Spanish woman with a rose in her black hair. No similarity between her face and Dolores's, but still... In the dim light of the darkened theater, even the look in her eyes changed.

4.

In front of the curtain, in a purple spotlight, stood a tall, burly man in a black frock-coat, with a smooth, round, womanish face, and in a disconcertingly high-pitched voice sang about a "little angel." The lips of his narrow mouth opened in an oval as he sang sweetly and languidly:

Give my regards to Mother,

Tell her I can find no other

Who'd love me as much as she...

In the row in back of them someone sobbed. Jennie-Dolores's volatile face was hard at work as her escort stole frequent glances at her and his faint smile curled the corners of his mouth.

After *Give My Regards to Mother* came, naturally, *Somebody Waits for Me* and finally a song about the tobacco leaves shining like gold and the cotton fields white as snow, where "the darkies" don't do anything all day but eat red ripe watermelon and dance by the light of the blue moon at night. All of which takes place "down by the Mis-si-sip-pee..."

Very nice. It struck him as odd that the three different songs seemed to be sung to one and the same tune, a tune he had heard a year ago, two years ago, six years ago, in all kinds of vaudeville houses. Only the words changed, or maybe he was mistaken and the words too were always the same...

After the 250-pound angel collected his several rounds of applause, out came a Black man who started singing a Negro song, but before he finished, it began to sound like the same song the "angel" had sung, except that he danced a little jig with it — and then disappeared into the wings.

Then, from both sides of the stage, came the following company: a girl dressed as a white lily, a tall, skinny, gray-haired sinner in a tuxedo twirling a walking-stick between his fingers. The lily and the tuxedo sang many couplets and danced opposite each other, and both the couplets and the dance transparently insinuated what they were supposed to insinuate. Dolores could not restrain her feelings, tittered, and with a little screech squeezed her escort's arm. Not to respond to this intimate gesture would have been an insult.

The stage presentation ended. The theater grew darker. The curtains closed. On the screen appeared THE WORLD BEFORE YOUR EYES.

Yale vs. Cornell. Cornell won the football game. A celluloid factory in Columbus, Ohio, is destroyed in an explosion. The damage is estimated at two million dollars. A kitten in the basement of the building was rescued and is photographed nestling in the arm of a policeman. An injured fireman is taken to the hospital. The bodies of the missing workmen have not yet been found. Miss Marian Terrence of Tacoma, Washington, went over Niagara Falls in a barrel. She is wearing knickers and her smile reveals a row of gleaming white teeth. In Japan they are planting rice in fields that are under water. Japanese men and women stand up to their ankles in water, their hands busy in the mud. A horse named Lightning won the annual British Derby. The animal fills up two-thirds of the screen and his nervous ears twitch atop his remarkably narrow head. In Los Angeles, California a young man has been sitting for 17 days tied to a chair on the roof of the Commercial Bank Building. He has seven more days to go before he wins his wager. John D. Rockefeller, Sr., plays tennis and hands out new dimes. Paris lays its annual wreath on the grave of the Unknown Soldier. Lucky Lindy flies 600 miles in his airplane to get married. Jack Dempsey works out on the eve of his bout with the Peruvian champ Zapatera. President Calvin Coolidge blinks his fish-eyes right into the movie theater, but because of the broad brim of his cowboy hat it is difficult to read the thoughts that are racing through his brain like a whirlwind. Whoops! The review of the world before your eyes is finished.

Now comes The Comedy. People run. People fall. People get up and hit each other over the head. They run, they fall, they get up again. They lose their pants. A flower pot drops from a window sill and scores a direct hit on someone's cranium. A man runs, trips, falls into a barrel of water. And so on, until he jumps off a bridge and disappears into the river, leaving behind only two monstrous air-bubbles that rise from the surface of the water. Ha-ha-ha!

"Are you enjoying yourself?" Manny asks his companion.

"Oh, yes, this is so funny!" Dolores's volatile features sprinkle a thousand smiles. The audience is still laughing at the antics on the screen. Humor — a gift of the gods.

Next on the program, the feature picture, *The Red Scarf.* Somewhere in Europe in the 12th century. Two brave knights, one rich, one poor. The first is brave in direct proportion to his wealth; the second, in the same proportion to his poverty. What will happen? Which of the two will — but let the high-placed lady of the royal court worry about that. What's true is true, though: the well-placed lady is very beautiful in her long gown and her high coiffure. How noble she looks. Manny wonders whether she eats or does other natural things, like ordinary human beings. He looks around at Dolores. The smile freezes on his lips. She is fascinated by the Lady on the screen. Her eyes are open wide in adoration. "Jesus! Maria!" she whispers, "how magnificent she is!"

"Dolores," he whispers in her ear, "excuse me. If I weren't so smart, would I be such an idiot?"

"What?" asks Dolores, unable to tear her eyes away from the screen. "Don't disturb the — look up there — why aren't you watching the movie?"

"I am, I am. Why shouldn't I be?"

It's true, he *is* looking, but at *her*, at Jennie. From beneath her black hair peeks the tip of an ear, a tiny ear, and next to it, glowing like an ember, the rose in her hair, as if it were growing out of her head. He picks up her hand in both of his; she responds with a light, tentative pressure. Little by little his hand sinks lower. The two strangers are sitting very close together now, but each of them is still in a separate world...

5.

"Oysters!" Manny decided as they were leaving the theater. "We ought to go and eat some oysters."

Dolores followed him silently, a shadow of a pensive smile on her lips. The weather had turned cold. Tiny snowflakes floated around singly in the air. Inside the big LUNCHROOM, POPU-LAR PRICES it was warm, bright and noisy with the after-theater crowd. Manny ordered oysters in their shells. Dolores ordered oysters in milk. She ate with the exaggerated manners of the "real New Yorker" — screwed up her mouth, took tiny sips, held the slice of bread daintily between two fingers, and pecked at her food like a bird. For dessert she had red Jell-O and whipped cream. Manny observed her with his head down. Once he asked her:

"You live with your parents?"

A cloud passed over her brow and disappeared. She did not reply. After a little while she said calmly:

"When you work in a restaurant you see all kinds of people."

So simple. Ignore the question that may have been too personal and introduce a new subject.

"What made you think of that?" he asked.

"Nothing in particular. Just remembering something. There's a man comes into the Automat. A smallish, skinny guy. A musician. Wears glasses and a five-year-old derby and a threadbare coat, like a scarecrow. One of those Russians or something. All he ever orders is hotcakes and syrup. I guess that's what made me think of him. You also ordered hotcakes. But this guy — he never orders anything else. A real comedy. I don't even wait for his order anymore. He just smiles and I get him his hotcakes. One thing he does have — a nice smile. A smile is a smile, but there's something about the way he does it...

"So what was I saying? Yes. He always sits down at a table not too close and not too far away. Looks at me once in a while. Well, why does a man look at a woman that way? But all he ever does is look. To tell the truth, at first I tried to encourage him. I smiled back. Just curious to see what kind of person this was. But he never said anything. Just smiled and looked. Well, it's a free country, you want to look, be my guest. Although it got on my nerves after a while. But what could I do? I got used to it. You could say we had a kind of relationship. A silent relationship. When he doesn't show up for a few days, I miss him! Did you ever?" She giggled, signifying the end of her story.

But she seemed happier now. Playful. As they left the restaurant she took hold of his arm and pressed against him.

"And now, young lady," said Manny, "it's time for you to go home."

She let go of his arm, straightened up like a soldier on inspection and looked at him mutely — puzzled and astonished.

"What's the problem? It's late. Time for you to get some sleep. For me too."

Still she said nothing. Ill-at-ease, he took a step away from her and then back to her. She took hold of his elbow. "Take me with you. Take me *somewhere.*"

"But it's not my — my habit," he muttered.

"What do you mean?"

"It's not my way of doing things. You won't understand. And where shall I take you? How do you know I don't have a wife and kids at home? You want me to introduce you to her?"

"But — what about a hotel?"

"A hotel? I hate hotels!"

Impatiently, nervously, he danced around her.

"What kind of man are you, anyway?"

"Like all other men. Not much worse." Something suddenly occurred to him. "Listen. I think I understand —" He put his hand in his pocket, but as he did so her Latin eyes blazed, her mouth twisted. He did not take his hand out of his pocket. Her hostile look vanished. She shook her head and said:

"Good night. Thanks for the good-time."

Before he could reply, she was ten paces away.

Disconcerted, he followed her.

"Wait a second — I'm sorry. That was stupid of me. Why are you running away like that?"

She narrowed her steps, but continued walking.

"I'm telling you — I was stupid. Don't be angry with me. It's okay. Come home with me, Dolores ... Jennie ..."

She stopped walking, but could not recover her composure all at once. He took her arm.

"Let's walk a little, Dolores. Then we'll see..."

A light snow was now falling. Tiny warm feathers, falling gently from above, floated in the air and came to rest momentarily here and there, ready to rise again and fly away somewhere else. Fifth Avenue began turning white between the high, now silent walls. From time to time an automobile slid by with a silken rustle. It wasn't that New York City was asleep; more likely it had sat down in a comfortable easychair, cigar in hand, too relaxed even to think...

At 59th Street Manny hailed a cab. The brief but emphatic burst of anger that had come between them left them with a sense that they were no longer strangers, but neither of them felt very much like talking. Inside the taxi he put his arm around her. She snuggled up to him and they sat this way until the cab pulled up outside a large apartment house in the Bronx. Dolores cast a surprised look at the entrance, but she said nothing. It was definitely not a hotel.

Inside, they crossed a large hall on the ground floor. At the stairway he halted.

"Take my hand," he said. "And don't rush. It's a long climb."

The corridors and the stairways were well illuminated, but they were empty and quiet. She leaned her head on his shoulder, and in this way they mounted the steps from floor to floor like a married couple returning home late from an evening of merrymaking with good friends.

6.

The day is so hot that the grassy earth under Manny's body is warm and pliant as a woolen blanket. The day is so bright that through his closed eyelids he can very clearly see the green valley far down below; he can see the sky, a pale, pale blue, as if it had been bleached by the sun, but it embraces the whole world. He can see the rich foliage on the chestnut tree high above his head. He is lying on his side, his left hand beneath his cheek, and every limb in his body is at rest.

It is very quiet, so he can hear a bee singing nearby in a thin, reedy tenor: *Scar-let red! Scar-let red!* What does the bee mean by that?

Sunk in his thoughts, he moves his right hand over the warm ground near his body and it lands on something that utters a weak, frightened peep. He pulls his hand back. On the ground sits a tiny bird, its little beak and its round yellow eyes gesticulating excitedly. Pink skin peeks out from between its sparse little feathers. Still a baby. Must have fallen out of a nest. Again he places his hand on the little body, carefully, tenderly. The bird trembles, barely perceptibly, but apparently the creature is not frightened. It stops moving, then starts again, in a regular, rhythmic beat. Don't-be-afraid, don't-be-afraid, afraid, afraid...

Somewhere in his own head he had stored away a thought that he now needed to retrieve and study more closely. What was it? Yes. How is it possible that he can see through closed eyes? If the light is so strong out there, how much more so will it be with his eyes open? Very peculiar. He forces his eyes open — pitch dark! Incredible! He closes his eyes again immediately. Darkness. Blackness. He opens them again. Beneath his hand the bird is still trembling, evenly, regularly, like a human heart. Yes, beneath his hand is a human heart...

He forces himself awake.

Night. If you lie still for a moment with your eyes open you can see that the darkness is not perfect. The light of the stars streams through the double window, into his bedroom; the night itself is immersed in a soft, white, diffused light. Must be the snow on the street. A moment later the walls of his room step out, the stains on the walls become pictures. Then the table, a chair. On the floor, a dark pile — clothing, women's clothing, dropped there in avid, joyous forgetfulness. He shivers, smiles, draws the air deeply into his lungs.

She is sleeping restfully, her body curled up, snug, exuding warmth. Her heart is beating evenly, regularly. The body renewing itself. Remarkable how many unbeautiful women have beautiful bodies. Or the reverse...

Carefully he sidles out of bed, slips on his robe, goes into the next room, closing the door behind him. He presses the light switch. This was the larger of his two rooms, very sparsely furnished. On the bare walls, a lone painting — a landscape by Isaac Lichtenstein. Two doors in a corner lead into the bathroom and the "kitchenette."

He rinses his mouth, drinks a glass of water, lights up a cigarette, looks into the mirror, grimaces. What a mug! A sleepy, swollen, grouchy face, the eyes protruding out of his head, gray wire sprouting on his chin. Fui! A hairy chest, a growing paunch, a body that looks used up. Although ... He waves his hand woefully and goes to the window.

A white, frosty night. A few moments earlier — a hot, sunny day, just as real — for me. And what more can I know than "for me"? *Scar-let red.* A juicy word, "scarlet." Fills the mouth like a sip of Malaga wine, or a slice of fresh watermelon. Scarlet red. There must be other words like that. Stalks of gold. Corn-stalks. Life asks no questions. Only death asks questions. What does that mean, anyway? Not too clear ...

That human being there on my bed. Apparently love that is bought is also a kind of love. How was one to know that? Tender — passionate — capricious — playful — deep — genuine. How can that be? Human beings need a ray of sunshine, a little bit of fun, a modicum of pleasure. And so simple, but earthy. A kiss. A touch. The naked soul? I've never seen a soul strolling on Broadway without any clothes on. For that matter, I've never seen a naked body strolling on Broadway either. The Ninth Symphony, without an ear made of skin and sinew to listen to it is — nothing. Yet people say that stuffed derma is "good for the soul." What does that mean? Ach! You impractical daydreamer! Brought a girl up from the street and philosophizes over her!

A few blocks away the El trains are already thundering. Heavy express wagons creak along in the snow. The day is just around the corner.

He paces back and forth in his bedroom slippers from one corner of the room to the other. Diagonally.

That little one in there is full of longing. But I've already gone through that discussion. What is the moral of the story? Bought love is also — love. Show a person a shekel and he starts singing the praises of heaven. Bah! A bad joke. Am I so stupid? All my life I never understood that? That would be too simple. Too simple is not good. Too complicated is also not good. Where is the truth? Oh, hell! He spits because he has just put the wrong end of the cigarette in his mouth. But also because his thoughts are in such a hopelessly tangled knot.

He went to the door and brought the milk in from the corridor, along with the odors of eggs, bacon and fresh coffee.

"Dolores! Breakfast!"

"Mm-m-m ... In a minute," she answered from the bedroom. She sat at the edge of the bed, her thoughts having stopped her in the middle of putting on her clothes. Violet panties. Naked above the waist. A youthful body, almost like a boy's. Her head, unexpectedly that of a grown woman, her black hair disheveled, her eyes open wide, her lips parted. A self-induced trance. Finally she pried her eye away from a spot somewhere in space, jumped off the bed, grabbed her clothes from the pile, ran through the front room and into the bathroom.

They ate their breakfast in silence, occupied with their own thoughts. Meantime the sun had peered out from behind a roof across the street and thrown a glowing golden sword on the floor, a long, sharp sword with a pencil-thin point. It happened so suddenly that they both looked up, waiting for the clinking sound of metal. When it didn't come, they stared at each other with faint, uncertain smiles.

Dolores finished her breakfast, put on her coat and hat, stepped over to the mirror and methodically made up her face. Manny stood up, took a couple of bills out of a drawer and handed them to her. She flinched, stepped back and shook her head vigorously: No!

"Take it, will you!" he insisted, with a look of impatience.

She put her hands behind her back, like a child.

"But — why not?"

For a moment she said nothing. Then, haltingly:

"I — this time — it was — for pleasure, for *my* pleasure."

"*Your* pleasure?" He chewed on this. Then he moved closer to her and pleaded.

"Listen to me, please. Take it. You can use it. A gift, you understand? Or maybe — buy yourself a good silk blouse that will cling tenderly to your skin — like this —"

7.

They stood that way for a little while, not saying another word. Then, without looking at the money, she stuffed it into her purse.

"Good-bye"... she said.

He took her hand and touched her fingers with his lips. Just a little bit mock ceremoniously. The brave knight in his bathrobe, with a shining bald-spot on his head, and the high-placed lady — in 20th century New York. But it was Jennie from Tenth Avenue who took it from him without a smile, seriously, almost sternly. She nodded, turned, went to the door and opened it. Here she turned and looked at him for the last time.

From behind this look, from somewhere very far away, a wave of intimacy struck him with such unexpected force that he shuddered. She stepped out into the corridor and pulled the door shut behind her. He rushed toward the door — and stopped in his tracks.

"My God! What? What happened here?"

BROWNSVILLE KRETCHMA
Kadya Molodowsky

KADYA MOLODOWSKY (1894-1975) — born in Poland; died in New York.

As a child Molodowsky studied the traditional Jewish subjects with her father, a Hebrew school teacher. She then attended the Hebrew Teachers Seminar in Warsaw. In the early 1920s she lived for a few years among Yiddish writers in Kiev, then moved back to Warsaw to teach in the Yiddish secular schools. In 1935 she emigrated to the United States, where she wrote From Lublin to New York, *a novel, (1942) and* Stories for Jewish Children, *published by the Yiddish Folk Schools in 1945.*

In 1950-52 she lived in Israel, where she wrote many poems expressing joy at the restoration of Zion; she also wrote a play in Yiddish, Toward the God of the Desert, *and a novel,* At the Gate, *about the life of the new immigrants in Israel.*

Moving back to the U.S. in 1953, she continued to write poetry and fiction for young people. Marzipans, *published by the Workmen's Circle in 1970, became an immediate favorite in Yiddish schools. In 1957 she published* House with Seven Windows, *a collection of stories which includes* Brownsville Kretchma, *and* On the Roads to Zion. *Between 1965 and 1971 she was awarded several literary prizes, including one from the American Jewish Book Council.*

Sh. Niger, the Yiddish literary critic, said about her: "Kadya Molodowsky writes so as not to scream, just as she laughs so as not to cry." Further information on Molodowsky, Miriam Raskin (also represented in this volume) and other women Yiddish writers can be found in Found Treasures. Stories by Yiddish Women Writers *(Toronto, Second Story Press, 1994).*

Brownsville Kretchma

The Kretchma

The boss of New York City is undoubtedly the Mayor, but the boss of Brownsville is Nyoma Khurgin. A goodly number of all the garment operators in New York live in Brownsville, and Nyoma Khurgin has lived there now for forty years. When he came to America from Zaritsa, he settled in Brownsville and has never moved from there.

"I still remember Brownsville when it was as big and as beautiful as Zaritsa," Nyoma says. "A few wooden houses and many herds of goats. Houses were dirt-cheap here, so the operators rushed in and made Brownsville their town. And now, behind every door lives an operator."

In Nyoma Khurgin's kitchen stands a big table, the kind you usually find in a tailor's home, and the table is there mainly for the sake of the "Friday evenings." Friday evenings the operators play cards at Nyoma's, but they also talk about world politics, and that's the *main* thing.

"The son-of-a-bitch made another speech, and again he barked at the Jews."

That's Harry talking. They call him Shorty Harry, but the truth is he's as tall as the rest of them. The reason they call him Shorty is that he's always complaining about being "short in the pocket."

You could give Nyoma Khurgin free tickets to the theater for Friday evening, but he would never accept them. Friday evening he doesn't "belong to himself" but to his community. The chairs around the big table in his kitchen are all occupied, and whenever it gets too crowded they move some benches over and start a "second row." Nyoma belongs to six organizations. He helped build the first Yiddish folkshul in Brownsville. He also helped build the Congregation Anshei Zaritsa.

The Board members of the folkshul were not too happy about this. "A synagogue you're building? Are you a rabbi or an operator?"

Nyoma doesn't even raise his voice. "Am I building it for *you*? I'm building it for other Jews..."

Nevertheless, they still stayed angry with him — until a few of them joined the congregation. But then the Anshei Zaritsa Congregation had complaints.

"A folkshul? You want to fill Brownsville with heretics?"

Nyoma gave them the same answer: "Did I build it for you? It's for other Jews..."

But they kept arguing with him until several members of the congregation began to support the folkshul.

When all the excitement began about *Eretz Yisroel*, Nyoma started collecting money for the trade union campaign.

"Am I asking you for so much? All I want is one dime." Nyoma could collect two hundred of these dimes as quickly as pulling stitches out of a cuff. Sometimes one of the operators would object:

"What do you need Eretz Yisroel for? Are you planning maybe to settle there?"

But Nyoma Khurgin is the kind of man who can wait. He knows that a person can't stay angry forever. So Nyoma waits. He has a little can of tobacco handy that he uses for rolling his own cigarettes. By the time he rolls one cigarette for himself and one for the angry guy, the latter has forgotten why he was angry. Nyoma pastes the cigarette paper down with one lick of his tongue and replies:

"Am I telling *you* to go to Eretz Yisroel? You have a job on 38th Street, so I'm not sending you to Eretz Yisroel. But what about the Jew back in Zaritsa who doesn't have a job on 38th Street, is it all right for him to go to Eretz Yisroel? Is he worth a dime to you or not?"

Nyoma isn't really asking a question. He knows the other man has no answer. Nyoma knows the town every operator comes from, and he always puts that into the question. Shorty Harry, for example, comes from a place called Seltz.

Kadya Molodowsky

"What do you think, Harry, everything in Seltz is hunky-dory? If they could get visas they would all come over here on the next boat. But you know it's easier to get 20,000 dollars now than to get a visa."

Nyoma takes his time and rolls the cigarette for as long as it takes the light to go on in Harry's brain. Then he ends his pitch with a slap on the table:

"Well, Harry, give me your quarter and keep quiet!" In some cases Nyoma raises the minimum contribution to 25 cents.

*

Nyoma's wife Rokhl calls her house "The Kretchma." Fridays she bakes cookies for the Kretchma. Hanuka she makes latkes for the Kretchma. May First they serve drinks in the Kretchma.

Nyoma Khurgin loves to tell you how he and Rokhl got married.

"Exactly like Isaac and Rebecca in the Bible. But exactly! When I first came to Brownsville from Zaritsa I rented a room no bigger than a baked potato. One night I'm sitting in my room reading the paper. Someone knocks at my door. I open it. There stands a girl — tall and skinny and dark. And she's laughing. Such a smile! With all her teeth! 'Maybe you have something for my goats?' she says.

"How do you like that? For her goats! In Brownsville! It turns out that her mother is raising goats. How many goats do you have, I asked her. 'Plenty,' she says. So I gathered up all the pieces of stale bread I had and gave them to her. The next day, aha, she's back. 'Maybe you have something for my goats?' she asks again. And again she stands there laughing with all her teeth. 'I'm not a baker,' I told her.

"But right from the beginning I liked her, especially the way she laughed. To this day she laughs that way. She doesn't have many other merits, my Rokhl, (he winks) but she does laugh a lot. And she doesn't put on any airs."

And Rokhl, who was standing there at the time listening, laughed. Whenever the talk turns to goats, Rokhl grows more animated.

"A goat has to eat too. So I went looking —"

Nyoma helps her out. "Saul went looking for donkeys and found a kingdom. You went looking for a meal for your goats and found an operator."

The operators, they love the Kretchma. They wouldn't trade it for any Society in the world. They also love to listen to the goat story, even though they already know it by heart.

That's how it is in Nyoma Khurgin's Kretchma.

SHOLEM-MOISHE

Sholem-Moishe has three things that he loves very much. He owns a three-story house on Saratoga Avenue, the one that Nyoma Khurgin lives in. He has a wife, Gina. And he has a silver cigar-holder shaped like the mouth of a wolf. For twenty-five years he has owned that cigar-holder, exactly as long as he has been carrying in his heart a grudge against Semek Filister ever since that day when they met in the Yiddish theater, sitting next to each other.

And although this happened a great many years ago, Sholem-Moishe remembers every little detail as though it were yesterday. He even remembers how Semek exchanged looks with his wife when he found Sholem sitting in the same row next to him. Semek had rubbed his hands together and called the usher over to change their seats. (Sholem-Moishe swears that at that moment he felt something happen to his heart.) But there were no vacant seats in that row, so Semek had the gall to go back to the cashier's booth and exchange his tickets. He took his bald head and his wife and sat down two rows further back, just so he wouldn't have to sit next to Sholem-Moishe, who was only an operator in his shop.

Whenever Sholem-Moishe tells this story he always inserts a parenthesis at this point: "One thing he forgot, Semekl. He forgot that he's in America..."

At that crucial moment in the theater, Sholem-Moishe made up his mind to open his own shop. The very next day he went out and bought the silver cigar-holder with the wolf's-head, exactly the same as the one Sam Filister used, and he came to work with the cigar-holder in his mouth. Two weeks later he found a partner with money and Sholem-Moishe thumbed his nose at Semek.

Sholem's wife is known in their building as "Mrs. Okun," but for him, the boss himself, they think Sholem-Moishe is enough of a name, without a Mister and without the Okun. And although Mrs. Okun calls him "Mr. Okun," it doesn't change anything. Everybody still calls him Sholem-Moishe.

Today Sholem-Moishe is sitting on top of the world. Yesterday he received enough votes to become President of Congregation Anshei Ahavas Yisroel. So he sits on the green bench outside his building and tells his neighbors, for the tenth time, how he became president.

"Once I made up my mind to shove that snob Semek Filister off his high horse, it wasn't hard to do. I handed the Anniversary Committee a check with two zeros on it and you should have seen how Semek's face turned white as a sheet. He knew right then and there that his term was already finished. So why didn't he just hand them a check with the same amount? Because he's so stingy with his money that he simply couldn't get himself to do it. Stingy as a dog, Semek is, but he struts around like a turkey. So they elected me President. Cost me a hundred."

Sholem-Moishe stares into the hollow of the wolf's-head on his holder, as if that were the source of his stories, of which he had a barrelful. Mrs. Okun doesn't like the stories that her husband tells the neighbors. When no one else is around she lectures him:

"Sholem, it's fifty years since you're no longer an operator. Why do you still keep telling those same stories? You have a son a doctor. It's not pleasant for him either."

Getting no response, she urges him to come into the house.

"Mr. Okun!" she calls out, her tone rising. "An important telephone call for you."

"Answer it yourself!" he says, and stays where he is, ready to tell another story about how Semek Filister wanted to become chairman of the Refugee Assistance Fund.

"Semek has a tongue that belongs to God and a pocket that belongs to the Devil. But his soul belongs to his wife Virginia, who writes his speeches: 'Our hearts are open wide for our unfortunate brethren, but now we must open our pockets...' So how much do you think he gave? A five-spot. And he still expected them to vote for him as chairman. But I was the one who came along and bought the birthright. When the crowd started handing out the round half-dollars, I raised the ante to twenty-five dollars. Semek started stammering — and the public voted for me."

Mrs. Okun tells him, through the open window: "Your coffee is on the table!" but he takes no notice. Mrs. Okun repeats her summons. "Mr. Okun, your coffee is getting cold!"

"All right," he says, but he doesn't get up.

When Nyoma and Rokhl came over to the bench, Sholem-Moishe went down to the basement and brought up another bench. He didn't need anyone to help him carry it. When Sholem-Moishe lifts up a bench, it's as though it were made out of paper. He put it down right next to the other one, and when Nyoma and Rokhl made themselves comfortable, he began another one of his stories.

"You think it's some kind of trick to become a president?" he begins almost diffidently. "The real trick is to stop the other guy from being elected." Everyone knows who is meant by "the other guy."

"Semek Filister almost dropped dead when they finished the new building for the Rodfei Sholom Congregation and they didn't invite him to be chairman of the opening ceremonies. How did I manage that, you want to know? I merely had a conversation with Anshl the Butcher. Anshl has four stores now in East New York and Brownsville. 'Mr. Sigel,' I said to him, 'It's time you became a *mentsh*.' He flared up like a match. 'What're you talking about? I'm no worse than anybody else around here!'

"They're going to dedicate the new building next month, I said. Why shouldn't you be the chairman? Haven't you contributed enough to the Building Fund? 'I gave plenty!' he said. 'But who will vote for me?'

"He who greases the wheels rides on the wagon, I said. Pay for the refreshments and they'll all vote for you. 'What are you talking about? That would cost me a hundred dollar bill!' he grumbled.

"I'll go halves with you, Mr. Sigel, I said. It's not every day we dedicate a new building. Well, what kind of man refuses an invitation to be Chairman? Not Anshl. I tell you, it was worth fifty dollars to watch Semek lose about fifteen pounds overnight ..."

Again Mrs. Okun tried to get her husband to come inside: "Mr. Okun, what's wrong with you?" And since Sholem-Moishe didn't budge, she came out herself. Mrs. Okun doesn't like to sit outside with her "tenants." She grants them a little smile, mutters a faint hello and takes their rent. But that's the extent of her sociability. This time she came down the steps and approached the benches, but she didn't sit down. She stood there a little while, then she very carefully lifted her skirt, as though she were wearing a glass petticoat, and sat down on the steps of the porch. An appropriate distance away, that is.

"Mr. Okun, please, it's time to come inside."

But her Mr. Okun was in no mood to pay any attention to her. He merely stared into the hollow of his cigar-holder and continued:

"When his son and my son were going to high school, mine always got better marks —"

But that was as far as he got. It was as if someone had sliced his words with a sword in mid-air. Mrs. Okun had gotten up suddenly and called out:

"It's the doctor!"

A big automobile with a long, shiny hood had stopped at the curb and out of it had come Doctor Robert. Sholem-Moishe, with a wave of the hand, excused himself, walked forward, took the satchel from his son's hand, and the three of them — Mr. and Mrs. Okun and Robert the Doctor — went upstairs. Sholem-Moishe turned his head only once toward his neighbors and winked an eye:

"I'll make it short and snappy. As long as I'm alive and breathing, Semek Filister will never be a president in Brownsville again!"

THE BROTHERS

When a man suddenly acquires wealth, it is noticeable no-where as much as in his eyes and in his lapels. The eyes grow stiff and so do his lapels. But with Jake, the older of the "Brothers," it was noticeable in something else: on the pinkie of his right hand, where a ring appeared with a green stone the size of a *matzo*.

The "Brothers" became rich in the space of only three-four years. From what? From horse-radish, believe it or not. In the Kretchma, people were expecting them to show up for the Hanuka latkes, and Rokhl had said that there would be not only latkes but "something" to go with the latkes. That same day, Shorty Harry had brought the latest news about "the Brothers" — they were no longer "Eisner Bros." but "Eisner Bros. & Company."

Nyoma Khurgin could remember when they had borrowed the first twenty-five dollars to rent the little horse-radish store they started in.

"I gave them five dollars. Shorty Harry gave them five. And I can't recall who loaned them the other —"

Before he could remind himself who the others were, the Brothers themselves arrived in person: Yankel and Itsik, or as they were known in America — Jake and Izzy. When they were still operators the Brothers had spent many evenings in the Kretchma, especially during slack times when there was no work "in the trade," so now, when they entered, they felt right at home.

Jake rested his eyes for a moment on Rokhl, then on Nyoma, and said:

"Nu, how are things with you?"

Having taken care of that amenity, he began cleaning his pipe, then he stuffed it with tobacco which he took from a little silver box, and then, when he had a good light going, and with the pipe still in his mouth, he turned to the crowd and asked: "Nu, so where are the latkes?"

Nyoma seemed to be getting ready to answer both questions at the same time, and, as was his habit, he was slowly rolling himself a cigarette, but before he could finish, two bottles of "Lord

Calvert" whiskey appeared on the table, put there by Izzy, the younger brother.

"Brother Operators!" he exclaimed. "Let's drink a l'khayim!"

Shorty Harry stared at the bottles.

"You don't drink anything but Lord Calvert nowadays?"

"If you drink, you may as well drink with a lord," said Jake. "You expect us to drink only with operators?" As he said this, he raised his eyebrows so high that his hat started jiggling on his forehead. Meanwhile, Izzy had opened both bottles. The crowd laughed:

"Bravo, Yankel! Bravo, Itsik!"

After the first drink, Jake left, even before the latkes had been served. He had a "business appointment" at the Astoria Hotel, he announced.

Nyoma tried to detain him. "What are you running away from? You never know. One of us might become President of the United States of America some day."

Jake winked. "A lady is waiting for me..."

When he left, however, the kretchma breathed easier. The talk turned to the "olden days" and, naturally, to the horse-radish business.

"Izzy, remember when I went with you to rent the store?"

"Do I remember!"

"That whole store on Amboy Street was no bigger than a paper box!"

"It sure was. I remember the first day I went to the market to buy the first sack of horse-radish. Carried it back on my own shoulders. I started grating it and stood there crying like a dummy!"

"It's a good thing you switched to horse-radish. You never were a good operator!" said Nyoma.

"We weren't doing so good with the horse-radish either. We were even thinking of going to Levenstock and asking for our jobs back. But then the miracle happened. And just in time too. I knew we were in trouble when I saw those little jars in the window piling up."

"What did you do, Izzy, for real?"

"I went to see a friend of mine, a printer. I asked him to print up a bunch of labels marked 'imported.' I took the labels and pasted them on the jars. A few days later the jars in the window were all gone. Like magic! We packed the 'imported' horse-radish in little green sacks and 'sealed' them with rubber-bands. And soon Amboy Street and Herzl Street and Strauss Street and Hopkins Avenue were all eating our imported horse-radish!"

It didn't take long and the Brothers moved to Saratoga Avenue, then Pitkin, with a big display window with flowers. And they did it all with horse-radish — domestic and imported. And Jake went out and bought himself that ring with the green matzo.

The audience in the kretchma listened raptly.

"And who tastes the horse-radish for you now? You remember how you used to bring the jar for me to taste?"

"Sure. But now we have a regular system and we don't have to taste it."

Izzy liked to tell these stories about his factory, especially to his brother operators.

"You want to hear something funny? I never told this to anyone. We had already moved to Pitkin Avenue. One morning a U.S. tax collector came to see us. How much horse-radish do you import, he wanted to know. And who do you import it from? That's all he wanted to know! My brother Jake got scared. He didn't know what to say. But I believe the best way is usually to tell the truth. So I said to the tax-man: 'Sir, the only thing we ever imported was our bubba's grater.' The tax-man happened to be Jewish, and he caught on pretty quick. He laughed so hard he had to sit down. When he stopped laughing he shook his finger at us.

"So you're fooling your customers?"

"Sir," I said to him, "Look at this label. Does it say 'imported horse-radish?' No, It says only 'imported.' If the customer would ask me what's imported, would I tell her a lie? But since they don't ask, I guess they must be satisfied with the horse-radish."

"You know something else, Brother Operators? Our best customers now are the ladies with the green feathers in their hats. 'Would you please give me,' they always say. Very polite. And they point to the jar they want. The bigger the feather in their hat, the smaller the ring on the finger they point with. Where did Pitkin Avenue get so many fine ladies? I tell you, I stand there sometimes and I think: Shame on you! The Mister is sweating somewhere in a shop, or in a store, and you walk around with your green feather and say please... Well, how about another *l'khayim?*"

After that came the latkes "with something." Rokhl demanded a nickel a latke.

"What!" complained Izzy. "Rokhl wants to get rich too?"

Nyoma gives him a little lecture: "Ever since you're on Pitkin Avenue you forgot what's going on in the world. What's-a-matter? There's no war going on? There's no refugees?"

Izzy had another latke and licked his chops. "Only a nickel a piece? A real bargain! You can't get such good latkes even in the Astoria Restaurant..."

When it came time to settle up, however, Rokhl insisted that Izzy hand over "paper money" for each latke. He tried to bargain with her, but Rokhl insisted. For the Eisner Bros., the price had just gone up. Nyoma interjected: "Well, at least one of the Brothers is still with us. The other one has gone off to the green feathers."

Izzy was pleased with the compliment. He made himself comfortable. Later, when he was already at the door, he said:

"Anytime, I'm ready to give up five dinners at the Astoria for one schnapps in the Kretchma. You hear? Anytime!"

When Izzy left, Shorty Harry said: "Let's see how long he keeps his word." Nyoma said nothing. As was his wont, he slowly rolled himself a cigarette.

THE CROW

All of a sudden, Shorty Harry began wearing colorful dollar neckties. At about the same time, Bella Montsinka, who worked at the corner drugstore, started patronizing the Kretchma.

One day Bella met Rokhl near the house and helped her carry some packages up the steps. Several days later she brought Rokhl a tablecloth that she had bought at a sale "for next to nothing."

Rokhl put the cloth on the table immediately and both women agreed: it simply "belonged" on that table, in that house. Brightened up the whole place. Rokhl couldn't take her eyes off her new tablecloth.

Ever since then Bella began stopping in at the Kretchma. She would come in with the three strings of beads around her neck and sit down at the table across from Shorty Harry. Bella was not pretty. Her lips were heavily made up. Her hair was combed with a ruler-straight part in the middle of her head, which somehow gave the impression that she had been up all night fixing her hair. For her shoes she never paid less than ten dollars a pair.

Bella had a strange reputation on Saratoga Avenue. First of all, people said she would never get married. Her first suitor had brought her to America when she was sixteen. Four years later he left her. She had vowed then that she would never marry. This story was well known. Secondly, it was rumored that in every house where she rented a furnished room, the man of that house fell in love with her. Because of this, women refused to rent her a room, and she therefore had to live as far away as Eastern Parkway. It's better not to let "The Crow" into your house — that's what people called her. Either Bella didn't know what people were saying about her on Saratoga Avenue, or else she had created a perfect facade of not caring what they said. The three strings of beads she wore, the straight part in her hair, her large, painted lips — they always looked exactly the same, as though they were a painting made by an artist.

One evening, as Shorty Harry was walking to the Kretchma, he heard someone calling:

"Yoo-hoo!"

The voice was happy and summery. Later Harry recalled thinking that it had actually been summertime, early in the evening, and that a warm breeze had been ruffling his hair. He recalled also Bella saying, "I'm going to the Kretchma, let's go up together."

The Kretchma was only one flight of stairs up, but Harry recalls liking the idea of going up together. This happened a few more times. Harry would be walking to the Kretchma and he would hear her cheerful "Yoo-hoo!" But it was on that first day that he decided to buy the neckties.

And that same evening she also told him that he put too much sugar in his tea, and sugar is not good for the kidneys. No one else heard her say it, though. Bella always spoke softly. Her bright red lips were like a flame, but her white hands with the long fingers gave off a coolness as refreshing as a summer evening.

"What does she want of me?" Harry wondered. And why do other women call her "The Crow?" It rankled him. She had such a cheerful voice and such white hands. Amazing what people will say sometimes.

When the neighbors in the Kretchma sat down to play cards, Bella would lean her arms on the table and silently watch. She could keep silent for hours at a time. Once in a while she would light up a cigarette. Or examine her fingernails. It was as though she were very busy keeping silent.

One Friday evening, when the card game had gone on later than usual, Harry left together with Bella and walked her to Eastern Parkway. They walked along in silence and Harry could imagine the warmth of the evening nesting in the broad sleeves of her white cape.

As Bella opened her door, she said, "Come up and I'll make some coffee."

Harry followed her up the stairs.

As he entered her room he began to understand why the part in her hair was always so neatly combed. The room sparkled with cleanliness and order. The ash-tray stood in a blue dish. The lamp rested on a freshly ironed white napkin. On a spacious sofa five pillows were arranged very neatly. On a shelf stood a few books and near them lay a bone-handled knife for cutting the pages. On the window sill bloomed a blood-red geranium.

Not at all like a crow's nest!

He could not restrain his curiosity. When she put the two cups of coffee on the table, he asked:

"Tell me, Bella, is it true what they say about you, that —"

She didn't let him finish his question.

"It's true, Harry. It's true what they're saying. Would you like to marry me?"

He looked at her brightly painted lips, at the blushing geranium on the window-sill. He felt as if all of New York City were in bloom.

"Would I — yes!" he replied without a moment's thought.

The next day he announced it in the Kretchma: Bella and he were getting married. Everyone, even Nyoma Khurgin — who had his own philosophy and rarely asked questions — was startled.

"You — and Bella?"

"Yes, this coming Sunday."

When Harry left, Rokhl shook her head sadly.

"May all our enemies last no longer than the Crow will stay with him ..."

Nyoma rolled a cigarette and quoted himself: "Nothing is impossible in this world. Even heaven and earth touch sometimes."

Since that Friday evening, two years have passed. The Crow often visits the Kretchma. And while the others are playing cards she sits with her head resting on her arms. Shorty Harry still wears his beautiful dollar neckties as he waits for the Sunday when he and Bella will be married.

BELLA SARADACCI

I. J. Singer

ISRAEL JOSHUA SINGER (1893-1944) — born in Bilgoray, Lublin District, Poland; died in New York.

Singer was the older brother of Isaac Bashevis Singer. His father was a rabbi; his mother, the daughter of the rabbi of Bilgoray. The family moved to Warsaw, and their family life there before World War I is graphically portrayed in the memoir by his brother, In My Father's Court.

At 18, "I.J." (as he was known) abandoned the religious home of his parents and joined other young left-wing Jews in Warsaw. While studying Polish, Russian, German, and other secular subjects, he worked as a machinist.

His first story, about a spinster, was published in Dos yiddishe vort. *In 1918, after the revolution in Russia, he moved to Kiev, where he published several novellas. His* Pearl and Other Stories, *which was rejected by European Yiddish editors, caught the eye of Abe Cahan in the United States, who published it serially in the* Forverts. Yoshe Kalb, *(English:* The Sinner*), a novel about a sainted fool, was dramatized by the Yiddish Art Theater in New York and became an instant "hit." In this novel Singer evoked the atmosphere of Hasidic life in the 19th century.*

In 1933 he settled in New York, where he published The Brothers Ashkenazi *in the* Forverts; *also* Chaver Nachman *(English:* East of Eden*);* The Family Carnovsky; *and a novel of American Jewish life,* In di berg *(*In the Mountains*). Several of these novels, translated into English by Maurice Samuel and Joseph Singer, trace the fate of generations of East European Jewish families. In 1946 he wrote an autobiographical work, published in English in 1970 as* Of a World That Is No More.

The story Bella Saradacci (Bela Saradachi) *is a departure from his usual subject matter but fits nicely into the mood of the present collection. It appears in* Springtime and Other Stories (Friling un andere dertsaylungen), *Warsaw, 1937.*

I.J. Singer

Bella Saradacci

1.

In her childhood, when her mother used to tie a big red bow in her curly dark hair, little Bella Katz already kept herself apart from her schoolmates — from all the Jewish and Chinese and Negro girls who attended the public school on Essex Street.

Her teacher, a tall, broad-hipped and sharp-boned Irish woman with straight flaxen strands of hair that kept falling over her bright blue eyes, sent for Bella's mother once a week to discuss the problem of her daughter.

"Mrs. Katz," she would say in a solemn tone, "Mrs. Katz, you must pay more attention to your Bella. She is nervous — and she tells lies..."

It was true. Bella did tell the wildest lies. She persuaded the other children of the most outlandish things. Once she told them that in the little town in the Ukraine where her mother and father came from, some of the people grow so tall that they are twice as big as Americans. The children did not believe her, but when Bella swore it was the truth — all the while beating her little breasts (which were prematurely prominent under her tight sweater), as a sign that she was telling the truth — the other children went straight to the teacher.

"Teacher," they asked breathlessly, "is it possible that some people can be twice as tall as other people?"

"No," the teacher replied. "That's utter nonsense!"

"Bella swears that there are such people."

The tall, sharp-boned teacher with one hand brushed back the flaxen strands of hair falling down over her bright blue eyes, and with the other hand she grasped Bella's swarthy chin so hard that the girl opened her lips and showed her big white teeth.

"Bella! Why do you tell the other children such things? It is not even possible for people to be that tall!"

"In the town across the ocean where my mother and father come from there are people who grow that tall."

The teacher flushed from her neck all the way up to her flaxen hair on her high forehead.

"You're lying, Bella!" she shouted, smacking her desk with her ruler. "And don't you ever dare repeat that again!"

"The people there are this big!" little Bella insisted, standing on her tiptoes and holding one arm up to its full length.

One day she came running in breathlessly with the news that a man was following her every day as she walked to school, that he was trying to entice her into his automobile. The teacher immediately took her by the hand and dragged her to the nearest police station and straight to the Sergeant's desk.

"Tell him what that man looked like," she said angrily. "Tell him everything, every detail."

The Sergeant, an older, genial, heavy-set individual with the face of a bishop, patted Bella's cheek in a fatherly manner and smiled broadly with all the creases of his honorable face.

"Tell me, little girl. Tell me about that robber who wants to kidnap you, you poor girl..."

He had understood at first glance that this little girl had a powerful imagination. He was an expert in such matters. More than once in his long experience he had had to deal with little girls with big imaginations. At the first questions they usually became all confused and began to stammer.

But this little Bella did not stammer. With the coolest aplomb she told him how the man lay in wait for her, on which corner, at what time. The whole story began to get on the policeman's nerves. In an instant he discarded the fatherly expression on his face and put on a sterner mask, just as the interrogators do in the movies.

"Well," he said, "I'll send a detective to investigate this. But if you have made this whole thing up, Bella, we'll teach you what it means to lie to the police." As he said this he winked at Bella's teacher. He knew that after a warning like this the little fantasizers began to cry.

But Bella did not cry.

"He was wearing a red tie," she said, looking straight into the Sergeant's eyes. "And two little green dolls were hanging in the windshield of his car."

The teacher was so upset she was speechless.

*

At the age of twelve, when her mother had already started teaching her about "women's problems," Bella single-handedly created a hell-on-earth for both her parents. One day she told her hard-working father, who made his living by junking old cars and who came home nights in time to go to bed — Bella told him that in the evenings, while he was away at work, a stranger came in his car to take her mother out for a walk.

Her mother beat her, pulled her hair, kicked her, in an effort to get her to admit she was lying, but Bella picked herself off the floor, wiped her bloody nose with the hem of her skirt and said calmly to her father:

"Three times a week he comes here. He blows his horn twice as a signal for Mama to come down..."

*

At sixteen she stopped telling lies. Along with this she also stopped talking altogether. She avoided people, never attended family functions, distanced herself from all her friends, and did nothing but work all day long, either at home cleaning and washing, or in the music publishing company where she was employed as a typist for eight dollars a week.

It was a small company, as old-fashioned as they come, dusty all over, full of faded, discarded notebooks and massive crumbling account ledgers. Equally old and dusty was the proprietor, a short, elderly man who always wore a high stiff collar, a soiled shirt with a starched front, and a white satin cravat with a big ivory stickpin. Just as old-fashioned were the letters he dictated to Bella and mailed to spinsters and clergymen in the forgotten corners of American cities. These were the customers for his "church music." Words and phrases which can be found nowadays only in old novels filled the old man's long "poetic" letters that he dictated to "his girl."

He ran his dingy little publishing company, which had come down to him as an inheritance through generations, the same way his grandfather and great-grandfather had done before him. He changed neither the furniture nor the books, and of course not the building, with its strong, thick walls, vaulted beams and inset, barred windows. Built originally by a great-grandfather of his down at the waterfront, it remained there, squeezed between the massive government buildings that surrounded it on all sides.

An accumulation of years of dust, rust and smoke lay on the unwashed windowpanes, riddled by sun, wind and fog. Right outside these windows, however, even through all the dirt, you could still see the ocean, broad, outspread, now a merry green, now an angry gray. Through these windows you could also see an endless procession of ships, with their haughty smokestacks and their lusty hoots. Evenings the red and green lights on the ships kept winking at you to come and join them on their journeys to distant seas, shores and exotic countries.

Bella would often pause in her work, take an old music sheet and wipe the dust off a windowpane, just enough for her to press her dark-skinned face against the cool glass and look out at the limitless expanse. She loved to listen to the ships' whistles bringing greetings from far-off countries. She followed the little red and green lights with longing as they moved silently out to sea and finally disappeared.

"Good-bye! Bon voyage!" she whispered as the vessels glided away from shore. Sometimes she would even wave...

On account of the ocean, the whistles and the outgoing ships that were always there for her eyes and ears, she continued working at the dust-covered publishing company, although they gave her only a one-dollar raise at the end of each year. On account of the little red and green lights she often stayed at her desk late into the evening. Every ship that passed by her window caught her dark eyes; every trembling hoot of the whistle spoke to her personally.

Her mother kept urging her to come visit family. Her friends dragged her to dances. Young men began hanging around, invited her out for "an ice-cream" or a movie. But she never accepted.

"No!" she would reply sharply, without a word of thanks or explanation. More than a yes or no was not in her vocabulary.

Her mother wanted to know one thing: what does she do with the few dollars she earns every week. She contributed nothing to the "house money." Her mother had never even asked her for any. She spent very little on clothes. Almost every day she put on the same tight red sweater which sharply outlined her breasts. Almost always she wore the same small, cheap, knitted hat which perched on one side of her thickly curled head.

"What are you doing with your money, daughter? Saving it for your dowry?"

"No."

"What, then?"

"Nothing!" Bella answered curtly, as usual.

At 18, her mother noticed two brand new features about Bella. First, two thin black mustaches appeared on her somewhat thick upper lip, second, her neighbor, the druggist, a blond, heavyset bachelor whom all the mothers in the neighborhood had in their sights, was sweet on her not-so-pretty and all-too-silent Bella. Whether it was the little mustaches on her lip, or the tight red sweater on her prominent breasts, or perhaps even her stubborn lack of response to all his many, graphic compliments that turned this young man's head (he was no longer so young), her mother could not fathom, but she was pleased, nay, very happy about it. Too much trouble this daughter had given her, with her wild antics at school and her stubborn silence later. As one waits with bated breath for the crisis period of a serious illness, so she waited to see what Bella's fate would be. Now, she saw, the worst was over. That tall young pharmacist with the blond hair, whom all the mothers and daughters devoured with their eyes, had come along at just the right time.

But now, precisely when the blond druggist began to visit the Katzes every night to repair anything he could get his hands on, from the clock that had stopped to a radio that wasn't working, Bella began to come home later and later every evening.

"Where are you going every night?" her mother asked her.

Without replying, Bella simply removed her sweater and stubbornly combed out her thick curly hair before going to bed.
Until —

Until one night she didn't come home at all.

Instead came a very brief telegram:

"Good-bye. Stop. Bella."

The telegram had been sent from the Mauritania at 12:43 a.m.

2.

Along with the fatigue in Bella's sallow face and the smudges on the tips of her stubby fingers from her constant pounding on the typewriter keys, the sharp ocean breeze also washed away her moroseness and her silence. Suddenly she became talkative again, a bit wild, as she had been when she was a child in school, when she exhausted the patience of her teachers. And in the same way, she regained her habit of telling lies, which came out of her mouth with no effort at all.

The head of the tourist agency, the well-dressed man with the ruler-straight part in his pasted down hair, suggested to her that she buy a return ticket, which would have reduced the cost considerably. Bella knew he was right, but — without knowing why — she blurted out that she was leaving the country for good and therefore she could not take advantage of his kind offer. Like any good American, the young man was hurt by the very thought that anyone would want to leave the United States for good.

"Oh? Why is that, if I may ask?"

"Because my husband is working in Russia near the Chinese border. He's an engineer."

The effect of this announcement was dramatic, both because of the long journey she was about to make and because of the thought that such a young woman should already have a husband working near the Chinese border. The young man was so surprised that he ran his hand through his hair and ruffled it a little bit. Bella emerged the victor in that encounter, but it cost her forty dollars more for the ticket...

On board the Mauritania, her imagination soared to new heights. In the dining-room she did not introduce herself as the young wife of an engineer working on the Chinese border but as a

Russian movie actress who had come to America to learn about "your newest film techniques." The young women to whom she confided this information wanted to know all about the dark secrets of Hollywood, including the private lives of the stars. Bella obliged them... She even taught them a few Russian words which she invented for the occasion. In her enthusiasm, she also told them about her fabulous wardrobe. Naturally they wanted to go to her cabin immediately to see for themselves, which forced Bella to tell more lies in order to get out of this tight corner.

To make matters worse, the ship's "social director" announced a "masquerade ball" for the following night. Bella, who had nothing in her valise but a few blouses and a few men's neckties (for which she had a weakness), had to sneak into the ship's store and buy — without trying it on — the one colorful gold-trimmed dress they had in stock. It cost her a small fortune.

The dress, however, made hardly any impression at the party. The young women who had been so fascinated by Bella's Hollywood story now commented audibly and sarcastically on her new dress, which was much too long and did not fit her at all. "Marvelous!" they mocked. "Must be the latest Hollywood fashion! What will they think of next?"

They now had serious doubts about Bella's film career and even about the "Russian" words she had taught them. She therefore avoided them and took up with a woman, no longer young but still very attractive, who had come down from the first-class deck to the tourist deck, looking for company. Apparently she was a well known passenger on the Mauritania. Blond, heavily made up but tastefully dressed, with many rings on her fingers and with a spoiled Pekinese which she never let out of her hands and which she never stopped kissing and petting. She looked much more the film star than the short, fuzzy haired, swarthy Bella in her tight-fitting red sweater. Everyone seemed to know all about her: that her husband owned a popular restaurant in Chicago and that she was going to Paris alone on a pleasure trip.

"Everyone knew" because she told them. Garrulous, effusive, quick to laugh, she could not abide the rarified first-class atmosphere. In the morning she greeted people volubly, asked how they were feeling, whether they had slept well, how they liked the food on this ship. Just as readily she told everyone about her husband the restaurateur, whom she no longer loved, about all the money he kept giving her because he was so much in love with her, and about her trip to Paris, where she was planning "to have a good time and enjoy myself." She never stopped talking, dragging strangers up on deck to have their picture taken with her, inviting them into the bar for a drink. She spoke with everyone, women or men, with the stewards and even with the few children on board. People began avoiding her, but this didn't bother her at all. She kept right on talking.

And she herself was a regular, frequent customer at the bar.

With this not-so-young but attractive woman, who still possessed many signs of her one-time beauty, Bella struck up a friendship. As she did with every one, the woman from Chicago told Bella all about her husband the restaurateur whom she no longer loved but who was still crazy about her. And about all the money he gave her, and about the trip she was making to Paris, where she was planning on having the time of her life.

Bella immediately confided in her new friend that she too had been married off to an older man, a pharmacist who owned ten drug stores, whom she didn't love but whom she had been forced into marrying because she was an orphan and he was very rich. The lady from Chicago sighed deeply at the bad luck of this little Bella, but Bella quickly assured her there was nothing to worry about, that she had stayed with her lover, a young prize fighter with whom she used to spend her evenings when the old man was working.

"Hurray for you!" the Chicago woman had applauded, happy to hear that the young woman had remained loyal to her lover.

Here, however, Bella's face assumed a hurt expression. Unfortunately, she said, her old man had caught them in the act. Whereupon the young prize fighter had broken her husband's nose, and she ran away — without her clothes, without her underwear, with only a few blouses and enough money only for a ticket to Paris, where she was going to stay, unless her old man personally came and begged her to come back.

In all their excitement, the two women suddenly realized they had never properly introduced themselves.

"Frances Hotchkiss," said Chicago.

"Bella Saradacci," her companion said, remembering the name of a student who had sat next to her in grade school.

From that moment, the older but still attractive woman never let Bella out of her sight. She sat next to her on deck. She moved Bella into her first-class cabin. She had her picture taken with Bella. She bought her all kinds of pins and baubles in the gift shop and plied her with cocktails at the bar.

"Darling! You and I are going to have such a wonderful time in Paris!"

She never let Bella pay for anything, but Bella insisted on treating once in a while. "Don't worry, honey. One word to my old man and he'll wire me whatever I ask for — and more." For every gift her new friend gave her, Bella bought her something in return.

Meantime Frances began regaling Bella with stories about all the romantic escapades she had been involved in. Bella soon learned to recognize the moment when another such secret was about to be revealed. Frances would lean closer to her ear, push her hair away and whisper the sinful details, punctuated by tittering and sometimes raucous laughter.

Bella, who had never even been kissed by a man, responded with romantic tales of her own.

"Excuse me, Bella," said Frances Hotchkiss one day. "I know you said your name was Saradacci. But what was your name before you were married?"

"Well, actually, Saradacci is my maiden name. My husband's name is Katz. But I prefer my maiden name."

"What does it matter, anyway! We're still in this together, aren't we? Look out Paris! Here we come!"

For some reason, Bella grew uneasy. Something about Mrs. Hotchkiss' behavior frightened her. But it was too late now to back out.

*

In no time at all Bella went through the crumpled bank- notes which she kept in her purse along with her powder, rouge and handkerchief. She no longer had any control over what was happening to her. Frances took care of everything. She moved Bella into the hotel where she was staying and even found her an apartment adjoining her own. Little Bella did not look too well in the big mirrors that were all over the hotel foyer; they all reflected the same ordinary lemon-colored coat that she wore over her tight-fitting red sweater. Bella felt embarrassed before the important-looking attendant in the official uniform who, a little too seriously and ceremoniously, took her shabby suitcase from her. She grew even more upset when he ushered her into her apartment — a spacious, elaborately furnished room full of mirrors and carpets — and put her suitcase down in a corner.

"Will that be all, Madame?"

"Yes," said Bella, not even knowing what he had asked her.

For a few moments she stood stock still and examined the room as though she were afraid to take another step across the enormous tigerskin rug. She was even more amazed by the bed, a wide French double-bed with a blue-silk canopy. In the midst of her reverie, Mrs. Hotchkiss knocked at the door between their two rooms. Bella opened the door. When the older woman began making suggestive jokes about the big French beds, Bella lost her fears and threw herself, coat and all, across the big bed.

"Funny!" she laughed. "Very comical!"

Just as funny, in her eyes, were the French restaurants, where one's feet sank into the rugs and where they served you dishes that you didn't even know how to eat.

They were such an unlikely looking pair, these two ship-friends, walking on the broad Parisian boulevards. Mrs. Hotchkiss, tall, willowy and blond, in her long red-silk dress down to her toes, which made her look even taller and more elegant, or in her white ermine coat, striding energetically along the sidewalks as though the whole world were spread before her feet. And beside her, the short, small-boned, dark-skinned Bella in her shabby lemon-colored coat which made her look even shorter than she actually was, and with her cheap, knitted red hat perched atop her mass of black curly hair. Her short legs could barely keep up with the long-legged Mrs. Hotchkiss. She trotted after her, exactly like the little Pekinese. Even in Paris, where people don't usually raise their eyebrows at anything, no matter how bizarre, they began to stare at this odd sight. Bella, feeling humiliated, wanted to hide herself in the farthest corner of some restaurant, but Mrs. Hotchkiss took an instant dislike to the restaurants in that city.

Like a hunting-dog she sniffed at the restaurants with her quivering, passionate nostrils. She would rush into the place, look around, inhale, leave, find another, repeat the process. She seemed in such command of the situation that the old experienced waiters there did not even try to stop her.

"No! No!" she would exclaim with a disparaging gesture as she dragged Bella with one hand and the dog with the other. "A disgusting garbage-can!"

Never in her life had Bella been inside such fancy restaurants. The waiters looked like the high society people she had seen nowhere but in the movies. She could not understand how anyone could compare such a place to "a disgusting garbage-can." But she didn't dare offer any opinions. She resigned herself to running after the tall lady through all the boulevards of all the cities in Europe. Until...

Until, from out of nowhere, appeared a strapping, well-dressed taxi-driver, a man with well-formed legs and a supple masculine figure, whose like can be found only among young cavalry officers. With a lightning motion his hand removed the cigarette from behind his ear and stuck it into his pocket. At the same speed he took off his stiff military cap, revealing a longish, handsome head — like a greyhound's — and with an elegant bow connoting both honor and servility, he offered — in pure, correct English — to "show the ladies Paris."

Mrs. Hotchkiss studied this man in leather for only a few seconds, from head to toe, as a practiced eye roves over a race-horse upon whom one is going to place a large bet, and then she displayed all the gluttonous teeth between her brightly painted red lips.

"Sure!" she said, looking the driver right in his green eyes. "Sure! But first we need a good restaurant. I'm ravenous as a wolf and I want something tasty!"

"Yes, Madame," the driver replied and started his car. He drove like an expert, weaving in and out of traffic and frightening Bella out of her wits, but providing Mrs. Hotchkiss with superb entertainment.

"You're a great driver!" she complimented him through the little window.

"Well, Madame, I got my training in the Royal Guard in Petersburg," the driver replied without turning his head.

"Oh!" Mrs. Hotchkiss cried with delight. "I thought as much!"

Gazing at the man's tough, masculine neck and broad shoulders, she knew she had stepped into this foreign city with her right foot first. This was a man they could depend on to take them to all the right places.

And he did not disappoint her.

But he did not take his passengers to only *one* place. It simply wasn't worth his while to do that. He received a percentage of the check from each restaurant to which he brought guests. Second, a man of expensive tastes himself from the "good old days" in Petersburg, he knew that one should never eat an entire meal in one restaurant. Every dish has its own specialists. During the years that he had been a chauffeur in Paris he had learned the city inside out. He was known in all the cafes, restaurants, American bars, Chinese tea-houses, Arab coffee-houses, Russian taverns and Caucasian wine-cellars. He was at home in all the nightclubs, a good friend of all the chorus girls, gigolos, drug-users, card-players, prize-fighters, bookmakers and ordinary Parisian pimps. He knew what would best suit his tourist clients. One glance was sufficient to tell him who was looking for romance, with Gypsy songs and a Russian princess, and who wanted to have a rousing good time with real Black jazz musicians, or with nude dancers, or who was looking for a more "cultured" atmosphere, or who wanted some cocaine and a glass of beer, or who had a weakness for his own gender...

So it was easy for him to size up Frances Hotchkiss from beneath the peak of his cap. This one was eager for the unusual and the piquant. And he always did his best to please his clients...

First he took them to an authentic French restaurant where they served unusual wines and aperitifs to awaken the appetite. Before she finished her first glass, Mrs. Hotchkiss was ready for another. Instead, he signaled her that it was time to leave this place. She did not object. He drove them to a Russian restaurant where they served genuine beluga caviar in little silver casks, accompanied by the purest, pre-war Russian vodka. From there he drove to a small, easy-to-overlook Italian restaurant that was known far and wide for its mussels, frogs, crabs, clams, oysters and all those other creatures of peculiar color and appearance. Bella could not even get the fork to her lips, so repelled was she by those slippery little monsters. Mrs. Hotchkiss, on the other hand, licked her fingers, ate with gusto and praised Bella's Italian relatives so highly — they knew how to live — that Bella herself was forced to put one of the creatures in her mouth — and almost choked.

She did not do much better with the delicacies at the other restaurants and cafes that the driver took them to. Accustomed at home to eating soup-meat or chicken legs and chicken soup, she had no tolerance for all the pungent dishes in the restaurants. The driver took them to a Greek place to eat turtle soup; to a Caucasian cellar where the waiters cut slices of meat from a freshly slaughtered sheep, roasted them over an open flame and served them to the guests on skewers. Then he took them for a long ride to a place where — for dessert — they had a selection of extra sharp cheeses which sent Mrs. Hotchkiss straight up to seventh heaven but brought tears to Bella's eyes. Never in her life had she eaten anything that looked and tasted like green soap...

Then they started on a round of cocktails, but each one in a different bar. After the first one, Bella's head started spinning. Her consumption of alcoholic beverages had been limited to the sweet Kosher wine she had imbibed once a year at the Passover seder. This French wine went straight to her knees. But Mrs. Hotchkiss kept filling not only her own glass, but Bella's as well.

Following her friend's example, Bella drank and threw dollar bills to the waiters. After a while, the wine began to taste better and go down easier. But her head spun around faster and faster in

a whirlpool of confused images: restaurants that looked like Eastern temples, smoke-filled saloons, all sorts of people dancing
wildly with each other, chorus girls doing the can-can, sailors and
soldiers of all colors bouncing half-clad women on their knees —
everything in one heap.

"Isn't this fun, Bella?" Mrs. Hotchkiss exulted.

"Sure is..." muttered Bella from a long way off.

She did not know how it happened, but mostly she was clinking glasses with a stranger who had sat down at their table. Mrs.
Hotchkiss was punctuating her drinks by kissing the leather-clad
driver, who could have passed for her son. Bella was embarrassed
and more than a little frightened by the stout, red-faced man next
to her who could have passed for her father. He reeked of alcohol
and cigarette smoke, shaving cream and animal masculinity. His
red neck, which protruded brutally from his too-white collar,
alarmed her. Even more fearsome were his hairy, veiny hands
which crawled like animals out of his snow-white cuffs. She
shrank back each time these hands fell heavily on her inexperi-
enced young shoulders. Bella had a sinking feeling it was Frances
Hotchkiss who had delivered her into the arms of this gross
stranger.

"This is Paris, Bella darling. Enjoy it. People kiss each other
in restaurants here all the time. Look around..."

So Bella let herself be kissed, but she blushed in fear and
shame. Her "escort" was quite free with his hands. When they
danced he held her so tight that her chest hurt. His bony knees felt
rough against her thighs. His toughened hands kept sliding down
lower and lower below her waist. But she could not summon the
strength or the temerity to resist in this welter of whirling couples.
The alcohol inside her was rendering her more and more helpless.
She was no longer moving of her own volition. Someone was
helping her put on her coat and having a lot of trouble getting Bella's arms into the sleeves. Someone was carrying her bodily out of
the restaurant and putting her into a car. Someone was taking off
her clothes. How she had gotten into the bed, she did not remember. And who was that big stranger lying beside her? What was he
doing?

In an instant the fog lifted from her brain. Her eyes opened wide. She did not know this red-faced heavy giant who was advancing upon her like a wild boar...

She opened her mouth, but no sound came out of it. Somehow she squirmed off the bed and stumbled to the door between the rooms.

"Frances! Help me! Help me!"

But no reply came from Mrs. Hotchkiss, although Bella was sure she heard sounds on the other side of the locked door. She uttered one frightened scream before the heavy man could get to her side. He put his big hands around her throat.

"Stop that damn screaming!"

Bella froze into silence. He let her go.

"Who needs you?" he hissed. "But you'd better pay me for my time! I was hired to be your escort. Don't make any more scenes. I'm not a kid who's still not dry behind the ears."

The explanation for the whole sordid business suddenly dawned on Bella. She pointed to her handbag.

"Take whatever you want! But get out —"

The man took his time, swore a few choice oaths, counted the bills as he was putting on his clothes, and left.

Bella too dressed quickly, put the knitted hat on top of her head and rushed down to the street and the cool air. Without knowing where she was going, she ran from boulevard to boulevard like a dog driven out of the house on a rainy March night...

4.

In the Latin Quarter, in all the artists' studios from the richest to the poorest in the cellars, in all the cafes, from the large, brilliantly illuminated ones to the smallest bistro, among all the restaurateurs, waiters, artists, political émigrés, Bella Saradacci, that dark Italian woman from America, is well known. She is part of the Quarter, like the painters, the lost talents, the real ones and the impostors. She is an item pointed out to tourists and foreigners, just like all the other rarities in the city.

All day long Senora Bella is on her feet. Her New York high-heeled shoes are worn out, which make her look even shorter than she is. The threadbare lemon-colored coat has turned into another color. The red knitted hat has shrunk so much from repeated washings that it barely stays on her hair, which has fluffed out even more. But Bella doesn't mind. She belongs to the Quarter.

She poses — free of charge — for impoverished Futuristic artists, who paint unreal, non-human freaks with short legs and frizzy heads. She edits manuscripts — free of charge — for modern poets, poems which they are constantly "rewriting for the printer," but which never see the light of day. She cooks up lunches in an attic somewhere for political émigrés who write impassioned proclamations. She visits lonely, sick foreigners, Montparnasse types, in the hospital. (She's the only person who notices when they stop frequenting the cafes.) All alone, she goes to the funerals of lonely cafe-habitues whose graves will not even bear their names. She drags immense paintings, larger than she is, to art dealers. She runs among American tourists, speaks to them emotionally about buying the work of unknown young artists who will one day be discovered and whose work will then be worth a hundred times what they paid for it. And as a result of all the above, she knows all the secrets, all the intrigues and all the gossip current in the Latin Quarter.

The day is not long enough for her. The Quarter is huge, with many cafes and even more studios. Everyone wants to see her, everyone needs a favor from her, so she keeps moving all day long, running along the streets with her quick little steps in her worn-out high-heels.

"Oh, Miss Bella, sit down and have a cup of coffee for a few minutes..."

"No, no, not now. Too busy," she insists in her comical French with an English rhythm. "Sorry... merci..."

No one can understand how she keeps body and soul together, when she sleeps, where she eats. Sometimes she herself doesn't know. Sometimes she can be seen at a table with a sandwich and coffee. Sometimes she even has lunch in a studio with an artist for whom she has prepared a meal. Bella doesn't need much on a regular basis except cigarettes. Her coat, her shoes, even her hair, always show signs of cigarette ash. Her stubby fingers are now as stained by nicotine as they once were with ink.

Sometimes she earns a few dollars by taking American visitors on a "tour" of Paris, of which she knows every nook and cranny. But that's the only qualification for this work she has. She does not know how to ask for "commission" from the proprietors of the establishments to which she brings guests. And she never allows any of the male guests to take any liberties with her.

"No! No! Sorry, M'sieur!"

Once in a while she gets a generous tip from a visitor. Sometimes she helps an artist sell a painting and is rewarded. But even that money doesn't stay with her very long. The artists in the cafes learn about it immediately, They gather round her like flies around sugar. The good news spreads:

"Senora Bella is buying..."

Her own rent is always overdue. The owner of the hotel, the blond Frenchman with the red Turkish fez, is constantly dunning her for his money. So she comes home very late and quietly climbs the six flights of stairs. The place is always busy anyway. Her neighbors — the street-walkers, the peddlers, the "illegal foreigners" — are always fighting and screaming at each other. Bella can't stand listening to it all, but it serves as a good cover for her entrances and her exits.

Despite all her "business contacts" with artists and foreign visitors, Bella avoids personal relationships with any of them. She has plenty of stories to tell about her extraordinary adventures and love affairs with men, but she is a master at finding excuses for "not going home with one." Her experience with Mrs. Hotchkiss cured her of that.

Bella has just received her latest letter from home. She takes it to bed with her. "The blond druggist still comes to our house to fix the radio. He is still waiting for you, Bella," her mother writes. The letter brings a strange warmth to her soul in that shabby sixth floor room in that rundown hotel in Paris. She sees a beautiful, comfortable bedroom with a red shade on the lamp. She is making her large double-bed. She removes the silk coverlet, She adjusts the blinds on the windows. Her husband calls to her, his voice full of tenderness:

"Come to bed, Bella darling ..."

She finishes reading the letter from home, lies there motionless for a moment. Then she slowly gets out of bed, sits down at the bare little table and writes the text of a telegram to her mother: "Send money for steamship ticket home." But she tears it up immediately and begins a letter:

"Mama darling: I have news! I have just married a well known artist here in Paris. We are very happy. I love him with all my heart and soul and he feels the same about me. Please tell our friend the druggist that I am sorry."

She addresses an envelope, takes out the packet of photographs of her many artist friends, selects the handsomest one, puts it in the envelope with the letter, and seals it.

ACTORS!

Leon Kobrin

LEON KOBRIN (1872-1946) — born in Vitebsk, Byelorussia; died in New York.

After studying in a traditional kheyder, he received instruction in Russian language and literature. In 1892 he emigrated to the United States and found work in various garment shops in New York, Philadelphia, and Hoboken. Meanwhile he wrote a few stories in Yiddish which were favorably received. He then turned his full attention to literary activity, writing for the Arbeiter tseitung *and the* Abendblatt. *Most of his stories up to this point were about American-Jewish life. A realist in the style of the Russian writers, he drew pictures of the chaotic life in the early years of mass Jewish immigration. (A collection of his stories published in 1910 ran to more than 900 pages.) Eventually he tried his hand at writing plays and soon became a builder of American-Yiddish theater.*

About Yiddish writing in America he said: "American-Yiddish literature has its own history. It is not a continuation of the older Yiddish literature in Russia. We, the pioneers of American-Yiddish writing, did not even know the European-Yiddish literature of that time."

His son Nathan notes: "Actually, for many years we had two writers in our house: my father was the playwright, and my mother, Pauline, was the translator of books from other languages into Yiddish."

Actors! (Aktiorn) *appears in* The Lost Melody (Der farloirener nign), *Yiddisher Kultur Farband, New York 1948.*

Actors!

This happened about ten years ago. One of the Yiddish theaters was preparing a production of a new comedy I had written. The leading actors in that company had good roles and spoke glowingly about the play during rehearsals.

"It's going to be a hit!"

"It'll run the whole season!"

And so on.

The cashier of the theater, who spoke only English when "business was booming" and only Yiddish when "business was rotten" — he too, hearing what the actors were saying, stuck his black curly head out of the booth whenever he saw me and greeted me enthusiastically in English:

"A double-G!" he predicted, which meant, I assumed, Good with a capital G.

The owner of the theater, who was also the manager, was an older, rather corpulent man with badly stooped shoulders, out of which a perfectly round head bobbed up and down, because he had no neck. His face was a full moon on which a smile appeared only rarely, certainly *not* when he was talking to a playwright who had just taken a thousand dollars from him. But he too was smiling at me as he scratched his right cheek with his pudgy fingers.

"A hit, right? A real hit?" His hoarse voice sounded like that of a forlorn old cat, but I could tell he had no doubts about my play.

The cast rehearsed for several weeks. The fervor of the actors increased from day to day and with it, their respect for me and my talent. I was the greatest Yiddish dramatist alive. Oh, there were others, but how could they compare to me? Rank amateurs. My sense of humor! My prose! Clouds of incense floated around my head.

They looked into my eyes, they responded to every little remark I made at the rehearsals, they smiled at me, especially those who had the leading roles.

The blond actress with the wise blue eyes, which exuded life as from a blue fountain, the star who had recommended my play to the manager — she positively beamed with happiness. In the first place, had it not been for her, he would never even have bought the play. In the second place, her role was a tragi-comic one and suited her to a T. Every word she uttered during rehearsals evoked laughter. In her scenes she was so moving in her tragic helplessness that the other actors were constantly blowing their noses and wiping their eyes with their white handkerchiefs. So her joy practically radiated from her blue eyes as she repeated the same story (almost word for word) at each rehearsal:

"As soon as I heard the first reading of your play, I laid my hand on the script and said: 'This one was made for me! Nobody but me can do this role!' "

And gazing at me, she would say: "How does he get so much fire into his words?"

The comic in the troupe, a short, skinny man who moved like quicksilver despite his sixty years, was ecstatic not only about the play but about me too.

"Never before has there been a comedy like this on the Yiddish stage!" he boomed. "A sure-fire success! A laugh a minute! It'll run till Pesach, I'm sure of that! I always said you were the only one who could create such a hit." And at that point he leaned over and spoke to me in confidence. "My friend, this play will make you immortal! You'll be able to tell the world to go to hell!"

The male star of the troupe, an actor with a dark, romantic curl on his forehead, just like a matinee idol, and who spoke in lyric tones, announced in my direction:

"Colossal!" Except he stretched out each syllable somehow. A trick of the trade.

After every rehearsal he would drag me to a restaurant to have dinner with him and he always insisted on paying the check, a sure sign of his confidence in the success of my play.

"You're the one who could write such a part for me. And I'm the only actor a great artist like you should write for!"

*

It is also true that the other actors, who had smaller roles, were not so pleased with me. But that's the habit of actors: the roles they get are always too small for them and always it's the playwright's fault. They never show their resentment, however. It doesn't pay to get on the bad side of the playwright, because if the play is a success the management will mount another one of his plays; so it's better, in the long run, to be friends with him. In any case, one of them always holds up a lit match whenever I put a cigarette in my mouth, as though he had been hired for just that purpose.

One young actor whispers into my ear that he knows a "beauty" who is "dying to meet me."

From an actress nearby, *sotto voce*, I hear: "He looks exactly like President Wilson, I swear."

From another: "No, more like Israel Zangwill."

The sum total of all this? If I had taken it into my head that day to go to that place from which no one has ever returned, my eulogy would already have been written by these actors rehearsing my play.

The manager, for his part, shows up occasionally at a rehearsal, and since he hears the actors themselves laughing at my lines, he laughs too, scratches his cheek and says to me: "Didn't take my thousand dollars for nothing, eh?" And he vanishes.

Meanwhile, word has been getting around the cafes on Second Avenue. People I know only casually seem to be smiling at me a little too sweetly. Except for my colleagues, the other Yiddish playwrights. They don't even look at me.

*

Here the plot takes a new turn.

The theater company that was rehearsing my "hit" was scheduled to put on another play in Hartford, Connecticut on the Wednesday evening preceding the Friday of the premiere of my new play in New York City.

The blond star, who is certain that she will conquer the world with her role in my play, now gets a brilliant idea. Why not do my new play in Hartford instead of the old one? This will give the cast an opportunity to become more at home in their roles. Nothing can do that better than a performance before a live audience.

The others go along with the idea. The manager agrees. I have no objections either.

Wednesday after lunch we are all on the train to Hartford. Everyone is in a good mood. Success is riding on the train with them. They can feel its breath on the backs of their necks. I can feel it myself. The man of the hour. The blond star notices that I'm sitting next to an open window.

"Shut that window," she insists. "You'll catch cold!"

The matinee idol gets up and shuts the window for me. He also invites me to play a game of 21 with him. Why not? We start playing. I lose the first few hands.

"Enough!" says the blond star, who has been watching.

The manager agrees. "It's bad luck! Throw those damn cards out the window!"

And they do.

We arrive at Hartford late in the afternoon and are taken to a large hotel. As we're mounting the white marble steps to the entrance we are welcomed by — a small, shiny, black kitten. The manager jumps back and almost trips down the steps. The blond star utters a little screech and grabs my arm. Only the comic doesn't lose his head. He emits a loud meow and the black kitten stops in its tracks.

"What are you all afraid of?" he asks. "It's only a *small* kitten."

"A small *black* kitten," the manager wheezes.

The blond star sighs deeply and a somber look settles on her now ashen face.

Later, in the hotel dining-room, the mood is even bleaker. The manager and the star barely touch their food.

Suddenly, a message arrives from the theater. The house is sold out. Standing room only.

The mood rises again. Smiles erase the glum looks. "Double-G!" the cashier bellows.

*

Later, before the curtain went up, I spent some time in the dressing-rooms, watched the actors make up, wished them all luck. They all had a look of fierce intensity on their faces, even the comic. It's always that way on opening night.

*

Five minutes till curtain time. I walk out into the "house." It is packed. The manager, cashier and I take out seats in a loge. We are all biting our nails.

The curtain goes up. The audience applauds the famous actors from New York. The play begins. Only the actors with minor roles are on stage. The audience is quiet. Then the blond star enters. She is a favorite here and the audience applauds.

"Now!" says the manager, scratching his right cheek, "Now we'll grab them! If it was funny at rehearsals, the audience here will be rolling on the floor!"

But what is this? The blond star is playing her heart out — and the audience is not even smiling.

"What's wrong?" the manager asks me, as if I know. "Why aren't they laughing?" I shake my head.

The comic enters. Same reaction. The audience applauds when he comes on stage, but his jokes fall flat. The entire cast has now been on stage, playing their roles perfectly, but they might as well be giving this performance in a graveyard.

The manager is now doubled over in his chair, a look of excruciating pain on his face. The cashier is talking to him, but in Yiddish now.

"A lemon! We bought a lemon! You know why they're not laughing? Because it's not funny!"

The manager turns and attacks me: "What have you done to me, you murderer! They don't even understand your wisecracks! Swindled me out of a thousand dollars — you Litvak! What am I going to do now? We don't have another new play. How can we bring this lemon to New York?"

What can I say to him? I'm bewildered myself. What's wrong with this audience? It's not the actors. They are all doing what they're supposed to do, and doing it well.

The curtain falls. End of Act One. The applause is feeble.

The manager and the cashier run out of the loge without even looking at me. I stay there, all alone. No use talking to the actors now. They too must be in an awful state.

An acquaintance spots me in the loge and comes over.

"This audience is disappointed. They came to see an operetta. That's how it was advertised here. Singing and dancing. This is not what they expected. How did it happen?"

His words are shocking, but they make me feel better. There is still hope. The audience in New York will be expecting a play, not an operetta. They won't be disappointed.

Act Two. The manager and the cashier are back in the loge.

"We've got to put a few songs and dances into your lemon; maybe it can still be saved."

"Absolutely not!" I object. "Read the contract."

"Contract, shmontract! To hell with your *literatsia!* Give me back my thousand dollars!"

The cashier gets his two cents in. "Without songs and dances it's sure to be a flop! Wait till you hear what the cast has to say."

During the second act the audience is even cooler. And the actors have lost their verve. The third act is a disaster.

*

As the final curtain went down the manager, white as a sheet, turned to me and pleaded:

"I'm dead! What did you have against *me?* Even songs and dances won't help this *shmaate*. It's worse than a lemon! You and your *literatsia!*" He spit on the floor and ran out, his cashier behind him.

In short: I went back to the hotel feeling miserable. They were all there — the actors, the manager, the cashier, sitting in the foyer in a group, as though they were grieving for a newly deceased relative. They didn't even notice me come in.

I sat down in a corner by myself. But I could not sit still. If it hadn't been one o'clock in the morning I would have taken the next train back to New York. If I had known my way around Hartford, I would have moved to another hotel.

Leon Kobrin

The voice of the blond star cut into my dreary thoughts: "Oh my God! It was that little black kitten!"

Then the voice of the cashier: "Why blame it on the poor kitten? Blame it on the man who wrote that crap!"

They all joined in, as though they were doing an autopsy on me, especially the ones who thought they had been given too small a role for their large talent. The actor who had been lighting my cigarettes announced with finality:

"I knew all along it was a dud, but since everyone else was praising it to the skies, I didn't want to be a spoilsport."

Only two of them did not join in the autopsy. The matinee idol sat there glowering, but did not say a word. And the blond star just sat there shaking her head, as if she could not accept the death of a dear friend.

The manager didn't stop talking for a second, but no one could understand what he was saying. Scraps of sentences hung in the air — killed me, thousand dollars, literatsia, lemon...

When I couldn't stand it any longer I retreated to my room.

The next morning, when I came down to breakfast, the entire company was sitting around tables. I said good-morning, but no one returned my greeting except the blond star, and even she seemed to be saying, "Good-morning, you murderer, why did you ruin my life?"

In the train going back to New York I sat in a seat by myself, thinking thoughts like "vanity, vanity, all is vanity," or sic transit gloria mundi.

When we got off the train at New York, again only the blond star said anything to me. There were tears in her eyes.

"Please do something. Maybe you can still save that play. I put so much effort into learning the role. He will make my life miserable because I persuaded him to pay you the thousand dollars."

"Nothing has to be done to it," I tried to reassure her. "The audience in Hartford was disappointed because they came to see another play."

"You're wrong," she insisted. "Your play has no humor. It's too literary."

That evening, when I came into the cafe where all the Yiddish actors hang out, no one "recognized" me. Not even the ticket-collectors. Everyone had already heard the news about my lemon.

Two or three of my colleagues, with lugubrious looks on their faces, did stop by my table to offer condolences. I thanked them.

Friday evening, at the premiere of my new play, I tried to sneak into the theater without anyone seeing me. The last thing in the world I wanted to do was engage in any kind of small talk.

Here too there was a full house. I found a seat in the back, off to a corner, and waited for the curtain to go up. The opening scene. A few people laughed. Then more and more people. The "stars" came on and began feeding each other their lines. As the first act ended, the entire house was laughing. They even applauded for a few minutes.

I stayed in my seat, still did not want to talk to anyone, especially the actors.

The second act was even more warmly received, and at the end of the final act there was a storm of cheering and applause. As they left the theater, people were smiling broadly, talking animatedly, having a general good time. It always happens when a play is a success.

The first one to greet me was a ticket-taker. "A hit! They loved it!" An usher came running over to me. "The star wants to see you! Right away!"

Not until that moment did I entertain any ideas about going back-stage.

She ran over to me, laughing and crying.

"God Himself came to our rescue! I prayed all night!" Then the manager was at my side, smiling. But there was a question-mark in his eyes. He wasn't a hundred-percent sure the play was really a hit. Hartford was still on his mind.

"Well, what do you think?" he asked me.

I didn't answer him. As I took a step back, I bumped into the comedian. He shook my hand warmly.

"You see what happens when you give the public something good?"

"Yes," I said. "When you give them something 'literary.' "

I thought he would burst a blood-vessel.

"They should all drop dead, those actors! They get used to the junk from the other playwrights and they can't digest something that's really good. You know I've always been an admirer of yours. Didn't I tell you this play was the best thing you've ever done?"

He burst out laughing.

"Remember that black kitten in Hartford? Everybody got scared but me. That kitten is a sign of success," I told them.

In short, my play was a hit. Even the critics praised it.

The cashier again spoke only in English. The manager always greeted me with a smile. The matinee idol again invited me to restaurants and picked up the check. I ought to write a play especially for him, he suggested, because the others don't understand the work of an important writer like me. And the blond star told me the same. The comic treated me with a cigar once in a while. In the cafes, the people "in the business" again came over to my table and inquired solicitously after my wife and children.

Only my colleagues the playwrights stayed away from me, as if we had had a violent disagreement.

And all I could think of to say after all this was a single word:

"ACTORS!"

THE PEST

Leon Kobrin

For a biography of Kobrin, see the introduction to the story
Actors!.

The Pest

A Thursday afternoon in July.

The darkness descended suddenly. The sky filled up with black clouds. A deathly silence seemed congealed in the atmosphere. There was not even a breath of wind. As if Nature's heart had stopped beating.

The big horses on the express wagons stood on Division Street, their heads bent low, twitched their ears nervously and breathed noisily through their enormous nostrils. The drivers ran around covering them with blankets and then hid inside the wagons or in nearby stores. Pedestrians hurried as fast as they could to escape the imminent storm.

On Division Street the people in the tenement houses who had that morning hung their featherbeds, pillows, blankets and other bedclothes out to air, ran to take them back inside again. The slamming of windows set up a staccato accompaniment to all this frantic activity.

Meanwhile the sky was growing blacker and blacker, and the darkness denser and denser.

A reddish-blue flash lit up the sky for a moment, then a muted clap of thunder came rumbling closer and closer, as if it were rolling across the rooftops of the tenements along the way.

The wind grew stronger. A discarded Yiddish newspaper lay in the middle of the street. A gust of wind picked it up, played with it, gently at first, then tossed it around and sent it sailing toward Seward Park.

Another thunderclap boomed closer this time, then the lightning-flash lit up the street, and the rain poured down in torrents, slapping the tenement walls relentlessly and overflowing all the gutters.

*

In the middle of this summer cloudburst Mary came running in from work. She raced up the five flights of stairs. Her clothes were dripping wet. From the red and blue flowers on her hat big drops of water coursed down her cheeks, leaving a trail of an unnatural color.

Gitl, her mother, with a wig on her head, was standing at a gas-stove in the kitchen, stirring a pot with a spoon. When she heard Mary's footsteps she slapped her thigh and cried out:

"Oy! May the lightning not strike me! Did you ever see such a thing! How soaked she is! Mameleh! Have you lost your senses! You couldn't wait till the rain let up? *Vey iz mir!* What a mess!"

Mary made no reply. She hung her hat on a nail by the door and started taking off her wet clothes.

"In this rainstorm — running like a crazy-woman —"

"Enough, Mama! It's none of your business."

"Whose business is it, then? Running home in all that rain! Did you ever hear such a thing?" Gitl had calmed down a bit. She stepped over to the closet where she kept her dishes, took out a glass and a saucer and filled the glass with hot tea. "You could catch yourself a cold, God forbid. Did you ever hear such a thing?" She put the tea down on the table. "Here, drink this. Running in such a..."

Mary walked past her into the front-room without a word. Gitl knew that her daughter's silence was a sign she was really angry or upset.

"*Mazl-tov!* She's the one who's mad yet! Running around in such a downpour... " She picked up the tea and brought it into the other room. "Here, drink your tea..."

Mary still kept silent.

"Well, do as you like. In one of her moods already! So don't drink it! Can't say an extra word to her. Did you ever hear such a thing? Even her own mother can't say a word to her... She's my daughter, isn't she? And who will have the heartache if she gets sick, God forbid? Well, will you drink this or not? It's cold already. I'll bring you some fresh... So suit yourself! Go bang your head against the wall..."

And she ran back into the kitchen.

*

Mary was not really angry with her mother. But she *was* feeling blue. She sat by the window in the front-room, staring out at the rain, listening to the thunder and the howling of the wind, and her heart was heavy.

All week long it had been raining. The Workmen's Circle picnic would be postponed. It was scheduled for Saturday and she was looking forward to it avidly. She had placed so much hope on this picnic. For two weeks she had thought about nothing else. She had paid for the ticket weeks ago. It was not the five cents that concerned her. Even if it had been five dollars, would that have mattered when she knew that Max would be there? She was certain he would be there — he was so devoted to the organization. So they would certainly meet at the picnic — and maybe they would patch things up. They must. Two whole months they had not been speaking. Enough! She would have made up with him long ago. But she was so stubborn, so unforgiving, Why did she always mess things up with her obstinacy? Had it ever done her any good?

A couple of times they had run into each other on the street and her heart had cried out to him, but her head — some overpowering force made her turn her head away so that she wouldn't look at him, so their eyes wouldn't meet... Only last week she had seen him in Jackson Street Park. She was sitting on a bench. Suddenly he came into view. He was walking toward her. Her heart started pounding, the blood rushed to her face. But she turned her head away. And when she finally looked in his direction, he was walking angrily away from her, or at least that's how it had seemed to her. She immediately ate herself up with regrets. Why had she done it? Her own worst enemy... Why did she act so high-and-mighty? Was she the only girl left in New York?

Staring out at the rain, her eyes welled up with tears of alarm and dismay.

And why had it happened? What had they done to each other? He objected to her going out with Krolik. He hated that Krolik. Krolik has a big mouth, he's a show-off, he's always criticizing America, disparaging New Yorkers, finding fault with the Movement, with the local socialists and their "bourgeois psychology." Krolik, Max insists, is nothing but an ignoramus who thinks he knows everything but who knows nothing, who quacks like a duck when he speaks and yet brags that in the Old Country he used to make fiery speeches at mass meetings.

"What does that shnook, that greenhorn, know about America? Not even a year in this country and he's already an expert! If he had come here as a two-year-old child, like me, maybe he'd have a right to criticize... Bluffers like him you should not even allow into your home!"

Mary always defends Krolik, not because she thinks so highly of him, but because she can see that Max is jealous of him. She can see that Krolik is not indifferent to her, which gives her pleasure. She's happy that Max is jealous; it shows that he loves her very much. She's only teasing him... but maybe she has carried it too far.

"Krolik is a fine young man, Max. You don't really know him."

"I know he's an incurable bluffer!"

"Why should you call him that?"

"Because that's what he is — a bluffer, an ignoramus and an idiot!"

"An idiot too?" Her eyes were laughing.

"A real one! A greenhorn! And a boor besides."

"Well, I'm not much more than a greenhorn myself, you know. Only five years in this country. Maybe I too am an idiot?"

"You're certainly not very smart, if you can enjoy his company!"

"He's smarter than you," she said, trying to sound hurt.

"And better looking, of course."

"That too," she smiled.

"So why are you in love with me?"

"Well, maybe I'm not..."

His eyes became two big question-marks. For a moment he was silent. Then he said: "If you're being serious, all right." And he got up to leave.

She laughed out loud. "Sit down, Max! You're the one who's an idiot! You don't realize what you're saying."

"What makes you think I don't?"

"Because...because..." She stood up, put both hands on his shoulders and looked deeply into his eyes. "Because *you* are a bad boy!" And she kissed him on the lips.

He responded. And they talked no more about Krolik.

But that wasn't the end of it. They kept having the same argument, whenever she told him that Krolik had been to visit her, or whenever he noticed Krolik looking at her, or whenever he heard Krolik boasting about what great revolutionary deeds he had performed in Russia. And whenever they got into one of these arguments, Max was miserable — and she enjoyed herself. Until one evening he got so angry that he walked out. And when he came by the next day to patch things up, he found her in her front-room with Krolik, who was sitting at the table drinking tea. She was still smarting from the abrupt way he had stalked out the previous evening, so she did not respond very cordially to his greeting. And just to make sure he got the message, she moved her own chair closer to Krolik's and put another cube of sugar into his glass. Max turned aside, lit up a cigarette and sat down in a corner to watch this domestic scene.

Finally she asked him: "Would you like some tea?"

"No!" he snapped. He turned his attention to Krolik. "And what is your opinion of American sugar? Not as sweet as Russian sugar, right?"

"It certainly is not! This is not even real sugar. In Russia, one cube of sugar is sweeter than a whole pound of yours."

"Is that so? Even our sugar is no good? Would you please tell me, Mister, is there anything at all in this country that *is* good?"

"My name is not Mister, *puzhalista*! Among civilized people it's customary to call people by their given names. My name is Krolik, *puzhalista*!"

"*Putz-alista*," said Max, with a derisive laugh.

Mary patted Krolik's shoulder. "Drink your tea, Krolik. If it's not sweet enough I'll put in another cube..." She threw Max a defiant look.

He rose from his chair. "Why only one cube? If you give him the whole damn box it still won't be sweet enough!"

"We don't need your advice," she said. "You were so mad yesterday that you walked out on me. Why did you come back today?"

He flinched, as though she had slapped him. His face flamed, and for a long moment he said nothing. Then he picked up his hat and said, a little hoarsely:

"All right! Excuse me! It was very foolish of me..." And he left.

She had ached to call him back, but was embarrassed to do so in front of Krolik.

*

"I was the foolish one," Mary said to herself now as she sat at the window, watching the rain and going over all the scenes that had taken place between them. "No good can come out of such encounters... But if I tell him that Krolik doesn't mean a thing to me, that he's a pain-in-the-neck, that I only did it to tease him... No, better not to say that. I'll tell him — what should I tell him, anyway? That I can't just chase a person out of my house for no reason? Yes! That's the truth. Oh, if only the weather clears up by Saturday! Yes, out there in the park, under the trees, on the green grass, I'll tell him I'm sorry. And never again will I do such a fooling thing, never, never!"

Meanwhile, the rain had stopped. She opened the window and looked out. Over the roof of the tenement house across the street hung a little cloud. As she watched, the cloud grew thinner and thinner, the sky brighter and brighter. The weather was definitely changing. Her eyes beamed with pleasure and she smiled happily.

She got up and looked into her mirror hanging on the wall. There were peculiar spots on her cheeks. She laughed out loud.

"What a face!" she grimaced. She picked up a handkerchief and wiped her cheeks, then ran into the kitchen. Her mother was simmering pieces of liver in a frying pan on the stove. The odor of fried onions filled the room.

"I'm going to have some tea, Mama! But first I must wash my face." She went to the sink and let the water run.

"Already? You're not mad anymore? Did you ever hear such a thing? Nineteen years old and still a foolish little girl!"

"All right, Mama, all right," Mary said, rolling up her sleeves and picking up the soap. "All right, you're a very nice mother, Mama." She rinsed her mouth, but didn't stop talking. "Please pour me a glass of tea... Saturday, Mama, I'm going to the picnic, Definitely."

"'Pour me a glass of tea,' she says. Did you ever hear such a thing? A mouthful of water and still she keeps on talking! Go drink your tea, go..." Thank God, Gitl says to herself. She's talking to me again.

*

Friday night Mary could not fall asleep. The sky was clear, but Mary wasn't convinced. Thursday it had also been clear, but Friday it had rained so hard that Mary, sitting in the shop over her shirts, felt she couldn't stand the uncertainty much longer. How could she be certain that the sky would not mock her again, that it wouldn't cover itself with dark clouds and then pour down a rainstorm that would last all day Saturday?

Several times during the night she threw off the sheet that covered her, ran to the window and stared up at the heavens. How beautiful! Up there in that deep blue sky, tiny golden stars were shining. If they could only read her heart! Dear little stars, shine and sparkle and have mercy on me. Make the sun shine tomorrow!

At dawn she fell asleep and dreamt there was a terrible storm. The black sky thundered and the red-blue lightning flashed and the rain poured down unceasingly. Even in her dream Mary knew it was Saturday and she was supposed to go to the picnic and her heart was being devoured by regrets...

Leon Kobrin

At seven in the morning, when her mother woke her, Mary stared at her blankly, then threw off the sheet and looked toward the window.

"Is it clear?" she shrieked.

"What clear? Did you ever? It's beautiful! It's a pleasure! Get up, Mirele, it's already seven o'clock."

"It's really clear?" She was still skeptical. "Mama, put the iron on the stove! I want to iron my white dress."

"You're not going to work today?"

"No. I'm going to the picnic this afternoon. Please put the iron on, Mama. I'll be getting up in a minute."

Gitl was glad to hear that Mary was not going in to work. Works hard enough, poor child. Let her have a little fun too. Only one daughter I have, and the poor girl has to work for her mother too...

"Good, Mirele, go to the picnic. Have a good time. Would you like a glass of tea before you get up?"

"No, Mama, I'm getting up now."

"What's your hurry? You're not going to the shop, so why can't you rest a little longer today? I'll bring you the tea —"

"It's not necessary, Mama. Really."

"Well, no is no. You think I can worry about every little thing you do? Suit yourself! Did you ever hear such a thing?"

And she left the room in a huff.

For a little while longer, however, Mary did stay in bed, indulging herself. She clasped both hands in back of her head and stretched her legs. She studied the golden sunbeams that glimmered on the floor beneath the window. She almost grinned.

"I'd better start out about three," she thought. "Takes over an hour to get there..."

She could already picture the park in Brooklyn. She was no stranger to it. She knew its trees, its hills, its meadows, its dance pavilion. And wherever she looked she saw him, and saw herself at his side.

"You're a bad, bad boy, Max! How could you ever doubt me, even for a moment?"

And they would both laugh playfully.

"Did you really believe that I could care for that idiot, that greenhorn, that ignoramus, that — that — aren't you ashamed of yourself?"

"You know I love you very much, Mary. That's why I'm jealous of that blockhead!"

And he would kiss her.

She trembled and roused herself from her reverie.

He really is a blockhead, she thought. Why the devil does he keep hanging around me? He's the one who got me into all this trouble! I should have told him a long time ago that Mama doesn't approve of him coming to see me... But that's the end of it!

Gitl came into the room again.

"Mirele, I thought you were getting up. Twice I heated the tea up already. It's a shame to waste the gas..."

Eventually Mary stood before the mirror all dressed for her outing. She examined her face, touched her round cheeks, her shapely breasts, and suddenly remembered she was out of facepowder. She would have to pick some up on her way to the park...

When Mary got to the park it was after four. She was wearing her white dress and white shoes. On her head was a broadbrimmed hat with a big white ostrich-feather. The hat itself had cost her two weeks' pay.

She was a rather pretty young woman, Mary. Average height, with fresh, comely features. Her nose was just a trifle too long, and her full lips were a deep pink. She would have been even more attractive had it not been for the stylish corset she had put on for the occasion. The corset spoiled her own natural figure, but she had convinced herself that it enhanced her appearance.

All around her were young Jewish workers, men and women, also dressed in their finest. And all of them were hurrying to get deeper into the park.

She studied the other women, the clothes they were wearing, their figures, compared them with her own — and was pleased.

From behind the trees and the hills came a babble of laughter and song, of coquettish little screeches and happy, boyish banter. And woven into this hubbub were the melodies of the dance music from the pavilion.

"Will I find him in all this crowd?" Mary wondered. Her heart trembled and her lips tightened in alarm. The bedlam on all sides was growing louder.

In among the trees sat little groups of young people, singing their favorite songs. The words of the Russian *Dubinushka,* of the Bundist Pledge and of popular Yiddish theater songs mingled under the clear blue sky and then blended with the passionate outcries of the relaxed picnickers and the joyful sounds from the pavilion.

Od lo ovda tikvoseynu, came the words of the Zionist anthem, ardently sung by a duet, a man and a woman.

In the meadow, they were playing "cat-and mouse," but both the cat and the mouse were happy to be caught. In another place young folks were disporting on swings, propelling themselves as high as the trees, and the higher they went the louder grew the girlish screams and the boyish shouts of Hey! Hey! and Up! Up!

How happy everyone is here, Mary thought. Where shall I look for him? Maybe he's dancing over there. He does so love to dance...

She headed for the pavilion.

Hot and perspiring, their faces and their eyes flaming, couples were dancing with might and main. The wooden floor burned beneath their feet. From the pavilion came a pungent odor of sweat and perfume and of something else — the sensual breath of desire.

When Mary entered the pavilion she was at first hesitant to raise her eyes; she felt that as soon as she looked around she would see him and she would be unable to look at him calmly. Why not? She herself didn't know — or understand. As if she were ashamed of something — or afraid.

She moved into a corner and from that vantage point began searching for him, first timidly, then more openly. But she could not find him.

She left her corner and went looking for him among the dancers. For a moment she thought she saw him with a white handkerchief tied around his neck, but it wasn't Max. Could it be that he wasn't even here and wouldn't be here at all today? Perhaps he wasn't feeling well? For a moment she was panic-stricken. Then she sensed someone staring at her. She looked around, There he was, with his jacket over his arm. In a white sport shirt, a white hat, and with a white handkerchief stuck behind his collar. And he was looking at her with questioning, pleading eyes.

She stood there confused. Her face turned bright red. He's going to come over now. What shall I tell him? Her heart was pounding. But no, he was *not* moving toward her. Come over here, come over here, she repeated silently, why don't you come over here? He took one or two hesitant steps. The smile on his face was strained. She turned her head away. Now he's walking over here! Finally. But I mustn't show him that I missed him...

*

From behind, someone touched her arm:

"*Zdravstvoyte!*"

She turned around. Krolik stood there, with his coarse, broad features and his fierce little eyes. He held his big, rough hand out in greeting.

She did not take it. She stared at him glassy-eyed, as if he were the Angel of Death himself.

He took her hand anyway and pressed it and shook it, in the Russian manner.

"*Zdravstvoyte!* Finally found one person I know here. Here your mother won't disturb us. Well, how are you? Almost a month that I haven't seen you. So what's new?"

Bewildered, she moaned to herself: "Oh, my God! The pest is here! At the worst possible moment! What shall I do?"

"You came here to dance?" he asked. "What a strange country this is! They don't even know how to dance like human beings. Jump around like goats! Look! Hup, hup, just like wild goats!"

She looked around to see where Max was. Yes, he was still standing there, looking at her in great agitation. Their eyes met and an expression of outright contempt flashed in his eyes as he turned his head away. Then he turned his back on her.

She felt abandoned. Now he's angry with me again. How shall I ever get rid of this nuisance?

"I'm looking for someone here," she whispered hoarsely and started to walk away.

"Oh, in that case, I'll help you look," he said, following her.

Shall I tell him plainly to leave me alone? How can I do that? She kept walking.

As she came closer to Max she stole a look at him. He was looking at her the same way. She breathed easier.

"Such music in America!" Krolik was saying. "In Russia an orchestra is an orchestra! The same instruments here, but *shto za raznitsa*!

"Is that my fault?" she exploded.

"No, of course not! Am I saying it's your fault? But it's a fact that America is a big bluff! Look, they are all sitting here to have a good time — all the *genosn* and the *genosines*, how can you compare that to our *skhodke*, where the brothers and sisters used to meet in the woods. With us they would be listening to a lecture on socialism and revolution —"

Mary looked around. Max was nowhere in sight. And this lunatic was still talking!

"And in my opinion, if all these brothers and sisters knew that a Cossack was going to attack them, none of them would have even showed up here. Furthermore..."

She no longer heard what he was saying. Her eyes were frantically searching among the dancers. Krolik's voice was now just part of the general clamor, along with the rhythmic thump of the dancing feet.

"I remember once, when I was speaking at a *masovka* in the woods — you remember the woods near Minsk?"

Where had Max disappeared to? Her eyes searched everywhere.

"Do you remember the woods near Minsk?" he repeated.

"What?"

"You haven't even been listening to me?"

"Excuse me. My head hurts."

"Let's get away from here. I want to tell you what happened to me in the woods. An interesting story about —"

If only she could say the words aloud, maybe —

"Shall we get away from this place?" he persisted.

She looked at him despairingly. Have mercy on me! Why have you attached yourself to me today?

"You really don't look well," he said. "Let's get away from here."

"I must find this person..." she muttered and looked around again.

Suddenly she saw him. He was standing behind her, near a stoutish young woman with black, shifty eyes. Who was she?

She stopped walking and stared at them and there, as through a fog, she could see Max's eyes, looking back at her spitefully, as if they were laughing at her... As she watched, he grabbed the girl with the black eyes and started waltzing her around the dance floor. They acted as if they didn't even know each other...

They kept moving closer-and closer to Mary, so close that his shoulder brushed against hers. Her legs almost gave way beneath her.

"Dance with me, Krolik!" she said suddenly.

"Yes, it's a mazurka!" And with the expression of a cat licking its chops he led her out onto the dance floor.

She moved along with him mechanically as something in her soul cried out for help. Finally she allowed herself to take a closer look at Max and his dancing partner. How pretty she was! They danced around the floor once more and came face to face again. It seemed to Mary that her rival was looking at her with a mocking smile. Mary stopped in her tracks and stood still as a statue.

"What's wrong?" Krolik asked.

Out of control, she beat his chest with her fists.

"*You* are! What do you want from me, you pest? Who asked you to come here? You've ruined my life! Get away from me! And stay away! Leave me alone, you idiot, you ignoramus, you big boor!"

The sound of her own voice shouting jolted her back to her senses. Mama! What's wrong with me? Have I lost my mind? Home! I must get home!

She ran out of the pavilion, her tears choking her. Now it was Krolik's turn to stand there bewildered. He shook his head.

"How strange the people are in this country! Well, I should have known. What else would you expect from Ameritchka?"

IN THE SHADOWS

Miriam Raskin

MIRIAM RASKIN (1889-1973) — *born in Slonim, White Russia; died in New York.*

In Russia Raskin was an active member of the Bund (Jewish Federation of Labor) and served one year in a St. Petersburg prison for these activities. Her novel Zlatke *reflects this experience.*

In 1920 she emigrated to the United States, where her first stories were published in Zukunft *and later in the* Forverts. *In 1941 a collection of her short stories was published by a group of her friends under the title of* Shtille lebns (Quiet Lives), *a remarkably apt description of the everyday working-men and working-women she knew best.*

Regrettably, there is no written record containing further details about her life and work. The three stories translated here appear in Zukunft: In the Shadows (In shotn), *October 1934;* Generation of the Wilderness (Der dor ha-midbor), *January 1935;* No Way Out (On an oysveg), *January 1937.*

In the Shadows

Light yellow hair. Yellowish eyebrows. A mole on the left side of her chin. Her light-blue eyes looked at you dimly, as through a glass, or even a sieve. A moment after you saw her you forgot her, as if you had never even seen her.

She had changed her name from Chaika to Annie, and — unlikely as it may seem — she was friends with the highly esteemed Shermans. Esther Sherman had been her friend since they were children, and Annie didn't want any new friends — or perhaps she couldn't make any.

Annie's week went by in a headlong but uneventful rush at her sewing-machine in the shop, but Friday evening, as all the other girls were hurrying to leave, in anticipation of upcoming pleasures, Annie was happy along with them, for she too had a celebration to look forward to, because every Saturday evening she visited with the Shermans. Annie spent a long time preparing for those visits. First she polished her stylish shoes, then she carefully selected a dress and ironed a white collar to wear around her neck. She moved quickly around her room, accompanying herself with a song. But when she was ready to inspect herself in the mirror and she stared at her yellowish face and her eyes that seemed to be looking through a sieve, her mood usually changed for the worse. She would stand there for a while with the powder puff in her hand, and with a pain in her heart, would torment herself:

"Why, oh why, was I born with such a face?"

*

Once she arrived at the Shermans', however, she cheered up. First of all, a better class of people gathered there, mostly writers and poets. Esther Sherman, a vivacious brunette with skin the color of ivory, and wearing one of her Gypsy skirts, always greeted her heartily, her long earrings quivering with every move she made.

The lights were always dimmed, but the furnishings in the room were colorful enough. The guests all stood around informally or sprawled on the sofas among mounds of little pillows.

Annie would find herself a corner where she could sit down alone, her hands folded in her lap, and look and listen. The people in this unusual intellectual "family" were accustomed to her presence. She was not too visible, and she never bothered anyone. And no matter how low she felt before she got there, she knew she would always feel better here in this festive, crackling atmosphere, in the exalted level of their conversation.

Entire evenings of endless animated discussions about art. Sometimes hair-splitting disputes over a word. Sometimes even truly fruitful ideas. Or marvelous insights which came with a sudden flash, like lightning. Annie often missed the point, because she grasped ideas more with her feelings than with her head, but she was an avid listener nevertheless. Sometimes her face flamed as she soaked up the talk, even when it might have seemed she was lost in her own thoughts.

Once, she let slip an opinion of her own. It happened so unexpectedly that she herself doubted anyone had heard it. But later Annie realized that Esther Sherman had indeed heard what she said because she picked it up and elaborated upon it as her guests listened with rapt attention. Annie was flabbergasted. She sat there with her mouth open. How was it possible for a person to make so much out of such a trivial thing?

Coming home from these evenings at the Shermans' Annie would think — and dream — about what she had heard. On this particular evening, as she lay in bed with her eyes shut tight, her fantasy was racing even faster than usual. She had become the favorite of those people at the Shermans' house. They loved to listen to her speak. They kept asking her questions and admired the wisdom and intelligence of her answers...

The next day, Sunday, she had nowhere to go, but it didn't matter. She was still bubbling over with the impressions of the previous evening and she felt fine.

Then came the long week. She plunged into her work as if it were a wave of ice-cold water. She tore open the bundles, worked on them with the quickness of an animal devouring its food. Undistracted by what was going on around her, she raced her machine faster and faster...

*

One evening at the Shermans', when the conversations were livelier than ever, the poet Isaac Lev was holding forth on the subject of art in general. Lev had a beautiful head of blond hair. His shoulders were broad and his eyes were always smiling.

"Art is like life," he was saying. "No, it's even higher than life. If the artist doesn't like the world we live in, he creates his own world. He lives in that world and forgets about the ugly things in this world."

Annie was sitting in her customary corner. The expression on her face was that of a person listening to her favorite music. Her head was tilted to one side. Her lips were slightly open. She may even have seemed a bit comical, with her right hand in mid-air as if she had raised it to fix her hair and forgotten what she was doing.

Later someone pointed her out to Lev, who became curious. He stepped over to Annie's side to speak with her. She looked up at him as if she were in a dream, wondering why Isaac Lev himself were standing beside her, asking her a question. When she finally attempted to answer him, her replies were disjointed, but his guileless face and his gentle, smiling eyes gave her courage.

"I wanted to ask you a question," she blurted out.

"Fine! Go ahead and ask!"

"It seems to me..." She couldn't find the right words and became even more embarrassed.

"What was it you wanted to ask me?" he whispered.

"When an artist retreats into his own world, how can he live — how can he get along without *this* world, the bad one?"

For a long moment Lev studied her face, as if that would help him understand what she was asking. Then he smiled.

"Don't take everything so seriously," he replied. She heard him saying something about her unusual appearance, but for the rest of the evening she was strangely upset. What was it he had said about her looks? She tried to recapture the expression she had had on her face while he was talking to her, then she stole into another room to look at herself in the mirror. Her face was flushed with excitement. She turned away from the mirror with disdain. She hated herself when she looked like that.

Sadder, she returned to her corner. But she knew that later, when she lay in bed and gave her imagination free rein, she would see him up on a pedestal, that Isaac Lev, and his face would be radiant with wisdom and beauty, and she would be standing nearby, looking up at him ecstatically, because he was her beloved, her man. And he would lean down and slowly kiss her on the lips, again and again.

*

One evening at the Shermans', as Annie sat in her favorite corner, Isaac Lev again stood before her.

"Where do you live, Annie? I'd like to take you home..."

For some time now he had felt a woman's veiled eyes following him with all her senses. He found this very puzzling.

Annie now appeared to be a bit sleepy, or else she was ensconced in her own thoughts. The man who now stood before her was certainly not the one who appeared in her dreams. Surprised, she asked him:

"I'm sorry, what did you say?"

"I said I'd like to take you home."

"Why?" she asked him, as though she really wanted an answer. He smiled. He really hadn't had any ulterior motives.

Other guests were preparing to leave. Lev helped Annie on with her coat. She struggled to get control of herself.

"Well, if you really want to," she said, finally. She did not trust him. At any moment he would turn on his heels and join the rest of the happy company.

But he walked her to the train and now they were sitting side by side in silence, both ill-at-ease, not even looking at each other. An observer might have thought they were a couple who had just had a bitter argument. It was partially true. Isaac Lev *was* angry — with himself. What had he gotten himself into? Well, too late now. Him with his exaggerated sense of duty!

When they were outside her building, Annie had still not uttered a word. He followed her up to her room, feeling foolish. She lit the lamp. He looked around. Small, but very pleasant. Bright, clean walls. A neat, woman's bed, covered with a white spread. The blue light of the lamp cast an air of restfulness over the place. Cozy. Yes. All at once he felt at ease here.

"A very nice place, Annie," he said.

"I'll put up some tea," she whispered, as though she were trying to keep it a secret. She wandered around the room like a sleepwalker trying to make herself invisible.

Lev watched her every movement with intense interest. Finally she came up to him, her hands carrying tea and cookies, her arms held out stiffly as though she were in a procession.

"Do you like your tea strong?" The question was prosaic but her tone had a suggestion of intimacy about it.

He kept studying her hands, listening to the voice that was speaking to him in this manner, and her solemnity transmitted itself to him. He got up out of his chair, put his hands on her shoulders, gazed steadily at her face, which was now very pale, but almost pretty, especially her eyes, now a radiant blue.

"You know, Annie, you're a very fine woman."

"Oh, go on!" she stammered as she moved away from him.

"I mean it, Annie. You're an unusual person. It's not always easy to tell about such things."

"Drink your tea before it gets cold..."

"And what about you, Annie?"

"Me?" She couldn't think of anything else to say. The whole evening was unreal.

Lev sat in her room a little while longer, sipping his tea and not taking his eyes off her. When he looked at his watch, it was after midnight.

"It's getting late! I'd better go." He stood up and moved closer to her. She got up from her chair. His voice was tender and warm, not light and playful and curious, as it usually was. He seemed more emotional, more serious. Annie felt his eyes upon her and it gave her such a warm feeling inside that she grew bolder.

"No, Lev, don't go yet." She touched him lightly on the sleeve, but then drew back, startled by her own temerity. She covered her face with both hands.

Lev gently pulled her hands away from her face. He drew her close. She did not resist. She felt as if she had drunk too much wine. But then a wild cry suddenly tore out of her throat, a long smothered passion. With unwonted strength she took his head into her hands. Then she pushed him away, still holding on to his arms. She wanted to see herself in his eyes. Then she pulled him closer again. And Lev, overwhelmed by her hot breath, his lips close to hers, murmured:

"You want to be my girl, Annie?"

That night, Isaac Lev never did get home.

*

Annie's life unfurled. Isaac Lev was her lover, her man. They lived together in two small rooms, their home. Her life became

82

fuller, richer. She now had a greater responsibility — for herself and for him. Lev did not earn very much money. Annie worked for both of them. But neither the work in her shop nor her housework made her feel tired. All her movements were light and airy. She felt full of new life.

And Isaac Lev, when he saw her this way — so carefree, so full of song, simply stared at her disbelievingly. It was he who had found this woman — who had discovered her. He couldn't help but smile.

"Annie, you are a truly great artist!"

Annie could feel herself being admired. It was a new sensation for her. She grew prouder of herself, more confident in her own inner strength.

Lev often felt guilty. "You're working too hard, Annie. Maybe you should stay home?"

"Doesn't mean a thing!" she said almost curtly. She didn't even want to talk about it. She felt fine. She felt so good she didn't even believe this was happening to her, especially on the days she was home.

Early evening. Her apartment is freshly cleaned. Lev sits at his desk, his head buried in his papers. Annie moves around the room on cat's-feet. Now and then she glances almost surreptitiously toward his corner. The blue reflection of the lamp gives his face a transparent look. His eyes are closed and he sits there motionless, his pen in hand. To Annie it seems that at such moments he is communicating with other worlds.

Suddenly he sits up straight, full of the joy of creation. The blessed moment when he has succeeded in finishing something he has been working on. He calls to her. They sit down on the little sofa, he takes her hand and reads the poem to her...

Her heart is open to him and responds to everything that concerns him. She is at his side when he is happy and when he is sad. She is always full of him. But she herself has somehow ceased to exist for herself — as though she has melted into him.

*

Annie always felt better when she was alone with her man at home. When she was among many people she always felt lost.

And now people have begun to visit *him* — writers, poets, and all of them cheerful and noisy. She was quick to see that Lev too became more spirited when he was among them. There were some women among them too, attractive women in their unconventional clothing. There were even a few plain women, like her. Lev was friendly with all of them. They were a peculiar breed. Talked about nothing but art and it was a pleasure to listen to them. Annie studied the women with quiet envy. She would have given anything to be like them, to speak like them, maybe then Lev would treat her as an equal.

Sometimes, when she was preparing the refreshments, and listening to their conversation, she would freeze in one position and then grow embarrassed. She felt it was too commonplace at moments like these for her to be offering food while people were so engrossed in higher matters. Luckily, Lev's smile had come to her aid on more than one occasion.

"Good! You brought it just at the right moment!"

Not that he actually said those words, but his manner plainly indicated it.

Later Annie would be so tired she couldn't keep her eyes open. And while her guests were preparing to leave her house and go somewhere else, Annie had to make excuses.

"It's a pity, but I'm very sleepy tonight for some reason."

Once Lev had commented to his guests: "It's remarkable how close she is to nature. In the evening she fades away like the day, and every morning she awakens fresh as the morning star." The guests had laughed at his clever observation, but they also praised Annie for her admirable habits.

There were two guests whom Annie disliked. One was Ezra, a skinny young man with a haggard look and a pair of restless eyes that looked up at the world from a deep pit. If he ever came to the door when Lev was out, he remained standing with one foot on the threshold.

"Lev isn't here? No one's here yet?"

Apparently Annie wasn't "anyone." She would bite her lips and say, "No, no one is here yet."

And then there was Lily. Annie knew her from the "gatherings" at the Shermans'. Annie had never paid much attention to her. A young, pretty girl who spoke only English, Lily seemed to have become extremely attractive. She too would come to the door, ask for Lev, and stand there crestfallen if he weren't at home.

After a while Annie stopped being the pleasant hostess to Ezra and Lily, although she didn't quite understand the depths of her own antipathy. Whenever she handed them refreshments she found herself calculating how much these two pests were costing her; then she was immediately cross with herself for having such picayune thoughts. "You're being pretty petty yourself, Annie..."

*

During the hours that she was alone in the house, with all her chores finished, she loved to sit in a corner of her little sofa, her eyes half-closed, her hands clasped behind her neck, and go over in her head things that had happened to her recently or conversations she had had. Yesterday a friend had been speaking to her about her own husband:

"Annie," she had said, "if everybody was like your Isaac, the world would be a much better place."

Annie smiled as she thought about it. She should have said to her friend: "No, I don't agree with you about that. Even if everybody was like him, it still wouldn't be good enough."

What had made her think of that? Nothing had happened between her and Lev. But she had been feeling uneasy. Lev was a wonderful person, certainly, but what about her? She was *not* a wonderful person? Why was she almost always in the shadows? Would it always be like that — always in *his* light? Did she not have a life of her own? Something that depended on her alone and that would raise her to his level? It was all so complicated and mixed up. She should speak with Lev about it. Only he could explain it to her.

She chose an evening when Lev was in good spirits. They had had a pleasant supper together and were sitting at the table across from each other.

"Lev, I want to ask you something," she said softly.

He looked at her with affection. Her face revealed an inner turmoil. Her eyes were fixed on him with the earnestness of prayer. His smile encouraged her.

"Lev, when you're writing something and you think it's very good — at such times it's *your* celebration, not mine. The feeling of happiness is yours alone..." She paused.

Still smiling, he said: "What makes you think so? Don't you know you have a big share in my work? You're a big help to me, with your job and everything."

"Yes, but what do I do that's really important?"

They talked for a while, until Lev said: "Annie, you think everything in this world is that simple? It's impossible to come up with a clear answer to every question, to give everything a name. It's never so easy..."

Annie saw his eyes start roaming around the room, a sure sign he had lost interest in the conversation. Stung, she said without thinking:

"How come you talk so much with that tall girl?"

"Dena, you mean? An extremely silly person! She has convinced herself she can write poetry."

"And you waste your time talking with a silly girl like that?"

"Oh, Annie, come on!"

Annie was sorry now she had introduced that tall girl into the conversation, but it was true she made Annie apprehensive. Those long talks that Lev kept having with Dena had grown so obvious that the last time it happened Annie felt she had to do something about it. She brought in a tray of sandwiches, which put an end to their conversation, but Annie was hard put to keep on acting the part of the gracious hostess.

Whenever Annie was home alone and began getting these feelings she tied a cloth around her head, attacked her household chores and sang some popular tune. Eventually this made her feel better.

*

One evening, when Annie and Lev arrived at the Shermans', they found the party already in full swing. The large living-room was full of young, talented, self-confident people, plus a few older writers who were still living on past glory. Esther, lively and lovely as ever, was wearing a black velvet dress with a red flower at her waist. Her husband had just come home from a long business trip and brought with him some marvelous wine. Smiling broadly, he was serving it to his guests. In this atmosphere of good wine and good conversation, everyone was feeling more important and more distinguished than ever.

In one corner, Ezra the poet, his face white as chalk, was reciting one of his "new things." About a giant who brings joy and new life to the world. To the weak he brought strength, to the timid, courage. Coming from the mouth of this pale, shrunken young man the poem about a giant seemed rather incongruous and evoked a few quips among his listeners, except for Lev, who had some kind words to say about the quality of the writing.

When the audience around Ezra had thinned out, Annie leaped to her feet, strode over to the poet and said in a tremulous voice:

"I've got to tell you something, Ezra. I'm angry with you!"

"Angry with *me*? Why?"

"Didn't anyone teach you any manners? You come to our house and always ask for Lev as if no one else lived there!"

Ezra tittered. "But what about my poem? Did you like it?"

Annie blushed. "You have to ask?" she said approvingly, but immediately regretted her words. Perhaps she should have waited until she talked with Lev about it. She was never really certain about her own opinion, especially when it had to do with poetry. But for some reason, she felt more comfortable talking with Ezra about it. They both found chairs in a corner. With her hands folded in her lap and a smile on her face she heard herself speaking to him effortlessly. Whatever the subject, her words flowed easily and made sense, as though she had been keeping them bottled up inside her for years. At the same time, she felt grateful to Lev for educating her. And Ezra was praising her for being such an intelligent listener.

During the course of the evening she noticed Lev only once more in that crowd of people milling around the room. He was talking with Dena again, leaning toward her with an ironic little smile on his face, but his eyes seemed to be devouring her. Annie could almost hear him saying: "You're a little fool, but a pretty one!"

For a moment she felt her familiar apprehension. But she turned her head away. Her conversation with Ezra filled her thoughts and the evening passed so quickly that when Lev appeared at her side and said "Time to go!" she awoke as from a reverie and murmured, "What? Already?"

Lev didn't utter another word, but she could tell he was peeved. Silently they put on their coats. Outside, some of the guests were planning to go somewhere "for coffee" and invited them to come along. Lev hesitated, then shook his head and turned away. On the way home, he and Annie did not exchange a word. She wondered what he was so angry about. As they entered their apartment she could no longer restrain herself.

"Why didn't you go with them?" she asked.

"What kind of nonsense was he filling you with?"

"Who?"

"That so-called poet!"

"Ezra? He was talking about his poem. I thought you liked it."

"I liked it?"

"Yes. You even praised that line — 'With faith in his heart and a sword in his hand.'"

"You know it by heart already?"

Annie bit her tongue. She wanted to argue with him, to defend Ezra's poem, but she thought better of it. She had had enough new experiences for one day. Then she chastised herself for making Lev angry. He had trouble working when he felt this way. And she really did love him — him and his writing too.

*

Ezra had said to her that a person lives fully only when he was using all the talents that had been given him. Annie was impressed by that idea and tried to apply it to herself. Maybe that's why things were so difficult for her. She was a very simple person. No special talents had been given to her. More than once she had asked herself how Lev could love someone like her. How could she ever measure up to him? He did not love her, of that she was now certain. He often grew angry with her for no reason at all.

And he no longer had the patience for any long conversations with her. Now that she thought about it, there was plenty of evidence.

One evening, when Lev had been sitting at his desk reading, she felt an urge — almost a craving — to talk with him. She pulled a chair over and sat down beside him.

"I want to ask you something, Lev." She didn't really have anything to ask him, but she had always been intensely curious about the creative process itself.

"Go ahead and ask," he said.

"How does a person start to write, Lev? What happens inside your head?"

Lev studied her with his smiling eyes. He didn't feel much like talking, though, so he tried to make light of her question.

"Many things happen all at once, Annie." And that was the extent of his explanation. For the rest of that evening neither of them said another word. This was happening more and more often. An inapt word could make her withdraw into herself. In the early days she had opened her heart to him like a plant that opens its leaves to the sun. All the following day, as she worked feverishly at her machine, she choked on her resentment. He had insulted her. Didn't have the patience to listen to her, so he dismissed her with a wisecrack.

She could think of nothing else. Still smarting, she came home at the end of the day. Lev greeted her with his usual smile, but Annie pretended not to notice. She turned at once to her pots and pans and started preparing dinner. They ate in silence as Lev stared at her in surprise.

"What is it with you tonight, Annie?" he asked, finally.

She almost choked over her answer.

"Tonight? And what about last night? You think it's an easy thing to forget?"

"What happened last night?" He really didn't know.

"You see. You've already forgotten," she said, bitterly.

Despite all his insistence, Annie only said: "It was nothing important. It's not worth talking about."

Always, whenever there were any cross words between them, Annie's anger was the first to subside. She couldn't stay angry with him for very long. But this time her resentment kept mounting, like a wound festering, A few days later, as she stood at the sink washing the dishes, she kept thinking, "Well, I may be a simple girl with no talent, but that's no reason why he should insult me..."

She wrapped the dish-rag around her hand and as she stood there motionless, the tears dropped from her eyes. He didn't love her any longer. Best that they separate.

At that time Lev was busy on a long, serious work. They seldom spoke to each other. But a welter of feelings had accumulated inside her, so that she could no longer contain herself. One evening after supper she said to him:

"Lev, listen. When two unequal people are living together and one of them —"

"Oh, Annie, not again...please!" And he burst out laughing. "You remind me of that old professor who kept discovering things that others had already discovered before him."

She said nothing, but she felt something tear in her heart.

After that conversation she was even more certain that their life together had ended. You wanted to fly high, she said to herself, but nobody really pays any attention to you. Mostly they laugh at you...

During the next few days, as she worked almost frantically at her sewing-machine, a decision took shape in her mind. And one evening she said to him simply:

"Lev, from the very beginning this was a mistake. The best thing now would be to separate."

She kept her eyes on his face and waited anxiously to see what his response would be.

He merely frowned — and said nothing.

This only strengthened her conviction that she had made the right decision. His silence was only a sign that he didn't care about her or her feelings. Well, good enough.

A few days later she came home early from work. Lev was not there. For a few moments she leaned against the wall and took a long look at her home. Everything was still in its place, the walls were clean and bright, his desk and books were still there. A quiet, comfortable corner for two people. Now she would have to take it all apart with her own hands.

Her eyes fell on a little heap of cut-up material lying on a chair. She had intended to sew herself a new blouse in one of Lev's favorite colors. Would she need it any longer?

She tried to look into the future. What would her life be like without him? But she saw nothing there. She did not *want* to see anything there.

Later that evening, when Lev returned, their possessions were already divided into two separate piles.

"This is mine and that's yours," she said, not looking at him.

Stunned, all he could say was "What is this?" For the first time it had struck him that she was really serious about all this. He could feel the anger mounting inside him.

"If that's what you want, I can't stop you!" He pointed to his "possessions" and said, only half in earnest: "A load of stuff like this you want me to carry out with me?"

Annie did not want to be there when he left. She slowly put on her coat. She had to be strong now, not sentimental. Let him not say later that...

Clumsily, Lev began packing his suitcase. Annie had never seen a man so impractical. It made her laugh.

"Look at him! Can't even pack a suitcase!"

She ran over and impatiently helped him pack. He did not stop her.

"You're going out now?" he asked.

"I've got an important errand..."

"Whom do you have to see at a moment like this?"

"People who consider my feelings, who don't take me for granted, who don't insult me..."

"You're imagining things. I've never intentionally insulted you..."

Annie stopped packing and started buttoning and unbuttoning her coat.

"What's the use of talking now?" she said with a wave of her hand and started for the door.

"Can't we at least say goodbye?" He practically yelled it.

"Maybe you'll still be here when I get back."

For a moment he said nothing. Then he smiled.

"Maybe I won't even go at all..."

"What!"

"I said, maybe I'll stay, and things will be as they were before. What do you say, Annie?"

He looked so forlorn, so guilty. Like a spoiled brat, she thought, smiling inwardly.

"But — but — you don't love me any more," she said.

"Now more than ever, Annie. I don't understand what's been happening to you lately —"

"What's been happening with *me*?"

"With whom, then, Annie, with *me*?" He took her hand. "Let's sit down here on the sofa..."

She felt like shouting for joy, but didn't want to show her feelings so soon. "Wait," she finally said, pulling her hand away. "Let me first put up some tea..."

And she floated into the kitchen.

GENERATION OF THE WILDERNESS

Miriam Raskin

For a biography of Raskin, see the introduction to the story In the Shadows.

Generation of the Wilderness

Bennie, an operator at dresses, woke up early in the morning and rushed off to his job.

In the garment center the streets were already full of movement and momentum. From the dark maws of the subways flowed a never-ending stream of people ready for the day's work. In rows they marched glumly through the streets like soldiers on parade. The day was gray, a sort of twilight in the morning. The air was damp and biting. A winter's day in New York City.

Awkwardly, Bennie pushed his way through the crowd. His limbs were still asleep, but soon he was sitting in the shop along with everyone else, working to the rhythm of the machines. Truth to tell, he loved his shop, especially in the early mornings, when he could feel the strength flowing back into his arms and legs, and when everyone seemed to be working in unison. A good operator, when he works in rhythm with his machine, feels his limbs singing along too. He and the machine are one. Each movement is calculated, so that not even a minute will be wasted.

For many years Bennie had resisted this rhythm of the shop. He had been a serious young man with a head full of plans about his "future." Perhaps he would even go into business on his own. But nothing ever came of it, until one day he said to himself:

"Too late. Now I have no other choice."

So these days his head is not full of plans, except that he is determined to perfect his performance at the machine. He gives this a lot of thought, often smiling to himself as he takes apart another bundle of work.

"It takes a lot of brains to make a dress! I wonder who thought of it first. And why is speed so important?"

With his broadboned face and his pensive eyes beneath his high forehead, he looks like a Hebrew teacher in the Old Country.

Bennie knows he still has much to learn. He is only a beginner. There is a union in the trade. There are right-wingers and there are left-wingers. Which of those makes more sense he has trouble understanding, but about one thing he is clear: when the Revolution comes, it will find him doing honest work. He has something to hold on to now and will no longer be suspended in mid-air.

*

Lunch hour in the shop is a time for rest and sociability. Bennie takes his paper bag of food and goes over to the pressers' table, where some of the men are already sitting in a circle, talking passionately about unions and socialism, subjects that interest Bennie very much. He sits down, takes out his sandwich and notices that out of this circle of pressers there has already formed a left-wing faction and a right-wing faction. Hershl, the blond presser and Yoske, the young operator, are embroiled in a dispute that apparently has been going on between them for years. Hershl is ready with facts and figures and Yoske contributes his young, hot blood.

"Where were you in 1909 when we laid the foundation-stone of the Union?" demands Hershl.

Without a moment's hesitation Yoske replies: "Your foundation was rotten right from the start!"

Bennie would like to know, for example, what will they do about the masses of workers who are still not "class-conscious" and approximately what year do they intend to start the Revolution, but he realizes that this quarrel between them has a long history and nobody remembers who started it. The other men are beginning to join the fray, trading insults and accusations, but concerning Bennie's questions no one says a word.

A couple of the older workers, with sad, worried eyes, stand nearby shaking their heads, as if to say: "We've heard all this before!"

At a window close by sits Sadie, who is no longer as young as she used to be. She is chewing her food lazily and staring out the window as if she has been sitting there all her life.

Johnny, the young Italian fellow, is listening to the argument with one ear until he moves to another corner where Florence the Redhead and a few other younger women are joking and laughing as if they had no worries in the world at all.

The shop is bigger than a football field. People of different nationalities are all mixed together here. The laughter of the younger women, whom the cunning foreman loves to entertain with double-entendre jokes, rings out like a bell, but in the pressers' corner the serious debate still rages:

"With you people the Union is the main objective!"

"The main objective? The main objective is to live like human beings!"

But Bennie is already back at his machine. He doesn't yet have a "handle" on this whole dispute. And while his hands are already working, his brow is still furrowed as he tries to get at the essence of all this, as he used to do over a difficult passage in the Talmud. One thought disturbs him:

"This Left-wing and Right-wing business. It's nonsense. They forget that the main thing is for all of them to be united in one purpose."

*

The later in the day it gets, the more strident grows the clatter of the machines. It is incessant. Bennie shakes his head in anticipation — at any moment someone will scream hysterically. The air grows more and more oppressive. Arms are swirling all around — arms of all colors, all sizes and shapes. Shoulders are rocking, rocking. The omnipresent foreman grows out of the ground now here, now there, and as he glides around the floor he seems to bump into the young Black "floor-boy" repeatedly, as if they were doing one of those popular dances.

Bennie is beginning to feel more and more uncomfortable, as if he had been dragged by the hair into some monstrous machine and cannot extricate himself from it. He wants to run away from this place, but he cannot. At such times he says to himself:

"I can't believe I came to this place of my own free will! I'm lost here and I'll never get out alive..."

At the end of the day, Bennie is the last one to leave his machine. He staggers like a drunk. He looks around at the other workers, their faces full of fatigue, but still they are resolute and confident, and they make him feel ashamed of his own weakness. Gradually his faith in the strength of the people returns. And when the foreman slinks by him with the little crown of hair atop his head, and with the nape of his neck smooth and stiff as cardboard, Bennie reminds himself that this man is only a lackey of the boss and a pompous fool besides, and when the Revolution comes the foreman will be the first to know it.

*

Often the other workers would say to him: "Bennie, you should 'orientate' yourself. You can't seem to make up your mind. One day you're with the Right-wingers, the next day with the Left-wingers."

"Orientate" himself? What kind of strange word was that? Bennie couldn't stand the sound of it. Lately he had been hearing nothing *but* new words. Besides, who could know for certain which side had the whole truth?

One evening Bennie wandered into a meeting of the "Lefties," though he himself wasn't too clear how he had gotten there. Everything was going well at that meeting. Young folks — and older ones like him — were gathered there. Bennie looked around and saw how pleased everyone was with the speaker. More than pleased. Enthusiastic. Why? Because he was burying the Right-wingers? After a while Bennie couldn't keep silent any longer. He decided to ask for the floor, to show them the error of their ways. He coughed, unbuttoned his vest and began:

"It's this way, friends. Whether a person is a Left-winger or a Right-winger is not all that important. Who cares? The main thing is that all of us workers should stick together."

He said a few other things as he wiped the perspiration off his forehead, and ended with his index finger pointing straight up into the air: "Because .. because the enemy is still strong!"

As he sat down he could feel stares of derision coming at him from all directions. From the platform someone asked him good-naturedly:

"And who do *you* represent, brother?"

Well, that was enough for Bennie. Hell would freeze over before he'd set foot in one of these meetings again. One good thing came out of it, though. A woman came over, sat down beside him and asked:

"What trade do you work at, brother?"

"What trade? I make dresses."

"Really? Me too. How come I've never seen you at a meeting?"

"Oh, I rarely go out anywhere..."

The woman looked at him sympathetically with her warm, brown eyes. Her oval face was a lackluster color, and from under her little hat brown strands of hair rested on her forehead.

"My name is Vera, brother. And you should come to more of these meetings. You'll find them interesting. Here, buy this ticket from me for a concert on Sunday."

Bennie took the ticket from her hand. Wasted money, he thought to himself, but as he looked more closely at the woman's sympathetic eyes he felt somehow more cheerful and broke out into a broad smile. He had always found it difficult to make friends with women, but this one seemed to be more his "type." As the meeting ended, he stayed close beside her.

Out in the street, the crowd acted like one big happy family. People from one group exchanged wisecracks with another group on the other side of the street. Vera joined in the banter, but from time to time she turned to Bennie and gave him an encouraging look.

But now it was time for them to part. Bennie held on to her little hand as her friends called for her to hurry.

"You know what, brother," she said. "You must have a lot of friends too. Why don't you sell them tickets to the concert? Here are the tickets and here's my address. Come on over."

Bennie stood rooted to the ground as he took the tickets from her and she walked off toward her friends. "What kind of mess am I getting myself into?" he thought to himself as he buttoned his coat and ran to the subway.

The winter dragged on doggedly. Snow fell. The gray sky hung low over the icy streets, with no promise of sun. As was his habit, Bennie got up with the dawn, beat a path for himself in the deep snow, and hurried to his job.

To make the day go faster, he speeded up his machine. He could hardly wait for the day to end, because evenings he went to visit Vera. Vera always greeted him with a warm smile. She liked Bennie for his simplicity. He was a little rough around the edges, but he could grow into a useful person for "The Movement." And Bennie liked Vera for what she was. She had a *yiddishe neshoma*, a Jewish soul, he said to her once.

Vera laughed. "Go on, Bennie! Why a *Jewish* soul?"

"Don't tell me any fairy tales!" he laughed back at her. He knew very well what he meant. What else would you call her concern for "higher matters" or her readiness to make sacrifices for the things she believed in? There was always an air of exalted spirituality about her, as if she bore a heavy responsibility for the world. Even her appearance bespoke this, with her brown hair and her bright, affectionate eyes.

In her youth Vera had been active in the Bund, the Jewish Labor Federation, and after those stormy years she had become completely withdrawn. But now that she had reawakened, she had become a "Communistke." To Bennie it seemed that she never had any doubts about anything. Everything was clear as day. Once, he asked her when she thought the opposing factions would make peace with each other. He confided to her his own doubts about the union and the shop. At such times her eyes were not fixed on him but upon some secret world of her own and she would say to him in a worried tone:

"Bennie, somewhere inside you there still lives a bourgeois..."

Whenever she said that, Bennie felt very much ashamed of himself. He wanted very much to become a real proletarian and not violate the "line" that Vera consistently maintained whenever she talked about the classes in society.

When Bennie is alone in his room, these thoughts trouble him as he strides back and forth, back and forth.

One evening Vera took hold of his lapels with both hands and chastised him: "Bennie, listen to me! Why do you always go out in this cold weather with your coat unbuttoned? You'll catch cold!"

In her hands he felt her femininity, in her voice he sensed tenderness and concern. He turned his head away, lest she see how moved he was. Because now there was no doubt about it. He was in love. He could feel all the old dreams return, dreams that he had long repressed. Had there been no one else in the room, maybe he would have summoned up the courage to bring these thoughts to his lips. But in Vera's room there were always a lot of friends. And like her, they were always very serious, although they were always in high spirits. And all of them seemed cut from the same pattern — each and every one of them was inflexible.

Jack, the college student, a young man with a finely chiseled Jewish face, and with an air of assurance, always shook his head in a way that reminded Bennie of a religious ritual.

"Well, Vera? What is *your* opinion?" He pronounced her name with an old-country accent, though he had been born in America.

Or there was Yankel the baker, who had been friends with Vera back in the Bundist days. Sometimes, her voice full of concern, she would touch his face and say: "My goodness, Yankel, what sort of cut is that on your face? Why aren't you more careful!"

"Don't worry, Vera, it's not from shaving. I got that cut on the picket line." Yankel was built like a Samson, but he had the smile of a young boy. Yankel "believes" in Vera. For her sake he would fight a whole army single-handed.

In Vera's little room it is always homey. Even when the talk is about everyday matters, it is still zestful. But Bennie can hardly wait for them all to leave. It's as though they were purposely staying as late as they could. For him, it is long past his bed-time. Tomorrow is a workday. But his own room is cold and dreary, so he'd rather stay at Vera's. He smiles at everyone and puts in a word here and there, so they won't notice what he's really thinking about.

Whenever Jack the college student comes to visit, Vera spends most of her time with him. She still has a lot to learn, she says. Bennie drops out of the conversation altogether.

"Did you all read what happened at the League of Nations meeting?" Jack begins in an authoritative tone.

Bennie resents this. In everything they have a share, and always they are on guard. He picks up a book but with one ear he listens to their heated discussion. Both Jack and Vera are ardent believers, ever ready for heroic deeds. Bennie's resentment mounts. Maybe he ought to have a serious talk with her. Maybe they could rent a room together or something.

The one occasion when he and Jack had had a serious conversation, Jack had called him a "nationalist."

"Is that so? And what about you? Have you already cut all your threads with the Jewish people?"

But Jack had no patience with Bennie's "flowery" talk.

"When the Revolution comes, people like you will disappear," he retorted.

Bennie was a little bit afraid of this young fellow and the fanatical fire in his eyes. He said no more, but as he was walking home later that evening he stopped in his tracks. It had suddenly occurred to him how he should have responded to Jack. But now it was too late, and Vera would think he'd had no reply to Jack's accusation.

A few days later he said to her: "That Jack is so removed from everything we know and feel. It's true what they say: 'A branch that falls from a tree will wither away sooner or later!'"

Vera disagreed. "You don't understand, Bennie. Communists should not have any sentimental beliefs. I wish everybody could be like that."

Bennie had no reply to that. He did not know yet that deep in her heart there still glowed a spark of sentiment for the old days when she had been a Bundist.

*

Some evenings Vera was not home at all. Bennie would sit reading a book, waiting for her. He was old enough to have the patience to wait until he could hear her quick steps in the corridor. It was not unusual for Vera to have two or even three meetings in one evening. But she was still buoyant when she could finally take off her little leather jacket and say:

"I'm starving, Bennie. Let's go into the kitchen and grab a bite!"

Vera was on friendly terms with her next-door neighbors, the Wieners, who had also once been active in the Bund. Boris was a tall, sturdy man with lively features and a full head of black hair touched with silver. Anna was slender and youthful looking, but with dark circles under her bright, shining eyes. Whenever Vera and the Wieners sat around the table drinking tea, they entertained themselves with reminiscences about their years in the Bund. Bennie, for his part, would lean his chair against the wall and smile inwardly about something.

But often this idyllic scene would be shattered by Vera's sharp words.

"That's all in the past! Today the Bundists are no longer revolutionaries —"

The air of peaceful nostalgia would be destroyed. Bitter words, designed to hurt, would fill the room. And Bennie could not understand what was happening. He could only bury his head in his chest and hope that the bitterness would subside. Boris and Annie would soon say goodnight, leaving Vera with her head in her hands. And as Bennie put on his coat he would stroke her hair gently.

"You must be very tired, Vera..."

"No I'm not! It just hurts when good people refuse to acknowledge the truth."

"I don't understand, Vera. Which one of you wants to know the truth? What kind of truth is it that makes brothers tear each other apart? You really expect to bring the Revolution this way?"

Vera was silent for a long time. Then she said softly: "That's how it is, Bennie. We're all children of this lousy time. What else can you expect? It will take a long long time — even *after* the Revolution — before people learn to be better human beings."

That night Bennie couldn't fall asleep. He kept seeing the words in the Bible that he had studied when he was still a child: "And Moses said to God: You expect these slaves to understand how to serve you and praise your Name? And Moses let the Hebrews wander in the desert for forty years."

*

The next morning Bennie, running to catch the subway, kept chastising himself: "Idiot! Why are you rushing like this? It's not late." But he knew it had long ago become a habit with him...

In the garment center the hullabaloo was even worse than usual, because this was the season for the "cheaper line" and if you didn't rush to get the goods out on time, you wouldn't earn very much.

That winter was a bitter one for everybody. Strikes kept breaking out, now in one trade, now in another. Rumors circulated about a "slack season" that could be the worst in history. The whole world seemed to be on shaky ground.

One morning Bennie read in the paper that the police had shot at workers in a long, bitter strike and that, in protest, the Right-wing and the Left-wing of the Union had organized a united front meeting. He couldn't believe his eyes. Something was starting to move. A "Committee for United Action" had been formed. It called upon the workers to come to a mass protest meeting. That evening Bennie came earlier than usual to the restaurant where he and Vera met often for supper. There was a holiday atmosphere in the place. The talk was all about the forthcoming "united" meeting.

At one table in a corner sat a former union leader named Okun. He sipped his coffee in a manner that showed his utter disdain for all the excitement. But Bennie had always respected his judgment. So he said to him:

"Well, Brother Okun, something is finally happening, yes? It's a good beginning, yes?"

"You think so? Good for you."

"And *you* don't?" said Bennie, taken aback.

Okun's only reply was a skeptical smile.

At that moment Yasha Mendel, the insurance agent, came through the revolving door of the Automat. Yasha, who was neither old nor young, always showed up everywhere where there was good company.

Noticing him come in, Bennie said: "Well, Yasha Mendel is here! That's a good sign!"

"Did you know that he's now a Left-winger?"

"Really, since when?"

Okun shrugged. "Doesn't matter."

Through the revolving door came new waves of people. The incessant conversation became one loud noise, until Yasha Mendel's booming, aggressive voice caught everyone's attention. His verbal challenge was aimed at Dovid, a Left Labor Zionist with sad eyes.

"I've already told you my opinion," Dovid was saying, a note of pleading in his voice. "You're purposely misinterpreting me."

Yasha was merciless. "Since you're a Zionist, I know what you're thinking. But these days there are no half-measures!" He seemed to be directing his barbs not so much at Dovid as at Bennie.

"Can you believe this guy?" Bennie whispered to Okun.

"He's giving himself away, Bennie. You know the old saying: The less sure you are of yourself, the louder you holler." And having uttered these words of wisdom, he got up and left.

Bennie didn't mind. Today he felt friendly to everybody, not only because he had lived to see a "united front" meeting, but because soon he would talk to Vera about a very important matter for them both.

*

Miriam Raskin

It was a cold evening. Chunks of dark clouds floated across the yellow moon. A frosty wind swept through the streets, tried to tear the clothes off people who had ventured out. Around the meeting hall, however, the lights were bright and the people were in a festive mood. From every street came streams of garment workers hurrying to the meeting, eager to be on time for this historic occasion.

The high-ceilinged hall was packed. People were still pouring in. The union leaders were all there, staid, serious-looking, with the self-assurance of artisans who have mastered their trade. Old and tried fighters were arriving, with their handsome gray heads and a youthful enthusiasm in their eyes. And the noisy, full-blooded young people were there, about whom you couldn't really tell whether they were Right-wingers or Left-wingers. And everyone had the same emotion in their hearts:

"Unity in protest against our oppressors!"

Bennie too is swept along by the stream of people. *His* people. And his heart is full.

"So many Jews!"

"Jews?" asks Vera, walking alongside him.

He smiles guiltily. He knows very well that in addition to Jews here there are also Russians and Spaniards and Irish and who knows how many other nationalities. But he still makes the mistake sometimes of thinking that everything good comes from Jews.

Up on the platform the "United Committee" was gathering. The noise in the hall abated. The speeches by leaders of both factions were beginning. They were experienced public speakers. The audience listened as though they were at a concert of fine music, familiar music that you want to sing along with. But not in unison. When a Left-winger spoke, one side of the hall cheered and applauded; when a Right-winger spoke, the other side of the hall did the same. It was like a deep wound in the body that takes a long time to heal. Not that people were arguing with each other; everyone was good-humored and agreeable and ready to compliment the oratorical abilities of the various speakers.

Still, the split seemed to have grown deeper. Bennie was worried. He moved around from one group to another. He could tell that the celebratory mood was being dissipated. This was not how he had envisioned the whole thing, and he grew more and more uneasy. Suddenly someone in the center of the hall called out:

"I'd like to say something! May I have the floor?"

There was something ominous in the sound of the man's voice, something that sent a shock wave through the audience.

"Give him the floor!"

"Let him speak!"

From the depths of the mass of people in the hall, something was seeking a way out. But already people were taking sides, calling names. And neither the Committee nor the leaders on the platform could stop the approaching avalanche.

In all the confusion, Bennie noticed that Vera was trying to get to the platform, apparently in an effort to quiet the crowd. But in their excitement, people assumed the opposite. One of the Committee members pushed her aside. Someone yelled: "They're beating up Vera!"

The cry went from mouth to mouth. The urge to fight spread like wildfire. Bennie stood flat up against a wall, pushed there by a wave of bodies. A sea of angry, distorted, hate-filled faces surrounded him. Women were screaming hysterically. Bennie covered his face with his hands, as one does against an evil spirit.

Then suddenly the hall grew still. The police had burst in with their wooden sticks and their wooden faces. Bennie noticed some suspicious looking characters grinning at each other. People began leaving. Those who remained stood there crestfallen. Suddenly someone in the front of the hall began singing the *Internationale*. Others picked it up. People stilled the pain and disappointment in their hearts by singing. Many had tears in their eyes. Gradually the voices grew stronger:

"Arise, ye prisoners of starvation!"

*

Much later Vera and Bennie took the subway home. Neither of them said a word. Neither one looked into the other's eyes until the train was above ground. Through the windows they could see the myriad lights of the city. A sea of tiny flames sparkled out there like gold dots against a black cloth. In the darkness the high buildings shimmered like massive fortresses, as if they were challenging each other to see who could grow taller.

Bennie peered into the night. He couldn't stop marveling at the way human beings never stop striving — or stumbling — through chaos and darkness, in their efforts to make the world better. Though wounded and tattered, they proudly continued their march.

NO WAY OUT

by Miriam Raskin

For a biography of Raskin, see the introduction to the story In the Shadows.

No Way Out

For the hundredth time Sam Rubin resolved to sell his store and give up the business. After all, how long can you keep throwing good money after bad?

On the "Avenue," a busy street jam-packed with stores, Sam Rubin had conducted his "butter and eggs" business for quite a few years. His little store, squeezed in between a butcher shop and a herring store, was so narrow that his wife Gussie, a short, stout woman with big hips, always knocked something off the counter whenever she pushed her way along the length of it. Gussie had therefore gotten into the habit of hurling deadly curses at her husband the *shlimazl* and her joyless, wasted existence.

Sam paid no attention to his wife's curses. All day long, day after day, with his hands in his pockets, he marked time in the doorway of his store, worried and overwrought, as his restless, anxious eyes searched for a customer. Not only his eyes, but his entire scrawny, stoop-shouldered body and his emaciated face, with its pointed little beard, created the impression of a wordless entreaty to the passersby on the street:

"Murderers! Why don't you come into my store and buy something?"

All around him the street swarmed with people, buyers and sellers, who kept moving back and forth busily in a bizarre dance. It was the hottest time of the year, and his store was surrounded on all sides by stands laden with all sorts of foodstuffs, as if there had been an overabundant harvest. A sea of fruits and vegetables shimmered in green and gold. The shopkeepers were dusty and weather-beaten from the sun and wind. Young boys with pale, gaunt faces hawked their wares at the top of their lungs. Untidy and unkempt women loudly protested shortages in the weight of their purchases.

But as though none of this concerned him, Sam Rubin stood silently in his doorway, his thoughts twisting and turning, gloomy thoughts about the big new dairy store that had opened less than a year ago right across the street. He kept his eyes averted from that establishment, but in his mind's eye he could picture the store with the freshly decorated windows and its brightly lit sign: DAIRY AND FANCY GROCERIES. He could see the owner, Julius Mendel, a big, strapping man with a ruddy complexion and a strong back, dressed in his clean, white apron, as he served his customers methodically and politely, in the manner of the "goyim."

People have respect for that kind of storekeeper, Sam said to himself. Customers appreciate that attitude. He bit his lips. He had come to realize that his own business was doomed. He no longer felt like a businessman. All the rest of that day he stood there staring straight ahead, his eyes full of apprehension. As he kept totaling up all his debts, he slowly came to a decision: He would gather up whatever money he had left, take his wife and children and get as far away from the Avenue as possible...

His thoughts were interrupted by a customer who entered the store and asked for a quarter-pound of butter. Sam snapped to attention and immediately "got busy." As he weighed the quarter pound of butter, his hands trembled. The slice of butter he had placed on the scale was too large. He cut some off and the scale showed insufficient weight. The customer, an attractive young woman, was growing impatient.

"Why do you make such a fuss about a little piece of butter? It's not gold, you know."

"For me it is," Sam smiled. Soon it would be the tenth of the month and he'd have to send out the checks. What could he tell this customer? And here he was, actually smiling at this young woman. He wanted to detain her as long as possible, but she had already gone out the door. Sam's face, which had shown some animation for a moment, again assumed its forlorn look. Suddenly he felt a deep dislike of all those people passing by outside. How could they be so indifferent to everything? A person could drop dead right before their eyes and it wouldn't bother them one bit. He felt the anger mounting inside him. He ought to set fire to the whole damn street and watch it go up in smoke, along with the big dairy store and its owner, Mendel the Crook.

*

No matter what time his wife Gussie called him for supper, he had no appetite. Instead of hunger he had a kind of sour taste in his mouth. When he did come to the table he ate in a hurry and gulped down his food without chewing it. Gussie prepared their meals in a "kitchen" in back of the store. Their two sons, Ikie and Jake, were big boys, and when they rushed in from school with their booming voices they brought in with them a world that Sam did not understand. Moreover, they made the place seem even smaller than it was.

Although it was summer-time and sunny outside, Sam's store was in semi-darkness. The sunbeams on the blistered walls seemed as if they had lost their way and wandered in by mistake. Empty cartons and week-old trash lay underfoot and unpleasant odors assailed the nostrils. Sam did not even sit down to eat his meals; he ate standing at a rickety old table. More than once he had picked up a hammer and some nails to fix it, but he never did. Why bother, when they were here for only a little while longer?

With no warmth in her voice and without a smile on her face, Gussie served Sam his meals as if she had been condemned to perform this duty. In her empty, troubled eyes there was an unspoken accusation against her husband: she would waste the rest of her years for the sake of this *shlimazl*, without a proper home and without a normal family life.

And Sam, on the rare occasions when his eyes lingered on his wife, on her protruding belly and her washed out hair, wondered where the beauty of her youth had disappeared to. Before they were married she had spent hours making sure she would look her best. Now she didn't care how she looked. Well, she wasn't the only one who acted like that. Everyone else did the same. Everybody made a fool of him...

One day, with thoughts like these in his head, he stood at his little table swallowing his lunch and washing it down with scalding hot coffee. His older son Jake was "minding the store." Sam heard him say:

"Missus, if you don't want it, don't buy it!"

Sam rushed angrily out to the store. "Is that any way to talk to a customer? Is it?" Then, his tone softening, he instructed his son: "A customer likes to feel she is being treated like a lady. On the other hand, if the lady is too picky-choosy, you have a right to tell her off..."

But Jake only looked at him with a sardonic little smile, as if to say: "Old man, why do you tell me things I already know?"

*

In the end-of-summer evenings, when there were fewer customers on the street, the storekeepers on either side of Sam's place would come out and chat: Wolinski the butcher, a man with a pair of mischievous eyes and an excellent command of English, and Moishe the Herring Merchant, with his unruly beard and permanently stuffed-up nose. Hymie the Vegetable Man, with the scraggly beard, used to sidle over. Then there was the mannish looking Mrs. Cohen of the Appetizer Store, who always kept her hands in her pockets and bragged to Gussie about all the outlandish things that had happened to her that day.

The mood was usually cheerful in this circle of shopkeepers joking about how bad business was. Sam listened with only half-an-ear as he stared at the brightly lit Dairy Store across the street. On this particular evening he suddenly found himself right outside the Dairy Store without knowing how he had gotten there. Like a thief he stood by the door, memorizing the prices on every article. Julius Mendel was engaged in the process of persuading a customer to buy something.

"These eggs? Try them once and you'll come back and thank me. They're practically fresh out of the chicken."

Sam beat a quick retreat, his gorge rising at this brazen lie his competitor was telling the unsuspecting customer. He returned to his store with a heavy heart. He didn't have — nor would he ever have — the *chutzpa* of a Julius Mendel. He didn't have the self-confidence, he didn't have the strength, he didn't have this, he didn't have that...

The circle of joking storekeepers was still standing outside his door.

"Hey, Sam, where've you been? You just lost two customers!"

"So what? Who needs them, anyway, my customers?" There was a crooked smile on his face. Gussie, who happened to have come out of the store at that moment, sang out:

"Listen to him! Now he doesn't even need his customers!"

Sam bit his lips. His own wife — his worst enemy. Now was the time to tell her what he really thought of her. But he restrained himself. He knew what would happen if he started up with her now — she had always had a knack of twisting his words so that she would emerge as the injured party.

The Avenue was now more subdued. Here and there a solitary storekeeper still stood looking out the window, hoping for a late shopper. But Sam locked his door and started walking home, and Gussie, just as unhappy as her husband, shuffled behind him like a shadow.

*

Their home, right under the roof of the apartment building, was small and stuffy. Its single window, in a side wall, was reminiscent of a man blind in one eye. In every corner lay a pile of rumpled clothing.

Sam took off his shirt and sat on the edge of the bed, lost in thought, one shoe still in his hand. Gussie dragged all her weight into the bed and lay there gasping for air.

"Why doesn't he turn out the light?" she mumbled. "Lectric doesn't cost money?"

Sam felt his previous anger melting away. He didn't like quarreling and was always the first to make up. Still, she had embarrassed him needlessly.

"How could you disgrace me like that in front of other people? Why can't you understand that?"

"What is there to understand?" Gussie sat bolt upright and ran her dimmed eyes around the room. "We might as well be in our graves — that's all I understand."

"What more can I do? If you can't bluff, if you can't take what belongs to someone else, then you might as well give up." With his honesty as a shield, he tried to protect himself against his wife's complaints. "Listen to me, Gussie!" He put his hand on her knee. "Listen to me! If it was up to me, I would make bluffing illegal! Everybody would have to be honest."

"Listen to him! He's feverish again! I wish it on my enemies .." She pushed his hand from her knee.

"Silly woman! Don't you think I want us to live like everybody else? With a real house, with separate rooms for the children and everything. Wait. The holidays are coming. We'll make a little money. Maybe even save a little..."

"Without fresh stuff, how do you expect to sell anything?"

"Fresh stuff? Like burying the living on top of the dead."

"God in heaven! It's either one or the other! How long can you hold on? Sell your store and be damned!"

Having said all that needed saying, Gussie stretched out to her full length and turned her face to the wall. Sam put out the light. Lying next to Gussie's back he felt as if he were pressed against a wall or being squeezed in a vise. At such times Sam turns to his imaginings, all sorts of fantasies in which he flies freely through the air. His overheated imagination brings him all sorts of good ideas, one more beautiful than the others:

Mendel the Crook has broken a leg, is lying in the hospital and his Dairy Store is empty. Sam himself, walking in the street, finds a bundle of money, grows rich, and his wife Gussie becomes very affectionate. But then, when he falls asleep, all the grief of the day returns — his unpaid bills, his past due notes, his lack of customers — and he keeps twisting and turning in his bed.

*

The summer mornings were clear and quiet. On one such morning Sam was taking a walk through "the market." He stopped at the Italian man's store and watched him arrange his stand, which became colorful as a garden in bloom. Sam shook his head in admiration. As he approached his own store a new idea was ripe in his mind. He would buy a new line of goods — biscuits, for example, or even fancy cakes — and with these he would decorate his show-window.

"Customers like a store that looks nice," he told Gussie excitedly.

Busy with a boiling pot, Gussie wrinkled up her nose skeptically. "Yeah, it will help as much as cupping a corpse," she hissed, and turned her attention back to the pot.

As if someone had doused him with ice-water, Sam shivered. "Stupid woman!" he muttered, but he felt a spark of hope glowing in his soul. His head was soon busy with new plans. After all, there are stores that do make a good living...

A few days later he was being solicited by a variety of salesmen, who somehow manage to sniff out such developments. They offered him goods "on consignment" and other such inducements. Standing behind the counter, Sam was "the boss."

"These crackers? I don't know. My customers are very particular about such things." Sam had not enjoyed the sound of his own voice so much in a long time.

Soon, trucks were stopping in front of Sam's store almost every morning. Strong, lighthearted young men jumped off these trucks and delivered beautiful boxes of cakes and biscuits and a new brand of cheese with vegetable specks.

Sam, all excited and wearing a vest to cover the pants that were too big for him around the waist, arranged his new merchandise carefully in his window. But in his heart he felt a sharp pain, a groundless terror, which he tried to dispel by singing old, melancholy tunes.

Just at that moment, a customer entered. A good omen, Sam thought. He permitted the woman to examine a basketful of goods from top to bottom.

"How old is this here cheese?" she asked, pulling back an edge of the silver wrapper and sniffing the cheese.

For Sam, this was the last straw. "Missus, you're not going to buy anything anyway, so why must you take it all apart like that?"

"Mister, you keep on talking to your customers like that and you'll be out of business in a week!" She threw the cheese back into the basket and stalked out of the store.

Sam's eyes followed her out into the street. "Damn her! She's ruined my good mood altogether!"

The heat that day was oppressive. A low-hanging, reddish-gray sky burned down over the heads of the people walking in the street. Merchants covered their wares with newspapers. But by early evening the market had grown busier. Hymie the Vegetable Man cut open a big green cantaloupe and shouted at the passers-by: "A big bargain, folks! Three cents a slice!" Moishe the Herring-Man, who usually sat calmly inside his store with a Yiddish newspaper in his hand, moved his jars of herring and sour tomatoes further out onto the sidewalk.

And Sam, standing in his doorway, rocked back and forth on his heels as crazy thoughts raced around his head. He felt as if he were trapped on a perpetual merry-go-round. He began to question the wisdom of his plan with the new merchandise. Very soon he would have to pay for it. All his effort would not have amounted to a damn.

Eating his meal that evening, he complained to his wife: "Maybe I was too smart for my own good." But Gussie had long ago stopped interfering in her husband's business. She looked at him coldly:

"Keep it up! Keep it up! You're going to be in trouble over your head!"

*

Sam really knew very little about the world outside his store. He rarely read a newspaper. But evenings, in the circle of his fellow storekeepers, he listened eagerly to what everyone said. The whole world was apprehensive, what with rumors of war and deep economic crises. Things were going from bad to worse.

Wolinski the Butcher, who always got the news first, told them a story about a storekeeper who was attacked by a mob that stole all his goods. It made the other merchants nervous, but Sam was positively petrified. He no longer worried about paying his bills, but things began falling out of his hands. The world was falling apart and he was sliding into a mysterious abyss along with everyone else. Sometimes this even made him feel a little better. When the whole world is on fire, what good is it to be clever?

Once, in his little circle, Sam felt bold enough to express his thoughts: "But look at that Julius Mendel, he's still going strong in spite of everything..."

"Mendel? Ha! If you had his money!"

*

A few days later Sam marched into the back of the store, where Gussie sat on an empty box trying to escape the stifling August heat.

"I've had enough!" he announced, and sat down opposite her on another box. "We'll sell out whatever we can, at any price, and then we'll get the hell out of here!" He spoke rapidly and his eyes were bleary, as if he had been drinking.

"And then what?" Gussie asked sleepily.

"Then what? Who knows? We'll see. Maybe I'll sell insurance. Or maybe we'll buy a farm in the country."

Gussie didn't utter another word. For a long time afterward she and Sam sat on their empty boxes in silence, Sam with a faraway look in his eyes and Gussie with the blank stare of a calf being led to the slaughter.

*

"An end to it! Enough!" Sam kept saying to himself over and over. Ever since he had decided to sell his "business" he felt as if a heavy load had dropped from his shoulders. He was never without a pencil and paper in his hand, adding up numbers. As he kept counting his remaining "stock," he kept hoping for a miracle that would transform everything into hard cash. He had spread the word in certain quarters that on the coming Wednesday evening he would be in the store ready to talk business with anyone who was interested.

As luck would have it, it had been a "good day" and a few times he wondered whether he was doing the right thing. He kept re-arranging the items in his show window. He kept checking his ice-box. Then he went down into the cellar where he kept his candling lamp, which he had made himself. "Damned if I'll give this away far nothing!"

Later that evening a tall Jewish woman with a determined look on her face came into the store. Sam knew at once that she had come to "talk business." Her "advisor" was her brother-in-law, a nimble fellow with a pair of dark eyes that never stopped searching. He examined every corner of the store as if his eyes were a torch. The expression on the woman's face indicated that if she had her way she would turn everything in the place upside down and inside out. She and her advisor kept shaking their heads mournfully from side to side and muttering, "the fixtures, the fixtures..." until finally Sam demanded.

"What's wrong with the fixtures?"

"Nothing," the woman said, "except they're too old! We'll have to replace every single one of them. And that old ice-box in the cellar..."

"It works better than your new ones!" Sam exploded.

This method of "negotiating" went on for hours as they talked mostly about other things and returned now and then to the matter at hand.

"You're asking too high a price —"

"I wouldn't sell it for a dollar less!"

"Then you won't sell it at all —"

"So I won't!"

Sam didn't like these people one little bit. Besides, he had already worked out a new plan to save the store.

"Listen to me, young man. I've made up my mind. I'm not selling. Nobody's forcing me. And my lease doesn't run out for a long time yet...."

The woman and her brother-in-law shrugged and started for the door. Meanwhile, Gussie stood in the back of the store with her mouth wide open and her eyes burning, Had her fool of a husband lost his mind completely? The buyers had no sooner walked out the door than she stomped over to Sam as if she were going to tear his eyes out. But just at that moment their two boys walked in.

"So what are you going to do now, wise guy?" she demanded.

She waited for him to reply. The two boys waited too. Even the walls and the fixtures were waiting for his answer.

Sam's eyes were even more bleary. With a grin on his face he laid out his new plan before his wife and children. He would open a low-price store and distribute circulars everywhere announcing the opening. Customers would come flocking in from near and far. Ikie would paint a new sign, with great big letters which would pull people in.

"What do you say, Ikie?"

Receiving no answer from his wife and children, Sam sat down on a stool and put his head in his hands, his body rocking, rocking...

The two boys looked at each other with a crooked smile.

"Must be dreaming..." Ikie said.

"Loony..." nodded Jake.

THE HAND OF GOD

Boruch Glazman

BORUCH GLAZMAN (1893-1945) —*born in a small town near Mozir, Byelorussia; died in New York.*

Glazman was born into a working-class family of shoemakers, carpenters, and glaziers. When he was 13 his family moved to Kiev. In addition to traditional Jewish studies he also studied secular subjects in a Russian high school.

In 1911 he emigrated to the United States, where he worked in various trades, finally becoming a house painter. In the evenings he continued his studies and graduated with a B.A. from the University of Columbus, Ohio. During World War I he served in the U.S. Army. After his discharge he continued working at his trade but devoted himself more and more seriously to writing in Yiddish and English. His first Yiddish story was published in 1913 in the Freie arbeter shtimme. *Thereafter his work was published in Zukunft, Shriftn, Yiddisher kemfer, and other journals in London, Montreal, and Warsaw, as well as in Yiddish and Hebrew dailies. In English his work was published in* Menorah, Jewish Sentinel, and Jewish Spectator.

In 1924 he toured Poland and the Soviet Union and then remained for several years in Poland before returning to New York, where he died in 1945. One critic called him "the most American of the American-Yiddish writers." He has also been characterized as a "disappointed Romanticist," a "debunker of Romanticism," and a "sobered up dreamer."

The Hand of God (Gotts hant) *appears in the series* Ateneo Literario en et IWO, *Buenos Aires, v. 86, 1981 (originally published 1921).* Garlic Wurst (Knobl-wurst) *appears in* Zukunft, *September 1932.*

Boruch Glazman

The Hand of God

Once upon a time, in the city of New York, there lived a certain man, an ordinary man, hardly any different from all the other men in that big city. A tiny grain on a boundless sandy beach. His name was David. David Steinberg.

David was a tailor. In New York there are, of course, thousands of tailors. One tailor more, one tailor less...

David lives a quiet, peaceful life. Or so it seems to the naked eye. In reality, however, it's not always so. From time to time something unexpected happens. A child falls ill. His wife feels poorly. Or, everyone in the household is in good health, thank God, but David himself is out of work. These are all minor misfortunes, however. They happen to everyone. And even the incident I want to tell about now is almost a trivial matter in the world-scheme of things, but it's a fine, cool morning, my head is clear, and well, I simply feel like telling you the story...

In the particular line of tailoring that David was working in, there happened to be a strike. It was really a nasty strike. That's what all the newspapers were saying — and people were grabbing up the papers faster than the presses could print them. It had been dragging on a long time, that strike. The Union's treasury was almost depleted. The "general public" was tired of sending in contributions. Even the measly strike benefits that the Union gave its members were not being paid regularly. The Union's executive board began scrutinizing the membership rolls — which members had a large family, which ones had a small family, which ones didn't have any family at all. They started going through their records with a fine-tooth-comb.

Still, if a man had put aside a few dollars a week during the season, he could now manage to scrape by and feed his family, at least, until he went back to work.

But suppose he had not been able to put any money aside?

At David Steinberg's house the wolf was howling at the door. And David, since he couldn't do anything useful at home anyway,

120

was now spending all his days at the Union hall. Smoke-filled. Noisy. Speakers orating from the stage, yelling, waving their arms, trying to breathe new life into the slowly dying flame. At least, that's what it said in all the papers. So every day they sit in all corners of the hall, playing pinochle or penny-ante.

In the afternoon, when David leaves the place, he feels as if he's lost his hearing. Not that he doesn't hear. Quite the contrary. He hears everything, all the racket, all the commotion, along with the faintest rustle. But he hears it through a thick curtain — isolated words, with no connection to each other... He feels like a country bumpkin at a fair. Flustered and confused. The main thing, however, he still understands: No settlement of the strike is in sight. So what use is all the excitement?

One other thing is clear in his head. That morning, when he quietly slipped out of the house under the despairing, silent stares of his wife, there was no food left in the house except half a loaf of bread. And no money. Not a cent.

Little by little all the half-thoughts and all the clamorous confusion that still remained in his head began to evaporate, their place taken by a tiny dot that kept growing larger and larger and soon filled his whole cranium.

"Food! Money to buy food! For my family! At least the kids! You can't expect little children to live on a crust of stale bread!"

And of course he was right...

*

In the corners of the Union hall the guys are sitting around, playing cards. For some of them the strike is something like a holiday. A time to rest. Because really, the situation is this: You can't go looking for another job. That's out of the question. You have to sit and wait... And the public is starting to worry. True, you're not earning a penny. But there's really nothing to worry about. So they feel as carefree, let's say, as soldiers in a barracks. The yoke of earning a living has been loosened a little around your neck. And if you're lucky enough to have saved a few dollars, the world is yours. Loaf around all day. Play cards. In front of each player sits a little pile of dimes or quarters, and maybe an occasional half-dollar.

And every once in a while, some talented young women get up on the stage and sing. Solos, duets. And ambitious violin virtuosos perform. Poor suffering artists! How humiliated they must feel when the proletariat in the Union hall shows no signs of appreciation of their art. Oh, they applaud — mechanically — but they don't even know whom they are applauding. So the artists leave the stage in a huff, their faces ashen and dismal. They have learned a harsh, unpalatable truth: there is no justice in this world.

But they are wrong. There *is* justice in this world. There is an eye that sees everything. As the reader will soon learn...

*

As that particular day was drawing to a close, David Steinberg left the Union hall feeling hopeless and woebegone, his eyes to the ground. As he opened the door leading out to the street, he almost stepped on a piece of green paper at his feet, all folded up into a little wad. His heart skipped a beat. He glanced to his right, to his left. No one was even looking at him. He bent down quickly, picked up the paper and stuck it into his pocket. Not until he had walked to the next corner did he put his hand carefully into his pocket and take out the green paper. Without even unfolding it, he could tell. A crisp, ten-dollar bill...

The bright setting sun hurled a powerful ray of light directly at his brain. He shuddered and almost fell. Touching the walls of the buildings along the way for support, he walked slowly home...

*

David and his wife spoke to each other in whispers. This was no ordinary event. Ten dollars! All the things they could buy with it! They started making a list. Wrote something down, crossed it out, put it back again. They tried to list them in order of importance. Enough for a week, at least. Goes to show. Never give up hope. Plain to see — it must have been the hand of God...

Mrs. Steinberg went to the grocery store. Meanwhile, David woke up the children, whom she had purposely put to bed early, so they wouldn't keep asking her for something to eat.

At the store, she filled up two large paper bags. Proud and happy, she looked around at the grocer and the other customers. She did not need to feel ashamed any longer. Her face beamed as though she had a priceless treasure in her possession. She put one of the bags on the counter.

She put her hand into her pocket — and turned pale as death. The bag she was holding dropped to the floor. She stared at the grocer, her eyes glassy. It had all been a trick of the Devil! There was nothing in her pocket at all. Absolutely nothing...

*

In the same apartment house where the Steinbergs lived, there lived a couple who had no children. The husband did not work in a shop. Actually, no one knew *where* he worked, or what he did for a living. The gossip among the neighbors was that he must be a professional gambler and in general a suspicious character. The lights in their apartment were on every night until four o'clock in the morning. And if, on some nights, the lights were not on in their apartment, you could be sure that the next morning he would be seen returning home about the same time everyone else was going out to work.

And his wife, well, she was not much different.

The evening that Mrs. Steinberg went out to buy some things for supper, this woman also went to the store — for her husband's breakfast. He had slept all day after a long night's work at whatever it was he did. She marched into the store and pushed her way in among the other women. As she brushed against the unsuspecting Mrs. Steinberg, she stuck her hand into the pocket of her neighbor's coat, deftly plucked out the ten dollar bill and transferred it to her own. The skill with which she performed this feat of legerdemain was evidence of much practice...

*

The desolation in the Steinberg home that evening was indescribable. It was not only the physical hunger. It was just as much the shattered expectations. David had already awakened the children and cheerfully described to them the wonderful things that Mama was bringing home to eat. The children, naturally, were now inconsolable. David, uncomplaining man that he was, choked back not only his tears but all his feelings, including the understandable anger he now felt toward his wife. How, but really, how, by what manner is it possible to lose a ten dollar bill out of your own pocket?

She couldn't explain it. She couldn't even imagine it. She had no idea how it happened. Once in a very great while there is an eclipse of the sun. Does anyone know how it happens? Could she have put her handkerchief into her pocket without thinking and then taken it out, along with the ten dollar bill? Maybe that's how the original owner had lost it? For the thousandth time she searched her pockets, knowing full well there was nothing there, not even a hole through which the money could have fallen.

But this time, in a corner of the pocket, almost covered by the edge of the lining, she *did* feel something. What was it? A tiny stone. Very carefully she squeezed it between two fingers and took it out...

David and his wife stared at it for a long time before they even dared to touch it. Then they both cried out — was it a cry of joy? of pain? Hearing this, the children screamed louder, then suddenly stopped. They had noticed that their Mama and Papa were standing like statues, as if they were afraid to move. And what did Mama have in her hand — something shiny, glistening, twinkling like a little star?

When they finally calmed themselves, the Steinbergs tried to reconstruct what had probably happened. The thief, conjectured Mrs. Steinberg, in his great haste to get his hand out of her pocket, had caught his ring in the rough cloth. Then, when he pulled his hand out, the stone stayed in the cloth.

"Why do you say 'he'?" David asked.

"It *must* have been a man. Would a woman be that shameless — to steal money from another woman — a poor one at that?"

"And a man — would a man wear a ring with a stone like that?"

But what did it matter? Joy returned to the Steinberg household, even deeper and headier than before.

They were afraid, however, to go out into the street now with that treasure in their possession. They would all go to bed hungry. In the morning they would figure out what to do. Even the hunger pangs seemed easier to bear now. Thoughts of the wonderful day ahead carried them off to sleep on the wings of zephyrs.

The next morning David ran all the way to the pawnshop. Running, he kept looking around to see if anyone was following him. He could not completely overcome a sense that he was doing something wrong. But how could it be wrong? The diamond belonged to a thief. Could he return it to that thief, even if he knew who it was? And he didn't even know that, did he?

The pawnbroker weighed the stone carefully. Very, very carefully. He studied it through his glass. He soaked it in some kind of chemical. Then he laid it down carefully on a piece of cigarette tissue, sighed, groaned, grimaced, complained about business, how bad it was, people were not even redeeming their pledges, in fact, they kept bringing in new ones...boxes full of diamonds he had in his store. But well, seeing as how he was dealing with an honest man here, he would give him, well, he would be extremely generous and give him, well, say a hundred dollars... But the gentleman should really come back soon to redeem it, because nobody was buying stones like this nowadays...

*

His heart was beating wildly as David ran out of the pawnshop clutching the money in his pocket so it wouldn't fly away... And back in the pawnshop, the man behind the counter permitted himself a broad smile. A good morning's work. A very fine stone. He could probably get five hundred for it...

David, meanwhile, had slowed down to a walk. His head was filled with unwonted thoughts and strangely uplifted feelings akin to blessings, like the earth in springtime. Someone was watching over him. He could feel it. God always knows who has been wronged. There is an eye up there somewhere that sees everything, Sooner or later, justice is served. Sometimes it seems that it takes too long, but here was proof. We do have a father in heaven... we are not orphans.

It sounded like the first line of a prayer, or a hymn. He was so filled with it that when he found himself at his door, he could not remember how he got there... He hadn't felt this way since the old

country, on a holiday, when he would come home from the synagogue filled with a tranquil lightness in his whole being.

But what was that woman doing in his house? What did she
want? He had recognized her immediately, despite the rivers of
tears flowing down her face. And what could she be crying about
this way? What crazy words was she babbling?

"Cursed be that sinful moment when Satan himself talked me
into doing it. I must have lost my mind. Something evil came over
me. The first time in my life I've ever done such a thing... O good
people, dear good people, take pity on me, forgive me! Please forgive me..."

And she fell on David's neck, and on his wife's neck, and she
kissed their hands and wept and moaned and repeated every word
she had said before.

"Forgive me, friends. I am the one! I am the thief!"

*

When she had come home the night before and realized what
had happened, and told her husband, he went berserk, started slapping her unmercifully.

"Some breadwinner you turned out to be! Steals ten dollars
and loses a diamond worth a hundred times that. You think money
comes easy to me, you butterfingered little crook! I risk my life
every day to earn the money I give you!"

And he was right to complain. But complaints were no use in
a situation like this. "You better do something right away!" he
screamed, as he kept beating her, until she agreed to go get the
diamond back first thing in the morning.

"I know those people," he instructed her. "I know how they
think. A few tears, a loud moan, a few pious words, a guilty expression on your face, a promise not to do it again, a look of des-
peration, like your whole life depends on their forgiveness — and
tell them your husband doesn't know a thing about it yet, and if he
finds out he'll kill you...because when he gets angry he's a mad-
man. You hear me, you clumsy idiot! Tell them all that, over and
over again, until they start feeling sorry for you..."

She did as she was told, sobbing and moaning and groaning all
the while. And truth to tell, the sobbing wasn't all make-believe.

The bruises on her body, where her husband had struck her, were still very painful.

David believed her when she said that her husband had threatened to beat her "within an inch of her life." The neighbors had often talked about this bully. So why shouldn't David believe her? He felt truly sorry for her. And Mrs. Steinberg, looking at this poor woman standing there disgraced and remorseful, a fallen sinner, calling herself all those degrading names — when she now saw all this contrition, almost broke into tears herself. How low this poor woman has been brought! Can I let her fall even lower? Can I let her husband beat her to death? Her life is now in my hands...

"Well," thought David, "stealing is a terrible sin. But she has already been punished for that. And which of us poor mortals is without sin? Didn't I myself just go and pawn that suspicious diamond? And if God has been so good to me, shall I be an ingrate and ruin the lives of two other people?"

He looked up and met his wife's eyes. They understood each other at once. Mrs. Steinberg handed the pawn ticket to her neighbor. David did the same with the two crisp fifty dollar bills.

"Go and redeem your diamond."

The repentant thief bent over, took a ten dollar bill from her stocking and handed it to David.

"Here's your money back. I hope you can find it in your heart to forgive me..."

And she ran out of their flat, restraining her giggles until she was on the other side of the door.

*

Again Mrs. Steinberg went to the grocery store. This time she held the crackling ten dollar bill carefully in her hand.

"Don't lose it again!" David warned her, although he was now feeling doubly happy. After all, he had lost nothing. He had found the lost money, he had prevented a tragedy in his neighbor's house, and he had the satisfaction one feels when he does something noble. Yes, it was clear that for the last several hours, God had been testing him. How many people would have given up a thousand dollar diamond, especially one that belonged to a thief who had lost it in the very act of committing a crime?

But he had passed the test. So he now strode around his house enveloped in a feeling of purification. He was a better human being now than he had been before. It was something to be thankful for, because although he had long ago given up any pretense at piety, David Steinberg was an honest man, and now he had to admit that yes, there really was a God in this world.

And as this honest tailor walked around his house at peace with himself, confident that he had done the right thing, the door opened and his wife came back from the grocery — empty-handed. Her face was yellow as an old newspaper...

She handed him back the ten-dollar-bill. Her voice was a hoarse whisper:

"The grocery man refuses to take it. He says it's counterfeit..."

*

David Steinberg felt a strong and mighty hand pressing down heavily, intent on squashing him. Like a felled tree, he tottered for a moment from side to side, then crashed against the wall. The chilling sound of unearthly laughter rang mockingly in his ears...

GARLIC-WURST

Boruch Glazman

For a biography of Glazman, see the introduction to the story The
Hand of God.

Garlic-Wurst

1.

In the City of New York, on the corner of Broadway and
30-something Street, in the busiest neighborhood in the country,
there is a confectionary shop that sells the best and tastiest caramels in the world — the caramels made by the firm of Clariss &
Lamont.

This particular corner — it has been established scientifically
by the latest acoustical instruments that measure noise-level —
this corner of New York City is the proven most tumultuous spot
not merely in the United States but in the world.

This is no trivial matter. Imagine: On that enclosed piece of
land — a few narrow asphalt valleys between gigantic mountains
of stony skyscrapers — there is more noise, bustle and confusion
than anywhere in the entire world!

When you think about it, your head begins to swim, your heart
begins to pound and your skin turns to goose-flesh. Nevertheless,
the caramels that you can buy there, on that particular corner, are
the kind that "melt in your mouth" because they are made of the
freshest butter, the most fragrant cream and the highest-grade
chocolate. They remind one of the toffee that *kheyder*-boys used
to enjoy so much in the small towns of the old country. Not that
they taste anywhere near the same; it's almost a sacrilege to make

that comparison. The comparison is only to the "holiday mood" that these caramels create in the heart of a grown-up who has become a bit jaded in the hustle-bustle of the big city.

2.

Mr. Jonah Kudla, senior partner and therefore president of the well known Broadway cloak manufacturing company of Jonas Kudel Bros., had intended to stop in at Clariss & Lamont's for a two-pound box of those marvelous caramels. Not for himself, perish the thought. He was occupied with more important things: coats, suits, raincoats, stocks, bonds, shares, notes due, mortgages due. Caramels were most certainly the farthest thing from his mind. It was the peak of the season. This was the time of year when he had to drive himself — as well as all the workers in the shop, young and old. The new spring line had to be finished as soon as possible, the sooner the better.

Winter was coming to an end. Buyers from all over the South had already been in the city for some weeks now, and Mr. Kudla, for some strange reason, was behind schedule in everything. If he didn't do something drastic at once, Jonas Kudel Bros. could be stuck with its entire stock.

Jonah Kudla had always thought of himself as the embodiment of the Company, and since he was behind in producing his merchandise, he was also a couple of weeks behind in making his payments to a series of banks from which he had gotten loans at the beginning of the season. And since his shop was late in finishing the new samples, Kudel Bros. was also late in getting the spring checks from the buyers. And since he was late in his payments to the bank —

The plain truth was that he was in trouble. And so far, he had no idea how he was going to get out of it. Worse than anything else: he couldn't figure out whose fault this mess was. Was it possible that he, Jonah Kudla himself, was to blame?

Lately a quiet war had been going on in the shop between him and his younger brother, the second most important partner, a silent but bitter feud, of the sort that happens sometimes between husband and wife. His brother, in fact, had been hinting that all the trouble in the shop was due to Jonah himself, because his mind was not on the business, the devil only knows why. "Walks around all the time distraught and absent-minded." And the shop felt the effects of this change immediately. No longer was Jonah Kudla's sharp eye on everything, so the shop had gradually relaxed and was now completely out of control. What's more, you couldn't put your finger on the problem. The work was simply not being done.

"A good ship must always be under someone's guiding and disciplining hand," his kid brother with the cold, blue eyes kept telling him, "otherwise it will get into some kind of trouble, like a machine that is never oiled."

And he was right. The penetrating oil of Jonah Kudla's determination had been missing from the shop machinery for several weeks. It was true. Jonah himself was to blame for the whole financial muddle, and who knows whether he could ever pull the company out of it. Yes, no one was at fault but Jonah Kudla himself.

3.

One thing was clear. Under such circumstances the last thing on his mind should have been caramels. Besides, anyone looking at Jonah could see that he was not a glutton, an over-eater or an epicure. This was a man of less than average height, with a boyish body on short legs, skinny and gaunt, like a new recruit after basic training; a little man with sunken cheeks, as though he had been fasting every Monday and Thursday for years. His arms, however, were hairy and longer than you might have expected; they reached to his knees. Even his hands were covered with hair, especially the knuckles, like a monkey's. Avid, aggressive, enveloping and powerful arms and hands.

He also had big eyes — sharp and with an icy fire. Gray eyes under thick, straight eyebrows that met right over his nose, creating one long single eyebrow that stretched almost from one ear to the other.

Yes, it was clear as day that Jonah Kudla did not need those caramels for himself. The person he needed them for was his wife. Every Saturday evening he would bring her a gift of caramels, and they had to be Clariss & Lamont caramels. His wife was a big expert on candy. She would not eat any other brand, couldn't even get them past her lips, she said.

So all afternoon the thought gave him no peace: "On the way home I must not forget to stop into that store on Broadway and buy a couple boxes of caramels."

This particular Saturday afternoon he had to try harder than ever to remember his errand. Lately he had become extremely forgetful. His brother must be right: "Something must be seriously wrong with you." So he kept repeating to himself: "Whatever you do, don't forget the caramels, don't forget to buy the caramels."

4.

It wasn't that Jonah loved his wife so much that he never stopped thinking about ways to bring her pleasure. In fact, Jonah Kudla didn't love his wife at all. For a long time now he had not loved her. Maybe he never had. Not that he hated her, either. That is, the first couple of years after they were married he did hate her because she had made him hate himself. Yes, he hated himself for marrying this woman. And he had married her because he needed the help of her wealthy and well-established family to get on his feet after wasting the best years of his youth in all kinds of garment shops. After so many years of bouncing back and forth unsuccessfully from job to job in New York, Chicago, Philadelphia and God knows where else.

But now he didn't think about it too much. He didn't love his wife and he didn't hate her, either. A home is a home. He had no complaints about the furniture in it. One problem was that his wife never stopped talking. Another annoying habit of hers was that she burst out crying whenever he did something she didn't like. So he tried very hard to avoid putting her into such a state. In the early years, whenever she got angry, she didn't say a word for days. And she did this in a very proud, honorable and aristocratic manner which he liked very much, because he found the silence restful. He almost felt at peace with himself and with all the furniture in the house.

As soon as she realized, however, that her sulking fits didn't bother him; when she realized that her husband was a very common, unfeeling individual; when she realized, in short, that "an immigrant remains an immigrant," she began to use simpler, more ordinary, feminine defenses, even fainting when necessary. And why not, when fate had joined her to such a backward, uncultured man as Jonah Kudla.

For what did Mr. Kudla really want? What he wanted was that when he came home after a long day of noisy peregrinations around the shop, he could sit down and do nothing but rest for a few hours in the evening. And the only way he could accomplish this was by acceding to his wife's every wish, no matter how trivial. What difference did it make? His real life was not at home, anyway; his real life was in the shop.

5.

Saturday. But during the height of the season they did not stop work at noon. The workers quit at four. Mr. Kudla stayed a little longer, so that he and his brother and the third partner could look over the accounts for the week. This activity never left him in a better frame of mind. But throughout all the most serious, most strained and most touchy discussions about the critical situation of the company, he never once stopped thinking about the caramels. Don't forget to pick up the caramels.

When he finally did leave the shop, it was already early evening. It had been a mild spring day. The sky over New York was clean and pale, as though it had been scrubbed clean in honor of the season. The blue of the sky was more like violet. The faces of the people in the street seemed similarly clean and pale, even a little drawn, the faces of people recovering from a serious winter.

Mr. Kudla had a headache. A walk in the fresh air would do him good. He therefore sent his chauffeur — and the car — home and headed toward Greeley Square, swept along by the insistent stream of big-city people. He was not really walking. The crowds that flowed here unceasingly for eighteen hours a day, in both directions, picked him up and carried him along as effortlessly as if he were a splinter. Mr. Kudla felt as though he no longer controlled his will to move, or the direction in which he moved. Those decisions were being made by the dark, dense mass surging through the street.

At the street corners, if the magician in the blue suit halted the stream with a wave of his white-gloved hand, then Jonah Kudla halted too. If not, then he proceeded straight ahead. It was really a pleasant state of mind to be in, he thought to himself. It was this mass of people that enabled him to think freely about his life for the first time in years.

The fact alone that he did not have to watch every step he took made him feel as if a heavy load had suddenly been lifted from his shoulders. He had left it all behind — his worries, the vexations of the factory, the problems with the massive ledgers and their millions of tiny figures that lay in wait for him in his small, restricting office like wild creatures locked in a cage — all of this suddenly disappeared. All except one thing:

The caramels.

Well, soon he would be there, only two or three blocks more.

Jonah Kudla started wondering about something. That mess in the factory — why wasn't it bothering him now? It had never happened before. What other connection with life did he have aside from the factory? But now — as if a slate had been wiped clean, and he, Mr. Jonah Kudla, had much more important matters to think about now.

Like what, for instance? Maybe his brother was right. Lately Mr. Kudla's head has been occupied with all sorts of silly things. For instance:

Because he had not been paying close attention to what Sam, his head cutter, was telling him, five bolts of cloth had been cut up for no apparent reason. Another thing. Dictating a letter to his secretary in reply to an inquiry about prices, he had mixed up the figures to such an extent that if his brother had not accidentally read the correspondence that day, before it went out, the result would have been such an absurd mish-mash that Jonas Kudel Bros. would have been the laughing-stock of the trade.

His brother had tried to stay calm. "Take a look at this piece of nonsense. Don't let it happen again!"

What was wrong with him, then? Here, in the midst of these thousands of elbows and feet on all sides of him, it had suddenly become clear to him: Something was wrong with him. What that "something" was, however, was not at all clear. Was he suffering some mysterious affliction? As one recalling a dream, he said to himself: "Yes, it's true. These last few evenings I've been doing some very peculiar things..."

6.

It had happened more than once. A few evenings ago he had found himself standing at a window in his house around midnight. He could not remember how he got there, how long he had been standing there, or what he had been looking at. What was there to see out there, anyway? The bushes in the garden that stayed green even in the winter-time? The little dwarf trees with their arms sawed off at the shoulders? A few patches of snow being eaten away by the oncoming spring? And that was all. And only when there was a moon. When there wasn't, you couldn't even see that much. So why had he been standing there for hours?

But then perhaps he hadn't really expected to see anything. No. What he had been doing was listening. Listening to sounds. Sounds coming from nearby, from far away. Sounds that were summoning him, commanding him, sounds that were not letting him sleep, keeping him up nights. He should get a good night's sleep every night, so he could get up in the morning ready to do a day's work.

His small two-story cottage of gray stucco and painted cornerstones is far from New York City, in Sheepshead Bay, not far from a fishing harbor and the open sea. That's where those sounds were coming from, but mostly at night, when all around was silence. The sounds of ships.

Strange. Up until recently he had never really heard those sounds, as one does not hear the clanging of passing tramways when one lives on a busy street. But these past few weeks the call of these ships was keeping him awake. In the shop the next day he felt groggy, his head full of thoughts that made him feel like a stranger there.

He had even tried pulling the blankets over his head, like a child frightened by a bad dream. He tried to force himself to fall asleep, but the mysterious call of the ships eventually got to him, as though it were addressed to him personally:

"Get a move on, Jonah Kudla... Crawl out of your warm bed in your underwear, get over there by the window, stand there all night in agony and listen closely with both ears..."

After several nights of this behavior Jonah learned to differentiate between the various calls that reached his ears from near and far. He could recognize the low, bass calls of the big Atlantic steamships, the hoarse baritone of the fishing vessels, the old falsettos of the anchored yachts and motorboats returning from exotic late-night adventures — either secret wild parties or dangerous liquor-smuggling.

What impressed him most deeply, however, was the droning of the restless night-sirens and the coldly regular clanging of the automatic warning-bells where Sheepshead Bay flows into the ocean. He could clearly see the massive bells that hover constantly over the water as if they were growing out of the depths; rocking back and forth listlessly, indifferently, their clanging so dulled that it seemed to come from the bottom of the sea. Every moment of the day and night they rocked from side to side, lazily, mechanically, rang continuously, eternally, as a warning to the ships that wander this way from all corners of the world, but themselves condemned to remain chained to one solitary place.

After standing and listening like this for hours, Jonah Kudla would feel a cold shudder over his entire body, as though these bells were warning him, demanding something of him. He then faced another sleepless night. And this was not good. He could not continue this way much longer.

7.

Jonah, walking down Broadway, suddenly grabbed his head. Good God! He had passed that confectionary shop a long time ago! He turned around and started back, but noticed that he was already at Union Square. It would take him twenty minutes to walk back there against this crush of people. A taxi? That would take even longer! What a mess!

Should he walk or should he ride? As he argued frantically with himself, he turned to walk back, but he was a splinter swimming against the current. And the current now streaming in the Broadway canyon between the high, massive stone buildings, was too powerful for Jonah Kudla's strength. Against his will he turned again, carried past 14th Street toward the East Side.

Jonah Kudla had a large, thick head of hair, but it could hardly be seen among the other heads in the crowd because it crowned a body on very short legs. So Jonah Kudla was also being swept along on the East Side by the powerful impetus of the mighty stream. At first he was very much concerned about not having bought the caramels. The image of his wife rose up before him — tall, stout, blond, overflowing. He could see her now, hands akimbo, a crooked, suspicious little smile on her fleshy lips, as she towered over him, her tiny husband, and stared at him destructively when he appeared on her doorstep without the familiar box of caramels wrapped in shiny wax paper...

Well, too late now, he consoled himself. How could he wage war against this irresistible army of thousands marching down Broadway? The giant clock atop the display sign of a jewelry store showed ten minutes past six. The confectionary shop closed promptly at six.

8.

He was already on Second Avenue, the downtown reflection of Broadway. Countless blue and pink and yellow arc lamps, electric signs, theater posters, greeted him joyfully.

That's when the sudden thought entered his head: Why not spend the evening down here?

A splendid idea. As if he were just arriving in a foreign city that he had never visited before. In a way, this was true; he had long since forgotten that there was an East Side in New York City. Actually he hadn't been down here in about ten years, ever since he had started going out with Gussie. She didn't like the East Side, even though she was born there. At every opportunity she was dragging him to Flatbush.

For Gussie, Flatbush was more a symbolic concept than a geographic one. In Flatbush lived the "higher and better" Jewish circles, where they were constantly talking about business, or about trading one car in for another, or about how their fortunes had grown; the circles where they either played cards or were busy packing to go to Lakewood or Atlantic City... True, Jonah Kudla always felt like a stranger among them, although he would join the conversation, play their games and smile back at everyone. But he felt no less the stranger even in his own home.

A peculiar home, when you thought about it. His wife stuffing him with oysters, scallops, an assortment of chops and minced pies... But what the hell, he had grown accustomed to his house, little by little. And there were so many empty rooms. So in one of them he would curl up in the corner of a chaise-lounge and read his newspaper. But whenever he was in those "other circles" he felt trapped.

And now, strolling leisurely through the East Side streets, he recognized a feeling that he hadn't known for a long time, an unexpected sense of liberation, as if he had come home and all these people around him were his relatives. And why not? As a young man, when he still worked in the shop ten hours a day for fifteen dollars a week, he had lived on one of these streets. On one of these streets he had spent the best years of his youth.

Magically, in a single moment, Mr. Kudla's mood had become almost celebratory. A little flame lit up in his eyes. His step became almost jaunty. Thirstily, eagerly, he studied the individuals around him and felt a kind of twinge in his heart. Who knows, he might meet a friend from the old days here.

Elderly men with unkempt mustaches and tobacco-stained beards wandered around here looking lonely and forlorn, lost in the great metropolis of Babylon. Happy, saucy American-born Jewish boys in knickers, with bundles of newspapers under their arms, darted between the clanging tramways and the speeding automobiles that missed hitting them by inches. Other boys seemed to crawl around under the parked cars to retrieve the rubber balls they were playing games with.

Faces, faces, faces without number. But not a single one that he recognized or that recognized him.

Hours passed. His legs — or his eyes — led him from one street to another. A very odd and unusual emotion enveloped him, the emotion of a man who has come back to his old hometown after years and years of rambling around the world and now felt both at home and like a stranger at the same time. And though he hated to admit it, the feeling of strangeness was stronger than the feeling of familiarity.

The streets are crowded and crooked. People don't even use the sidewalks, which are occupied by pushcarts full of notions, displays of exotic fruit, Japanese figs, persimmons, brown bananas, Indian nuts, carob, butternuts from Brazil. And over all these pushcarts, smoky torches tell the world about the perpetual motion of the Big City and the stubborn Jewish lust for life.

Jonah Kudla's thirsty eyes drank all this in, including the stream of faces that kept ceaselessly changing, like the current of a mighty river. Thousands of faces, yet he did not recognize even one of them. Mr. Kudla felt hurt by this. If only he would meet some of his old friends now — he would invite them all to come home with him that very evening.

He grimaced. His wife Gussie never did like his old friends — his "brothers" from the Union, from the Workmen's Circle branch, from the Yiddish-speaking branch of the Socialist Party. A couple of times he had invited them to his home in Flatbush, but to Gussie they were all alike — the "lefties," the "righties," the moderates, the socialists, the anarchists, even the Labor Zionists. She had one name for them all: Yids, a word that she uttered with a crooked sneer in one corner of her mouth. No sooner were they out the door than she would open all the windows wide, scrub the table-tops, dust the chairs, all the while mumbling and grumbling:

"Why can't you see it yourself? What do you want of me, anyway? Look at all these ash-trays I put out — and they're still not enough! Ash-cans I should have put out for those 'brothers' of

Boruch Glazman

yours! My God, where did they think they were? In a restaurant? Or in one of those noisy little synagogues downtown?"

9.

What finally happened with Jonah Kudla that evening on Broadway was not really so unusual; it can all be told in a few sentences.

He kept wandering around until he started feeling hungry. Then he entered a small, dingy Jewish restaurant on Broome Street, where you can still get a five-course meal for the unbelievable sum of 35 cents, with all the bread you want. A restaurant where the tablecloths are always stained with yellow grease-spots that have been there so long they look like flowers, and where the strudel in the window is so thick with flies that you can't tell which is a fly and which is a raisin. But it had been a long time since Jonah Kudla had enjoyed a meal as much as he did that one.

Afterward, he was one of a crowd of people that stood outside a phonograph store bathed in the bright glow of an electric lamp hanging over the entrance. The crowd, young folks and old, stood silently, transfixed. They all held their heads a bit to one side, literally lending an ear to the hoarse tones coming out of the store through a loudspeaker. People strolled by, stood there for a few moments and left, but the crowd remained the same size. Inside the store, as soon as one record finished, they put on another one. Cantor Yosele Rosenblatt, singing the *U'mipney khato-eynu* prayer. Then a woman very movingly sang *Di Grine Kuzine*. Then Cantor Shliskey chanted a portion of the Yom Kippur service. Then Tito Ruffo followed with *Figaro*.

People listened, then suddenly remembered there was a real world out there. They had to rush off, but they did so reluctantly, to be replaced by other listeners. And they all listened intently, a look of ecstasy and wonderment on their faces that would sometimes express itself in a sweet sigh, accompanied by a look that said, "Well, did you ever hear the like? Pure gold, isn't it?"

When Jonah Kudla finally tore himself away from there, he realized it was time to go home. Not that he felt like going home. Quite the opposite. He was now filled with a kind of dull, deaf indifference to his home, to his wife, and to whatever might happen when he got there. So he was in no hurry. He walked slowly — lazily, almost — without any feelings at all, good or bad. Except that he knew this "night out" of his had to end some time.

But then he found himself outside a rundown little delicatessen on Rivington Street, not far from the place where Shimmel sells his knishes. He peered into the window for a moment, then went inside and bought two one-pound garlic-wursts. As he ordered them, however, he felt as if he were getting even for a wrong that had been done to him over a long span of years. No, it was more than "getting even." It was a moment of revenge, of rebellion. Why had he never done anything about that injustice? Oysters and lobsters, yes, but garlic-wurst no? Frankfurters and sauerkraut, yes, but garlic-wurst no?

Imbued with these feelings of vengeance and battle-readiness, he made the long trip home.

The wursts were hard and dry as a rock, They were twisted into the shape of a bagel. Underneath the wrinkled, brown, somewhat mouldy skin were large grease-stains, suspicious-looking yellow grease stains, which emitted a not-so-pleasant odor.

10.

It was long past midnight when Jonah Kudla again stood by the window of the darkened parlor in his home in Sheepshead Bay. The window-panes were a watery blue. The early spring night was bright and pleasant. A razor-thin slice of the young moon hung on a pale, cold sky. But this time Mr. Kudla was not listening to the mysterious calls of the distant ships out there somewhere on the water. What he was listening to was the continuous bawling, blubbering and complaining of his wife Gussie, which cascaded down upon him from the bedroom on the second floor. The sound had been following him and chastising him for over an hour.

"More than a week I've been asking him to bring me a box of caramels! And what does he bring home? Garlic-wurst!"

In the house across the moonlit street he could see a Saturday night party going on. People were drinking and having a rousing good time. They weren't even worried about a hangover the next morning, it being Sunday. He could hear the hooting, boisterous laugh of a saxophone. He could see the silhouettes of couples embracing as they danced. To Mr. Kudla they seemed to be creatures from another planet, dancing and hopping around in other-worldly ecstasy, while here, in his home, Mrs. Gussie Kudla was going on and on in her lament over her desolate ill-fortune.

And in her kitchen, on the neat white-enameled table, lay Jonah Kudla's distant and disgraced relative from Rivington Street — the slightly mouldy, hard-as-a-rock wurst with the yellow spots. In shame and disgrace it lay there curled tightly into a bagel, as if in excruciating pain, listening with its ear-like ends to everything going on around it on that moonlit spring night inside the stucco cottage in a remote corner of New York called Sheepshead Bay...

DISASTER

by Meir Blinkin

MEIR BLINKIN (1879-1915) — born in Pereyeslav, the Ukraine; died in New York.

After Blinkin's traditional Jewish education, he attended the Kiev Trade School. When he emigrated to the United States in 1904 he was already the father of two children, but he was not able to bring his family over until later. In this country he learned carpentry, which provided him with an "irregular" living at best. He died in 1915 in New York at age 36.

His first story appeared in the magazine Zukunft. *He then wrote for a number of Yiddish publications which were then sprouting all over the place with poetry and fiction written by the new generation of Yiddish writers who called themselves "Di Yunge" (The Youth). (The group included David Ignatov and Isaac Raboy, both represented in this volume.) Many of Blinkin's stories reveal that he was, in the words of the modern critic Ruth R. Wisse, "fascinated by the volatile interaction between men and women."*

The author's son, M. L. Blinken — the spelling of the name was changed by immigration authorities — rescued much of his father's work from oblivion by instituting a thorough search for published writings as well as for his father's correspondence with other Yiddish writers. As a result, Stories by Meir Blinkin *(translated by Max Rosenfeld) was published in 1984 by State University of New York Press.*

Disaster (An umglik) *appears in* Zukunft, *August-September 1910.*

Meir Blinkin

Disaster

If — in this story — someone should recognize himself, and if it should serve as an example for anyone, then I have accomplished my purpose. I will publish it at my own expense, so long as people read it. But about my own past life up to the incident described here, I shall say not a single word.

I fell in love with a woman who was my best friend's wife. To this day, I still love her madly.

Don't ask me how it happened. I don't know that myself. For several years — almost every day — I went to visit my friend. We were very devoted to each other, but one day, out of the blue, I knew I had to do something drastic. I was faced with a temptation I could not resist. Exactly what to do, however, was not at all clear to me.

I began to collect my thoughts, to study my own personality. What was the matter with me?

Answer: Rachel, or "Rochele," as I called her. In a word, I was in love with Rachel, my friend's wife. No doubt about it whatsoever.

The emotion of love made me feel exceptionally tender. I vividly recall the evening when I first identified that feeling. I loved all of humanity! But Rachel herself had a look of puzzlement in her eyes.

How pleasurable it is when two people like each other as loyal, devoted friends. It doesn't necessarily have to be a woman. I had been feeling that kind of love for all my close friends, until I began to realize that my love for Rachel was something else again. I loved her so fiercely it made my heart ache. I could think about nothing but my love for her. I was embarrassed by my own feelings. Finally, I had to confess to myself that I no longer had control of my own actions. My fate was now in the hands of a delicate woman named Rachel. And I felt that this was no secret, that people could read it in my eyes. To go on suffering like this without saying anything to her about it became impossible. My heart would break in two. And anyway, why should she *not* know about it?

But what about my friend?

Even if it was hateful to do so, even if one should never feel this way about a good friend's wife, what can you do if your thoughts are beyond your control?

2.

One evening we were sitting around the table — Rachel, her husband, their children, and a few other friends of the family.

I don't recall what we were talking about, but at one point Rachel gave her husband a peculiar look. He responded with an insulting remark. I felt my blood rush to my head. Dark thoughts scalded my mind. I had to do something.

But Rachel could always tell what I was thinking. "What's wrong, Sholem, don't you feel well?"

"It's nothing. The pigeon in my head is falling asleep." Everybody laughed, except Rachel.

I asked Joseph for a pen and a sheet of paper and I wrote her a note.

"Most respected Rochele: No matter how much it hurts me, I must now tell you the truth. I am not indifferent to you. If you tell me to stay away from here, it will be better for both of us. Your friend, Sholem."

I handed her the note. "This is confidential, Rochele."

As she read it, her face turned white as the sheet of notepaper. Finally she said: "We have to talk about this, Sholem."

No one around the table had any inkling of what was happening. To this very day, no one knows about it.

Afterward we all went down into the street for a little "walk in the air." Her husband took a cigar from his silver case.

"I have only one left, Sholem. You take it. I'll smoke a cigarette."

"Thank you, Joseph. You walk on ahead with the others. There's something I want to discuss with Rachel. We're going to stab you in the back."

Poking me playfully in the ribs, Rachel said, "Don't be so fresh, you devil!"

"But it's true, Rachel, it's true."

She suddenly grew very quiet. Even after I spoke to her, she was silent, which gave me the right to hope.

"Why don't you say something?" I asked.

"I've nothing to say."

"Then I'll tell you again. I love you, Rochele."

This time she smiled. "Is that all? Don't you think I know that?"

"Drive me away, Rochel!"

"Listen to me, Sholem. You're not stupid. Don't play the fool!"

I took her hand. "At this moment I want very much to kiss you."

She laughed out loud. "What a baby you are! Who's stopping you? Come home and give me even two kisses! Who are you afraid of? Believe me, if I felt like kissing you, nobody would stop me."

"But I want to kiss you when the two of us are alone."

"Don't talk nonsense, Sholem. It doesn't become you."

She leaned over, looked into my eyes, a lovely smile still hovering on her lips. But there was something in her smile that made my heart ache.

"Don't make a fool of yourself, Sholem, you hear?"

That was the end of the conversation. Walking home, neither of us said another word, except that she sighed deeply once or twice. But she didn't take her hand out of mine until we approached the door of their house. Then she broke away and ran inside. I ran after her. A few minutes later the others caught up with us.

She went into the bedroom, lit the gas lamp and began tidying the bedclothes. I stalked her like a thief. As she turned toward the bed, I put my arms around her from behind and kissed her. The way I did it was offensive and contemptible. It frightened her. She cried out and struggled free.

"Please forgive me, Rochele," I said, like a simpleton.

"Sholem, what's wrong with you today?" Her voice trembled. She was visibly upset, and she had practically shouted those few words, which I didn't think she should have done.

On my way home I went over the scene in my head again and again, and I saw myself kissing her on the ear. For two weeks I stayed away from their house, the first time in all the years we had been friends.

3.

My God, what I went through during those two weeks! Every insane thought that bit my brain like a poisonous snake I wrote down in my diary. Night after night I paced back and forth beneath her window. I cursed myself over and over again. You idiot, why don't you just walk in there and put an end to it! But I didn't want to give in to my corrupt heart. And the worst part was that he — not she — came to visit me every day to find out "how I was feeling." The situation was driving me crazy.

One evening, as I paced back and forth across the street from their house, I could see her figure through the curtains. A chill ran through my bones. I crossed the street. One corner of the curtain was folded back a little. I could see her standing by the bed in her night-clothes. I felt my head split, as if someone had hit me there with a steel whip. I ran crazily all the way home. In my street clothes I fell onto my bed and — apparently — fell asleep and dreamed I was falling from a great height. The pain in my heart grew so excruciating that I woke myself up.

I must go see her! How could I have waited so long and not gone to see her?

No, that was out of the question! No matter what happens to me, I would not go there!

But I simply had to go there, if only to quiet the beast that had taken up residence inside me. The thought itself calmed me down a bit and I was able to think a little more rationally. But all I could think about was Rachel.

I looked at my watch. Only past five. I got up, smoked one cigarette after another until my head started spinning. I lay down again. I got up again. I went outside. Six o'clock. I went back inside again, lay down on my bed. The next time I looked at my watch it was nine o'clock. Incredible! I splashed some water on my face, ran out the door and all the way to her house. She was alone, her face white as chalk when she saw me. She held out her hand. It was trembling.

"Why have you stayed away so long?" she whispered.

"Rochele, dear Rochele..."

"How could you have controlled yourself and not come to see me all this time?" she insisted.

"Well — and what about you?"

"Me? You have to ask that?" Her voice quivered. "I was so miserable, so heartsick. All I could do was talk with you in my imagination. It made me feel a little better. Oh! What am I saying? Do you understand?" She brushed my cheek lightly with her fingers. Her face reddened in embarrassment.

"I've been going crazy, Rochele! Do you love me? Tell me! Tell me!"

She gave me a peculiar look. Somehow, it lit a fire in me. I talked and talked, hardly hearing what I was saying.

"Why are you asking me such a foolish question?" she whispered.

"Rochele, you've made me so happy!"

She sighed deeply, grimaced. "Happy? You think we'll ever be happy?"

4.

Week after week passed.

One day I said to her: "You know, Rochele, our love is a sin."

"What are you saying? A sin? Our love is the rarest, the most beautiful, the purest —"

I stared at her.

"You think I love you the same way other people love each other?" she continued. "No! My love for you is not of this world, you understand me?" She embraced me, pressed her lips against my forehead. "I don't deserve such happiness. I won't even kiss you... it's torture —"

"But Rochele, no matter what we do, our love will make someone unhappy..."

She stared. at me with fear in her eyes. I tried to soften the blow of what I had just blurted out. "Rochele, how much is our suffering worth?"

She stroked my hair. "Sholem, my suffering is the best thing that's ever happened to me..."

I embraced her. "Tell me, Rochele, whose are you?"

"Yours, Sholemke, yours. Yours — and my children's. My soul and my heart are yours." She flicked my lips with her finger. "Is that enough for you?"

"But Rochele, I want to be even more secure with my happiness. I want to experience it more deeply."

"What!"

"I want you to demand something of me, you understand? I want to bring a sacrifice on the altar of our love. Tell me what that is, Rochele, demand the most difficult, the most impossible —"

She buried her head in my chest. "You want to make an even greater sacrifice for me?"

"Rochele, I haven't made any sacrifices yet for our love. Nor have you."

She jumped back out of my arms. "Can I make a greater sacrifice than hearing you say you want to be secure in our love?"

What could I say to that? I began pacing back and forth across the room.

"You misunderstood me, Rochele. What I'm asking of you I'm asking in the name of our love."

She moved away from me and curled up inside herself like a hen in a downpour. I felt sorry for her. I stepped over to the window and looked out into the street. She came over to me, her face white.

"Sholemke, Sholemke, calm yourself. Tell me what to do."

"Do you love me, or not, Rochele?" Her eyes filled with tears. She wanted to answer me but could not find the right words.

Scoundrel! I said to myself. Why are you torturing her?

When I spoke, my voice was louder than usual. All I said was "Listen, Rochele!" but she jumped back in fright.

"Sholemke, Sholemke calm yourself," she begged me again. "You're the only one I love, the only one. You have made me so —" She could not finish and broke into a weeping so desperate that her shoulders shook.

I could feel my heart breaking. "Rochele," I said, "I don't want anything from you, not a thing, except that you calm yourself as well."

She took my head in her hands and pressed it to her bosom. "Enough, Sholem, I've calmed down now. It's all right."

I took her in my lap, kissed away her tears. For a while we were both silent.

"You've made me so happy, Sholem," she finally said.

"Listen, Rochele. Did you love Joseph as much as you do me? I mean when you first met —"

She grew livelier. "Did I love him as much? I don't know. But I did love him."

"When did you first begin to feel that you had stopped loving him?"

She was looking at me with utter devotion. "How can I describe it? I began to feel that with each passing day we were drifting further and further apart. So far apart that it scared me. A cold autumn settled over my life. The clouds were heavy as lead. Sometimes I had the feeling that big mountains were hanging over my head on flimsy threads. The slightest puff of wind and the threads would snap."

She put her arms around me and exclaimed happily: "And then you came along. Now I'm happy — the happiest woman in the world..."

"Why are you so happy, Rochele?"

"Because I have you — because I love you so much..."

5.

A few more weeks go by.

I cannot think straight. Nothing matters to me. I am possessed by the need to attain my goal, otherwise life has no meaning for me.

And Joseph? More affable than ever. Every time he utters a friendly word, it poisons my heart. He is worried about me. Why do I look so forlorn, he wants to know. And I am fonder of him than ever...

But whenever I see him (in my imagination) embracing her, kissing her, I could split his head open — and hers too.

No! It can't go on this way any longer! I must put an end to it!

One day I said to her: "Listen, Rochele. You know it does not matter to me if I have to deceive the whole world. The world means nothing to me. But I don't want to deceive *you*. And I need to be true to myself."

"Now what's bothering you, sweetheart? Tell your Rochele what's making you so unhappy." She caressed me. "Tell me everything."

"What I have to say to you will hurt you, Rochele. And you know how I worry about causing you pain..."

"Tell me, Sholem, tell me. So long as it makes you feel better."

I swallowed hard, moved closer to her, and said: "My happiness is now in your hands, Rochele."

"What do you mean?"

"I want you to be mine, Rochele, all mine..."

She blanched, stood stock still, as if she couldn't move. I was afraid to look her in the eyes. The sound of my own words alarmed me.

Finally she spoke. "Sholem, what — what did you say? Did you think before you said it?"

Her questions pierced me like a sword.

"Did you really say that, Sholem? How could you allow yourself to even think such a thing?"

"Rochele..."

"Oh my God, has it come to this?"

"But, Rochele, can't we even talk about it?"

She didn't answer me. She stared at the floor for several minutes. I didn't know what else to say. When I finally spoke, my voice resounded in my ears as though I were shouting.

"If you really love me, it's not such a terrible thing to ask. Love sanctifies everything."

Her next words squeezed my heart like a vise.

"Is that so? Love sanctifies everything? Then who permitted you to degrade *my* love?"

"That's nonsense!" I shouted again.

"Nonsense, hah?" She began tearing at her hair, scratching her face, as if she had lost all control.

I tried to calm her.

"Keep away from me! You frighten me! Leave me alone! Nonsense, hah?"

"But what are we to do, Rochele?"

"Nothing! Nothing! It can never happen! Go away!"

"But Rochele, what do you expect me to do? I did not want to utter those words to you, I swear." I tried to kiss her.

"Get away from me! Don't touch me! I'm afraid of you!"

"Why? Why are you afraid of me, Rochele?"

She didn't even hear me.

"What else do I have in my unhappy life except my love for you?" She was now crying uncontrollably.

The children came running. Soon Joseph would be home. Crestfallen, I left the house, not even saying goodbye to her.

6.

What to do now? Stop seeing her? That was out of the question. I could not live without her.

The next time I went to visit her, she greeted me in a friendly way. I could see that my arrival had cheered her up. But I could also see that she was trying not to show it. She took a sudden step forward, as if she wanted to embrace me, but then she suddenly grew somber. She looked older somehow. It was painful to watch. I thought to myself: She gets that expression on her face whenever she sees the ghost of "Thou Shalt Not." I don't know how long we sat there without saying a word. I could not have spoken about anything but my flaming desire for her. I sat there looking at her and it seemed to me she was vanishing in a thick cloud, like a ship sliding out to sea. Her eyes, staring at the ceiling, were full of fear and anguish. What dark thoughts were going through her head? I grew frightened myself.

"Rochele!"

She threw her arms around my neck. "Sholemke! Sholemke! My only consolation! Forgive me, Sholemke. I cannot do it... It must never happen, never. Joseph, the children... I will not demean my own children... No! Never!"

"Calm yourself, Rochele, please..."

Again, silence. Then she said, coldly:

"Tell me the truth, Sholem, the absolute truth. Do you really love me? Are you really my friend?"

I did not understand what she was asking me. I wanted to answer her, but I didn't know how.

"Why don't you answer me, Sholem?"

"How can I answer a question like that?"

"I asked you a simple question."

"Your question is not so simple. It sounds like you're insulting me."

"I'm not insulting you. Maybe I should have done that before. Now it's too late. Listen to me carefully, Sholem. Help me carry out my plan."

"Your plan? What plan?"

"I want to take my own life."

"Rochele!"

"Be a man, Sholem. Help me find the easiest death. I've been thinking about it for a long time..."

"God help you, Rochel, what are you saying?"

"Exactly what you heard. There's no other way out for me. You — and I myself, even more — have brought matters to this point..."

She was now speaking coldly, her eyes were filled with tears, but she was not crying.

"Rochele, dearest, I really don't understand you."

"You don't understand me?" Her question was a mixture of sadness and irony. "Well, Sholem, I understand myself very well. Or maybe I should say I know what I feel. Listen to me, Sholem. You want me to give myself to you. But that can never be. Not

because I don't want to betray Joseph. About him I've been thinking very little. Maybe I would have suffered afterward, but for the
time being I'm not worried about him. What I *am* worried about is
my children. I don't want to hurt them. But even that is not all.
I'm concerned about myself too. I know for a certainty that once I
crossed the line, I would stop loving you too. Yes, yes, Sholem.
Don't look at me as if I'm crazy. So what would I be left with?
Humiliated and deceived my husband and my children — and sadder than anything else — I deceived myself. Ach, how awful..."

This time she wept openly, uncontrollably, as one weeps over
an open coffin.

"So there's nothing left for me now except to kill myself. I
thought: Joseph is my friend, the father of my children, and you,
you are my spiritual comrade. But that wasn't enough for you.
Well, if that's how it has to be —"

She began pacing back and forth, wringing her hands.

"Oh my dear precious little children! Forgive your mother,
who has left this world so young because she loves you —"

"Rochel, stop it! For the sake of your children you have to
live. For Joseph's sake, for my sake — you have to live! You understand? Otherwise you'll be the death of us all! And there is another way out."

Her eyes opened wide. I wondered how I myself was going to
live through all this. But it was too late now. I had destroyed several lives. Better I left the scene.

I held out my hand. "Good-bye, Rochel."

"Where are you —"

"Don't worry, child. I'm only going home."

7.

That was the last time I ever set foot in that house.

What I lived through afterward is impossible to describe. I became a stranger to myself and to the world. I saw everything
through a haze. The most trivial thing could upset me.

Rachel acted wisely and never came to visit me. But Joseph,
that true friend, never suspecting a thing, came every evening to
ask what was wrong with me. But we barely exchanged even a

word, and as quietly as he had come, that's how he left, until one evening when he became insistent.

"Listen, Sholem, I can see that something is the matter with you. You can't fool me. Why can't we talk it over?"

The blood rushed to my head, She must have said something to him.

"Talk what over?" I said.

"Have you gone crazy, man? Don't you think your pain causes me pain too?"

"What exactly do you want, Joseph?"

"What I want is that you should borrow a few dollars from me every week until you find a job."

The next words came out of my mouth before I even knew they were in my head.

"You're a real idiot, Joe! I'm your worst enemy, and you come here offering to lend me money!"

"You *have* gone crazy, haven't you, Sholem?"

My God, what was this honest, generous friend of mine trying to do to me?

"Okay, Joe, sit down here beside me and let me tell you a story. Once upon a time there was a murderer, a lowdown, shameless murderer. Many a time he killed a person for a lousy few dollars. Then, one day, this criminal learned that in a remote corner of town there was a man who kept a great deal of money in his house. He went out there. The man was sleeping soundly. The murderer lifted up his axe, raised it over his head and — suddenly — the sleeping man let out a deep sigh. The murderer let his arms down very slowly. He couldn't hurt this man. This bloody murderer, who killed people over a few dollars, couldn't bring his axe down on a sleeping victim."

"Why are you telling me all this, Sholem?"

"Why I'm telling you this? Because I took unfair advantage of you, Joseph."

"What the hell are you talking about?"

"Interpret it any way you want, brother. Think anything you want of me — the worst — and you won't be wrong."

There was a long silence. Finally Joseph said:

"Sholem, you're in love with Rachel?"

"Yes."

"And she with you?"

"You'll have to ask her that."

"But you just told me that terrible story —"

"I was speaking only about myself."

"But why tell me that story? You have insulted her."

"How?"

"You have to ask that? You don't know?"

"Hear me out, Joseph. I can say whatever I want about Rachel."

"What do you mean by that, for God's sake?"

"Your Rochel is too honest, which is how she ruined my life. She stamped out my life as if it were a glowing ember."

"You're talking a bit too symbolically for me, Sholem. Tell me plainly, does Rochel know about this?"

"About what?'

"That you love her."

"You'll have to ask her that."

"You've known me too long for that kind of answer, Sholem. Neither of you has to deny anything."

"Who are you talking about now, Joseph?"

"You *and* Rachel. You should have told me about this right away."

"Told you about what? Don't be a fool. You don't believe her? Your Rachel is an angel. She's the most honest woman I know."

Joseph lowered his eyes. He paled. Then he asked me, almost unemotionally:

"But why didn't you both tell me about this?"

"Tell you what?"

"About your — relationship."

"What relationship?"

"That you loved each other."

"You *are* a fool, Joseph. She has nothing to tell you, and I was ashamed to. Don't you understand? Aside from the fact that I always felt guilty."

"Why?"

"Now you're insulting my intelligence, Joseph. Hear me out and try to understand me. I love you, Joseph. I respect you. But I hold myself higher than I do you, in every way. And it hurt me very much that Rachel chose you instead of me."

"What do you mean — she chose me?"

"You know damn well what I mean. I loved you like a good friend. But when I finally worked up enough nerve to tell Rachel that I love her, and she rejected me — what was I supposed to do then? We are all egoists — and that's what drives us to do the basest things. And once I had taken the first step, I couldn't go back. I felt I was still a friend — and therefore a betrayer — but I couldn't help myself. I would have stopped at nothing, especially if Rachel had agreed. But she didn't. Don't you understand that? I lost. So good-bye, Joseph, and I don't think we should ever meet again."

"Don't be such a sentimentalist, Sholem. Let's erase the whole thing, as if it had never happened."

"No, Joe, it would never work. I can't stand your generosity — that hurts me more than anything else. Let me just kiss you good-bye. Have a good life with your dear, saintly wife. And if you can, forget me."

"Sholem!"

"Good-bye, Joseph! And not another word..."

EQUALITY OF THE SEXES
Avrom Reisen

AVROM REISIN (1876-1953) — born in White Russia; died in New York.

In Reisen's long, productive life he was a poet, short story writer, editor, and champion of the Yiddish language. His father was a Hebrew-Yiddish poet; his mother, an avid reader of Yiddish religious books. As a child he studied Russian and German and general subjects, and at age 14 he became a teacher in his home town of Koydonev. A few years later he began corresponding with I.L. Peretz, and his poems were published in various literary magazines.

In 1895 Reisen was drafted into the Russian army and became part of a military band in Kovno. When the Russo-Japanese War broke out in 1904 he moved to Cracow, Poland, where he made plans to publish a weekly "according to my literary taste and convictions, especially to proclaim Yiddish as the national language of the Jewish people."

Reisen visited the U.S. in 1908 and again in 1911 and did readings in Paris and Brussels. With the outbreak of World War I he came to the U.S. to stay. Up until the day of his death there was an unusual harmony between Reisen and his readers, including his younger readers whom he visited frequently in Yiddish schools. The Yiddish critic Nachman Meisel said of him: "Like his poems, Reisen's short stories are mostly descriptions of reality, of something that has just happened. But taken together they add up to far more than the sum of the parts." His many volumes are an inexhaustible treasure of short stories and poems which, in simple and sympathetic language, illuminate the everyday lives of three generations of European and American Jews.

Equality of the Sexes (Glaykhheit) *appears in Reisen's* Gezamelte shriftn (Collected Works), *v. 9, 1916.*

Avrom Reisen

Equality of the Sexes

For almost a year now Harry has been going out with Ida.
Harry is tall, slim, dark-haired and twenty-four. Ida is petite,
comely and twenty. Their love is secure, firm and already encir-
cled by a small, five-dollar gold ring which Harry gave her as a
present, and it is further tied together with a 49-cent necktie which
Ida bought him in return. Neither one of them has parents here to
push them into marriage. They themselves believe that *khosn* and
kalleh, lover and sweetheart, are much more beautiful words than
"man" and "wife." "Man" doesn't sound too bad, but "wife" —
that is a word neither of them can stand.

"An ugly word!" Ida exclaims charmingly.

"A vulgar word!" Harry agrees.

It is much more pleasant for them to meet several times a
week at certain pre-arranged places — at an "Elevated" station, or
on the corner of a quiet little street. Ida is never punctual. Usually
she is ten minutes late, that is, in addition to the first ten minutes
that Harry has learned to expect. By nature, Harry is a very impatient person. "A big fault, her tardiness. I really should talk to her
about it." But when he sees her coming he strides forward to greet
her with a friendly smile on his face.

And when she asks him: "Have you been waiting long,
Harry?" he always replies good-humoredly:

"It's nothing, Ida. I don't mind..."

Harry is convinced that his sweet expectation of her arrival
will vanish once they are married. She will be waiting for him in a
home where two beds stand close together, and people who come
to visit them will immediately perceive everything and smile
knowingly.

Isn't it better when he steals into her room, with its one
sparkling-white narrow bed that he doesn't have the nerve to sit
down on, even on the edge, until she assures him that she does indeed want him to sit there because the only chair her landlady put
in the room will "shorten your years"?

Or what about the moment when he and Ida leave together, surreptitiously, and her cheeks are aflame from his kisses and from the ice-cold water she has just washed her face with, so people won't suspect — not that it does any good.

"My cheeks are hot as fire, Harry!" she says in mock anger.

And Harry assures her that she is only imagining things, that a thief always feels as if the hat on his head is burning. She laughs her charming little laugh, and going down the stairs Harry falls in love with her all over again. A brand new love affair. And right there on the stairs he kisses her again, and again she is "angry" and lectures him:"Harry, you're not being careful! People can see us..." And suddenly she bursts out laughing in such a delightful way that you've got to be stronger than iron not to kiss her again. But now they are already out in the street and must be content with squeezing each other's arms and snuggling up to each other.

All this — they are both convinced — will cease abruptly the moment they get married. The happy couple therefore does not even want to think about it...

From the standpoint of practicality, it definitely does not pay for them to get married. Harry's fifteen dollars a week makes him a real "sport." He owns three suits, one of them "made to order" for twenty-five dollars. One suit he bought ready-made for fifteen dollars. And one, for which he paid ten dollars, he wears to work. As for neckties, in addition to the one Ida bought him, he owns six of them — they still look brand new — plus three others that only have to be ironed, except for the red one, which he wears on May First and sometimes when there is a strike demonstration.

And collars? He must have two dozen of them. As soon as a new style of collar comes out, Harry is the first to buy three. Even dress shirts, which are a more expensive item — he has two that are part silk, and one a hundred percent silk, that he bought on sale. And shoes — he has two pair, black for winter, tan for summer, and sandals for sunny days when he goes to Coney Island.

For a single man, fifteen dollars a week is real money. You even have some left over for cultural things. Every day Harry buys two newspapers — a radical one, where they write about his working-class interests, and a "Jewish" one, where the interests of his mother and father in the Old Country are discussed. Sundays he buys *The World*, which costs more — a whole nickel. The World runs beautiful pictures, which he clips out and gives to Ida. For himself he takes the faces of pretty actresses and keeps them in his vest pocket to show to his friends in the shop.

In a word, as a single man, Harry lives comfortably. He has everything a "sport" of his status needs, and he still has enough left over to take Ida out a couple of times a week purely for pleasure.

And his greatest pleasure is to sit with Ida in a restaurant and order "the best" — strawberries with sour cream in the summer, or a baked apple with sweet cream in the winter... And when he gets the two checks from the waiter, he adds up the totals, which usually amount to no more than forty cents and no less than twenty-five. And like a true sport, he leaves a nickel on the table for the waiter. Then he lets Ida go out first, while he stops at the cashier's, which signifies, "Ida, you go on ahead. Paying the check is *my* business..." And after he pays it, Harry has a feeling of pride, as after a very important accomplishment.

Out on the street again, Ida's curiosity gets the better of her and she asks:

"Harry, did it cost very much?"

And he answers with a wave of the hand:

"A trifle..."

But in that very reply one can hear the pride of a man who can afford to pay for what his lady wants.

Then Ida puts her dainty hand in the crook of his arm and they take a leisurely walk to the moving-picture house. Here again he stops at the cashier's booth, puts down two nickels for two tickets and the treat is on him again.

This entire process of "treating" makes Harry feel not only proud but gallant, and he carries it off with ease, even with a certain grace.

Ida accepts all these treats as part of the natural order of things: of course the man should pay the bill. But afterward she comments:

"You know, Harry, sometimes I feel like I want to pay for *you...*" This comment is punctuated with a little laugh, and she adds: "Yes, sometimes I want to treat *you!*"

But for Harry, the idea is insulting. From the expression on his face you would think that a belief he holds sacred has been violated.

"That's nonsense, Ida! Out of your seven dollars a week you're going to treat *me*?"

"Well, of course," Ida stammers in embarrassment, "not now. Of course not. But later on, when I start working at dresses and earn fifteen dollars —"

"You? Fifteen dollars a week?" There is a trace of mockery in his tone.

"Certainly! Why not? You think a girl can't earn fifteen dollars a week?"

"Well," he grumbles, "maybe there are some who can, but what do *you* need it for?"

And when Ida starts telling about her future fifteen dollars a week wages, Harry listens, shakes his head, smiles, and as though jealous of this manly sum, he mutters:

"Get that nonsense out of your head, Ida."

"Why is it nonsense? It makes good sense to me!" And gazing into his eyes, she teases him: "Because then I will be the one to pay the cashier! I'd like to do that sometime."

Here Harry becomes really upset and cuts her off with an artificial smile:

"Well, we'll see, we'll see..."

*

Finally Ida's day came. A friend of hers, after trying for a long time to get Ida into her shop where they manufacture dresses, finally succeeded and taught her the skill at which she could earn the long-hoped-for sum.

For about two weeks Ida kept it a secret from Harry. In the first place, during those two weeks she didn't even earn the full amount, since she was not yet able to finish the required number of dresses. But by the third week she had mastered the work and on Monday, when she opened her pay envelope, she counted out fifteen dollars.

That same evening she and Harry had a date. This time she was not late, not even by a minute.

Harry was amazed. "You're here on time! Is something wrong?"

"No! But I've got good news!"

"Good news? What happened?"

"Let's get something to eat first. I'm hungry..."

She took his arm and they headed toward a familiar restaurant nearby. On the way she stopped for a moment and, looking straight into Harry's eyes, exclaimed:

"Harry, today you're the one who's getting a treat — from me!"

Startled, he smiled feebly and said:

"Don't be foolish!"

"I'm serious, Harry." Her voice had a little heat in it. "Otherwise, this whole thing won't work. Today I am paying for our supper." And she couldn't help giggling.

Again Harry started to protest, but she interrupted him and continued nervously:

"And then I'm taking you to the theater, you understand? A real theater, not the movies. A serious play. You know where? Fifty cents a ticket. And I'm paying..."

Again she stopped walking and, with a happy grin on her face, took the envelope out of her pocketbook.

"Count it!" she said, handing him the envelope.

With trembling fingers he took it, opened it — a ten and a five.

"Fifteen dollars!" There was a hint of fear in his voice.

"Yes! I'm already working there! At the dresses!"

"You're a silly girl, Ida." He himself could not understand what was making him so angry.

"You're silly yourself!" she smiled. "But it's still my treat tonight!"

He trailed along after her, as if he had just learned of some terrible disaster. Ida kept laughing and joking. He could not find the right words to say to her in this strange mood she was in. Finally he muttered witlessly:

"You know something, Ida. In that case, we can get married..."

"Now you want to get married? Really?" She laughed out loud. "You like the idea of a rich bride? Well, wait a while. First let's save up a few hundred dollars, then I'll see whether it pays me..."

And looking at him to see what effect her words were having on him, she started laughing again.

This time he laughed too, but his heart wasn't really in it.

They entered the restaurant.

Still smiling, Ida beckoned to the waiter.

"It's not nice," Harry whispered into her ear. "The lady is not supposed to call the waiter. The man does that."

"It won't hurt," she said. "Today I'm playing *your* role. I've always envied you when you did it... Well, Harry, what do you want to eat? Get something special, for a change. I'm paying."

And although Harry knew she was only playing a game with him, he replied gravely:

"I'll just have some soup. I'm not hungry..."

"Whatever you wish," she said magnanimously.

After the meal she quickly picked up the two checks as soon as the waiter put them down on the table. She squeezed them triumphantly in her fist.

"All right, Ida, enough!" Harry objected. "Give me those checks."

Though there was a smile on her face, there was also a definite steeliness in her tone.

"Not on your life!" she said resolutely as she marched toward the cashier's booth.

Still smiling, Ida handed over the checks, along with a five-dollar bill. The cashier, a tall, slender brunette, stared at her quizzically. Then she looked over at Harry. The shadow of a smile passed over her face.

"For two!" said Ida, pointing to Harry. She took the change and walked proudly out of the restaurant with Harry behind her.

Outside, he was too angry to utter a word. They walked along in silence for a few minutes. Finally he blurted out:

"You just acted in such a — you insulted me."

"I did? How?"

"By paying for me."

"Then why have you been insulting *me* for such a long time?" She had stopped laughing.

"I insulted you? When?" He had no idea what she was getting at.

"Whenever you paid for me... You think it's really so pleasant? All the time, *you* pay? Sometimes I want the pleasure of paying. You begrudge me that pleasure? Oh, you egotistical little boys!" She was laughing again. "You still don't want us to have equal rights with you!"

Harry had no reply to this. He even smiled. Then he grew serious again. This equality business was so new and so radical that he felt threatened by it.

But that evening he held Ida in his arms tighter than usual, differently somehow, as if he were afraid of losing her.

AT THE THRESHOLD
Peretz Hirshbein

PERETZ HIRSHBEIN (1880-1948) — born in Lithuania; died in Los Angeles.

Hirshbein is known primarily as one of the most prolific playwrights of the Yiddish stage. His father owned a mill in an isolated corner of Lithuania where he was born, and the natural surroundings there left a mark on him and his imagination for the rest of his life.

At 20 he became a teacher of modern Hebrew and also led an illegal circle of young Jewish workers, men and women. Around 1902 he began writing stories in Yiddish but did not publish them. Two years later, however, he visited I. L. Peretz in Warsaw, who read some of his things and encouraged him to continue his writing in Yiddish.

In 1911 he emigrated to New York and a year later had written Di puste kretchma (The Haunted Inn), *a four-act play which became popular and was performed throughout the world. In 1914 he began writing fiction for* Der tog, *a new Yiddish daily. In 1918 Maurice Schwartz staged Hirshbein's* A Secluded Corner *and* The Blacksmith's Daughters, *dramas which marked the beginning of Yiddish art theater in America.* Green Fields *followed soon thereafter. Regarding these plays, the Yiddish poet Yaakov Glatstein mused that when Peretz Hirshbein began thinking about his youth, he ended up by writing the four best plays in the Yiddish repertoire.*

In 1924 he and his wife Esther Shumiatcher, a young Yiddish poet whom he met in Canada, embarked on a world tour that lasted five years, travels about which he wrote extensively. In 1942 he published his trilogy Babylon, *which encompasses five years of Jewish life in America. In 1940 he and his wife finally settled in Los Angeles. Five years later he was stricken by an illness which left him an invalid and from which he never recovered.*

At the Threshold (Baym shvel) *appears in* Zukunft, *June 1934.*

At the Threshold

1.

She stood stiffly on the top deck of the ship as if her hands had become part of the railing. With her whole being she imbibed the little blinking fires which — from behind a transparent cloud — were sending points of light in her direction. The City of New York and its stone and steel towers, together with the breeze from the east, breathed upon her with a cool metallic whisper. The shadowy Hudson River alongside the ship flowed inexorably toward the sea, linking the cool autumn night with the approaching dawn.

And although the ship had been anchored since midnight at the outskirts of New York, and although she would not be meeting him until nine o'clock in the morning — the man to whom she was bringing her young life all the way from her small Lithuanian home town which she had left two weeks earlier with a troubled spirit — she nevertheless could no longer sleep a wink.

She knows very well that it would have been better for her if she had slept that night because ever since she had started on her journey to America to meet this man whom she barely remembers — ever since then all the blood had drained from her face. And a sleepless night would certainly do her face no good. But how could one lie there on that damp, sea-salty bed when the ship was already touching the shore of the city? She could almost feel the breath of that stranger upon her skin, the stranger whose wife she was about to become.

The tiny blinking lights kept multiplying. A harsh, whispering sound came from the dark silhouettes of the city. For some reason she did not understand, those sounds threw her into a panic. She tried to conjure up an image of that man who had visited her town a few years ago to find his old mother. As fate would have it, her own mother was living in a rented room in that same house. But try as she might, she could not separate his image from the immense silhouettes of the skyscrapers. Why had she not had the sense, eight years ago, when that broad-shouldered stranger with the clean-shaven face and bald head had visited them, to take a good long look at him and store his image away in her brain?

Her heart began to pound, as it did whenever her mind cast back over those eight years. Had her own mother already known that her only daughter would have to marry that man? Why had her mother not asked her: "Sterna, my child, do you like this Mister Berl Kaplan?" Maybe if her mother had asked her that, she would have taken a better look at him.

The thought kept boring into her mind. How could her own mother have taken money from Mister Berl Kaplan, a complete stranger, to buy a new sewing machine? Mister Kaplan had also left enough money for her mother to buy a cow, so that her only daughter could drink a lot of milk. And from that day forward, Mister Kaplan's mother had stopped taking rent from Sterna's mother. What had all that meant? Had her own mother sold her only daughter, who was still a child, to this stranger?

The chilling thought cut through her body, made her shiver. For a moment she felt ashamed of herself for having such thoughts. All her life she had loved her widowed mother who sewed and sewed day and night to raise her child. True, later, the child had begun to help her mother and was soon earning more money than she. But still, he got his way. Sent them a ticket, second class, on a big ship, and two hundred dollars besides. And so many letters he had sent from this city which now breathed so heavily upon her. She had answered all his letters, every one of which, she now realized, was a love letter.

Still, the startling thought kept drilling into her head: "Her own mother had sold her — sent her own daughter away to a stranger. How was that possible?"

2.

She hurried back to her cabin. She wanted to curl up on her cot and relive her last days with her mother... She wanted to conjure up once more her mother's face, look into her eyes, examine her intentions. It all brought a sharp pain to her heart. How could a person suspect her own mother of such things?

Inside her cabin was a woman who shared it with her — an elderly woman from Poland who was coming to the United States to join her children. She was sitting on the edge of her seat.

"They don't let you sleep, eh? Me neither. Not a wink the whole night long. It's a sin. The ships arrive here around midnight and they don't let anyone off until morning, and they don't let anyone on board to meet you. I can see you didn't get a wink of sleep either..."

The woman's voice grated on her nerves, but she couldn't restrain herself. "What do you think, Mrs. Silverstein? Is it very smart for a young woman to travel across the ocean all by herself to meet a complete stranger?"

"If you're sailing across the ocean to meet him, he's probably not a complete stranger. Didn't you tell me he came to your town to see his mother who's a neighbor of yours?"

"Yes, that's true. Still, I feel ashamed. And frightened, too. I've been staring out at the big city all night — and I'm scared."

"If he's rich, you don't have anything to worry about. They say that in America a wife can live like a princess if her husband has the money. My daughters-in-law are living with my sons like real ladies. That's what everybody says."

"I grew up in a poor family, Mrs. Silverstein. I learned how to sew. I wore out my feet at the machine. But that didn't bother me. And now I don't know. It's not as if I was in love with the man..."

"Dear child, love is not everything. I myself married my husband before I even knew him. If we hadn't had children, I wouldn't even have wanted to know him. Soon, soon, in three or four hours, you'll get a good look at him."

"And what if I don't like him?"

"You should have thought of that before you got on the ship."

"I thought about it plenty. When I was back there, my heart was over here. And now that I'm here, my heart is over there."

"You never had a serious talk with him?"

"I was still a child. He put me on his knee and kissed my forehead. 'When you grow up,' he said, 'I'll bring you over to America.' And both mothers — his and mine — were so proud."

"Well, at least, he's a man of his word."

Sterna stood up. She wanted to go up to the top deck again, lean on the rail and stare out at that fearful city. Her anxiety was palpable.

"A young heart is always uneasy," Mrs. Silverstein said. "But you have no reason to feel that way. If he was able to help *your* mother and *his* mother all these years — and now he sends for you — that's not a trivial matter."

"Then why do I feel so — so — nervous?"

Her neighbor laughed, but didn't reply.

"You're laughing at me —"

"You should have forced yourself to get some sleep last night, so you wouldn't look like —"

"I know. I know how I must look. I feel as if my face has turned green..."

She lay down and tried to sleep. The skin on her face felt dry as parchment and her eyes were weary. If she could only get some sleep, even for half an hour!

Her mother's face was clear as crystal before her closed eyes, wrinkled by age and worries and complaints: "How long will you depend on a poor widow? Your father left me all alone with you when you were still an infant. I did everything I could to bring you up right. You never went hungry. We never had to ask for help. Now, my child, it's time for you to help your poor mother. A millionaire in America wants to bathe you in luxury. God willing, you'll be very comfortable, and maybe in her old age your mother will have a place to rest her head..."

When she opened her eyes her neighbor in the other bed was snoring loudly. Must have fallen asleep... But Sterna was wide awake. On her tiptoes she left the room, quietly closed the door and climbed up to the top deck.

3.

The sky above the city began to pale. The high shadowy buildings turned a darker gray. The lights lost some of their sparkle. The metallic roar became more distinct, vibrating between the buildings and echoing in her mood like distant peals of thunder.

She tried mightily to distance herself from her mother's image and from the "lecture" she had just heard from her neighbor. Instead, she tried to call up the image of her "betrothed," on whose knee she had sat eight years ago without ever taking a good look at him, His dark, sympathetic eyes — that she did remember. She could still feel his kisses on her cheeks — the first time in her life a man had done that   and in the presence of both their mothers And both mothers were pleased that the gentleman from America was holding the young girl on his knees. But he had also whispered many fine words into her ears, words that both mothers did not hear: "When you grow up, Sterna, I'll bring you over to America... With me you'll have a life of luxury... and your name will no longer be Sterna but Sadie..."

A warmth streamed through her limbs, a warmth that originated in her heart and traveled to her face and down to her knees. Her cheeks were hot as fire, a fire that left her weak in the knees, so weak that she felt she was about to faint right there on the deck.

Now his old mother's words rang in her ears, words of praise she constantly repeated about her son. "He is goodness itself, my Berl." Yes, he certainly was a good man. But why was it that at that time when her mother bought (for his money) a new Singer machine, and Sterna had begun to work on that sewing machine and earn money for herself and her mother — why had her mother not thought about his goodness then? The sewing machine was not a mark of his goodness, not a mark of the fine words he whispered into her ear. Quite the opposite. She had grown up at that machine. And when her feet moved the treadle and caused the wheel to turn and the needle to stitch and stitch — then Mister Berl Kaplan's image disappeared as if into a cloud. She never believed that he would bring her to America. And it was the machine that caused her to disbelieve that, even though he wrote her letters and even though she answered every single one of them.

Nevertheless, something inside her protested. "I am on this ship because of him. He must remember me as I was then. It doesn't matter that I sent him my photograph only a few weeks ago..."

Now she was sorry she had been neglecting her appearance lately. If only another 24 hours were left before she met him, maybe...

4.

With quick steps she returned to her cabin, determined to do whatever she could to improve her appearance a little. She studied her face in the mirror. It was as if she were seeing it for the first time. Dark eyes. Dark, thick hair, uncombed. Under her eyes, dark circles. The face that stared back at her from the mirror was serious and frightened. A face that seemed to be scolding her: "Such neglect! Such stupidity! To let yourself be persuaded by two old women! Because of two old mothers and a man in America who bought you a sewing machine you failed to notice how your youth had bloomed and then faded! You let yourself be persuaded by two so-called mothers who sold you to a man in America whom you don't even know. Love? What do you know about it? Choosing the one your own heart yearns for? You forgot all about that! What are a young woman's years, after all? Only everything in the world, all the spring-times, all its beautiful mornings... Serves you right, to let two old mothers take your youth and bury it alive..."

Her cabin-mate, although herself a mother of grown children in America, looked up from her cot toward the mirror in which Sterna was studying her face. As if speaking to herself, she said: "Who knows, maybe even a mother can make a mistake?" Then, a bit louder: "Is it really true that you've forgotten completely what he looks like? What if someone else comes to meet you? They won't let you get off the boat unless the person responsible for you is present. In fact, you'll have to marry him before they let you into America. What a world! Whoever heard of a young woman sailing to America to marry a man she doesn't even know!"

Sterna turned and looked at her neighbor with the mocking smile on her face.

"You're making fun of me," she said softly. "It must seem ridiculous to you. Here I am making up my face for a man I don't even know. You're wrong. I wouldn't have come all this way to meet a complete stranger. I do know him. I remember him well. He wrote me love-letters and I answered them. I wouldn't have come all this distance to meet a person I didn't love."

The woman's voice softened. "That's exactly what I think. I never thought any different. A mother would never sell her own child like that. Your mother has eyes too. You're doing the right thing, fixing yourself up a little. Your face looks better already. Bend down and let me give you a kiss — after all, I'm a mother too. I'd like you to meet my children. I'll give you their addresses. Who knows what can happen? At least you'll have someone to turn to..."

Sterna's heart dropped. This stranger in her cabin had spoken the truth, plain and simple. "Who knows what can happen?" Still, she persisted. "Something like what? What sort of thing could happen to me?"

"I shouldn't have said that. It slipped out for no reason at all."

"No it didn't. Tell me the truth. What did you mean?"

"I mean — suppose you don't even like him?"

"And what if he doesn't like *me*?"

"He still has to marry you..."

"What!"

"Don't worry. He'll like you. You're still young. And from what you told me — he's no longer a young man."

Again the blood rushed to Sterna's face. Why had she revealed her secret thoughts to an utter stranger? It would be best now to keep quiet. What she was trying to express now could not be expressed in words. So she had committed a terrible injustice to the years of her youth. So she had hidden her youthful bloom from the young men of her town. How old had she been when she "pledged her troth" to the man from America? Thirteen? At thirteen a girl already knows something about the world she lives in. What did she have to fear from him anyway?

But Mrs. Silverstein knew about life too. She stood up, put her arms around Sterna and kissed her like a mother.

"Your face is hot, my child. Don't let it grow cold. You're blooming like a chestnut tree. I'm sure he'll like you. But you have nothing to worry about. In America a girl like you won't be overlooked. In America, they say, a woman can earn just as much as a man. And if you have to marry him for appearance's sake, that's not the end of the world either... Look! It's almost morning..."

5.

Three men came aboard to meet her. Mister Berl Kaplan was the oldest and the only one with a bald head. That was how she recognized him, not by his face or dark eyes. The two younger men had light hair, were both clean-shaven and neatly dressed. There was an expression of surprise on their faces. And Berl Kaplan, who at first was the most animated of the three, grew silent after the first few moments.

She noticed this with a feeling of panic. During those first few moments he seemed to shrink. She could not understand whether this happened because she was a disappointment to him or because she greeted him in such a cold, unfriendly manner. During those first few moments all she could think of was his mother, who always had such complimentary things to say about him. And *her* mother's image appeared before her and stood between her and this man with the bald head and the short neck.

And although all this took no more than a few seconds, in those few seconds she relived both her childhood years when this man had held her on his knee, and also the later years when she was growing up with the knowledge that a man in far-off America was waiting for her. It was as if an unseen hand in back of her were pushing her toward this stout man with the bald head, delivering her into his arms.

And although she had never known her father and had no memory of him except what her mother had told her, she now felt as if she were falling into his arms. In that fraction of a second her entire being wanted to cry out with a great weeping: "Take me away from this place, as a father would take his child, and as soon

175

as we enter the streets of this unknown city, let me go and don't even follow me with your eyes. Let me disappear..."

But this man in front of her was now talking excitedly. "This is Sadie, my bride Sadie, you know. In the old country, you know, she was called Sterna." Mister Kaplan introduced her to the two younger men. "When I first met her in the *shtetl* she was still a baby, ha ha. Now look at her! Sadie, meet my friends, my partners. This is Mister Berman and this is Mister Fagin. They are here to be our witnesses, you know. In America you need witnesses for everything, ha ha. Uncle Sam wants us to have the *chupah* ceremony right away. I myself, you know, wouldn't want to have it without love, you know, ha ha..."

The two men giggled along with him. She felt like giggling herself. But the pressure behind her eyes kept building up, and her heart was feeling more and more constricted. She bit her lips but couldn't keep the tears from flowing freely and rolling down her cheeks. Yet anyone who had known her would have recognized the face of the child she had been eight years earlier.

To hide her tears, she once more threw herself into the older man's arms and tried consciously to awaken the feelings which once — even from a distance — had set her blood racing. She tried to imagine herself in the arms of a younger man. She raised her head from his chest and — unexpectedly for him and for herself — covered his face with kisses. Her dry lips felt the warm skin of this stranger, but it was a warmth that did not excite her in the least.

"What happens now?" she asked him with a certain equanimity.

"Everything has already happened," Mister Kaplan replied with a smile. "Everything. Certain formalities and nothing more. Maybe they'll send you over to Ellis Island for a couple of hours. But don't worry about that. A comfortable home is waiting for you on Riverside Drive. The whole city of New York is waiting for you, ha ha. But first we have to go through a ceremony."

"A *chupah*?"

"You could call it that. Without it they won't let you off the ship."

She glanced at the two younger men who stood nearby. They seemed to be commiserating with her. How she would love to take them aside and ask them a few questions! They certainly knew one thing — she was the bride for whom their partner had been waiting patiently all these years...

The seconds turned into minutes, but there was no longer any time for waiting. The steady stream of passengers impatient for freedom swept her and the three men along. But instead of going out to the sunlit street, she and the third-class passengers were shunted to a small boat and taken back to the "Isle of Tears" — Ellis Island — where they were led through cages and cells, part prison and part freedom. And even though the three men were still with her, her head began to spin. No time now to think rationally, no strength even to study her surroundings and the swirl of people around her. Even the three men, who were now her closest "relatives," seemed to be floating in the air before her very eyes...

6.

She was painfully aware that time was short. It was too late even to think about it. The unknown mammoth city, which had stared at her all night long with its thousands of eyes, the broad-beamed buildings, so big they touched the clouds, blotted out all memory of her little corner back home. She tried to picture her new home in this city called New York, but the man called "Mister Kaplan" blocked her vision. The image of her native town was blurred and indistinct, but the image of the two frightened mothers there was clear and distinct as they pinched their cheeks in shame.

"I want to ask you something," she said to Mister Kaplan breathlessly. "I know your mother. I know you've been supporting her for many years. You are a good, considerate person. So I beg you — let me go free. I'll pay you back for everything you have done for me."

"There's no reason for you to be so scared," he tried to assure her. "I will not force you to do anything you don't want to."

"That's good, Mister Kaplan. So I beg you — let me go."

"I'm not stopping you."

"But what am I to do? Please tell me..."

"They won't let you off the boat unless —"

"Unless what?"

"Don't be so afraid. I won't force you to go with me. And my partners — they are both gentlemen —."

Mister Kaplan was obviously at a loss. In his mind, too, he could envision that afternoon at his mother's when he held this Sterna on his knee and told her a story about what would happen to her when she grew up, that he would bring her to the Golden Land called America. She had been so delighted with that story...

"You think you're the only one who was waiting, Sterna? I waited for you eight long years, you know. During that time I could have gotten married eight times, ha ha. Talk to her, Mr. Berman. You too, Mr. Fagin. Tell her about her intended, who is a good boy, an honorable man. Tell her not to disgrace me. Everything is ready for you. A furnished home is no small thing. And what a holiday is waiting for you as soon as you rest up from your long journey..."

Mister Kaplan fell apart. Not only was he being put to shame in the presence of his two partners, but he felt as if everyone else aboard ship was staring at him with suspicion. Any moment now the police would come and arrest him for debauching an innocent young woman.

"I beg you, Sterna. Don't disgrace me..." He wanted to say something else, but the tears in his throat choked him. He turned aside with a desperate look at his partners.

These two gentlemen stared at each other helplessly, not knowing where to begin. Mister Kaplan had been singing the praises of this girl for years, describing her beauty, her cleverness, her love for him. Now they didn't know which one to feel more sorry for. Finally Mr. Fagin said:

"You know, Sterna, America is a free country. Everybody can do as they wish. But that's true only after you have already entered the country — and you are not inside the country yet. This gentleman here is trying to do you a favor. He will not do anything against your wishes."

"Mr. Kaplan is a nice man," said Mr. Berman, following his partner's lead. "Eight long years he's been waiting for his bride.

By this time I'll betcha he could already have been the father of three children, ha ha. Be a good girl. They won't let us stand around here very much longer. There is a Reverend on board this ship, and Mr. Fagin and I are prepared to act as witnesses."

She pulled her hand from Mr. Berman's and cast a glance at her bridegroom, who was standing with his back to her. She really wanted to assimilate those broad shoulders into her life somehow, but she couldn't do it. She wanted to find a connection between this man and her own youthful years, but she could not do it. She had grown up in his mother's house, but now she could find no affinity between this well-fed man and the old, wrinkled, bent-over woman who lived back there in the shtetl on his charity. He had told Sterna that a fully furnished home was waiting for her in the city. She tried to picture all sorts of richly furnished apartments, and in every one of them there was a bed waiting for her. That very night she would have to lie in that bed and watch this bald-headed man approach her with the right to spend the night with her, to share that bed with her, all because he had —

Mister Kaplan turned to look at her. His face seemed to shrink and his head sank even deeper into the space between his shoulders. She could feel the anger rising in her throat. She bit her lips. Her fingers spasmodically sought a pocket in her coat where they could hide and there freely pinch her body...

7.

Meanwhile the eyes of the three men were boring into her. She could feel it all over her body. For a moment she caught a glimpse of the nocturnal city, the cold, unfamiliar lights blinking at her unceasingly. The next moment her imagination carried her back home. She could see the window that looked out into the courtyard at the ancient, drooping willow-tree. And there in a corner was her sewing-machine covered with her dotted blue-and-white apron. At the last moment before saying goodbye she had taken off that apron and draped it across the machine. She wondered why she could not see her mother's face in this picture. But the outline of the sewing-machine grew clearer and clearer. The apron flew away. The wheel on the machine, of its own accord, began spinning, and the needle kept stitching and stitching over the vacant spot. Why was there no cloth under the needle? A stream of bright sunlight burst in through the window and cut the machine in half...

Her entire body shook. Mister Kaplan stepped closer to her and touched her arm hesitantly, as if he wanted to awaken her from her reverie without alarming her. When she shivered, he stepped back a pace or two, and with his eyes staring down at the deck, he said:

"I'll do whatever you say, Sterna. I'll send you back home on the same ship because if you have left your real betrothed back there, you know, you shouldn't have kept it a secret. In America everybody is straight. American girls know exactly where they stand. I won't force you to marry me. If you made a mistake, then you should know that I too have made a mistake. We'll leave you here now. Don't worry. They won't put you in prison. I'll come back later to see what you need..."

She was unable to utter a word in response. She turned away and her whole body contorted in a suppressed weeping.

The same ship that had brought Sterna to America carried her back home again. Around midnight she stood holding tightly to the rail, staring at the towering silhouettes of New York. The man with the bald head had taken great care to see that nothing unpleasant would happen to her on the "Isle of Tears." He even examined the cabin in which she would have to sleep. But he did not have the fortitude to wait until the ship pushed off from shore. He even forgot to send greetings back to his mother in the little Lithuanian *shtetl*.

When he left, Sterna tried to imagine the place where her new home was to have been. But to no avail. No sooner did she close her eyes than she saw clearly the house and the room where her sewing-machine stood facing the old willow-tree. A breeze blew through its branches and the leaves dropped to the damp autumn earth outside her window...

THE NEWCOMERS:
NEW YORK IN THE 1890s
David Ignatov

DAVID IGNATOV (1885-1954) — *born in the Ukraine; died in New York.*

When Ignatov was 18, he joined the Russian Social Democratic Party and was arrested for "revolutionary activities." In 1906 he emigrated to the United States and found work in various factories in Chicago, St. Louis, and New York. For a brief period he was a union organizer.

When he turned to writing fiction, he could not find a place to publish it. Soon he found himself the leader of a Yiddish writers group that was in rebellion against the literary conservatism of the Yiddish press. Characteristically, they called themselves "Di Yunge" (The Youth), a group which also included Meir Blinkin and Isaac Raboy. For a period of 20 years Di Yunge published their own literary magazines, which were really anthologies of their writings that would never have found a place in the Yiddish newspapers. These publications gave the young literature a chance to breathe and grow.

Ignatov's first story, published in 1907, was well received. His trilogy Vistas (Oyf veite vegn) *describes the rise of the Jewish labor movement in the United States. The hero, Berman, is easily recognized as Ignatov himself. Sol Liptzin, in his* History of Yiddish Literature, *notes that "Ignatov's activity as a writer alternated between a colorful romanticism which casts a halo about Jewish tradition and a radical realism which linked him with proletarian literature." This combination existed in the work of many of the American Yiddish writers of the time, but in Ignatov's work this alternation between romanticism and realism is more apparent than in the work of other writers.*

The Newcomers (Di ny-gekumene) *appears in* Zukunft, *March 1929.*

David Ignatov

The Newcomers:
New York in the 1890s

Happy is the person who has no complaints against God's world. Even happier is the person who *enjoys* God's world. And one of these was named Berman.

Who can count the thousands and thousands of workers who get up each morning and crowd the streets, the tramways and the profusion of overhead and underground trains of New York City as the metropolis and its hulking buildings begin to bathe and swim in the early morning light?

Berman. He can count them. They add up to millions. And as soon as he utters the word "millions," he knows that he has counted them.

On this particular morning, as he made his way to his job, he was thinking: In my trade alone there are about a thousand people. If I could only succeed in organizing my trade, or even just that part of it that makes the frames for ladies' hats! If I could do that, I would then appeal immediately to the workers who make the wire itself: "Look, we, the frame-makers, are well organized; we can now demand that our shops stop using wire made in non-union shops. Organize, brothers and sisters, and you'll soon have an easier life! We'll help you in every way we can!"

The next step would be to organize the workers who make the silk that covers the frames. Soon the whole city would be organized. Then city after city, country after country. In this manner — in Berman's head — everyone in the world would be united, and everyone would live in peace and harmony. Every morning the sun was born anew — and along with it, Berman's faith in his dream.

And along with the morning sun, rising bright and free, Berman's spirits would soar as he envisaged the organization of city after city, country after country. All the inhabitants of the entire world would be happy and content — as would Berman himself, with his dark brown beard and his dark brown hair and his radiant expression. What a glorious place the world would be!

Thinking these thoughts, he felt as if he were soaring into mid-air, as if a wintry breeze had lifted him high up on its wings. "What a glorious place the world would be!" To whom had he said that, only yesterday? Zena? No. With Zena he had been talking about a monk with dark hair and a dark brown beard who walked in the snow in his bare feet. Today his purpose was to get everyone to come to the meeting. About Zena Frankel, the editor's daughter, he was remembering how she had come uninvited to his room, how she had sat down on the only chair in the room, how she had gotten up from the chair and then abruptly sat down again...

Berman felt the blood rush to his face. He remembered how, afterward, walking her home, he had raced down a hill and how she had said to him, her cheeks aflame, "I had no idea you were such a —" Such a what? He grinned, felt a warmth suffuse his heart.

He looked around, pleased. All around him an endless web of human beings, like a medley of colors that had just been tossed on a painter's canvas.

*

The city of New York is enormous, and its buildings are high and massive. They have been constructed in long, dense rows. Between one row of buildings and another flow countless long, straight streets. Anyone standing in a factory on an upper floor of a building that is higher than the buildings around it can look out the window and see an endless succession of roofs, then the long streets that have dug a way for themselves between the roofs like deep canals of gray asphalt.

The people and the wagons and the tramways that run up and down the streets look like floating dark stains. When winter comes and the snow lies on the asphalt like a congealed white foam, and the snow-covered roofs spread out across the city like rising waves, the uncovered places shine like pools of water in the wintry sun.

There are also in the high-walled City of New York large broad roofs from which rise tall, slender towers. These towers are ten stories high and are crowned by golden cupolas of various styles. The wind guards these cupolas and crowns and keeps them free of dust and snow. These towers therefore stand high and free and watch over the roofs of New York as though they were put there for that purpose.

*

"Good-morning, Freedberg!"

"Good-morning, Berman! Why so early?"

Berman smiled. "I think my clock fooled me today."

The foreman comes out of the wash room. "What's this I see? Berman here already? I don't believe it! What's going on? Anyway, *mazl-tov*! I hope it's a good omen."

He smiles and offers Berman his hand. Berman shakes hands with him, feeling a bit foolish, then has a startling thought: Before the day manages to get them in its grip, people act like decent human beings.

The shop is large, with many windows and a lot of long tables. Suddenly laughter fills the room. Four or five young women have come in together, accompanied by Bennie, the shop comedian. They are laughing at something he said. Then his voice rises above the others.

"No, Rosie, I swear the wind today has made your cheeks so pretty I can't take my eyes off you!"

The young women send another peal of laughter around the shop and Sadie says to Rosie:

"Don't believe a word he says! Yesterday he told me the exact same thing!"

Taking a step toward her, Bennie exclaims: "Sadie! If this place didn't have so many windows I'd put my arms around you right now and give you a big kiss!"

Here the girlish laughter reached its crescendo as they walked away. Half the length of the shop they turned into the ladies' washroom. As they did so, Bennie grabbed the elbow of the closest one.

"Frances, please find out for me which one of them loves me best!"

"Certainly, you poor child," Frances assured him, the curl of her lip belying her promise to be helpful.

*

As workers kept entering in groups, the shop filled up. People sat down around the tables. The cracking of the pliers and the hum of the freshly opened wire-coils grew louder. On the other side of the shop, where the women worked, came the forelady's order:

"Let's go, girls!"

Immediately following that command, one machine took off like a dog from its leash, and then the other machines woke up, one after the other. The racket filled the shop. For a little while the operators held on to the thought that outdoors it was a beautiful morning, but it very soon slipped out of their heads.

On the men's side, someone shouted: "Hey, Mendl, turn your head this way a little bit!"

Bennie immediately chimed in: "You call that a head?"

"What is it, then, Bennie?"

"A block of wood!"

"A block of wood? Then why does it have eyes?"

"You call those things eyes?"

"What are they, then?"

"Two little holes!"

"What does he need holes for?"

"For the water to come out."

"Stop it, Bennie! Look how he's blushing!"

Mendl had had enough. "I'm not blushing!" he shouted, furious. "Such a loafer he is! Always picking on me and barking like a mad dog!"

Bennie mimicked Mendl's rage. "Listen to that son-of-a-gun! A barrel of laughs!"

Through the whole exchange, Bennie kept twisting the wire faster and faster. Mendl, however, had lost his temper and his hands were trembling.

"You lousy bum, you! Lay off me, Bennie, you hear? Or I'll split your head open!"

"Did you call me a bum? Didn't your mother teach you any better?"

"You leave my mother out of this or I'll—"

A third operator joined the fray. "Our Bennie is not a dummy, but he's always starting up with somebody!"

For Bennie this was not even an interruption. "Why should I leave your mother out of this, Mendl? What kind of woman would give birth to —"

This was too much even for Mendl. He picked up a spool of wire and hurled it at Bennie. "You lousy stinkin' bum, you!"

More operators encouraged him. "Let him have it, Mendl! Shut his fresh mouth for him!"

But Bennie had ducked the wire and started laughing at the top of his voice. "Didn't your mother bring you into this world? Ain't that why you're so tall and skinny, like a telegraph pole?"

The foreman, who had been at the other end of the shop, now caught sight of the spool-throwing. He ran through the shop, shouting all the way:

"What kind of monkey business is this, you loafers — "

"Bennie's the one who started it, that bum, that tramp! Tell him to keep his filthy mouth shut!"

"Never mind his filthy mouth! You want to fight, call him outside. I don't care what you do to each other out there! But wire costs money. And look at your work! What is this — a new style of ladies' hats? Looks more like a baking-pan!"

Mendl had run out of retorts. The two red spots that were always on his cheeks now looked as if they had been painted on. The other workers froze as the foreman began yelling even louder. "Mendl, you'll have to go! We can't tolerate work like this in our shop. Look at your hooks — they're more like knots!" Mr. Berstein, the boss, had sized up the situation, however. He turned to Bennie.

"What are you doing with that wire? Don't you know better, cutting such big pieces for such a small hat?"

Now the foreman rushed over to Bennie and yanked the wire out of his hands. "This one never knows when to keep his big mouth shut!"

Bennie, still laughing — though not as boisterously — shouted back at the foreman. "I know your tricks! Give me back the wire and let me work!"

"Never mind! I've warned you twenty times about wasting wire, but talking to you is like talking to the wall!"

Bennie couldn't help himself. Bennie had to be Bennie, no matter what. "A wall, you say? I could pick you up by the ankles and make a stew out of you!"

"I'm telling you for the last time, Bennie! Don't ever open your big mouth to me again!"

Bennie started to say something, but Mr. Bernstein took the cigar out of his mouth and bellowed:

"Enough is enough!"

*

Bennie went back to his work. The other men smiled at his defeat, although they could feel the acrimony seeping into the shop. The foreman, meanwhile, appealed to Mr. Bernstein.

"I don't know what to do with them any more. No matter how many times I holler at them, it doesn't help. Look at this — two inches of good wire wasted!"

Mr. Bernstein took the cigar out of his mouth again, flicked off the long ash, and said:

"Next time you see anyone cutting wire like this, fire him on the spot."

As soon as he and the foreman left the floor, the comments coming from the workers were generously sprinkled with curses.

"A nasty worm!"

"May his hands drop off!"

"As soon as he notices that the boss is around, he starts picking on people!"

"Lately he's becoming impossible."

"Lately? All his life he's been a louse! But ever since he married that strike-breaker he keeps getting even worse!"

"Still, what do you make of our Bennie and his shtick?"

"You ought to be ashamed of yourself, Bennie. Feh!"

David Ignatov

Bennie tried to put a good face on the situation and, as usual, laughed out loud. "You turkeys — you've turned on me too? I'll squash you like a herring and throw you into a barrel!"

"Out of a turkey you're going to make a herring?"

"Listen! I'll tell you what. I bet you a quarter I can make a herring out of that turkey. Let Berman hold the money."

Berman, who had not uttered a word during the whole fracas, smiled and turned to Bennie: "You really have some money on you?"

Bennie put down his wire-cutter, fished in his pockets and came up with a quarter. "Here's the cash!" Bennie held out his hand.

"I really need this money..."

"What for?" Bennie asked, sensing something unusual, but not sure what it might be.

"We need to print leaflets about a mass meeting."

"What? The union again?"

"Yes!"

"Twenty-five cents each!" Bennie exclaimed, slapping the silver coin on the table. He liked the idea of the union so much that he shot out a few more pungent curses and began passing the hat among his fellow-workers.

"Moishke, give us a quarter!"

"What for?"

"Don't ask what for. Just give me a quarter."

"And then what?"

"Don't ask so many questions! Berman wants to put out a circular. It will state in big red letters that you and I can stretch our foreman out on the floor and spit on him."

"Now you're talking! That's worth a quarter! Here!"

"Hey, you long noodle!" Bennie said to Mendl. "Out with a quarter and we'll be friends again!"

"Who wants to be friends with you?" Mendl muttered.

"Come on, Shorty! If you give us a quarter, Berman will call a meeting and pass a resolution that you and I are allowed to catch our miserable foreman and stuff his ears with cotton. If you don't, I'll have to find another partner."

"I'll give you a quarter anyway," Mendl agreed. "Maybe if we have a union they'll even make a *mentsh* out of a *zhlub* like you..."

Eventually all the operators handed over their quarters, each quarter accompanied by a wisecrack. It made Berman happy. And to add to the magic of the moment, it happened that just at the moment when they handed Berman the collection, there was a sudden flash of light in the shop. A worker standing near Berman's window pointed his pliers toward the sky and cried out, his voice trembling: "Look at this! Look at this!"

All eyes turned toward the windows.

Across the rooftops, in the distance, where the city's highest towers stood, the white winter sun reached the upper windows in the dark crown of the tallest tower, and the massive dark crown began to reflect the boisterous white sun-columns. The high dark tower in the midst of all the towers seemed to be looking around at the others, as golden grids began to spread across the shops and the people inside them in varicolored triangles. In one triangle stood a man holding a hammer, in another a man holding a pliers, in another a block of wood, another a coil of wire, as if they had all been constructed with sharp, shadowy and bright pieces made of some mysterious light.

And in this natural phenomenon which had happened just at that moment, Berman saw a good sign, and he smiled an ambivalent smile, a smile of happiness about the sign, and a smile at his foolish eagerness to believe that it really *was* a sign.

AMONG THE INDIANS IN OKLAHOMA

Shea Tenenbaum

SHEA (Joshua) TENENBAUM (1910-1989) — *born in a village near Lublin, Poland; died in New York.*

At age 13 he learned the craft of typesetting and then moved to Belgium, where he worked in various printing houses in Antwerp and Brussels. His first published work was a poem, My Beloved *(Antwerp, 1926). In 1934 he emigrated to the United States and spent several years in the Denver Sanatorium to cure his tuberculosis.*

His short stories and essays were published in a wide variety of Yiddish journals. A novel, The Sphinx, *was published in the U.S. in 1938. From 1935 to 1948 he wrote articles and observations which were collected in 1949 and published in a volume of over 600 pages as* Harvest of My Field. *Among his other published works are* Children of the Sun, *1942;* Writers and Artists in New York, 1938 to 1968 *(*Essays, *1969);* A Lock of Hair from Maidenek, 1978. *It seems that none of his works have been translated into English till now.*

Among the Indians in Oklahoma (Tsvishn indianer) appears in Zukunft, *May-June 1977.*

Among the Indians in Oklahoma

It was during the winter of 1935. At that time I was living in the small town of Norman, Oklahoma. The owner of the house was Elvira Glenn, a woman in her nineties, who traced her proud family lineage all the way back to George Washington. Evenings she would sit by the fireplace like a matriarch and tell stories about our first President, stories that were told to her by her grandfather, the captain of a slave-ship, when she was a little girl.

I was then paying Mrs. Glenn the grandiose sum of five dollars a month for my modest room. It happened that she had known my older brother Jonah, who died when he was only 22. Jonah was a tailor and had come to America in 1912 with my father and my brother Moishe, who still lives in Oklahoma. He is now about 75. The walls of his home are papered with my father's Russian banknotes. The old stone-faced Czars and their stout wives look down upon my brother Moishe as he prepares his supper — a thick pea soup with chunks of meat.

The remarkable thing is that years ago my brother Jonah had also lived in that one room in Mrs. Glenn's house. It's as if he remained stuck somehow in the cracks in the walls; I could hear his voice during my sleepless nights. Mrs. Glenn told me that his brown-skinned sweetheart, Pocahontas, used to come there often, wearing her amber beads. After Jonah died, she took his tiny Psalter, as well as his watch with the six-pointed Star of David engraved on the case, and rode back to live with her tribe in a small town called Seminole.

I myself lived in Norman for about a year. Not a day passed that I didn't think about my brother Jonah and his mysterious Indian bride.

I often used to visit the Zeidmans in Oklahoma City, which was an oil-well center. Mr. and Mrs. Zeidman were educated people who loved Yiddish literature and who were proud of the Jewish people. Ossip Zeidman had come from the city of Yekaterinoslav in Russia. In his youth he was a Socialist

Revolutionary and had been exiled for several years in far-off Siberia. He escaped, however, and went to Central Europe, which was then a bee-hive of revolutionary activity. In Switzerland he met his "intended" and there they were married. Zeidman's stories about his experiences as a revolutionary were complete literary memoirs in themselves. All that was required was to write them down.

I always felt comfortable in the company of the Zeidmans. I was then about 24 and had already seen some of my stories published in the *Neie Folks-Tseitung* in Warsaw, which was sent to me in Norman. My friends the Zeidmans praised my literary talent warmly and introduced me to the few Jewish professors at the university in Norman. The Zeidmans had five young and beautiful daughters.

At the Zeidmans I met their friends the Tanzmans, whose family consisted of Mr. and Mrs. Tanzman and their only son Charlie. They lived in Seminole. One evening in late November, as I sat at my desk writing, the Tanzmans came to visit me. Shimshon Tanzman sat in his little Ford with an old Indian chief, who talked about the war with the White Man at the end of the 19th century as though it had happened only yesterday. Tanzman told me to put on a warm wool shirt and a heavy jacket and then he packed me, almost by force, into his rusty old Ford.

"Now we're going on a visit to Seminole!" he announced.

In Norman I had been occupied mainly with two things: During the day I worked as a "salesman" in my brother David's second-hand clothing store. I could not yet speak a word of English. I was feeling depressed and in a pessimistic mood. For six months I didn't make a single sale. But toward the end of the year, when I was already thinking about going back to New York, an old Indian gentleman with a fiery red beard came in. It happened that I was alone in the store.

Without any attempt at bargaining he bought a pair of heavy boots, a leather shirt and a fur hat. I wiped the dust off these items with an old Yiddish newspaper and wrapped all his purchases in one package. The Indian then thanked me in a very friendly way...

and promised to pay the following week. He never showed up again anywhere in that neighborhood.

My brother David told everyone in Norman about my renowned ability as a shrewd merchant, namely, that during the twelve months I worked in his store I made only one "sale" — I sold a pair of boots, a fine leather shirt and a fur hat, and I generously loaned the unknown but friendly Indian the money to pay for the "transaction"... So I was thinking to myself: who knows, maybe that noble Indian, who actually looked to me like a Jew from my Polish shtetl all dressed up for Purim — maybe he lives in Seminole where I was now going with the silent Shimshon Tanzman?

My other occupation was to write my autobiography, beginning way back with my mother's pregnancy. Then my childhood in the Polish woods, picking mushrooms and cherries. Then my ten years in Belgium. And then my first few months in New York in my parents' home, where I listened all night to the monotonous chiming of the wall clocks that my father, a watchmaker, had brought with him from Poland.

I wrote feverishly and soon there was a swollen manuscript of about a thousand pages. Before I left the house to make the trip to Seminole I tied these copybooks securely with a couple of old silk neckties I had brought from Antwerp and I hid the package in my metal trunk. But riding over the red roads of Oklahoma, I was almost in a panic lest thieves break into the house and steal my precious manuscript.

The truth was that I now deeply regretted having allowed myself to be squeezed into that little Ford. The uncomfortable trip through the darkness, cold and howling wind took years off my life. I felt my depression deepening. I seemed to be riding straight into the great unknown. Who knows what other misfortunes I would have to endure in Seminole? Up in the sky, there was a gathering of dark and monstrous clouds. The frozen stars hung in the heavens as though they were made of tallow. It all reminded me of my childhood in the Polish villages, where the dogs yowled at the stars all during the long dark nights...

We arrived at Seminole together with the dawn. Shimshon Tanzman led me to my bed in a sort of attic, where his son Charlie slept. Also sleeping there were three young Indians who worked in Tanzman's oil-fields. To combat the bitter cold, they had lit several open gas stoves. The sour smell of the gas kept choking me and I didn't get to sleep at all. It became clear to me that I had acted like a weakling when I left my warm, quiet room in Norman.

In Seminole I was the loneliest person in the world. Mrs. Tanzman — Soreh-Minke — looked like a big duck that had been fattened for Pesach. She was, however, a delight to my Jewish ears. Whatever she said was pure Jewish folklore, polished by generations of use. She reminded me of my mother. For me and for the entire household she had prepared a delicious meal. Wine bottles glittered on the table. You could smell the roasting meat throughout the whole house.

But I really wasn't very hungry. And Soreh-Minke soon began sharing her troubles with me. It seems that Charlie, her only son, who was such a desirable match for the bright and good-looking daughters of the local wealthy Jewish families, was actually in love with an Indian woman who was not even particularly pretty. And it wasn't long afterward that I saw Charlie walking arm-in-arm with his Indian sweetheart in the miniature city park. She was not very young and not very pretty, according to our conception of feminine beauty. Her diminutive face was yellow and pock-marked, making her look like an old woman. When she laughed, it sounded to me as though she were crying. From her small brown eyes peered an ancient sorrow, the sorrow of her old, weary and aggrieved people, which had once owned an enormous territory — all of America — with its fields, forests and rivers, over which roamed the hunch-backed buffaloes that let themselves be caught to serve as generous meals for the Indian tribes.

One day, as I studied her face, I suddenly noticed certain Jewish features of ancient days, when King David ruled the Jewish country. She sang sad songs filled with a kind of Jewish nostalgia. But she also smoked cigarette after cigarette and drank glassfuls of whiskey like water. Charlie must have been attracted to her in the same way a restless butterfly is drawn to the wick of a burning candle.

I did a lot of walking around in the poor section of town where the Indians and the Black people lived together as neighbors. I walked over fields coated with ice. Underfoot the ice crackled like pieces of shattered glass that might have fallen out the windows of an ancient palace. Snow and icicles hung from the branches of trees like miraculous gems.

The people in Seminole lived in abandoned automobiles, in broken-down wagons, in huts no larger than kennels, fastened together with strips of rusty metal and rotting boards. Looking at this terrible poverty I thought to myself: God gave humans such a glorious wealth of sunny landscapes shining by day with the gold of the sun and at night with the reflection of the moon, and this insane species deforms everything with the ugliness of hate, envy, lust and brutality. It is Man who has sullied and bloodied God's handiwork with his wars, destructiveness and devastation.

There were many saloons here, gambling houses, bawdy houses. Every Thursday afternoon the Indians would come here from surrounding villages, from their "reservations," in order to get their "remuneration" from the oil companies for "permission" to pump the flowing gold from the bowels of the primeval earth.

For me, the Polish Jew, it was exciting to observe the Indian men and women, with their multi-colored shawls and carpets over their broad shoulders. The men, with their crisp new dollar bills, headed mostly to the gambling houses. The women, with their children ensconced in the baskets over their shoulders, went "shopping" in the stores for household necessities. To me they all looked like actors in some exotic production who were leaving the stage momentarily and flooding the streets, still wearing their grotesque makeup and their colorful costumes.

In the little room that I now inhabited I sometimes wept out of sheer loneliness, but I also discovered there a small cabinet of Hebrew and Yiddish books. It was like finding a treasure: several thick volumes of Mordecai Spector's *House Friend,* a collection I had read while I was still back in my Polish shtetl. Thanks to the *House Friend,* at age 14 I had already become familiar with the classical writers of world literature — Knut Hamsen, Bjornsterne Bjornson, Gerhart Hauptmann, Hermann Sudermann, and also the Russians — Tolstoy, Dostoevsky, Chekhov, Gorki. I also found in that cabinet a story about a dybbuk. I found a copy of *Sefer Josifun*, written in Old Yiddish, which had once stirred my imagination. There were other rare Yiddish journals dating back to pre-World War I, magnificent publications about literature and art.

Seminole, meanwhile, had been attacked by a storm of red dust. It made me think of the biblical city of Sodom, where such a hot volcanic dust must have fallen, destroying houses, burning up the gardens, incinerating the people, while Lot's famous wife stared sadly at scenes of her childhood. Then it turned her into a pillar of salt, a piece of sculpture fashioned by God Himself. Like Lot's wife, I too thought of my youth in the villages of Poland.

And as the red dust attacked me, I saw two sensational prostitutes arriving in the shtetl. They laughed a lot and howled with the wind. They paraded through the dismal old streets. People gawked at them through the dust-covered windows. Drunks followed their long shadows. For no particular reason I suspected one of them as being my brother Jonah's bride, his Indian sweetheart Pocahontas. She too studied me in a peculiar way, much as a dog sniffing a stranger, as I broke into a cold sweat.

Meanwhile, in my utter loneliness, a homeless dog attached itself to me, became my mute friend. I bought a roast chicken and devoured it, tossing the dog the bones with the skin and bits of feather stuck to them. The dog was ravenous; apparently he had been "fasting" for a long time. Suddenly, as he chomped on the bones, he fastened his eyes on me so intently that I could read his mind: What kind of creature is this who has nothing better to do than sit there and throw me his chicken's sweet-tasting bones? From that moment on, the animal never left my side during all the time I spent in Seminole...

The doctor in Seminole was a Jew from Kiev. He had first settled with his parents in Tulsa, capital of Oklahoma, in 1904. He owned an expensive home and a fine library, including a large collection of Russian books, as well as several volumes of Peretz, whom he considered a better writer than Sholem Aleichem. The masses of Jews, he explained to me, love Sholem Aleichem's work because he thought their thoughts and chattered in their language. But Peretz was the aristocrat. In order to evaluate Peretz's genius one must be on a higher spiritual plane. Dr. Boruchowitz even quoted Peretz to his patients. He knew no other Yiddish writers, nor did he want to know them. He was satisfied with Peretz alone.

Remarkable as it may sound, this doctor performed complicated and risky operations on patients in the city hospital. He had even operated on my brother Jonah for a stomach ailment. In me he aroused not only curiosity and wonderment, but also fear. By the light of a lamp he turned the yellowing pages of a Yiddish book by Peretz. He sipped drops of phosphorus-colored wine from a crystal goblet. The cuff of his shirt glowed a flaming red, like the bloody eye of an Aztec god during human sacrifices. But I always imagined spots of my brother Jonah's blood on his hands. It was not wine he was drinking but my brother's blood. Strange thoughts filled my head. Supposedly he had attempted to cut out a dangerous cancer from my brother's insides, but who knows what the real truth was — maybe he had actually killed him instead...

After the operation Jonah lived only a week. My older brother Moishe, who visited him in the hospital the day before he died, talked "at" him for a long time before Jonah finally said:

"Moishe, stop talking already. Don't bother me now. Can't you see I'm close to the end?"

The next day he died. When I was in Oklahoma City, Moishe and I visited his grave. A small gravestone — as for a child — lay there on the ground. On it perched a bird, sharpening his beak on the gravestone, as if it had just finished a hearty meal.

One week later I left Seminole, but not before the Tanzmans arranged a "farewell" evening for me. Present was also Dr. Boruchowitz. Soreh-Minke Tanzman placed a small silver cup on the table and poured a bit of sweet wine into it from a large golden cup, as she said to me:

"You see this little cup? It's about a hundred years old. When my father married my mother, my grandfather gave them this cup and a few other rare things."

I couldn't help touching that cup, whose silver had already darkened. I wanted to kiss it, to taste those beautiful old days. As I sipped the wine I felt I was actually kissing those heroic generations of Jews in ancient Poland.

Shimshon Tanzman then brought out a pair of slender candlesticks and stood them on the white tablecloth. The candlesticks had been made in Warsaw. I could read the name of the manufacturer engraved on the silver: Shenkman. They were the proverbial 120 years old and had once stood on the table of Tanzman's parents.

People were offering toasts in honor of the "young writer" (me). But Dr. Boruchowitz could not stop lauding my dead brother Jonah.

I tried to express my gratitude to the Tanzmans for their hospitality. Then I said goodbye to everyone and returned to my little room "because I was so sleepy," but actually I was wide awake. It was only a few minutes after twelve. Through a back door I slipped out into God's glorious outdoors.

The dust storm was still active, painting the roofs of the houses the color of red honey. Like a rust stain, the moon hung in the low-lying sky. From the saloons came the strains of *Besame Mucho* and other popular melodies. I peered into the windows of the taverns and wine-cellars. I convinced myself that before I left this place at dawn I would somehow find my brother Jonah's Indian bride, with her rust-colored hair, as Mrs. Glenn and the doctor had described her to me. I floated through the narrow streets like a ghost. I searched among the heavily perfumed women. I wandered through the dim, noisy drinking places like a moonstruck somnambulist. Among the prostitutes I must have created the impression that I was looking for a young beauty that I could take into a room in one of the nearby hotels.

I was looking for my brother's Indian bride, but who do you think came forward to greet me? The lonely, loyal dog with whom I had shared my supper of roast chicken. His eyes were wide with surprise. They seemed to be saying: "What's wrong with your memory? Don't you recognize me?" Somehow he made me feel guilty...

Shea Tenenbaum

In the reflection of the moon the red dust seemed to have covered the entire town of Seminole with a layer of cooled lava. Only
up high, in the sky, could I see the rusty moon striding across the
dust clouds as if they were the surviving stairs of a burning palace.
But as I looked closer at the quiet moon, I could see the sad face
of Pocahontas, my brother Jonah's Indian bride...

MABEL'S SECRET

Shimshon Apter

SHIMSHON APTER (1907-1986) — *born in Poland; died in New York.*

After completing his traditional Jewish education, Apter went to Warsaw to prepare himself to teach in Jewish schools. His first poem, Our Hope, *and a short story were published in 1928. Two years later he emigrated to Canada, where he wrote several short stories and essays for the Toronto Yiddish press. In 1936 a collection of his stories was published in Toronto. That same year he moved to New York, where he attended the Jewish Teachers Seminary.*

In 1946 he received a literary award from the Yiddisher Kultur Farband (Yiddish Cultural Association). In 1977 he received the Congress for Jewish Culture award for his novel The Preisingers, *which was translated into English by Joseph Singer and published by A. S. Barnes in 1980. Among his other published works are:* The Roman Ghetto, a historical account of Jewish life in the 16th century *(later translated into Hebrew);* In A New World, *a novel about the first Jews to settle in America (1956); a collection of short stories (1973); and* The Marrano Family da Silva, *a novel (1981).*

Mabel's Secret (Maybls sod) *apears in* Zukunft, *July-August, 1976.*

Mabel's Secret

That Friday afternoon the heat in the Eastern Frocks building became absolutely unbearable. The motors drove the sewing-machine cylinders with a weary, monotonous drone, spreading a foul odor of oil and grease. The workers — Italians, Greeks, Jews, Puerto Ricans, African-Americans, men and women — sat with their heads buried in the machines, sweat dripping from their flushed faces.

"A real sweatshop," Pearl said to Mabel, her neighbor. She wiped the perspiration from her face and brushed back her damp, dark-blonde hair that was stuck to her forehead.

Mabel did not respond. Mabel was one of the quiet ones. In order for her to speak up, there needed to be some very important matters in her head. She sat at the machine, breathing with great difficulty. In her middle years she had become so overweight that she looked almost blown up. Her feet lay heavily on the pedals of the Singer machine without moving. Were her thirty years at this machine coming to an unhappy end, she wondered. Her feverish cheeks hung down over her flabby neck. The narrow slits of her eyes were narrower now because of the excessive heat, so that her eyes were barely visible. Her small, turned up nose, almost flat against her face, was whiter than usual.

"Aren't you feeling well, Mabel?" Pearl asked. Her voice was full of concern.

Mabel grimaced. Her mouth opened, as if she could not get enough air to speak.

"Michael! Get a glass of water, quick!" Pearl called out to the man at the machine on the other side of her. He raised his head, sized up the situation at once, ran to the water cooler and hurried back with the water. Mabel wiped her face with a handkerchief, took a little sip of the cold water and breathed deeply. Her expression relaxed a little.

Michael stood there for a moment, looking out the half-raised windows. Over the high buildings across the street hung a sky full of thick clouds, as though the sunlight had gotten lost somewhere between the buildings.

"It's going to rain again," he grumbled. "Just when I've got to make that long bus-trip to the Catskills. My wife and baby are there." He turned off the lamp over his machine, waved his hand at his neighbors and headed for the cloakroom to change his clothes.

Mabel watched him leave. Then she lowered her eyes to her machine, but she no longer saw the wine-colored dress that lay there. Before her was a panorama of green fields, lush hillsides of pine and maple trees. In the town of Roscoe, on one of the Catskill mountainsides, where she was born, lived her two brothers and their families. Joel, the oldest, still lived on the chicken farm that her father Isaac Resnick had left for his sons when he disowned her.

Mabel had never told anyone in the shop about this, because then she would have had to reveal why her father had done it. Even now, after all these years, it was hard for her to talk about it, and anyway, it was too late.

Her other brother had put up a dam across the gushing stream on the farm and built a small hotel with a kosher kitchen. Summertime the place was filled with pious Orthodox Jews. Mabel had never even seen the place, but she had heard about it from others.

Years ago, when her father's close friend Sam used to go up there for weekends, she would walk over to Sixth Avenue on her lunch hour. Sam worked in the Felstone Building in a shop where they made ladies' hats. She tried to time it so she would "accidentally" bump into him as he was going out to lunch. He would tell her about all her brothers' accomplishments and about their families. She assumed an air of indifference, but inside, her heart ached with such a longing to see them that she had to put herself to sleep that night with whiskey.

But Sam Blocker too had grown old and died, and the only news she ever got about her brothers now came from stories in the afternoon papers where they advertised the Roscoe Kosher Hotel. In the fall, before the High Holidays, the ads would have a picture of a cantor with a little prayer-shawl on his shoulders and a high silk hat on his head. But even that was now so far-removed from her life that it was almost completely foreign to her. All that was left was a curiosity about what was happening to her brothers, and a longing to see the fields and woods where she grew up.

How could it have happened that even her kind, gentle and generous father had let himself be persuaded by his sons to write her out of his will? Not that she had any complaints. Right from the start she never blamed anyone but herself.

Ordinarily her father Isaac would never have chosen to settle in the Catskill Mountains. He would have been content to spend the rest of his days on Gorick Street in the East Side. But then he took sick. From the working conditions in the shop, the doctor said. His lungs were accustomed to the good, fresh air of his native Polish village. But here in New York he had to carry the head of his Singer machine every morning and evening on his back, which was not as strong as it used to be. There was hardly any air at all in the shop, and the tuberculosis began to dry him out. He did not want to be the first to be buried in the empty space that his fellow townsmen from the Old Country had bought in the Mount Moriah Cemetery. So one day he rode up to the Catskills and bought an abandoned farm in Roscoe.

By that time Mabel no longer remembered her mother. Later, when she was already a tall young lady with a tiny nose squashed into her face, the family used to sit around the long wooden table in the kitchen and talk about the "olden days." They laughed and they cried and always it ended with the story about Mabel.

It had been a long, hard winter. The snow piled up higher than the windows. One day her mother began to feel the birth-pangs. Isaac sent the two boys out of the room. Mrs. Callahan, the Irish midwife who lived nearby, came rushing over. But it was too late. Mabel's mother had died after she heard her baby's first cry...

Mabel brought no happiness into her father's house. Later, something about her features became troublesome. Her older brother Joel "explained" jokingly why his mother had given birth to a freak. She had always wanted to be a real farmer, so one of the neighbors had been teaching her how to raise pigs. But she had looked at the pigs too long...

Isaac did not think that was funny. He merely looked at his first-born son with a forlorn little smile. But Mabel's brothers laughed so hard they rolled on the floor, as though they were getting even with their father for holding Mabel on his lap or bouncing her on his knee. He even made little dresses for her on his old sewing-machine and fussed with her appearance more than he did with his sons'.

Mabel recalls that once, when her brothers were teasing her, she ran out of the house in tears and hid in the barn. To comfort herself, she had snuggled up to a little calf that lay on the ground a little distance away from its mother. She had patted the calf and then the calf had licked her face with its rough tongue. Later that evening, after searching for her all over, they had found Mabel asleep in the barn next to the calf. That same evening Isaac took his sons aside and warned them never to ridicule their sister again. Mabel recalls that they took their father's stern words seriously, but that didn't stop other pests from doing it. The school term had just begun. Mabel was wearing a brand new dress. Her father harnessed up his wagon and they rode over to Roscoe, where he dropped her off at the public school.

Among the boys in her class — most of them with blond hair of various shades — there was one who stood out because he was so different. His skin was dark and his hair was curly. Mabel already knew him. His name was Abner. Abner Hays. His mother, Bess, worked in the big Livingstone Manor Hotel. During the winter months, when things were slow at the hotel, she sometimes came over to Isaac's to clean his house, and often she brought Abner along.

One day he and Mabel went skating on their frozen stream. Her older brother Joel saw them from across a field and came running over. He snatched Mabel up in his arms and smacked her backside. She screamed and kicked her feet and scratched at his face, but he carried her into the house, where she crawled into a corner and cried for a long time. The worst part of it was that he had warned Abner never to come to their house again. Later Joel explained to his father that he had done it because the ice was too thin and the children could have fallen into the water and drowned. But Abner never came to their house with his mother again.

In school the other boys picked on Abner all the time, inventing new ways to trip him and make him fall and scatter all his books. Mabel would help him pick them up and then she would walk with him. When the teacher found out about this she made the boys stop it, but she also told Mabel and Abner to sit in the back of the room.

It didn't end there. A few days later, as they were leaving the building, the boys tore Mabel's notebook out of her hands and started tossing it back and forth to each other. When she finally retrieved it, it was all torn and dirty. Abner watched with doleful eyes as this was going on, trying to think of a way to help her. He moved toward her but the boys started to surround him. Mabel grabbed his hand and they ran all the way to Bakersville Road, where she lived. The boys stood there screaming after her:

"Piggy-face! Nigger-lover! Piggy-face! Nigger-lover!"

Mabel felt so hurt and humiliated that not until she was halfway up the hill did she realize that Abner was right behind her. She stopped and smiled at him. He smiled back. Later, at home, she stood before the mirror for a long time, studying her face. Was it true what the boys were calling her? She had practically no eyebrows; only a few flat brown hairs over her squinting, almond-shaped eyes. She sighed a deep sigh and felt a sudden stab in her chest. She shut her eyes and saw Abner smiling at her, his sad eyes filled with fear and anxiety.

Mabel opened her eyes. The motors on all the machines had grown silent. The operators and the pressers were hurrying to the cloakrooms to change their clothes. The day's work was over. She tried to stand up, but felt a sticking pain in her chest. Her head spun. Pearl was at her side immediately.

"You're not feeling any better, Mabel?"

Mabel turned her head to look at her neighbor. The whole shop turned with her — the dresses on the racks, the befogged windows, the lights on the ceiling. She put her arms down on the machine and rested her head on them.

"Come, Mabel, I'll take you home."

Bennie, another operator nearby, offered his opinion. "She should rest all week-end. Monday she'll be able to run her *katerinka* again."

Pearl bent over and, with her fingers, took a little water out of the glass that stood on the machine. She sprinkled a few drops on Mabel's face and wiped off the perspiration with a napkin. Mabel took a deep breath. A little color came back into her face.

"You won't be able to get home alone today, Mabel. Where do you live?"

Mabel hesitated. For all the years she had been working with these people, she had never told them anything about herself or about her husband or where they lived. She could not start now.

"Thank you, Pearl. I'm sure I'll be all right." She stood up — and almost fell over. Pearl helped her sit down again.

"I live in Harlem, Pearl. Do you really want to take me home?"

Pearl stood there confused a moment, saying nothing. She exchanged a look with Bernie, then said:

"Of course I do. We'll take a taxi."

"I didn't know there were any white people still living in Harlem," Bernie said. And then, talking to himself, he said, "I sure don't envy her..."

Pearl dug her heel into his foot. The damn fool never *could* keep his mouth shut.

Mabel looked up at him with a feeble little smile. Pearl helped her change her clothes. Joe, the janitor, was already turning off the lights. Mabel took a last look at the rows of machines standing in the shadows, the chairs now resting on them upside down with their legs sticking up in the air. She smiled. The sight always struck her funny. Would she ever see it again?

They got into the taxicab. Pearl gave the driver the address. He turned around, an indignant look on his face.

"I don't go that far, Miss! I work in center city!"

"This woman is very sick," Pearl pleaded.

"Get an ambulance! I can't afford to have my cab vandalized!" But he put the car in gear and they started moving.

Mabel sighed and leaned her head back on the soft seat-back. Now everyone in the shop would know that she lives in Harlem with a Black man. Not that she was ashamed of that, but things would get so damn uncomfortable. And none of them could ever know the hurt she'd had to endure all these years.

*

After that incident at the Roscoe public school when she had come to Abner Hays' defense, he had walked her home every day on Beaverkill Road. Sometimes they wandered deeper into the woods. Abner had grown up tall and slender and a good student His skin was a light brown, his eyes always smiling but often perplexed. He told her stories about Abraham Lincoln and about his own grandfather who was a slave in Georgia.

One day Mabel's brother Joel happened to come upon them in the woods. They were both lying in the tall grass, looking up at the blue sky. Abner was tickling her face with a little bunch of black-eyed Susans. Mabel had bitten into the yellow edges and was squealing delightedly. Joel, driving his pick-up truck to Livingstone Manor with a load of eggs, had recognized his sister's laugh. He parked the truck on the road and crept over to them in the grass. Mabel still remembers how terror-stricken she felt when he came into view. She had jumped up and started running, trying to button her blouse at the same time, but Joel caught up with her. This time he didn't slap her bottom. He punched her on the breast, picked her up bodily, carried her up to the road and tossed her into the back of the truck like a trussed-up calf. As he drove away he screamed at Abner:

"Stay the hell away from her! If I ever catch you around here again, one of us is going to end up dead!"

*

After that tempestuous incident her family held a long, secret meeting and didn't let her out of the house. Days later her father informed her that he was moving back to "the city" and that she was coming with him. In New York they had the best doctors in the world, they would find a cure for his condition. Joel got the truck ready for the long trip and they drove back to the East Side.

They parked on Gorick Street near the home of Isaac's friend Sam, who was now a widower. His grown children lived out on Long Island, so there were now plenty of empty rooms in his house. The windows looked out on a little square where children played all day on the swings and in the sand-boxes. The park even boasted a few trees; they looked tired and scrawny, but still, they were trees. Sick trees, like her father. The city was foreign to her. The air stank, choked her with its smells of rotting food, gasoline and sooty smoke.

One morning Sam Blocker asked her to take a subway ride with him. He was going to visit friends at Eastern Fashion Frocks, where he used to work. In fact, he knew Jacob Rich, the old boss there, very well. He could introduce Mabel to him. Who knows, maybe something would come of it. After all, her father had taught her a long time ago how to sew on one of those new machines...

It happened such a long time ago. Why did it seem like only yesterday?

*

"It's hard to believe, Pearl, but I've been working in this place for thirty years..."

"I believe you, Mabel. Life is like a dream. Some people have good dreams. Some don't. But we have to go on living. What choice do we have anyway?"

Mabel nodded her head, and a cold sweat covered her face. Pearl wiped the perspiration off her forehead and tried to fan some air toward her.

*

The taxi stopped in front of a building on Lenox Avenue. Nearby, little Black girls and boys were playfully jostling each other. When the taxi pulled up they all ran to the curb and surrounded it, poking their heads into the open windows and wondering what the sudden appearance of these white folks portended.

"Scram!" Mabel scolded them. "Mr. Hays will come down soon and beat you!" The effort was too much for her. Her head fell back. The driver blew his horn a few times and the youngsters re-treated. A few older boys came running and started pounding on the yellow metal with their fists, laughing uproariously.

From a dark corridor came a tall Black man. He looked strong, but his shoulders were already a little bent. The dark curly hair on his head was sprinkled with gray flakes. His long arms hung out of his brightly colored shirt. The gang of kids melted away.

"Mabel, honey, I heard your voice from inside. You scared me to death. I warned you this morning not to go to work today in this heat..."

He opened the door and, with Pearl's help, got Mabel out of the taxi. Pearl paid the driver and asked him to wait, but he quickly slammed the door shut and fled like the wind.

They helped Mabel into the house and into her bedroom. She collapsed onto the bed, wheezing. The air in the room was hot, but at least it was being moved around by an electric fan in the lower part of the window. On a chair hung a gray jacket with the silver buttons of a U.S. mail-carrier. On the dresser near the mirror stood photographs of Mabel's family: her father, his face wan, his cheeks deeply sunken. On his chin, a short beard. On his head, a yarmulke. On one side of him, his two sons, one of them on the day of his bar-mitzva, wearing a little *tallis* on his shoulders. On the other side, hugging her father, Mabel — a small, fat little girl with long straight hair down to her shoulders. In a corner of the room, on a little table, an empty whiskey bottle and an unwashed glass.

Mabel opened her eyes. "Abner," she called softly, "please go down and find her a taxi. This is Pearl, my best friend in the shop."

"Mabel has told me so much about you, Miss Pearl. I feel as if I've known you a long time."

Pearl bent down over the bed. "Mabel, I'll see you Monday at work. You'll be all better..."

Mabel looked up at her and tried to smile, but her crooked lips said clearly: I don't expect to be back at work so soon, if ever. Pearl said goodbye and left, with Abner behind her. At the door, he stopped, turned around and looked at Mabel, his mournful eyes making his thin face look even more haggard.

"I'm going to call Dr. Saunders! Maybe you should be in the hospital. He'll have to call an ambulance —"

"No, no! Please, Abner! I don't want to die in the hospital. And I can't stay here. Call my brothers. Let them come and take me home. I want to go home, Abner..."

He shook his head sadly and followed Pearl out to the street.

*

Mabel shut her eyes, tried to sleep. Instead, her mind went back to the October evening exactly one year after they left the farm. It was after a hard day's work and she was very tired. A cool breeze came up out of the Hudson River. The sun was dropping quickly toward the horizon, setting the rooftops on fire. Her heart was filled with longing for the hills, the fields, the woods that would now be aflame with autumn reds and golds. As she came closer to the house on Gorick Street she saw him. Abner, standing nervously near the entrance, leaning on the metal railing along the steps and waiting with a stubborn patience.

She had shuddered with some kind of strange mixture of joy and fear, because through Abner she had had so much heartache and was forced to leave her home, and who knows what other kinds of trouble her closeness with him might bring her, and him as well. She knew that his presence here had to do with her. He too could no longer remain at home with his mother. She could see that in the helpless little smile around his big, quivering eyes. During the year she had not seen him he had grown taller. On his upper lip were a few curly hairs. From the sleeves of his tan coat, which he had outgrown, stuck two longish hands on which the veins were showing, as if he had been doing hard physical labor here in the city. He noticed her staring at his hands and stuck them into his coat pockets. She knew that he had always been a good student and that he had wanted very much to get some sort of managerial position in the Post Office or at least a job as a mail-carrier.

Very slowly she walked over to him. She wanted to ask him: Did he ever come with his mother to the farm? Did he ever see her brother at the hotel? But then she caught a glimpse of her father looking out the window of the house. She changed directions and hurried into the dim hallway. From the other side of the door she called out to Abner:

"Tomorrow evening come to the Leffert Building on Broadway. I work there..."

When she came into the house, her father said nothing unusual. But when he served the meal he had prepared for her, he announced that the time had come to go home. The doctors here in the city could not help him at all. And Sam Blocker was giving up his house. He was planning to get married again. And the woman owned her own home in the Bronx.

Shortly afterward, Mabel's father took sick. He could see she had no intention of moving back "to the country." How could she have done such a cruel thing to him, Mabel asked herself. After Abner moved to the city she began coming home later and later. Her father was too sick now to prepare a meal even for himself, let alone for her. He knew she was with Abner. He could not fall asleep until she came home. Time and again he talked to her about this. Sometimes he could not restrain his tears.

"You'll be lonely and miserable the rest of your life. You won't be welcome in our family — or in his —"

His gentle scoldings tore at her heart. She wanted to stuff up her ears. She locked herself in her bedroom and wept. What if her father were right? But she couldn't help herself. Often she fell asleep in her street clothes. Until finally one day she came home to find no one there. Her father had left without even saying goodbye.

Not too long afterward he died. From a heart attack, they told her, not tuberculosis. But it was Sam Blocker who told her about it. Her brothers didn't even let her know about the funeral. Sam hinted that although she was no longer considered part of the family, and her father had left the farm to his sons, she could come home — without Abner — and live there, any time she wished.

*

Again, as she had earlier at work, she felt a burning sensation in her chest. She had difficulty breathing. She tried to sit up, but her head spun around and she fell back helplessly. Her body felt so leaden that she imagined she was tied to the bed with ropes.

The frantic tooting of a horn awakened her. She felt a searing heat all over her body. With a great effort she opened her eyes. Several faces hovered over her. She shivered. A pale, round face. Blond mustache. Her brother Joel. So many years she hadn't seen him. She shut her eyes for a moment. No, it wasn't Joel, it was Dr. Saunders, a stethoscope hanging out of his ears and a stiff smile frozen on his thin lips.

"Abner!" she called. "Where's Joel?"

Joel appeared again. Not as clear as before. His rough hands were caressing her cheeks, her forehead.

"Joel! You've come to take me home? I want to go home and see Papa," she babbled.

She smiled, and closed her eyes...

JOE THE TAILOR
Isaac Raboy

ISAAC RABOY (1882-1944) — born in Kamenetz-Podolsk in the Ukraine; died in Los Angeles.

Raboy's father, a bookkeeper for a lessor of state forests, moved the family to Rishkan in Bessarabia, where he made a living as a lessee of the royal mail. Soon after his bar-mitzva, Isaac joined a group of maskilim (Jewish "modernists") in Rishkan and began studying Russian language and literature. (The group also set up a modern Yiddish school.) Several stories he submitted to Russian newspapers were rejected.

In 1904 Isaac emigrated to the U.S., where he worked as a hatmaker. At this time he wrote much and published little, and even thought of suicide. Two of his friends, Joel Entin and David Pinski, kept encouraging him to continue writing, and in 1906 the newspaper Wahrheit *published his first story. By mistake they spelled his name "Rubin" instead of Raboy! Around this time he connected up with the literary group* Di Yunge, *which also included David Ignatov and Meir Blinkin, and published his story* Di royte blum (The Red Flower) *in their journal.*

In 1908, fed up with the city and the shop, he enrolled in the Baron de Hirsch Farm School in Woodbine, New Jersey. Upon graduation he got a job as a farm hand in North Dakota, but after two years there he returned to New York and persuaded his father to buy a farm in Connecticut. This venture failed.

The Yiddish literary critic Sh. Niger said: "Raboy wrote prose poems about the prairie, the sun, the rain; about longing, joy, and sorrow. His novels are pieces of congealed lyricism."

Joe the Tailor *(untitled) appears in the magazine* Shriftn, *third collection, 1914.* Among us in America (Bah undz in amerike) *appears in* Yiddish America, *1929.*

Joe the Tailor

No one knew where Joe had come from or how old he was. He moved into a place on Ninth Street and opened a Ladies' Tailor Shop. He did all the work himself, at the machine and with the needle. With his own long, slender fingers he added a wealth of energy and craftsmanship to the cloth. Then he draped it lovingly in the show-window of his "place of business."

Step by step he built up a clientele of older matrons and younger single women. One of them ordered a dress made, then told her friends about it. Soon Joe had more orders than he could handle, no matter how many hours he worked. But he did not wish to add another tailor, so he compromised. He bought another Singer machine and hired a young seamstress to run it. Then he had to buy a third one, and later a fourth. Finally he had to move into another place with two show-windows.

The more work his helpers did, the less work he had to do. Soon he was standing around his shop with a tape-measure around his neck. Whenever a customer came in, he bowed low and was very gracious and engaged her in polite conversation. After he learned what she wanted, he would describe the finished dress to her so there would be no misunderstanding.

"It will be just long enough to show only the tips of your shoes. In back and on both sides, small pleats. With each group of pleats, three buttons. In front, over the right knee, a pleat shaped like a flower. Naturally, with a button. And down the left leg, a narrow split..."

His descriptions were so vivid that the lady could hardly wait for her new dress to be finished. Cost became secondary.

Business went from good to better until one day he could no longer do all the work himself. He was forced to hire an assistant tailor to take measurements and to check the garment when the customer came in for the first fitting.

Among his helpers on the machines was a red-haired young woman with a slim, lithesome figure. All day long a gentle smile lit up her milky-white face. She did her work with enthusiasm. Even the sound of her name was soft and gentle.

One afternoon Joe had a confidential conversation with her, but not so confidential that the other operators could not hear.

"Esther, I need someone to assist me. I think you could do it. You won't have to work at the machine any longer. Let me see how you would take the measurements for a dress. Pretend I'm the customer."

Esther's face reddened as she stood up from her machine. The other women exchanged knowing looks.

So that became the new system. Whenever a customer came into the shop, Joe spoke to her first to see what kind of dress she had in mind. Then he turned her over to his assistant, who did the rest.

In the evening, when the other women left, Esther would stay behind to go over the day's problems with Joe. In recognition of this duty, she was permitted to come in an hour later in the morning. During the day, when all the machines were running noisily at the same time, and if there were no customers in the shop, Esther and Joe were usually engaged in earnest conversation.

*

On the other side of the ocean, in Kolomeya, Joe has a wife and two children. His wife lives with her father, Shimon the Bathhouse Keeper. She also lives in hope, and writes letters to America and waits desperately for the letter she will get any day now from her Yudel. After a long time of running back and forth to and from the post office, and crying her eyes out, she finally receives a letter. Then she runs home with the letter and skips into her father's room and starts dancing around and kissing the children for joy.

She tosses the shawl from her narrow shoulders as if she never wanted to see it again, and she starts looking for a seat where she can get comfortable and read the letter. She sits the children down on the table. Her father, Shimon the Bathhouse Keeper, puts on his spectacles and sits down on the long bench next to the table. And she sits down beside him.

But after every letter her heart is more empty than it was before, because there is really nothing much in the letter to read. Her

Yudel writes to her very briefly; sometimes he even forgets to ask about the children. If only her mother were still living now... What can she tell her father — a man who puts on his spectacles but who cannot even read. And when she finishes reading the letter and remains sitting there helplessly, he repeats the whole letter word for word as if he enjoyed pouring salt on her wounds. "Not a bad little letter," he says, as if he cannot even read the pain in her eyes.

Later he will turn to his daughter and say:

"Why are you walking around the house like a shadow?"

"What?" Hannah says, and as if she were looking for something, she begins running around the big house from room to room.

"You look as if you can't find a place for yourself, Hannah."

And Hannah feels that if her father would now give her a beating, as he used to do when she was a little girl, she would hurt as much as she does now from his fatuous words. But she tries to get hold of herself.

"All morning I've been looking for the pen and ink. What happened to it?"

"I put it away where the children can't reach it. They might drink the ink, God forbid, or hurt themselves with the point of the pen."

"So you do know where it is, Papa. Please. I want to answer Yudel's letter."

"You can save the postage. Hinka, Motel the Tailor's daughter, is leaving today for America. You can give her the letter to take with her."

"I'd rather mail it. She might lose it in the ocean."

"Don't be silly. People don't sail to America nowadays on a ship. It says in the papers that they have invented a kind of bridge that hangs up in the air and trains go across the ocean on it. Give Hinka your letter. It will get there sooner."

"Please, Papa! Hinka's husband went to America long after Yudel did, and now she is already going herself. But I'm still — no! I'm going to mail the letter!"

"Your time has probably not come yet, daughter. But when it does, oh! will Yudel be glad to see you!"

*

Itzik-Meier from Kolomeya, a man with a short, pointed beard and light-gray eyes, was once taking a walk, as was his habit ever since he had been in America. That is, he was stopping more often than he was walking, because he liked to look in all the show windows. This time he stopped to look into the window of the Ladies' Tailor on Ninth Street, and thought he saw a familiar face. The man looked just like Yudel from Kolomeya, the Bathhouse Keeper's son-in-law. Itzik-Meier wiped his glasses and looked again. Yes, he was right. He pushed open the door and went inside.

"Good afternoon, what can I do for you?" asked Joe, as if he were talking to a complete stranger, although he had recognized the man immediately as a *lantsman*.

"You don't know me, Yudel? Look again."

Unable to help himself, Joe said, "Oh! It's you, Reb Itzik-Meier," and his stomach turned over. He spoke in a whisper, praying that his visitor would disappear.

And Reb Itzik did turn and leave, after a moment, but not before taking note of a "lady" with red hair who seemed to be on very friendly terms with Yudel. Not like the other sewing-machine operators. But apparently, here in America, a ladies' tailor must have a "lady" to manage the shop.

Itzik-Meier practically ran all the way home and even before he had one foot in the door blurted out the news:

"Chava, you'll never guess who I just saw on Ninth Street!"

"I give up."

"Yudel from Kolomeya!"

"It can't be. You must be mistaken. He was making a good living in Kolomeya."

"Maybe. But he's doing much better on Ninth Street."

The same evening, after supper, Chava said:

"You know what, Itze, I'd like to see that Yudel with my own eyes."

So both of them took a walk on Ninth Street. As they entered the Ladies' Tailor Shop, it was Esther who approached them and invited them to have a seat. She herself went "in the back" to tell Joe he had guests. She returned almost immediately.

"He'll be out in a minute," she said very hospitably.

Itze and Chava exchanged puzzled looks.

"Must be a younger sister of his in America," said Chava.

"Yudel never had a sister," said Itze. There was something ominous in his tone.

Meanwhile, Yudel had come into the shop. His *lantsman* from Kolomeya was here again. Twice in one day. He felt a sharp pain in his chest.

"I brought my missus over, Yudel. She loves to talk to a *lantsman* once in a while. Like a voice from home. You know how it is..."

"So how are you, Yudel?" asked Chava, but her eyes could not stay away from the lady. Something, her woman's instinct told her, was not quite right here.

Joe's legs felt as though they had turned to rubber. Only Satan himself could have brought him such guests now.

"Look at the fine business Yudel is running here, *k'n'hora,*" Chava said to her husband. "We'll write home and tell them we visited you, Yudel. Your Hannah will be overjoyed. I remember her as a little girl..."

When they left, it did not even occur to the "lady" to ask Yudel who they were. And Joe, all he could think about was: should he move the shop to another location? But that would not be good for business. Besides, what would he tell Esther?

*

So one day Yudel received a letter from Kolomeya. It happened to be one of those days when the red-haired lady stayed after work to discuss some matters that had come up during the day. Joe did not know how much longer he could keep his inner disquiet from coming out into the open, especially when she asked him:

"Who was that letter from that you received today all the way from Europe?"

"From my parents."

"May I see it?"

Joe handed her the envelope and the letter, knowing she could not read Yiddish.

She turned the letter this way and that. One thing she could tell was that it seemed to have been written by two different people.

"This part must be from your Papa. And this part must be from your Mama."

"You're so smart!" Joe exclaimed as he put his arm around her and kissed her on the forehead.

"Don't be so fresh, Joe! Read me what your Mama says."

Joe studied the letter and broke out into a sweat. For a moment he could not recall which part she had "guessed" was from his mother. His little girl's handwriting?

"My dear son Yudel," he began, as a feeling akin to guilt almost overwhelmed him. "My name in the old country was Yudel," he explained. Esther beamed. "Read further, Yudi," she said, hanging on his shoulder. How exciting her proximity was! He stared at his daughter's labored handwriting. How much effort it must have cost Hannah to teach the girl to write those few lines! He started over again.

"My dear son Yudel. I wish you mazl-tov from very far away. May you and your bride have a good life together. May you both live out your days together, God willing, in happiness and in comfort... Please send us your wedding pictures." He "read" the last sentence after a long moment of hesitation.

"Your old Mama is almost as fresh as you are!" Esther laughed as she turned away and began fussing with a dress hanging on a figure.

"Why do you call me 'fresh'? We're neither of us youngsters, you know. Or don't you love me any more?"

"Don't talk like that, Joe."

*

Mr. Itzik-Meier, meanwhile, was conducting his own investigation and he soon discovered that Yudel, the Ladies' Tailor from Ninth Street, was actually planning to marry the red-haired lady in his shop. At first he refused to give this rumor any credence, but then he began to feel so bad about it that he decided he must share his information with some of the other *lantsleit* from Kolomeya. This was easier said than done, because they were spread over the length and breadth of New York City. But the more people he talked to, the hotter the fire burned, and this worried him.

"That's not the way," he told them. "Let the fire simmer quietly for now," he advised.

"What do you expect to accomplish by that?" asked one.

"We could take it to court," suggested another.

"Better to talk to the girl's parents," said a third.

"No, that would be foolish," insisted Mr. Itzik-Meier. "First we've got to bring Yudel's wife over. And to do that, we must keep the matter quiet for a while." Eventually he convinced them, because he spoke from the heart, but at the same time, he did not leave his head out of it.

So they took up a collection. One gave a dollar, another gave ten. And when they had enough money, they chose Itzik-Meier to go back to the old country and bring "her" here. There was no need to give him a "letter of authorization" or anything official like that, because back in Kolomeya everybody knew Reb Itzik-Meier better than Jacob Schiff is known here in America.

He sailed with the first ship possible, and as soon as he arrived in Kolomeya and washed his hands and face, he sent for Hannah the Bathhouse Keeper's daughter.

"Tell her," he instructed the errand-boy, "that I have just this minute come from America and that it's urgent that I talk to her right away. But right away!"

The first to arrive, however, was not Hannah but the Bathhouse Keeper himself. He shook hands with Itzik-Meier and wished him welcome.

"And how is my son Yudel in America?"

"I sent for your daughter, not you! Go back and send her here right away!"

Hearing his tone, the Bathhouse Keeper paled in fright. And old as he was, it didn't take him more than nine seconds to run home. Even less time did it take Hannah to come running, and even more wildly did her heart pound, and in her fear she even forgot to say good-morning, let alone all the other amenities.

*

Esther was her father's youngest. And since Julius Kornwald had married off his other daughters in style, he was determined that Esther's wedding would outshine them all. Though he was only a small merchant on Ludlow Street, he somehow accomplished things that his friends — even those who were more successful than he — could not manage to do. So Ludlow Street was abuzz with the news, and Julius was enjoying it.

They went to Orchard Street and rented the same large hall in which Julius' other daughters were married. To perform the ceremony they engaged the same stoutish Reverend with the square brown beard and restless little eyes, who had recited the blessings at the marriage of his other daughters. They also engaged the same overweight woman with the glistening forehead to cook the wedding meal, and the same *klezmer* to play the music.

In a word, Julius Kornwald spared no expense. "Annie," he said to his wife, "don't stint on anything. We don't have any more daughters to make weddings for!"

They went to the butcher and ordered 200 chickens, and 50 calves' livers, and 200 pounds of rib-steak. And just to make sure, they ordered another 200 *miltsn*.

They went to their favorite baker on Essex Street and ordered enough white rolls for twice as many people, plus a large assortment of cake. They went to their favorite saloon on Suffolk Street and ordered 20 barrels of beer, an equivalent number of gallons of wine and a few cases of Slivovitz.

Up and down Ludlow Street, where Esther was born and grew up, the news spread overnight: Esther the red-head had fallen in love with a successful businessman from Ninth Street corner of Second Avenue.

As for Esther herself, for a few weeks before the wedding she did not appear as often as usual in her betrothed's tailor shop. Annie, her mother, a tall, thin woman, took her aside one day and cautioned her to be wary of strangers, because she was a bride-to-be, and most important, she must not remain alone with her husband-to-be for more than a few minutes. True, these maternal warnings sounded comical to Esther, but still, she was curious to find out if there really was any truth in them.

So one day, when she happened to be alone with Joe, she watched carefully and she did notice that there was something disturbing about the look in his eyes. Making excuses, she left the tailor shop and went straight home and thought for a long time about her mother's warnings, and finally she had to admit that there *was* some truth in them. And since this was so, she was very, very careful.

*

Even more careful was Joe the Ladies' Tailor. On the surface he was cheerful and in his usual good spirits. With each of his customers he politely and diplomatically shared the good news that he and Esther would soon be husband and wife. At first, Esther was embarrassed by this "publicity," but she soon grew accustomed to all the attention, because Joe had many, many customers, and good wishes like these are dear to the heart of everyone. She was no longer embarrassed for herself, and it never occurred to her to study Joe's face again so closely, though she did notice that somewhere around his eyes a warm blush seemed to appear as soon as the conversation turned to their forthcoming wedding. Otherwise, however, his pale, clean-shaven face showed no emotion.

He prepared for his wedding with a generous hand but a dejected spirit. Esther wanted a home up in the Bronx. If she had wanted a home up in the sky, wouldn't he have gotten it for her? It took them ten days to select the furniture. They bought matching pieces, mostly dark brown, very hard mahogany. And, of course, rugs for all seven rooms in their new home.

Alone in his bed at night, however, Joe had trouble falling asleep. He kept trying to justify his actions to himself, he was guilty of nothing, he had no other choice, it was destined to be this way. Why had God sent him such a precious woman? Was his the only tailor shop in the city? That first day her feet crossed his threshold she had walked right into his heart.

But how could he forget about his Hannah across the sea and his young children?

The red-haired Esther dominated his tailor shop. Her charm and her good taste were in every piece of work they turned out. And that same charm had gotten to him. How was a man to know what the right course was? For that matter, does anyone really know who he is? Or what life has in store for him? Is not one's own happiness the only thing that really mattered?

Embroiled in this conflict with himself he kept putting off his letters to Hannah on the other side of the ocean. Those he did manage to write grew shorter and shorter. He knew that sooner or later he would stop writing to her altogether.

*

The great city of New York is one big, dark secret. And even more secret and more dark is the past of the people who live in it.

Even those of Joe's *lantsleit* who finally learned the truth about Joe the Tailor have promised to keep it a secret.

So Joe himself has no inkling of the net that certain people are spreading out before his feet...

Before Kolomeya itself got word of anything amiss, Itzik-Meier met with Hannah behind locked doors.

"Are you getting any letters from Yudel?" he asked her.

"Just recently I got one." Her voice trembled.

"What did he write to you?"

Hannah's face changed color. She loved Yudel and she believed that what he wrote to her in his letters was between them and God and was nobody else's business.

"Listen to me, Hannah. Everybody here in Kolomeya knows me well. So do you." His voice was filled with fatherly concern. "And over there in America I have a good name too. May my name be obliterated if I have any intentions of doing you harm."

For a moment he was silent. Then he looked straight into her eyes and asked her:

"Hannah, do you really love Yudel? I must know."

"Do I —?" She could not say any more. She turned her face to the wall and covered it with her thin, toil-worn hands.

Itzik-Meier knew this was the moment to deliver his message.

Isaac Raboy

"Hannah, I came across the ocean to tell you something. Your Yudel has found someone else..."

"Someone else?" Hannah pivoted and stood face to face with Itzik-Meier. She was no longer crying, but her face was the color of death. If anyone had stuck a pin into it, she would not have bled.

"Yes, someone else. But it is not too late. It can be stopped, if we act quickly. You must go home now and get yourself ready to go with me to America now. We have enough money. Go!"

The next day Mr. Itzik-Meier and Hannah were on a ship bound for New York. The children were left in the care of her father until God would help.

*

And this is how the folk finish the story:

A carriage with two festooned horses flew through the entire length of Ludlow Street and came to a halt outside the home of the bride. On both sides of the street more carriages with festooned horses stood ready.

The groom stepped out of the carriage, went into the house to fetch the bride. On both sides of the stoop groups of neighbors stood tightly pressed together. A few minutes later the groom came out of the house with the bride. The train of her wedding gown was carried by two small children, a girl and a boy. A shower of rice and rose-petals came down over the bride and groom. The groom was put into a separate carriage with two young women, friends of the bride. The bride was put into a separate carriage with two young men, friends of the groom. Into a third carriage stepped the bride's parents. This process was continued until all the carriages were filled. Then the procession drove to Orchard Street.

As soon as the bride and groom walked into the darkened hall, all the lights were turned on. Bride and groom sat down on chairs at one end of the room and received the good wishes of relatives and friends with great joy and much kissing.

At the other end of the hall sat the musicians with their clarinets and saxophones and fiddles. Also, a little man with a big bass fiddle and a drummer with all his equipment.

When the turn of the bride's parents came to enter, along with the bride's sister and their husbands and children, the musicians played a special *freilakhs*. The little man with the pale face gave the signal to start — a smack of the bow against the back of the bass fiddle. He also ended every number with a few words accompanied by the rolling of his eyes and the shaking of his head from side to side.

The big hall was filled to capacity. The young folks danced the waltzes and the quadrilles. A long table, laden with bottles and baked goods, also occupied a prominent place.

One of the bride's aunts wondered aloud: "Look at this, will you. Everybody here is from the bride's side..."

And a cousin of the bride replied, with a note of pride in her voice: "A rich groom, but all alone in the world like a ship at sea...."

The proceedings went on.

The Reverend arrived with all the necessary papers. Two strong young men unrolled the wedding canopy and stood it upright. The musicians began playing the heart-warming *khosn-kalle* dance...

Suddenly, a commotion at the door.

Everyone stood up, heads turned toward the door.

A gust of wind pushed the door open.

Over the guard's objections, some people pushed their way into the hall: three witnesses and Mr. Itzik-Meier from Kolomeya led a woman into the hall, a pale woman wrapped in a dark shawl.

Someone called out: "From the groom's side..."

The music stopped.

With tight lips everyone stared at the man with the short beard who was already standing on a chair. His voice trembled as he called out:

"From the groom's side! Here are three Jewish witnesses who will swear that the groom already has a wife... And here she is. Her name is Hannah... "

He pointed to the woman, who was covered almost from head to toe by the shawl. Only part of her sharp-featured, chalk-white face and her piercing dark eyes were visible.

227

All she did was look at Yudel...

Evil spirits immediately began dancing in the big hall. But the klezmer were not playing...

Shouts. Wailing. Sobbing. For a long time.

Bells ringing, alarm bells, harbingers of catastrophe. Ambulances came racing up. Doctors in white coats leaped out, rushed into the hall, rushed out again. Again the clanging of the bells. The ambulances were barely able to force their way through the dense, dark crowd of curious onlookers that had come running to Orchard Street.

The bridegroom had collapsed and died. The bride had fallen on top of him with a broken heart

Only Hannah managed somehow to escape from the hall. To this day no one knows where she is...

AMONG US IN AMERICA
Isaac Raboy

For a biography of Raboy, see the introduction to the story *Joe the Tailor.*

Among Us in America

Precisely at 2 p.m. the workers at Rosenzweig's clothing factory heard the loud, shrill whistle they had been expecting all day. Shears were put down, aprons flew in the air, sewing machines took one last breath and grew still, workers leaped over overturned chairs. Men fell on each other's necks, hugged each other. Women kissed each other as tears glistened in their eyes. Soon the whole place was empty.

All except for Mr. Rosenzweig, the proprietor, a short, sturdy, middle-aged man with a bald head, who was now so dejected and so upset that he did not know what to do with his hands, which shook uselessly inside the wide sleeves of his office coat. With him were his foreman and his secretary. The row of wide, white columns that supported the ceiling of the factory building now looked menacing. The silence itself was fearsome. Only a few minutes ago the place had been pulsating with life, with human voices, with the cheerful clatter of machines and the soft clink of scissors.

Mr. Rosenzweig felt strangely indecisive. Should he lock the doors and go home or should he stubbornly stay where he was? This was the first time in his life he had had to suffer such an embarrassing blow. Ever since he had been in business for himself he had always gotten along well with his workers. Now he could not understand how matters had deteriorated to the point where his workers felt they had to go out on strike. Someone else must be behind all this, maybe one of his competitors trying to trip him up, trying to hurt him financially, or maybe even just ruin the season for him.

Mr. Rosenzweig sat in his office thinking about this. Mike, his foreman, sat at his own desk totaling up time-cards. Suddenly he remembered something and walked over to the other side of the factory, where the women worked. He stopped in his tracks, feeling faint. But he recovered quickly, went to one of the machines and opened a drawer. It was empty.

"Sophie. She must have cleared out of here," he thought. "Why in the world would she do that? She went out with the strikers?"

He could not believe it, much less understand it. He stood looking at the machine where she always sat. All sorts of reasons went through his head to explain why Sophie would do such a thing. His own wife! Finally he gave up, waved his hand resignedly and went directly to Mr. Rosenzweig's office.

"Well, Mike," said Mr. Rosenzweig. "Trouble, eh?"

"There's trouble and there's trouble," replied Mike, his face flaming.

"Not to worry, Mike."

"We've got to show them who's boss here, Mr. Rosenzweig."

"We'll show them, Mike."

"But what do you think of Sophie? Seems like she went out with them."

"Right." Mr. Rosenzweig's cheeks puffed out and he spoke in his low bass voice, to give his words more importance. "She had to do it, Mike. She had no other choice."

"What do you mean?" Mike asked, pacing around in a circle, as was his habit when he was upset. "I won't have anything more to do with her. It's all over. I won't even be able to look at her."

"Take it easy, Mike. Don't be stubborn." Mr. Rosenzweig liked to weigh and measure his words in situations like this. Having spoken, he closed his mouth and smiled, revealing his strong white teeth. "You know how I dislike hasty decisions, Mike."

"This strike won't last long," Mike said, his tone softening under Mr. Rosenzweig's influence.

"That's the least of my worries, Mike," smiled Mr. Rosenzweig.

"Of course!" Mike agreed, trying to figure out where his boss was coming from, but taking heart from his attitude. "I still have a little work to finish. What happens next?"

"What happens next, Mike, is that we shut down the factory."

Mike slapped his forehead. "Scare them! Of course! What a great idea! I never would have thought of it!"

"Who will they strike against if Rosenzweig is already closed?" Mr. Rosenzweig liked the idea even better, now that he had articulated it.

"They'll come to you on their knees, begging you to reopen."

"Like I told you, Mike — don't panic." He stood up and slapped his foreman on the back.

"What do we do about the orders, Mr. Rosenzweig? That's what's bothering me. They don't let me rest."

Mr. Rosenzweig seemed to have something to say about this too, but apparently he was not ready. "Mike, what would we do about the orders if there was a fire? For now, let's just close up the place."

2.

That afternoon Rosenzweig, his secretary and his foreman left the factory together. Mike locked the last door to the passenger elevators, stuck the key in his pocket and said to the elevator operator:

"We're shutting down the place, Harry."

"Is that the truth, Mike?"

"We always mean what we say, Harry."

Stepping into the imposing marble corridor, the three of them walked to the street door, but with heads high, like people who had just been insulted but who were above such annoyances.

Out on the sidewalk, along the length of the building, two of Rosenzweig's workers marched side by side. Picket signs hung around their necks, front and back. Each sign read, in big black letters, STRIKE AT ROSENZWEIG'S. The pickets did not give the three persons coming out of the building a second look.

Mr. Rosenzweig, however, stopped, studied the scene for a moment, and said to himself: "You think you're striking against Rosenzweig? Ha! There is no more Rosenzweig!" And he smiled knowingly at his two companions. As they were about to take leave of each other, however, he handed them each a slip of paper.

"That's my home telephone. Don't come back to the factory without my permission. The place is closed. That's all you know. There's nobody in the factory to strike against, you understand?"

And they each went their separate ways.

*

Mike ran into the house with his arms spread out, and when his mother-in-law looked at him questioningly, he sighed deeply once, then again, but said nothing.

"So it's true?" she asked. "They went out on strike?"

"Even worse. Better you shouldn't ask." On the verge of tears, he could barely get the words out.

"So where is Sophie?"

"With them."

"What do you mean?"

"What I said. She joined the strike."

"It can't be!"

"Believe me, *shvieger*, I know what I'm talking about." He ran his hand over his prematurely bald head. If there had been any hair there, he would have torn it out.

"So it's true? She went out with them?"

He nodded his head gravely.

"Then you can tell my daughter: I never want to see her again!"

"Sure. I'm going right out to the picket-line and tell her. Better you should save me the trouble and go tell her yourself."

"I won't let her into my house!"

"Yeah. I'll see it when I believe it."

"You'll see it! Just wait!" She punched her left hand with her right fist. "Let her just try to come home... Not unless she apologizes for what she did."

"Women." Mike laughed. "You're already getting soft!"

"If she comes and apologizes, I'll forgive her."

The house suddenly grew dark. Dusk seemed to have fallen all at once. Rifka lit the gas light and then brought Mike his habitual glass of tea, which he never drank unless it was piping hot.

"Hits the spot," he said, and took another sip. The hot liquid seemed to dissolve his anger.

The door opened and in came Mike's father-in-law, a man with a sparse blond beard and cheeks like two red apples. His wife called him Itche, but she managed to elongate the second syllable. Reb Itche was a *shokhet* in a big chicken store, which he referred to as "the shop." The first thing he always did when he entered the house was to remove from his pocket the long, black leather case in which he kept his knives and put them away very carefully in a drawer of the bureau. From another drawer he took out a velvet yarmulka, then, in one motion, he removed the rabbinical-looking hat from his head and slipped the yarmulka onto his fiery red hair. Only then did he turn his attention to his son-in-law.

"Why so early, Mordkhe?"

"The horses ran away."

"What does that mean?"

"A strike!" Rifka interjected. "A strike!" Her tone was full of impatient mockery.

Reb Itche disregarded her tone. He knew only too well what it meant. She would have preferred her husband to be a business-man, or a peddler, or even a tailor, anything but a *shokhet*. With his usual artlessness he asked Mike:

"It's a real strike?"

"No, a make-believe one!" Mike exchanged looks with his mother-in-law. "A strike is a strike."

"Something must be hurting them. The workers, I mean," Reb Itche said simply, without a trace of guile. "When things are not good, people go out on strike."

"Ha! You think Itche would miss this chance to give us a les-son in *peyrek*? Tell him about his pride-and-joy," said Rifka.

"About what?" said Reb Itche, stroking his beard.

"About your daughter!"

"Oh. I understand." Reb Itche's face fairly lit up with pleas-ure. "She always takes the path of truth and justice."

"I'll split her head open!" shouted her mother. "If she dares come home! Would to God she doesn't!"

233

Reb Itche stared at his wife and muttered something between his red whiskers. Then he was silent. He marveled at the depth of his dislike for her. But he would never have the strength to tell her. She was still his wife, after all. Sometimes things are good between them, and then there's nobody as kind as she is...

3.

Mike went into his room to change his clothes, a habit of his. When he comes home in the evening after work he must put on something more comfortable — an old pair of pants, his carpet slippers, a shirt with the sleeves cut off. Then he hangs up his good clothes in their place, puts shoe-trees in his good shoes so they will keep their shape. In this house he is the beloved son-in-law and even a little more than that.

The house had four rooms: a kitchen, a dining-room and two bedrooms. One bedroom, facing the street, was the young folks'. The other bedroom was for the old folks.

Head of the household was Rifka. She kept house, She paid the rent. She cooked for everyone and she kept the house clean. Payday, everyone's wages were put into her hand. Whatever her husband earned in the chicken market, Mike's pay as foreman in the shop, Sophie's wages as a seamstress — it all went into Rifka's pocket. Of this money, she spent most on the house. Whatever was left, she deposited in the bank; some day, she hoped, they would buy their own house. But that was her own private dream. She told no one about it. She never told anyone about such private matters, but she managed them so that she always turned out to be the smart one.

"In America," she explained, "a man should never handle the money. After all, what can a man learn about money when he's buried all day in the shop or in the market?"

Her husband was a quiet, reserved man. Were it not for Rifka, who had persuaded him to work in the chicken store, he would have resigned altogether from the material world in America. All they require here is a throat-slitter. Not a day goes by in "the market" that he doesn't die a thousand deaths, doing things that are against Jewish law. But what is the alternative? To fight with the missus? If she wants him to work in the market, then God in heaven must want her to want it. And if God in heaven wants something, there's no use opposing it. So whatever Reb Itche earns, he brings home and turns it over to his wife. It belongs to her. He has placed himself in her hands. God only knows he doesn't love her very much. He has no sympathy for her whims, but he could never tell her what to do or what not to do. Not that she would listen to him.

Whatever Mordkhe-Mike says is also right, Mordkhe that ignoramus; Mordkhe who is *treyf* from head to foot, has become her chief advisor. Look at him, strutting around the house in his bedroom slippers and his circumcised shirtsleeves, and with those old pants that are so tight he doesn't even need a belt. He's the new boss here, the *baalebos*, the Master of the House.

Reb Itche pours a glass of tea for himself and sits down at the table, trying to calm his nerves so he won't argue with his wife or carry anger in his heart against any of God's creatures, especially Mordkhe.

The door opens. Sophie comes in like the wind, runs over to her father and kisses him on the forehead. He gently pushes her away, as he always does. Women, even daughters, shouldn't kiss men like that. Rifka comes running in from the kitchen, folds her arms across her chest, and issues her ultimatum:

"I'm giving you two choices, Sophie. Either you go in to work tomorrow or you move out of here!"

"Mama —"

"I don't want to hear it. You're a stupid cow and so are the others."

"Let me hear what Papa has to say," Sophie pleads, white as a sheet.

"Papa has nothing to say about this. If you go in to work tomorrow morning, you can stay here in my house. If not, get out of here right away. March!" Rifka stepped over to her daughter and attempted to take her by the arm. Sophie resisted, shaking the long hair that stuck out of the little black hat she wore. This time her voice had an edge to it.

"Try to imagine it, Mama, if you can. I'm not going in to work tomorrow."

"No? Then get your things out of my house right now!"

"Don't worry. I won't stay here another night. But first I've got to find another place to — "

"That's none of my concern. Get out right away!"

"So my own mother is driving me out into the street? Papa, why don't you say something? Don't you hear how she's threatening me?"

Papa said nothing. Merely waved his hand in a gesture of helplessness.

Deeply hurt, Sophie ran into her room to gather up her belongings, but then changed her mind. Where would she take them? She must first find a room, or else she would have to stay out in the New York streets all night. She went back into the kitchen and looked at her father, her two big eyes full of pain. She knew he was on her side. She stepped over to him and kissed him on the forehead again. But this time he did not push her away. He took her hand in his.

"Take me with you, daughter," he whispered.

"I'll come back for you," she said, and left the house, slamming the door behind her.

The silence that ensued was that of a house with no one in it. Mike wandered from room to room with his hands deep in his pockets. He kept chewing his lower lip. His nostrils quivered. He tried to understand what had happened. Was he right? From whom could he seek advice? The old man? I hate him, he reminded himself. His mother-in-law? For her approval you had to show you were strong. He called into the kitchen.

"She must think I'm going to run after her and beg."

"I don't want her in my house!"

"And when the strike is over? I won't give her back her job! She's finished in our shop!"

"Crazy!" Rifka shouted from the kitchen. To herself she added: "And you, my dear son-in-law, are crazier than she is..."

Reb Itche sat where he was, staring into his empty tea-cup. He felt as if he were in a big empty place, all alone and helpless, that he was shouting and shouting, and the echo kept bouncing off the bare walls.

THE OLD MAN AND HIS SONS
Fishl Bimko

FISHL BIMKO (1890-1965) — *born in Kielce, Poland; died in New York.*

Bimko was born into a family of merchants and Hassidic rabbis. His parents ran a small food store. At age 15 Bimko served six months in the Kielce jail for "revolutionary activities." In 1917, when he was 27, he was arrested by the German occupying power and served a short sentence in the Warsaw Citadel prison. In 1921 he came to the United States and worked for a few years in garment shops.

Bimko began writing when he was 12. When he was 19 his first story was published in the Lodz Tageblatt, *a Yiddish newspaper. Realizing he had a talent for dialogue, he turned to drama and comedy. (Around 1910 he had worked as a prompter in a Yiddish theater in Lublin.) His first play,* Dembes *(Oaks), was produced by Julius Adler in 1914 in Lodz. In 1922 Maurice Schwartz produced the same play in the New York Art Theater.*

Bimko's characters are raw and earthy. They speak a natural, juicy Polish Yiddish and their milieu is from "real life." His play Ganovim, (Thieves), *which was in the repertoire of every Yiddish theater in the world, was first performed by the Vilna Troupe in 1919 in Warsaw, then in 1922 in New York, and later in Hebrew in Israel. By 1936 Bimko's collected works filled seven volumes of plays, novellas, and short stories. In 1967, two years after his death in New York, CYCO (Central Yiddish Culture Organization) published a 5-volume collection of his later works under the title* Oyfn veg tsum lebn (On the Way to Life).

The Old Man and His Sons (Der tatte, dem tatns kinder*) appears in Bimko's* Collected Works (Geklibine verk), *New York, v. 8. This story is adapted from the original by Max Rosenfeld.*

Fishl Bimko

The Old Man and His Sons

His two sons owned the shop. It was a first-class shop, lively, active, busy all year round, a regular bee-hive. Employed in that shop were cutters, designers, sewing-machine operators, helpers, the whole works. The bosses' father, a man in his sixties, still had an irrepressible need to work in the shop. And he could work like a demon. The Union, however, whenever he tried anything like that, stopped his hand in mid-air.

"Just a minute, Mr. Nadelman. For you this is off-limits!"

The workers — like workers everywhere — were sometimes full of pep, and sometimes they dragged their feet a little. So sometimes the shop foreman had to remind them, in his own particular style, that the factory was "sitting on hot coals." In other words, get the lead out. He did not have to mince any words with them, because they were "his people," some of whom he had known personally for a long time.

"Moyshe," he would say, "what's your head doing down there on the machine? Your wife didn't let you sleep last night?"

Or, to a young American-born fellow, he might say:

"Hey, Teddie! During lunch hour you can tell your buddy all about the game!"

Unfortunately, the father of the two owners, who wanted so badly to do something practical in the shop, was not permitted to do it. Here is a piece of goods that he would just love to work on. Over there is a sleeve that is just waiting for him to finish on the machine. But all he is allowed to do is stand around and look, or walk around and look, on condition that he keep his hands to himself. And if he ever did manage to get something into his hands, the shop chairman would not even have to leave his machine. All he did was yell out: "Mr. Foreman!" and that dignitary would already know what that meant. He would look around, find the old man and take him aside.

"Please do me a big favor and keep your hands off that roll of cloth. How many times do we have to tell you?"

Now the old man gets angry, because he was interrupted in the middle of an important job. He goes on the offensive, in a voice heard all over the shop.

"In my own sons' shop I don't have any rights?! You want me to stand around and watch other people work and I'm not even allowed to touch the cloth?"

In a tone so oily that you could apply it to a wound, the shop chairman says:

"Take it easy, Mr. Nadelman. You know that all work in this shop must be done by union hands. That's why it's called a union shop."

"And what about me? In a union shop I have no rights? These two hands of mine — they weren't once dipped in the holy water of the union?"

The voice of the shop chairman becomes a little louder, because now he is not talking only to Mr. Nadelman, Sr.

"Even if they do give him a union card — which if I have anything to do with it won't happen till hell freezes over — he still won't be allowed to work here, because he is the father of the boss, which makes him nine-tenths a boss too!"

*

All his life, when his children were young, Mr. Nadelman, Sr. worked in garment shops, and old-time shops at that: dark, depressing, with never any sunlight or warmth, where his very bones were always frozen. And when his children grew up and opened a nice modern shop, airy and light, it was to be expected that their father, who was born and raised in this work, and whose hands showed it, would finally have a decent place to show what those hands could do. Imagine — his own children's shop! Here he could work as long as he wished and as hard as he wished. But right at that point, the Union proved to be a bone in his throat.

"He's not allowed to work there, period."

What was he supposed to do — get on his knees and beg for mercy? *He* was not allowed to work? It wasn't the money. He didn't need it. He just wanted to live as he always had lived, in a way that was most comfortable for him, with shears and iron in his hands. He had no complaints about his sons. They provided him with everything he needed. But how could he stand around all day and do nothing? His bones and his blood were not used to it. Does an old horse put out to pasture stop neighing? Or stamping his feet? Why was he any worse than all those other people who were working in the shop? It didn't make sense. And the more he thought about this injustice the more stubborn became his position, which he held onto with tooth and nail.

Look at that neat row of machine-heads. How sweetly they sing. But look at the operators. You call that sewing? Do they know the real meaning of the word "stitch"? All they know is how to put the thread through the hole and drive it as fast as they can. God forbid that one of the machines should drop its head like a sick chicken and refuse to move. The only thing they know how to do then is send for the doctor. That's the union rule.

Well, if they won't let him sew, he'll be happy to press. He can dance around with the iron as gracefully as any of the other pressers here. First of all, for a tailor it's second-nature. Second of all, these operators were still stuck somewhere in their Galician, Rumanian or Polish towns when he was already slinging the press-iron around in America. And what's the big deal in handling that lightweight little iron they use nowadays? You don't need to puff up your cheeks, you don't have to be ready with a mouthful of water to spray on the cloth, you don't have to heat up the iron and cool it off, you don't have to be careful not to burn a hole in the goods. The iron gets ready all by itself. The only thing they haven't figured out yet is how to use it without any hands at all.

He'd like to see these modern bigshots lift one of those old-time irons. If they didn't weigh 23 pounds each they didn't weigh an ounce. An easy life they're looking for, these pressers. And to add insult to injury, they always look so sleepy. What skin is it off their backs if an old man wants to keep his hand in? Does the iron belong to them?

If he's not allowed to sew and he's not allowed to press, then let him at least be a cutter. You have to go to college to learn that too? Using a shears — who can do that better than he? He's a Jew, isn't he? What Jew doesn't know how to handle a shears? Isn't that what our sages said: *Amkho sher un eizn*! My people, shears and irons!

But it's a new world — everything in the shop is theirs — the shears, the irons, the machines, everything. So what belongs to him? Nothing, Yet they keep trying to drum the opposite into his thick skull: Everything here is his: the shears, the irons, the machines — nobody is trying to take anything away from him. He can grow old together with all that stuff — more power to him. The only thing is: he can't use it! What's the good of owning something if you can't use it?

And to make matters worse, they talk about him amongst themselves as if he already weren't there.

"If *my* children owned such a shop, I'd be so far away from it they'd never find me! ... What an old fool — wasting his old age in a shop!... Let him get arthritis and stay home and not take the bread-and-butter out of our mouths..."

Go explain to them that "the old man" can't sit still, even for a minute, that something inside him drives him, he himself doesn't even know where it comes from. Who can he discuss it with? The other workers? That big a fool he's not. Doesn't he have his sons he can complain to, right here in their own office? But that's the problem — it's their shop, so he's not allowed to work here. If they were somebody else's children, he could work there. That makes sense?

*

Not too long ago, when the factory was still an "open shop" he did work in it. Not like the other workers, from 8 in the morning till half-past-five. No. After everyone left, that's when he really enjoyed himself. Day or night, it made no difference. No one could tell him: "Stop! You're not obliged to do everything yourself, especially when your sons pay you whether you work or not. Leave some work for us — that's how we earn our living." Even his own sons would get sore and yell at him: "Don't make us rich, Pop!" But sons or no sons, they couldn't stop him.

Now that it's a union shop, however, there was someone there to slap his hands.

"You've worked enough in your time, old man. Give other people a chance, people who won't eat if they don't work."

But then, when the union called a walk-out, the old man went out with everyone else; forgot he was the bosses' father.

"I've been a union-man all my life," he insisted. "My sons — they pay me, but not because I'm their father. They pay me because I give them an honest day's work. If I didn't work, I wouldn't even want to look at their money. I was a working-man before they were even born. Why can't I be one now?"

Not so, said his sons. "We're not paying you for your work. We're paying you because you are our father." They thought it was the funniest thing since Charlie Chaplin. "Why do you want to join the union, Pop? You want to work fewer hours? You want to go home five o'clock with all the other workers? You want the union to help you get a raise? You want time-and-a-half for overtime?" To them it was all a big joke.

But even before they finished talking he saw that they were right. The last thing he wanted to do was embarrass his own children, who were now riding high in the saddle, who had unlimited credit and two new automobiles and lived in a high-tone neighborhood and who had completely forgotten that his "pedigree" was different from theirs, that all his life he had been a tailor, and that his father and grandfather before him were also tailors. No. The last thing in the world he wanted to do was embarrass them. So he began to brag about his newly discovered status:

"I am not working in their shop as a regular worker but as their father, because it gives me pleasure and I really enjoy it."

He didn't even realize that he was digging his own grave. Now he was neither fish nor fowl. It didn't bother his sons that he could no longer sit down at a machine. They never *had* been in favor of that. They had put up with it, however, because it kept him busy and out of the office.

Among the workers in the shop, on the other hand, he was not only a boss but a father — and therefore a stubborn jackass and a damn fool besides, who was not satisfied to work like an ordinary human being but who had to take bigger bites than anybody else and leave them with the smaller pieces. But now they had a longer whip in their hands, with which they could punish him not only for his present sins but also for the sins of his past.

"A boss? Okay. We'll give him all the honor and respect that's coming to him. He can stand and watch, or he can walk around as much as he wants and give orders — if the foreman doesn't object. But work? Not on your life. Forget it. A union shop is a union shop. The work belongs to us."

The old man, before he put in his 60-some years in the trade, had most likely been a reasonable human being. It must have been the realization that he was now superfluous in his own sons' shop that unscrewed his brain. All day long he roamed the shop, tense and out-of-joint, and over a mere nothing, a triviality which didn't even merit opening his mouth, he could stir up a storm, a whirl-wind, a volcano. His screams of "Crooks! Murderers!" sounded as if the factory were about to be destroyed by dynamite.

On such occasions his two sons would come running out of their office and, since they had already guessed what the trouble was, they would not even ask him any questions, but only try to sit him down and calm his nerves. "It's not nice for the customers, Pop. We have buyers in the office — you want them to know there's a fight going on in this shop?" And if this didn't work, they would try scolding him:

"Why do you come here, Pop? To holler? You enjoy making trouble? Go home and stay there. You think we won't be able to get along without you?"

This would, of course, make him even angrier and he would start all over again, but louder, as if they had stepped on his toes.

"So that's what you want? I should go home? Why? So your wives will have a steady babysitter and be able to go shopping for hours at a time? Your own mother couldn't harness me to you when you were little kids; you want your wives to do it to me now?"

"Who's telling you to stay home with your daughters-in-law? You can't find a place for yourself where you'll be able to rest your bones for a while and not work your guts out the rest of your life?"

At this point some wiseacre on the floor joins the fray, which sets off a landslide.

"All the synagogues in the neighborhood are empty — there's plenty of room!"

"Other men his age have to go digging in garbage cans for their daily bread!"

"Time for him to take it easy. He's not as young as he used to be!"

"Not him — he thinks he's going to live forever!"

This is too much. The old man suddenly realizes there is a plot against him: his own sons have joined forces with the union to drive him out of the shop. The idea makes him furious.

"The workers don't want me here? All right! But my own children? How will your shop keep running if I don't keep an eye on it? Look what happens even when I'm here! I hate to imagine what will happen when I'm not!"

"The less you see, Pop, the better you'll feel."

"You think your foreman can see everything that goes on here? You're dead wrong. Ask him how much work has to be done over here because people are bungling their jobs!"

This part delights the workers. Now the old man has even made the foreman his enemy. Why not stoke the fire a little bit? They love to hear the old man carry on. Livens things up. Every day the same old routine, the same clatter of the machines. Every day, all day long. With him here, at least, you can amuse yourself once in a while, get the blood pumping faster, so you don't fall asleep...

*

It is a well known fact of life that even bosses are human. And every boss, when he pays for something, wants a fair return on his money. It's only natural.

With the help of their accountant, the sons began to notice a drop in their rate of production. They began to investigate. Too much time was being wasted on "fixing mistakes." Inside the shop it was an open secret and had been for some time. Much of the problem could be traced to the old man's interference in the "production line."

So one day, after discussing the problem for two hours with their foreman, the two sons agreed that drastic measures were now called for, including a bit of melodrama that would impress the troops. They burst into the shop and stopped work for a "special announcement."

"We gave you everything you wanted in the contract! In return, we expect an honest day's work out of everybody! Your wage-scale is the highest in the city, so we expect our money's worth! Stop wasting time with the old man — we don't want to hear about that any more! We have enough problems without such nonsense!"

The old man, seeing his sons so distraught, misunderstood the whole situation. He didn't even know they were talking about him. Like any good father, he immediately came to the defense of his children:

"Crooks! Murderers! Bunglers!"

The effect was disastrous. The high drama of his sons' well-planned harangue lay in ruins. The workers turned their heads aside and smiled. The less inhibited ones laughed out loud. The gravity of the situation was now upside down.

"What a funny man!"

"How did they ever get such a father?"

The sons, instead of continuing their "special announcement" to the workers, now turned their attention to their father, and none too gently.

"They're not so far off base, Pop. But it's not funny any more."

"They're right and I'm wrong? Because I let you put me in the middle?" He felt an old stab in his chest.

Afraid of what all the excitement might do to him, they softened their tone.

"For a long time we've practically been begging you to stay out of the shop. We have a foreman and we're paying him good money. Why do you have to interfere?"

"Your foreman is more important than your own father? Where is it written that a foreman can't have someone over him?"

The sons ended the discussion with a wave of the hand that could mean only one thing:

"No use arguing with him any more. Better for everybody if he doesn't come in at all." The finality was unmistakable.

*

Still, he did not retreat all the way.

When the workers are still in bed asleep, when they are just turning over on the other side, not even dreaming about the shop, he is already standing by the door like a guard. And when the first operator arrives, the sleep still in his eyes, and finds the old man standing against the wall like a condemned man before a firing squad, he says to himself in great puzzlement:

"Why does he get here so early? There's nothing for him to do here anyway."

The second man to arrive thinks the same, but he says it aloud: "Wouldn't it be better for your health if you slept a half-hour longer?"

And then the other workers start arriving, singly and in pairs, and they all say the same:

"You're maybe expecting crooks to break into the shop if you're not here?"

"You think if you show up an hour late someone will give you a black mark — or deduct it from your pay?"

The old man no longer jumps at the bait, however.

One worker shakes his head lugubriously: "The poor man is in a bad way."

Another: "He's got a screw loose, is all."

A third: "His sons ought to buy him a little shop somewhere..."

The old man is bloody but unbowed. He is hard and stubborn, like a piece of old fur that you can't get the hair out of, no matter how hard you pull. These workers — they seem to be making sport of him, if not worse, but he keeps his head down, as if he were digging a hole in the ground with his eyes.

When the foreman arrives and opens the doors of the shop, and they all take their usual places at the tables — this one starts pressing, that one starts cutting — the old man is still standing where he was before, his eyes still full of sleep, and something in his mind starts moving, but very slowly. A thought began to take shape when he first arrived and assumed his place beside the door and stood there looking at his still strong arms, his still capable hands that were not allowed to touch anything in the shop. And this was the thought: Would it not be better for him to go with the workers into the union, so that he could sit down like them and do his work, rather than remain the father of those children and have to be satisfied with looking, just looking and looking?

*

At the height of the season, when the shop is in full swing, and the work is burning in everyone's fingers, and smothered voices begin to make him drowsy, the old man shuffles into the shipping-room and stands there looking. So what if he made a fool of himself? Here in this quiet, fenced-off little corner of the big shop through which all the raw goods enters on giant rolls and then later goes out into the world as finished, stylish garments, here in this little anteroom, where all the work is under the supervision of a 17-year-old clerk whose entire claim to fame is that he comes in to work an hour later than the "inside" workers (and goes home three hours later than everybody else), here in this safe place, the old man is now all alone. Here, with the entire treasure of finished garments, over which no union has any power yet, he feels better. Here his hands are unfettered, nobody can stop him from burrowing, from shifting the hangers around, straightening out the garments. He does not approve of the way all the sizes and colors are mixed together. It would make more sense, he reasons, to keep all the blue dresses together and all the red ones together and similarly with the sizes, so they will all be in groups of the same length. A line of green garments, size 16. A line of blue garments, size 18. That way, they would be more pleasing to the eye...

What he does *not* know is that the shipping-clerk purposely arranged them that way according to orders to be shipped, and that he worked two hours overtime the previous night to get them ready. So when that conscientious, trustworthy young man arrives promptly at nine o'clock and takes one look, he suddenly feels faint. Then he starts running around like a poisoned rat. Who did this to me? Who? In one minute the whole shop is on its feet. Everyone. Even the bookkeeper. And the salesmen. Gales of laughter roll through the factory.

Except the shipping-clerk, of course. "I'll have to work all day to put the orders together again," he weeps.

The old man defends himself feebly. "I thought it would look nicer that way. I didn't do it to hurt anybody..."

And strangely enough, the young man does not bear the old one a grudge. He rather likes the idea of having someone work with him. As he explained to the two sons:

"In time, after he learns the ropes, he can be my right-hand-man!"

*

This might be an admirable place to end the story, but it wouldn't be true. Too many hurtful things had happened along the way.

And so one day, at lunch time, after the shop workers had lulled the old man into thinking he was again one of them, they began a harmless pummeling of each other, all in good fun, as workers will often do. During that hour there is no foreman, no boss, no one who really cares what the workers do — it's *their* time, isn't it? The horsing around begins slowly and gradually picks up steam. Workers can take a good-natured punch in the ribs or a slap on the behind any time. It's all done in boyish fun.

This time, however, the good-natured slaps and punches landing on the old man carried a little more steam, and soon he realized that he alone had become the target. His right eye was black and blue, his cheek was swollen, his head bare, his nose bloody.

"You wanted to play, hah? If you want to be a soldier, you've got to be ready to smell the gunpowder!"

Who knows what the outcome would have been had not one man taken pity on him and made his way unobtrusively into the bosses' office.

"If you guys don't get out there right away your father is going to be hurt real bad!"

The two sons ran out into the shop, alarmed and furious. This was too much. Only drastic steps would be of any use now.

When the smoke had cleared and the old man's wounds had been dressed, they issued their ultimatum:

"You will stay on the payroll, but you are positively forbidden to enter the shop!"

For the old man this was the last straw. So one day he went to the Union office on West 16th Street and poked his head into the window where the cashier collected the dues. And in the same stentorian voice in which he had previously cursed the workers in his sons' shop, he bellowed:

"LEMME INTO THE UNYA! LEMME WORK! AND IF NOT IN MY SONS' SHOP, THEN AIN'T THERE PLENTY OTHER SHOPS IN THE CITY? GOD FORBID I SHOULD HAVE TO TAKE MY PAY FOR NOTHING!"

And as though there had reawakened in him the toiler of old, when he had helped his father in the shtetl sew patches on the peasants' bulky breeches, or when he had wielded the 20-pound iron forty years ago in the gloomy downtown sweatshops, he kept hollering at the innocent young woman behind the window:

"TAKE ME INTO THE UNYA! WASN'T I ONCE A GOOD UNYA-MAN MYSELF? IS IT MY FAULT THAT MY OWN SONS HAVE BECOME BOSSES?"

MAKING A LIVING IN AMERICA
Der Lebedicker (Chaim Gutman)

DER LEBEDICKER — *Chaim Gutman (1887-1961) — born in Pietrkow, White Russia; died in New York.*

Gutman's father was a successful freight shipper. His mother was a cultured woman who read Yiddish books and loved to talk about them. She was also the family "accountant," a vivacious woman who loved to tell jokes. Gutman recalls: "Life in our house was peaceful and quiet. My life flowed smoothly, like the river opposite our house; but also like the river that was only on the surface. The sound of the ships' whistles worked on us like a call of liberation."

At age nine Chaim was already writing Hebrew verses. In 1904 he emigrated to the U.S. to live with his uncle, who, he had been told, was a prosperous farmer in Woodbine, New Jersey. What he found there was a rundown farm and a houseful of children. There he enrolled in the Farm School (founded by the Jewish philanthropist Baron de Hirsch), but he left after the first year, moved to New York, and wrote for the Forverts *and* Der arbeter. *For a short time he owned a Yiddish bookstore in Brownsville.*

In 1909 he began writing for the humorous magazines Der kibbitzer *and* Der groiser kundes *under the pen-name "Der Lebedicker" (the lively one). In this genre he achieved wide popularity. A few years later he turned to writing literary and dramatic criticism. In 1922 he became a regular columnist for the Yiddish newspaper* Morgen-Jurnal. *Over the years, collections of his columns and reviews of plays were published in book form.*

Making A Living in America (Me' makht a lebn*) appears in* Pithom un raamses, *Achisefer Publishers, Warsaw 1928.*

Chaim Gutman

Making a Living in America

The well of Jewish livelihoods is so deep that it's difficult to exhaust it.

What do Jews make a living from? The best answer I know is: from what do they *not* make a living?

Throughout the world, and also in America, Jews are constantly looking for a way to make a living, and if they don't find a way, they invent one... One thing Jews have is imagination.

That Jews live off one another is not news. But that Jews make a living out of nothing, out of air, is a fact.

I myself know a wide variety of people with an equally wide variety of ways of making a living. For instance, I know a man on Orchard Street whose pushcart is almost always empty. Let's call him Yoshke. The only thing you ever see in his pushcart is an old log and an even older hat. So how does he earn his living?

It took me a little while to figure it out, but eventually I did. He makes a living from pushing — not the pushcart — but himself, plain and simple. He is a strong, healthy man with a couple of pointy elbows, sharp eyes and a voice that rings out like a firebell. So this is what he does:

Every morning he wakes up very early and wheels his pushcart over to Orchard Street before anyone else does. He stakes out the best spot and just stands there. Before long another pushcart peddler comes along who needs that spot more than Yoshke does— and they make a deal. For 40-50 cents Yoshke gives up his spot to the other peddler. Then he takes his pushcart and pushes it into another place — which usually leads to a protest from somebody, but Yoshke has a louder voice than anyone else, and he stands there with his pushcart until somebody gives him half-a-dollar to get the hell out of there.

And that's how Yoshke makes a living in America.

*

I know another man — let's call him Feivl — who "does business" right in the synagogue. How? Simple! He sits in the synagogue and keeps track of the kaddish-sayers. As soon as a person enters who is a mourner or who wants to observe a *yohrtseit,* he approaches him.

"You're going to say kaddish?"

"Certainly!"

"You want me to respond amen?"

"Certainly!"

"Then you've got to pay me. Everybody around here pays me for that, because that's how I make my living..."

Most mourners accept this as normal. They don't bargain with him. They simply slip him a coin. But there are always trouble-makers everywhere.

"And if I don't pay you, what will happen?"

"Then I won't respond amen."

"I can get along without your amen!"

"Without my amen your kaddish won't be worth anything, because we barely have a minyan here."

This is a very convincing argument, so the mourner agrees to pay.

Once Feivl even organized a strike — a strike of amen-sayers. It happened this way. A mourner came into the synagogue who wanted to observe *yohrtseit.* This man had not only a sizable belly but also strong principles. He absolutely refused to pay. "I don't pay money for such things," he insisted.

So what did Feivl do? Right on the spot he organized a strike of all the amen-sayers in the synagogue. And the strike wasn't settled until that man agreed to pay double — ten cents a piece for nine men, and not a penny less.

*

I know another young man who makes a living from an even more unusual occupation.

He is an "observer" in a restaurant where fellows come to play cards. He himself doesn't play. For one thing, it doesn't pay him to play, and for another thing, he prefers to watch and, where necessary, to give advice. As is well known, experienced card players hate this, so they put up with it as long as they could, then they made a deal with him: Brother, we'll pay you ten cents a game, but only on condition that you keep your big mouth shut.

Ever since then, this young man has made a pretty good living. Some days he makes three — four dollars a day.

Several times, however, he couldn't restrain himself. "Play your deuce!" or "Don't play that ten of hearts!" For that transgression they fined him: no payment for the next three games. But after that happened a few times, our businessman grew silent as a fish. And believe it or not, he's been making such a success of this business that he's even thinking of getting married. As soon as he finds a girl...

2.

A man of about 30, maybe ten years in America, with a pair of darting eyes that are always looking for something. One afternoon we got to talking, until I finally asked him the inevitable question:

"And how are you making a living in America?"

"From agitation," he replied immediately with an infectious laugh.

"Agitation? For what cause? Zionism? Socialism? Unionism? Life insurance?" I laughed too. I thought he was kidding.

"None of those," he said. "I tried that once. But it didn't pay enough."

"So what are you agitating for now?"

"For accidents."

"I don't understand."

"You will, in a minute. Do you know that in America there is an ongoing business with accidents?"

"Yes, I already learned that."

"Then you also know that in a city like New York there are hundreds of people who sue the streetcar companies and the subways, and who get money from them."

"Oh, you're a lawyer?"

"I wish I were, but so far I'm only working for one."

"Now I'm beginning to understand. But what does that have to do with agitation?"

"It has a lot to do with it. How many people are there who can sit around waiting for natural accidents to happen?"

"So what is *your* job?"

"I agitate. I persuade. I convince. All day long I hang around the streetcars and agitate for accidents..."

"How do you do that? Can't you get caught?"

"You certainly can! But you've got to use your head. You have to know who you can agitate. You need to have a sixth sense about people, you understand? Every day in New York there are thousands of people waiting for streetcars. So I stand there with them. For example, if I see a greenhorn — I can recognize them already — I start a conversation with him. What number car is he waiting for? He tells me. I say I'm waiting for the same one, and as I say that, I sigh. Columbus and his trolley cars, may they all burn in hell! I know my greenhorns, you see. All the greenhorns love to hear you curse America. In that way you become bosom pals with them."

The man warms up to me. We talk about this and that, until we get to *parnoseh*, that is, making a living. He complains bitterly. Already six months in the country and still has no job. I comfort him: "Don't worry, you will. Listen, a *lantsman* of mine, also a greenhorn, last week earned 600 dollars for doing nothing."

"Of course, he doesn't believe me. I tell him the whole story, with details. My *lantsman* was getting on a streetcar, he slipped, he fell, he bruised his arm..."

He still has trouble believing me. "For that they pay you in America?"

"You really are a greenhorn, aren't you? You get the names of witnesses, you write down the number of the streetcar, you get into bed, you call a doctor, a lawyer — and you get the money."

"Very strange," says the greenhorn. "Did your *lantsman* really get hurt?"

"A few scratches. They'll heal. But you've got to understand, brother: this is America. Some people don't even wait until they fall. (And here I lower my voice). Take you, for instance. You're nobody's fool. As you're getting off the car you trip, you faint, then you get the money."

"But listen to my 'English.' I can hardly speak a word. If I fall, who will see it, who will write it down?"

"Don't worry about that. If you wish, I can wait here until you slip and fall. I'll write everything down and call the doctor and hire the lawyer. I'll take care of everything."

"Why? Are you my father's servant or what?"

"I feel sorry for greenhorns. Besides, I'm not working myself now. It's slack season. No work, you understand? What have I got to lose? And if you're a gentleman, after you collect your few hundred dollars, you'll slip me a couple of tenners."

"So that's the way I agitate and do business," concluded the young man from the East Side.

"And do you really get customers?" I wanted to know.

"It's not as easy as it sounds. Most greenhorns don't believe me. Sometimes I get too excited with my own agitation. But once in a while, one of them trusts me. A few more of that sort and I'll start making a living. And of course, sometimes a real accident happens too..."

3.

One day I met a man in Bronx Park, a Jew like all other Jews, of the type that are half-clean-shaven and half-bearded, in a threadbare alpaca jacket, but still there was something different about him. It was an ordinary weekday. He was sitting on a bench, reading a book. This in itself whetted my curiosity. He wasn't young, but he wasn't old either. A middle-aged man, how come he was free in the middle of the week to sit in the park and read a book? I tried to see what he was reading, but I wasn't close enough and anyway, he soon became aware of me too.

"It's a novel, a very exciting story called *The Red Prince*. Have you read it? I recommend it, if you have the time. If you're wondering how a man like me has time for such foolishness, you don't have to wonder any more. Rest assured that as I sit here reading, my business is taking care of itself..."

I guess he could read the question in my eyes.

"Here in America, if you use your brains, you can make an easy living. At first I struggled like everyone else, but now, thank God, I'm making a living. Even putting a few dollars in the bank."

"And what is your business, if I may ask?"

"I'm the owner of a trust. Well, almost a trust. Actually Rock-enfeller makes more money from his trust than I do from mine, but who can compare to him? He's been here in America so long already. If I were in America as long as him, I would be a Rocken-feller too. If you promise not to tell anyone, I'll tell you what my business is, because in America you have to worry about the com-petition. But I can see you're not the type to give away secrets.

"My business is coupons. How I got into it? I'll explain it to you simply. Every good business starts by chance. Mine was no exception. One day I'm in the Bronx and I get thirsty. Near the subway station is a soda water stand. I buy a glass of seltzer, and as I pay for it, they hand me a coupon. And would you believe it, before I even have a chance to see how much the coupon is worth, a little kid is at my side."

"Mister," he says, "give me your coupon, please."

"So I give him the coupon. What do I need it for? But I got curious and watched him for a little while and that kid — every-body who bought a drink, he asked them for the coupon. And al-most everyone gave it to him. Now, what you should understand is that at that time I had already been without a business for six months. The milk business I'd had in Harlem I was forced to sell because of the competition. It was really a good business, but then along came this crook, this murderer, this lowdown scoundrel — and one of ours, at that — and opens up a milk store right across the street! And you know the women in this country — give them something new and they'll come running. So I had to sell my busi-ness and lost my shirt in the bargain.

"Then one day I watched that kid doing business with the soda water coupons. You don't need a big investment and the work isn't hard. I figured I could hire ten or twelve kids, place them all around the city, and let them beg for the coupons. A business like that, you have to put it on a solid foundation before you see any profit. If each one of those kids brings in 200 coupons every day, which is a total of 2000 coupons, you've got yourself a little business."

"But of what use are all those coupons to you?"

"Don't you see? You exchange them for useful little items, then you sell the items at a reasonable price. Anyway, the boy I first met at the stand, I asked him if he wanted to work for me, and could he find me another ten kids like him. To make a long story short, I now have 26 kids working for me in all parts of the city, including four 'captains' who watch out for thefts. The way I worked it out, every kid must bring me 250 coupons every day. Those who bring in more get paid extra. Sometimes I can make fifty dollars a week. Depends on the weather. But all in all, I'm making a living. A big spender I'm not. What I am is a widower with no children. And I'm not in a hurry to get married again. That's why I have time to sit in the park and read a novel."

Personally I can't swear he was telling me the truth. Maybe he not only reads novels, but writes them.

4.

I realized at once that this man would have a really unusual way of making a living. His old straw hat was pulled down over one ear and his coat pockets were overflowing with Yiddish newspapers. I met him on a streetcar going to Brownsville. I sat down beside him and, although I'm not one of those people who likes to read a newspaper over a stranger's shoulder, he said to me immediately:

"Mister, you don't have to strain your eyes. You want something to read, here's another paper."

"Thank you," I said, "but I've already read that one."

"So what do you think of our guys flying around the world like this?"

Since he had asked me a question, it was only polite to answer him. "What can I say? They sure know how to fly..."

"Knowing is not enough. How much do you think they earn a week?"

I smiled. "Who knows? I guess they don't do too bad."

"What does 'not too bad' mean?" he insisted.

"Not too bad means they're probably making a good living."

"You're a greenhorn!" he hooted. "They're making a living? So am I. So are you. But I'm talking about getting rich. You don't fly around the world for pleasure. People don't risk their lives for peanuts. I'll betcha they're millionaires..."

"Possible," I smiled again.

"Not only possible. It's a sure thing. No doubt about it. I myself wouldn't do it even for a million. What good will all that money do me in the next world? But if I absolutely had to do it, I'd make sure I was well paid."

"How much, for instance?"

He ticked it off an his fingers. "First of all, they'd have to put a million in the bank in my name. If I came back alive, good; I'd know I was set for the rest of my life even if I never flew again. But if, God forbid, I didn't make it, then at least my wife and kids would be taken care of. They would always remember me as a good provider. Although, when you think about it, today's kids aren't worth it. You think I'd be doing the right thing? How far are you going, anyway?"

"Pitkin Avenue."

"Good! Me too. You're going there to look for a business?"

"No. Just visiting a friend."

"Looks like America treated you okay." He shook his head. "If you can afford to go visiting in the middle of the week. I can't do that yet. Although to tell the truth, I'm not so busy myself."

I took a chance. "And what is your occupation?"

"Occupation? Six years now I've been riding these streetcars."

"You work for someone else?" I was getting really curious now.

"No. I'm in business for myself."

"What kind of business?"

"All kinds!" He smiled, pulled his hat off and put it right back on again.

"For instance," I pressed on.

"Six years now I've been looking for a good business and I haven't found one yet. I wouldn't mind a grocery store, a drugstore, a candy store, a hardware store, a gents' furnishing, or even a moving pictures."

"And in all those six years you haven't found anything?"

"Don't be such a wiseguy! Did you ever look for a business in America? No? Then don't talk. Don't get me wrong. People are always trying to sell you a business in America, but it's all thievery and highway robbery. Everybody's out to skin you alive. Ask me; I know. "

"So, Mister, how *do* you make your living?"

"My living?" His lips twisted in a crooked smile. "A good question. But I already told you. I make a living from riding around in the streetcars looking for a business."

"Really? How does that work?"

"Mister, I can see you're still a greenhorn." He closed one eye In what I assumed to be a conspiratorial wink. "In America, if you're in business, you can always find people willing to lend you money. And I really am in business. My business is looking for a business. I'm ready to buy one any time. Well, here's Pitkin. Today I'm looking at a delicatessen store... Goodbye and good luck!"

*

I met this young man in a cafe late one evening. He was sitting at a table dozing (or so it seemed), but when I took a table nearby, he invited me to join him, as if he needed someone to talk to.

He was still single, he told me, and he had no job, nor does he have a trade, except that he used to write poetry. He soon realized, however, that everybody else in New York was writing poetry, so it was no longer a novelty. All his life he wanted to be different. It was beneath his dignity to do what everybody else was doing.

"So how do you make a living?" I asked him.

"For a long time," he sighed, "I went to bed hungry. But now I'm all right. For the last six months I've had a steady job."

"Doing what?"

"You might not believe me if I told you."

But he apparently wasn't in a big hurry to tell me. First he beckoned the waiter and asked him to bring a Wiener Schnitzel. He loved Wiener Schnitzel, he told me. He himself came from Vienna, that is, not exactly from Vienna, but from Galicia. He had visited Vienna once; a very beautiful city. "New York can't compare with it, although New York isn't bad either."

I waited patiently for him to continue his story, which he did, after the Wiener Schnitzel came.

"I've got a very unusual job," he said, "probably the only one of its kind in the world. But what's the difference, so long as you're making a living. Not hard work, either. I'm working for a friend of mine ever since he bought his own car. He can well afford it. Earns a lot of money, so he suddenly decided he had to have his own car. And you know why? He loves the girls. And the girls love men who have their own car. But my friend soon got into trouble. Not because he drives too fast or anything like that. His problem was in signaling when he had to make a right turn or a left turn. Why was that a problem? Because he has only two hands, and both of them were usually occupied; one on the wheel and the other, well, I leave that to your imagination. So he kept getting one traffic ticket after another. It wasn't the money that bothered him so much as the nuisance of appearing in traffic court to pay the fines.

"Well, it happened one evening my friend invited me to stay over at his apartment. Before we went to bed we went out for a little ride in his car. Naturally, he had also invited one of his lady friends to come along too. And at one busy corner where he had to make a turn, the idea suddenly came to me to do him a favor. I put my arm out the window. That evening he didn't even get one ticket.

"The next morning he treated me to breakfast. On our second cup of coffee he says to me suddenly:

"You know, Berka (that was my name in the old country), I think I have a steady job for you. You're not working now anyway."

"What kind of work is it?" I asked him.

"The idea came to me last night when you put your arm out the window before I made that turn. You can stay at my place as long as you like. You won't lack for pocket money. All you have to do is ride with me and be ready to put your arm out the window. You'll just have to learn my habits so you'll know when I'm about to turn right or left."

Chaim Gutman

I laughed. "You betcha I'll take the job! And don't worry about what I see or don't see. Leave that to me."

"Why shouldn't I have taken such a job? How many jobs like that are there lying around loose? Besides, every once in a while I get a day off. Like today. He's too busy to go driving. So I can sit here and take my own sweet time and enjoy this Wiener Schnitzel. I'm getting paid anyway..."